Anomalies

Books by John Litchen

Memoirs:
Fragments from a Life
Fragments that Remain
Ephemeron
Grab that Moment
Run with It
Beside the Sea
Between the Mountains and the Sea
Changing States

Fiction:
Convergence — Aspects of the Change
A Floating World
And the waters prevailed (eBook)

Non-fiction:
Cinematography Underwater
Aikido - Basic and Intermediate Studies
Aikido - Beyond Questions often asked
Attributes a writer needs
Dreams of Mars - 130 years of stories about Mars
More Dreams of Mars - 150 years of stories about Mars

As editor - book designer:
Journey of a Lifetime
The Central Zone

Co-editing and design:
Remembering Sensei

Anomalies

John Litchen

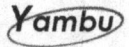

ISBN: 978-0-6459983-2-0

Published by *Yambu*
3 Firestone Court Robina, Qld. 4226.
jlitchen@bigpond.net.au

Dedication:
For Monica
For her constant encouragement...
Que recordaré para siempre

Contents

Rockbones

As she walked along the street from her unit Anne could see already a group of men on the grass verge beside the road had gathered around two parked Toyota SUVs. They clustered together studying what looked like a map. It was early and already getting too warm even though the sun was barely above the horizon. The sky was clear, not a cloud in sight. The air smelt of freshly bundled bales of hay with a hint of dust, but she knew that was from the dried grass verge that was recently cut. It made her nose tingle, gave her the urge to sneeze. There's too much dried grass and dust, she thought, as she looked beyond the cluster of men to the road that left the town, cutting through extensive grazing land filled with yellowed dead stalks of a poor wheat crop. She would have to take an antihistamine tablet later. It had been one of the hottest summers on record and though they were officially past the end of it, the weather did what it wanted and so it remained as hot as it had been during the last month of the summer.

"Hey Professor, you find any rock bones yet?" a stocky man with a heavy black beard asked.

He wasn't with the group but was sitting on a low wooden rail fence. He had a notebook and was writing something down. Beside him was a crudely constructed sign depicting a leaping black cat, with crudely painted words above and below it.

```
┌─────────────────────────────┐
│                             │
│       REWARD                │
│                             │
│       $1000                 │
│                             │
│       EASTER                │
│       PUMA                  │
│                             │
│       EXPEDITION            │
│                             │
└─────────────────────────────┘
```

"Rock bones, I like that," Anne said as she walked towards him. She lifted her tan cap and brushed back a lock of auburn hair that had escaped and was annoying her. "I'm not really looking for bones," she added.

"For someone not looking for them," the stocky man said, "you certainly seem to find plenty."

"I suppose that's true, but what I'm really looking for is evidence of dramatic climate change that could have brought about mass animal extinctions."

"Heavy stuff…"

"Yeah." Anne laughed. "It depends on how you look at it, Jimmy. If we can understand the causes of past changes, then maybe we can see the things that are happening now that will cause future changes. Knowing this, we can plan in order to survive them."

"Like I said, heavy stuff. You should leave that for the future Professor and concentrate on the here and now."

"Wouldn't you like to know what the climate is going to do over the next few decades?"

"Some folks around here would like to know what it's going to do next week. They would like some rain for a change. You know it hasn't rained at all this summer. Can you predict that?"

She smiled at him and shook her head. He always asked her stuff like that. Each time they encountered each other over the last few weeks that she had been here he had managed somehow to ask her if she could tell them when it would rain. They were desperate for rain. Everything had dried up, everything was dead. The wheat had been stunted and poor because it hadn't rained when it should have after they planted the seed, and the little bit of irrigation they could manage hardly made any difference. The town was drying up and they would have to start bringing in water tankers soon.

"You know, when it does rain, you'll probably be complaining about the river flooding."

"What river?" He looked at her with a twinkle in his eyes.

"Yeah, there's not much of a river here now is there? A scummy trickle in a gavel bed."

"That's always the way, isn't it? If isn't a drought, it's a flood." And glancing around he added, "it doesn't seem likely at the moment though."

A heavy 4-wheel drive vehicle slithered to a stop on the gravel at edge of the road in front of the sign leaning against the fence.

The driver leaned out. "You don't want to go with those guys Professor," he said, a hint of a chuckle permeating his voice. "You come with us, and I guarantee we'll find you a puma."

"I'm not looking for pumas."

"Yeah, I know," the driver said. "You dig up old bones. Now how much fun can that be?"

"You'd be surprised," Anne said. She turned and looked at Jimmy, "Is that what everyone thinks, that I'm looking for old bones?"

"Don't take any notice of him," Jimmy said. "He's never even seen a puma. The only thing he's ever shot is a bunch of scraggy rabbits."

"That's what you think. I'll bring one back this year Jimmy, you can bet on it. Why don't you just give me the $1000 now, and we can save a lot of mucking about?"

"Get out of here," Jimmy said, waving him off.

The driver laughed as the 4-wheel drive took off with all wheels spinning, digging holes in the gravel by the roadside, flinging up enough to make Anne jump. Because of the heat, she was wearing shorts and the gravel stung when it hit her bare shins.

She hadn't planned on going on the puma hunting expedition. She thought the likelihood of them finding anything like a puma was remote. How many times had the local townsfolk gone off in search of these mythical pumas and never found anything? And the stories they tell of American soldiers bringing puma cubs here during the beginning of the Second World War and then abandoning them in the bush near the mountains when they were transferred to Brisbane in preparation for a possible invasion by Japanese forces; there was no proof. No American serviceman was ever willing to talk about it. Yet the myth persisted. It's a good way to get tourists here to spend money, she thought. And this old town could certainly do with an influx of money and tourists.

As the dust from the dry gravel settled Jimmy asked, "Do you want to come with us Professor and hunt a live animal for a change?"

"You really think there pumas out there in the remote bush?"

"A lot of people around here have seen them."

"And you believe that?"

"Yeah. I saw one myself. About three years ago. I was coming back along Far-Creek Road. Drove through some mist in a hollow and damn near ran over it. It was in the middle of the road tearing at a Roo that had been hit by a car." He shook his head, still marveling at how composed the animal had been, and how it had not been frightened of his vehicle's bright lights. "When I slammed on the brakes it looked up and glared. I'll never forget the way its eyes glowed in the headlights."

"Sure, it wasn't a feral dog?"

"Hey, I've got big dogs," Jimmy said, grinning affectionately. "Dobermans, so I know what dogs look like. I'm telling you this was a big cat, dark as hell and powerful. It bent down, picked that Roo up in its mouth and carried it into the scrub. Just like a house cat picking up a rat it's caught taking it away somewhere private to eat."

"Was it black and shiny?"

"Why would it be black? You're thinking of a panther not a puma."

"Sorry. I was thinking of a panther I'd seen years ago in a zoo. Pumas are mountain lions and they're not black but usually fawn and brown."

"Come to think of it," Jimmy said as he stood up, "The one I saw was more a dark brown than fawn, but with stripes near its back legs. It was very heavy around the shoulders and neck."

"Like you." Anne said and regretted it the moment the words came out. *You're not flirting with him, are you?* She imagined if you ran into him, you would bounce off. He was a solid hefty man from head to feet. His beard and scruffy hair made him bear-like, but charming none the less.

Jimmy laughed.

"No," he said, "like a thylacine." He used that word instead of 'Tasmanian Tiger' hoping to impress Anne, who nodded and smiled. She understood.

Beyond the rail fence on the dried grass swathe behind them, several people were still engrossed in studying a map spread across the bonnet of one of two well-used Toyota SUVs. A gusty hot north wind had sprung up while they'd been talking, and it kept lifting the edge of their map up even though it was held down by a couple of small rocks. An untidy hedge separated the grass from the sidewall of a service station where another crudely painted sign displayed a leaping black cat and the name: BIG CAT PETROL.

One of the men by the Toyotas came over. He was taller than the others and thin but wiry. The top of his shoulder had a forward lean as if he had spent so many years bending down slightly to get through doors without banging his head, and the posture had remained. "Jimmy, you telling the Professor your story? I seen them too," he said, looking straight at Anne. "I saw two of them. They must have been asleep in the tall grass because when I came into the paddock with the slasher, they leaped up and bounded off.

Went right over the fence and up into the trees by the foothills."

"You think they were pumas? Or Mountain Lions?" Anne asked.

"I don't know. They had the tawny colour of a lion, but darker. They were dark by the tail. They ran up the tree trunk like a cat would."

"There used to be thylacines in this country up until about four thousand years ago," Anne said. "But I don't think they ever climbed trees. All the bones we've found cut off about that time. After that it's nothing but dingo bones. The dingoes killed off the thylacines, with the help of the Aborigines. That's how they became extinct on the mainland. It's now thought that most of the mega-fauna disappeared during the first 20,000 years of occupation by humans, either through burning off the trees and long grass, as those first people did to herd the animals they hunted, which eventually killed their food supplies, as well as changed the kind of bush that survived. They were easy prey because they had no fear of humans. It's still thought possible that in the remotest inaccessible bushland you may still find a Thylacine. Now wouldn't that be something?"

"There are a few people over in Gippsland claim they've seen Tigers. They don't believe they're extinct, but they're damn hard to find. It's rugged country there."

"It's rugged here too," Jimmy said. "Maybe there's still something out there, still surviving in the wild. Nobody goes there much. The bush is too dense and comes right up to the edge of the farmland."

"I'd like to believe it," Anne said, "but climate changed as the ancient continents drifted apart over millions of years, with the recent introduction of dingoes, and humans hunting…" she paused for a moment, then concluded, "all the evidence points to the extinction of our mega-fauna around 20 thousand years ago. Just think, these magnificent animals survived millions and millions of years unchanged, but when humans first appeared here 40 or 50 thousand years ago, it only took 20 thousand years before they became extinct. The whole country was changed in such a short time..." She felt momentarily sad as she contemplated just how recent these extinctions were. And the Tasmanian Tiger was only half a century ago if that, because it had been isolated in Tasmania once the sea level rose and Tasmania became a separate island. She discounted reports that Tigers had been seen in remote Tasmanian bush as recent as the 1980s. It was wishful thinking and forlorn hope. No photos had been taken and no evidence brought forward to sustain the claims. *What would be next?* she wondered. *Koalas? Every time there's a bad bush fire, they lose part of their habitat, and too many animals die.*

The two men fell silent as they contemplated what they had been told.

A battered Range Rover pulled up. The driver got out and came over to register his name with the list Jimmy had of those ready to head out in the morning to spend the weekend hunting for the mythical pumas thought to be killing local farm animals and wildlife.

"I reckon that's about it," Jimmy said as the new arrival drove off. "Most of the local landholders are joining in. It gives them a break from their usual work at a time when we're in between seasons." He put the notebook and pen in his pocket. "There'll be at least half a dozen loads of hunters out there looking for pumas. Some have already left, but the others will leave early tomorrow morning."

"Let's hope they don't get in each other's way, and end up shooting at each other," Anne said half-jokingly.

"It could happen. It has happened before, but fortunately no one has been killed yet. But to answer your earlier question, what we saw here was twice the size of any Tasmanian Tiger," Jimmy said with assurance. "Definitely a Big Cat. We all reckon the Americans left a few here during the war. The troops brought some puma cubs over as mascots. When they were shipped north, they released them into the bush, in the Grampians."

"Why would they do that?" Anne asked. "I mean, would the American authorities allow their troops to bring a wild animal like a puma or a mountain lion on the transports that brought them to Australia? And more than one according to the stories you hear, which I find hard to believe. Australia is very strict about bringing strange animals, or plants or anything different into the country. There's no way they would allow it. But what gets me is that if they went to the trouble of bringing them here and smuggling them in, why leave them to run wild?"

"Who knows. Americans always do the weirdest things."

Anne smiled. She had decided to join Jimmy and his son on the hunt the next morning. Her assistant had gone back to Melbourne for the long weekend, and she had nothing much to go on with. *It'll be a nice break from digging through old bones in hidden caves scattered amongst the foothills and valleys, studying sedimentary layers attempting to determine climate timelines. It was time I did something different for a change.* "It's a lot of bullshit," she said, referring to the Americans who may or may not have left puma cubs in the bush. "Just one of many conspiracies floating around, but I would like come along with you, if that's okay?"

"You're more than welcome." Jimmy said enthusiastically.

"By the way, my name is Anne."

"I'd rather call you Professor," Jimmy said. And before she walked off, he added, "You'd better wear long pants and boots. Those shorts and sandals are no good in the bush."

"Don't you worry about that," she said as she walked off. "I'll dress appropriately. See you tomorrow."

There was a feeling of excitement, of anticipation permeating the town as the various groups of hunters left early in the morning. There were a few more people than usual out and about to see off the hunting parties as the late summer sun peeked over the horizon. The grass sparkled with dew left after a cold inland night. Everyone was sure that this year they would solve the mystery of the pumas. Kids ran around waving at the SUVs and Land Rovers as they left. Several women, wives and relatives of the various hunters, gathered to chat about this year's prospects and to keep an eye on their kids. Not much happened in this town during the year and the annual puma hunt was exciting enough to get them up and out earlier than usual.

The final two Toyotas to leave slipped quietly out of town; Jimmy's with four and the other with three on board. The sun was barely above the horizon casting long shadows from the trees along the roadside. Apart from those leaving this morning, several vehicles had gone out into the bush the day before, each containing farmers and hunters from the surrounding area. And with Jimmy and his group finally departing, there was no one else.

They drove a few miles along the road, crossed a bridge over a dry riverbed, and turned into an unpaved track that led across a wide plain of dried grass, beyond which shimmered the trees of the dense forest covering the land leading to the foothills of a distant mountain range.

The great puma hunt was something they did every year at the end of summer. So far no one had ever shot a puma or any other big cat, but it was a good excuse to get away from the farm or the town for a few days, to not think about how much you owed the bank or next season's planting and harvesting and whether it would rain enough in time for the seeds to germinate. Besides, it was great fun hunting feral dogs, rabbits and domestic cats that had been dumped in the bush and left to go wild. They would drink lots of beer, sit around campfires for a couple of nights and swap yarns about everything under the sun except farming and how much they owed the banks.

Anne was in the Toyota Jimmy drove, along with the tall lanky man who had come over to speak to her while she was with Jimmy. Big Bill, everyone called him. The fourth person in their vehicle was Jimmy's teenage son William, who was naturally called Billy. He was the spitting image of his father, only slightly less solid and minus the beard. He was obviously excited to be with them though he tried not to show it. He wanted to be seen as 'Cool', but he blew it by continuing to fiddle with a rifle he held in his lap. Finally, his father told him bluntly to put it away.

"We're not here to shoot pumas. We just want to see if they exist."

"Not me." I'm gonna shoot one," Billy said defiantly.

Jimmy shook his head in exasperation.

"I want to bring back a trophy," he added, but he did turn and put the rifle behind his seat.

Anne said, "I would like to take some pictures of them to prove they do exist."

"They exist alright," Big Bill said.

"How do you know it's not dingoes or big feral dogs that are killing the sheep?"

"You might know about bones Professor, and I don't, but I do know what a sheep looks like when a dog kills it. It's a mess. Bits of wool everywhere, flesh and bones scattered about. Dogs eat standing up and they are always messy. Now a big cat will sit down on its haunches and eat its way into the sheep. It will take everything out and leave the wool and the skin in a neat heap. It's almost as if a butcher has boned the animal."

"He's right," Jimmy added. "We've had a lot of sheep killed that way this year. Too many to ignore. The farmers are angry and pissed off about their losses. You can bet they'll shoot anything they see that they think might be killing their sheep."

The other vehicle following along behind them bristled with rifles and shotguns, and the men driving it were determined to bring back a trophy or two. They weren't interested in seeing if pumas existed. They simply wanted to kill them. They wanted to prove to the world that the stories about the pumas were true. They were absolutely convinced American wildcat mascots roamed the bush, and they wanted to get rid of every one of them. And if they couldn't find any, then at least they would bring back a few rabbits for the dinner table.

They followed a dusty track across a wide stretch of grassland. The sun was hotter now that it was well above the horizon. It promised to be a scorcher. A dry inland wind ruffled the dead grass making it shiver in waves across the plain. The track led toward distant granite hills and several worn extrusions that jutted up through dense scrub and scraggy trees. These extrusions had once been the cores of active volcanoes. Over aeons the ash cones and the sandstone the volcanoes had punched through had been weathered away to expose the harder core material. This was the rugged country where the pumas were supposed to be.

After the driving settled into a steady run across the plain no one said much, preferring to keep their thoughts to themselves. Anne was hoping that they would find something different. She would be disappointed if the so-called pumas roaming the rugged country ahead turned out to be nothing more than mangy dingoes, foxes, or feral dogs. Some small animals long thought to be extinct had been rediscovered in remote areas of the bush. A Tasmanian Devil had been accidentally killed in Harcourt, Gippsland as recently as 1991, and these were not supposed to be living anywhere on the mainland. If they could still be found in Mainland bush, then it was possible Tigers could also be still living and hiding in remote inaccessible areas. She would love to find a living mainland thylacine. What a sensation that would be. But she knew it was not possible. The last Tasmanian Tiger that was known died in captivity over half a century ago, which makes them an extinct species. From the descriptions of big cat sightings over the years she thought the probability a small family group still surviving in a remote area was possible, although unlikely.

"Do you think we'll find anything?" Billy asked her, interrupting her train of thought.

"I hope so." She patted the camera bag on the seat next to her. "I've got my camera ready, and it has a 64-gig flash drive. With an auto focusing zoom lens I can bring the image up in an instant. As soon as we see anything, I'll shoot continuously," she said, full of confidence, "It takes 7 frames per second. I won't miss it."

"Let the guys in the other truck do all the shooting." Big Bill said from the front seat." I would just like to see it clearly, so I know what it is, that's all. Whether it's a puma or a mountain lion doesn't matter. Be nice if it was a Tasmanian Tiger though."

"Wouldn't that be something?" Jimmy said echoing Anne's previous thoughts, "To actually find a live tiger."

Jimmy was thinking how famous they would be if that occurred. There would be pictures of them in all the papers across the country, TV interviews, and magazine features. He couldn't help smiling as he visualized himself on TV.

They hit a patch of corrugated track. Everything vibrated and rattled. Jimmy's daydream vanished. He took his foot off the gas-pedal and let the Toyota slow down to diminish the force of the vibrations.

Rain followed by harsh sun had cracked the surface, so it was slow going for a while, then once again on a smoother sandy stretch they picked up speed. Running away from the approaching vehicles several Emus trailed puffs of rising dust across the plain.

Entering the scraggy trees near the foothills Jimmy decided to stop for a break. Even in the shade of the trees the wind was hot and dry. Looking back the way they had come, Anne could see mirages on the plain where rising heat shimmered in the air giving the illusion that they had traversed a series of lakes. She could see the dust from the other vehicle floating across a water mirage as it followed the track they had come along.

"How come they're so far behind?" Anne asked.

"They gave us some room," Big Bill said, "so they wouldn't be swallowing our dust."

"What do you think they'll do if they come across something?"

"They're mad bastards in that truck. All they want to do is kill things. If it moves, they'll shoot it. Wildlife is vermin as far as they're concerned."

"Be a real shame to shoot something everybody thinks is extinct." Jimmy said. "Whatever it is that's been killing our sheep recently, it belongs out there in the bush. We should leave it be. We're the invaders. We're the ones putting easy prey in its territory."

"You're not a sheep farmer, are you?" Anne asked even though she knew the answer.

"No. I'm a mechanic at The Big Cat service station."

Before Anne could say anything else the other vehicle slithered to a stop about ten metres away from them. Dust swirled around but no one jumped out of the vehicle until the dry hot breeze blew the dust away. When they did come out, they were all laughing at a joke shared between them.

"Hey professor how about taking a photo of us," the driver called out.

"For posterity," another said.

"Why not," Anne said. She reached back inside Jimmy's Toyota and grabbed her camera.

She didn't mind Jimmy and his son calling her Professor, but these other guys said it with a hint of sarcasm and disdain which she found intensely annoying. It was as if they had no respect for the work she did; like they thought it pointless. Perhaps it was for them, but not for her. They were people of the land and she was an academic. For them she would always be an outsider, an intruder who used fancy language to explain what they knew intrinsically to be true: The climate was changing. They had seen the affects it caused on their land, and they knew nothing that scientists and academics could do would alter that in any way.

Anne waited as the three men from the other vehicle held their rifles at an angle across their chests as they slouched against it. They looked like a bunch of guerrillas from a third world country rather than farmers out on a hunting expedition. She took the photo and put the camera back into Jimmy's vehicle.

After that, they had a snack and drank hot tea from a large thermos. From here on they would really be off-road, not following any tracks. The plan was to travel together for a while until setting up camp for the night. The two groups would then separate and head up into the more rugged country towards the foothills of the mountain range. Pumas liked rugged mountainous country, where the hunters couldn't take their vehicles. The actual search for the pumas would be on foot, each group going in different directions into the jagged foothills and narrow gullies where big cats could hide.

Jimmy wanted to set up a hide and put some bait out to attract the pumas. They all knew the spots where pumas had been seen before, so they would begin their individual searches from there. They would meet back at the general camp after two days.

Their short break over, they drove between the trees with the windows up and the air conditioning on. It was now so hot outside the air above the ground shimmered. On the plain they had traversed, dust devils swirled, sucking up leaves, dry grass and dust with ferocious but short-lived intensity. In the foothills where they drove the leaves on the branches of the trees hung listlessly, their life drained by the sun and the long drought this part of the state had endured over recent years. Everyone wished for a drop of rain, but they knew that when it came it would be torrential and they would then be enduring and complaining about floods. It was always the way with this country; droughts followed by floods, then more droughts. Now people complained about climate change, but nothing had changed. It was always the same; years of drought followed by a couple of years of flooding rains. The pattern was the same as far back as records had been held.

Anne had used 'studying climate change though fossil remains' to garner funding for her research. Everyone was jumping onto the climate-change-bandwagon. There was no money for anything else. If you wanted funding you had to somehow tie your research project to 'climate change,' and then there was no problem with funding.

Both vehicles were separated by four to five hundred metres as they entered a wide gap between two hills of huge granite boulders. It looked greener ahead as the gap narrowed. The air shimmered and a mirage further along the way gave a false promise of cool water. None of them thought it odd that a mirage would appear in a narrow valley, instead of on an open plain.

As Jimmy drove towards the mirage it didn't retreat but swelled and rolled towards them. A shimmering wall of air. They drove into it.

An uncontrolled shiver ran down Anne's spine. The hair on the back of her neck stood up and her arms goose-pimpled. She caught a glimpse through the side window of several ragged people staring at them as they drove by. What the hell are they doing way out here in the middle of nowhere? One of them pointed towards her. She seemed to be yelling something. Suddenly they vanished, gone in an instant.

Billy's face paled. Saliva welled into his mouth, and he swallowed convulsively, trying not to vomit. "I feel sick," he said. "Can you stop?"

"Me too," Big Bill said. His face had paled. A layer of sweat glistened on his forehead.

Trying not to vomit, his stomach convulsing, Jimmy slammed on the brakes. The vehicle bounced and skidded to a stop. Jimmy shoved open the driver's door and launched himself from the vehicle. Bent over he couldn't stop himself from spewing up his breakfast. The others piled out, each trying to control the welling nausea.

The vehicle following a half a kilometre behind slowed as the occupants realized Jimmy's Toyota was no longer in front of them. The dust had cleared and there was no vehicle in sight.

"Did you see which way they went?" the driver asked his companions.

"No there was too much dust."

"They must have gone up that valley between the two hills," the guy in the back said as he pointed off to their left.

"Then we'll go a different way," the driver said. "We can meet them tomorrow as planned, back where we had that break." He gunned the vehicle and headed towards a wider gap between several low hills a kilometre away.

"I thought we were going to set up camp together before going our own ways."

"Obviously they had other ideas about that."

None of them noticed the point where the tracks from the vehicle in front had abruptly stopped. Beyond that point the dry half dead grass was untouched.

As suddenly as it had come upon them the nausea subsided. Anne took an involuntary deep breath of air that was hotter and more humid than it had been before and shuddered. She looked around and stared uncomprehendingly at the lushness of the countryside. *How is that possible? Only moments before it had been hot, dusty and dry, with everything desiccated.*

They were standing in knee-high grass that was lush, rich green, and much thicker than what they had been driving on only moments before. Heavy cumulus clouds layered the sky above the granite hills. Sweat broke out on their faces and their clothes started to stick to them even before they began moving. The air felt so thick and heavy with moisture it like being in a steam-bath.

"What the hell happened?" Jimmy demanded. He looked back along the way they had come to see the tracks where he had skidded on the thick grass only went back about fifty metres. Beyond that the grass was untouched. He walked slowly back along their track. The others followed, their clothes already sticking to them in the humidity.

As far as they could see all around them the lush knee-high grass extended to the horizon. A warm breeze made slow ripples across the grass, so it looked like gentle waves on a wide inland lake.

This is wrong, Anne thought. She felt more goose bumps forming along her arms.

"What the hell happened?" Jimmy asked again. "And where are the others?"

"They were right behind us," Billy said.

"They're not with us now. I can't see any sign of them. The grass looks unmarked out there." He stopped abruptly as he realized how different the grass looked. "What kind of grass is that? It's too tall and thick, too green."

They stared at the spot where their tracks abruptly began. There was not a mark in the grass beyond where they stood, nothing to show that they had driven across the wide plain stretching away from them. There were no signs of the other Toyota SUV that had been only a couple of hundred metres behind them. Jimmy stared at the grass which was thick, lush with moisture, and intensely green, as a hot sun blasted the landscape. The air was heavy and humid with the feeling that a tropical downpour was imminent. What the fuck is happening? He was having trouble trying to make sense of what he was seeing. The grass tops close to them quivered, and all of them felt the faintest vibration in the ground beneath their feet. It only lasted a few seconds. They ignored it, too taken by the tropical landscape that surrounded them.

"It looks like Arnhem land," Anne said, "in the wet season, but without the swamps."

"It's as if we were just dropped onto the grass here," Big Bill said as he stared at the point where their tracks had flattened the grass and showed how they had skidded until they came to a stop. He looked at Anne. "Professor?"

Anne shook her head. She was as bewildered as the others. "I have no idea what happened," she said. "Look at the trees. They're tropical. These are not the same dried up half-dead eucalyptus we drove through before. There is nothing like that anywhere near here."

"Why don't I park under that tree over there," Jimmy said. "We should get out of the sun while we try and figure out what happened."

Under the tree the shade was deep, the air cooler though no less humid.

"You know this is impossible," Jimmy said.

"What are you talking about?" Billy asked. He stared across the valley they had driven into at a dark clump of scrub trees. He edged back towards the vehicle never for a moment taking his eyes away from the deep shadows under the trees. Sweat trickled down his back making his t-shirt stick to him. He reached in and grabbed his rifle from the vehicle. He was sure he had seen something large moving in there, but the glare bouncing off the lush grass made his pupils contract, partially blinding him to what could be in the deep shadows under the trees.

"What I'm saying is we shouldn't be here; we should be somewhere else."

Billy turned back to his father. "You're not making any sense Dad. We drove in here, didn't we?"

"Of course we drove in here," Big Bill said. "But we all know this kind of tropical country doesn't belong here. This is supposed to be a dry riverbed. The only time there's water here is after a rainstorm in the hills. Look around Billy. Does this look dry to you? Does it even look like a riverbed?"

Anne walked slowly back along the flattened track the vehicle's wheels had left in the grass to the point where the grass was untouched. How is this possible? She asked silently. The word echoes flashed into her mind, but before she could grasp its meaning, it disappeared as the voices from the guys surrounded her.

"But where the Hell are we?" Big Bill asked rhetorically. "We didn't drive across that grass. There aren't any tracks, except from this spot here to where we skidded to a stop."

There was no track beyond that showing where they had come from. The lush grass stood thick and deep green, totally unlike the dusty dry shriveled grass they had driven over to get here. As far as she could see towards the horizon the grass was rich, and trackless. The sky was blue, only marred near the horizon by early morning cumulus clouds starting to build up. There was not a hint of dryness in the air. And the smell, was tropical, redolent with the perfume of unseen flowers that barely masked the smell of rotting vegetation. It only reinforced her earlier thought that it looked like the far North Gulf Country that Anne a few years back on a project to count Cassowary numbers. Not too many had been seen over recent years and someone had suggested that they may have disappeared or were on the verge of extinction. She had been lucky and had seen enough to convince her they were not becoming extinct but that they had retreated further back into denser bushland where they were less likely to be disturbed. She looked up. The sky they had travelled under before had been greyish blue with dust and streaked with high cirrus clouds. The air here was clear, a vibrant blue and humid, but with not a speck of dust.

Perspiration beaded her forehead, and she wiped it away with a brusque flick of her hand.

"What do you think Professor?" Jimmy asked as he moved closer to her. They were both standing at the point where their tracks had flattened the grass.

"Did any of you see a group of people waving or pointing at us as we drove in here?" Anne asked.

They shook their heads.

"What people?" Billy asked. "There's no one else here but us."

"We drove right past them as we skidded to a stop."

"Where are they then?" Jimmy asked.

They had not seen them, which made Anne wonder whether she had seen them or whether she had been hallucinating during her moment of extreme nausea.

Each of them slowly turned, searching for a sign of the people Anne thought she had seen. There was no one nearby. No marks in the thick grass to indicate anyone had been standing near or walking along where their vehicle's tracks commenced. There was now a stillness about the place that reinforced the uneasiness Anne felt. Not a blade of grass moved, neither did the leaves in any of the nearby trees. The air was even heavier, laden with so much moisture that Anne almost convinced herself that she was trying to breathe underwater. The silence unnerved her. There should be bird sounds at the very least, but there was nothing, not even the buzzing of flying insects, or the sound of something slithering away in the grass.

"I must have imagined it," Anne mumbled after a long moment of silence. Once again, she looked around trying to absorb why everything was so different to what it had been only a few moments earlier. "I don't think you can turn around and go back."

"Why not?" Billy asked. He walked along the tracks in the grass, and stepped past where they began. He took several steps into the untouched grass and stared across the plain.

"Because down there," Anne said pointing towards the distant horizon, "is not where we were before. The shape of the whole area is different, the trees are different, and the grass is different. Even the hills are different. Look around you. They're taller and more rugged."

The ground underfoot again vibrated so softly hardly anyone noticed.

"Did you feel that?" Billy spun around to face them.

They shook their heads and stared at him. What, feel what?

"Why don't we drive further into this valley?" Big Bill said.

"Yes, why don't we do that?" Anne agreed. It was as good an option as any other.

"Come on Billy," Jimmy said. "Let's go."

They drove slowly between groves of huge trees, some with hanging vines, until the valley opened out into a wide circular basin devoid of large trees but full of scrub partially obscured by tall grass. They stopped and got out of the vehicle. The air seemed even more thick and oppressive. It lay heavily on them like an invisible weight pushing down, sapping their energy. Their clothes stuck to them as if glued on. Nothing moved. There were no sounds of birds singing, no sounds of insects. Anne couldn't imagine anywhere in the bush being as quiet as this.

They stood a long while before Jimmy muttered, "Where the hell are we?"

No one could answer.

This was so unlike any country they were familiar with.

It felt wrong. Each of them sensed that.

As they stared across the basin the grass and shrubs near the centre started quivering. This movement rapidly spread like ripples on a large pond from the point they had first seen the movement. The ground began to vibrate. At first it was imperceptible, but it coincided with the ripples spreading out across the grass and as the ripples became more visible, the ground vibrated enough for them to feel it.

"I don't like this," Anne said.

"We should get out of here," Jimmy said but couldn't make himself move. He couldn't take his eyes off the ripples spreading out across the grass.

The grass in front of them started quivering. The air now moved past them, heavy and sticky. Suddenly the ground beneath them vibrated fiercely against their feet. There was a deep groaning sound. The ground moved once with such force they almost toppled over. The trees behind them shook violently, branches rattling, leaves rustling. The sound increased in volume, making a noise like a giant piece of wood slowly splitting along its length.

"Shit." The word exploded from Jimmy's mouth, and suddenly he was moving, climbing into the driver's seat as fast as he could.

"It's an earthquake," Billy yelled above the noise.

Then it stopped as suddenly as it had started. Something crashed through the trees behind them. They spun around. Two large Roos, bigger than anything they had ever seen before bounded with giant leaps back along the valley. In the centre of the basin there was a loud cracking sound like the noise lightning makes when it hits the ground. A suddenly glowing spot burst and vanished, leaving them blinking as their eyes tried to adjust to the flash of light. A trickle of grey smoke drifted sluggishly upwards. Beyond that, other smoke plumes emerged, to drift upwards.

Before the sound had faded away, they were all scrambling back into the vehicle, almost getting in each other's way. Jimmy started the motor, crashed it into gear, and spun the steering wheel. Turning quickly, they drove back the way they had come as fast as the terrain would allow. They saw no sign of the two giant Roos.

Now Anne knew why it had been so eerie, why there had been no insect sounds, or bird, or animal noises. Everything, except for the two giant Roos left long before they had arrived. They would have sensed the coming earthquake and moved out of the area.

They drove past the point where their tracks began at the start of the valley.

They drove out onto the grassy plain. Far ahead of them they saw a herd of Roos bounding away, but they couldn't tell how big they were. Behind them a thick dark grey smoke plume rose steadily into the air. It rose several hundred metres straight up then started spreading out.

There was a tremendously loud crack a long way behind them. The ground shook violently. The vehicle bounced up and down several times, wheels spinning, engine screaming.

"Shit," Jimmy snarled as he struggled with a steering wheel that seemed as if it wanted to fight him.

The vehicle lurched, and with all wheels spinning regained traction and surged ahead.

Heavy dark cumulus clouds towered ahead of them, ominous flashes of lightning spearing through them. Behind them smoke and ash filled the sky spreading into a huge stain. A shadow fell across them as the sun was obscured.

They drove as fast as the terrain would allow until Jimmy suddenly slammed on the brakes and twisted the steering wheel to turn them to the right. The vehicle skidded and shuddered, the back wheels sliding on the grass. They slid sideways until they came to a stop beside the lip of a wide gorge. They could go no further.

"Where did that come from?" Big Bill said, astonished that such a chasm could be in the middle of this plain. He had driven around here many times and had never seen anything like that before. He shook his head to clear it. This is not the same place, he told himself, still not convinced that they could possibly be anywhere else.

"How are we going to get across? is what you should be asking," Anne said.

"What the hell is happening?" Jimmy asked Anne.

"An eruption."

"You mean like a volcano?" Billy asked.

"That basin we drove up the valley into must have been the caldera of an ancient volcano that blew its top. Now it's getting ready to erupt again. We should get as far away as possible."

"I've never seen a volcano erupt," Billy said, wondering whether he should be excited at the prospect.

"I don't think that's something you really want to see," Anne said.

As if to emphasize what she said the ground beneath them shivered again. Dust rose up from the edge of the gorge but fell back quickly in the heavy humidity. They could hear stones and rocks falling into the chasm. Jimmy started to drive along the edge but not too close after seeing a large chunk break away to fall into a narrow river far below.

"Try and get closer to the Roos," Anne said. "I want to get some pictures of them."

"Are you crazy?" Jimmy snapped.

"They're running away. We're running away. Why not catch up so I can get some shots."

"You're right," Big Bill said, "Something odd about those Roos. I wouldn't mind a closer look."

"You're both crazy," Jimmy said, but he gunned the motor, turned away from the edge of the chasm so they headed after the Roos. Before they could get close enough to get a good look at them, they disappeared into a massive clump of giant trees. The vehicle skidded to a stop at the place their quarry had gone in amongst the trees.

"Now what?" Jimmy asked.

"We go in after them," Billy said. This time he was excited. He had always wanted to shoot a big Roo but his dad never let him. This was the first time he was close enough to perhaps do it. And they were the biggest he'd ever seen.

He had his rifle in his hand as he opened the door. "Don't forget your camera Professor," he said, jumping out. He knew this was the last time for a while that he would be going on a hunting trip, and he was determined to make the most of it. Come the beginning of the new school year he would be off to Melbourne and boarding school before going on to university. He would only get home during term breaks and would probably have too much studying to do to think about hunting trips.

"Billy," Jimmy called.

Billy ran towards the trees. Anne cautiously followed, still uneasy. Maybe it was only the sultry air, but there was a kind of achy feeling deep inside her bones. Something isn't right, something about that old volcano…

Pushing that thought aside, she turned at the edge of the trees and looked back at Jimmy and Big Bill standing beside the SUV looking a bit lost. She took a shot of them, making sure she had the plume of rapidly rising massive ash clouds in the background. Lightning flashed in the cumulus clouds forming higher above the billowing ash from the eruption. She thought the clouds of ash seemed to be rising faster than before, huge billows merging with the black cumulus clouds forming high up above the rising ash. Massive lightning bolts split the air momentarily blinding her. Thunder rolled across the plain almost instantaneously, almost like a shock wave instead of a sound wave.

"We might as well have a look around too," Big Bill said to Jimmy, and he followed the path Billy had left in the tall grass.

The ground shook again. *Another aftershock or a prelude to something bigger?* Anne wondered as she continued to follow Billy.

With the thickening of the heavy cumulus clouds a wind had arisen, sucked in by hot rising air near the eruption. The air around them seemed cooler because of the wind. It evaporated the sweat off them. The tops of the trees spasmed. The rising smoke and ash cloud from the eruption began to spread wider, rapidly obscuring more of the sky.

She stopped at the edge of the trees. "You know what?" Anne said when Big Bill and Jimmy caught up to her." It hasn't been tropical like this," and she pointed at the huge trees and the lush grass they stood in, "for about two million years."

"What are you saying?"

"The last time a volcano erupted in this area was 2 million years ago, that's what I'm saying."

"What's that got to do with anything?" Jimmy asked.

"The more I think about it the more ridiculous it seems, but it's the only thing I can think of." She waited a moment for them to say something and when they didn't, she blurted it out. "Somehow, we've jumped back into the past."

A shot rang out.

"Shit." Jimmy said.

There was a crashing sound in the scrub under the trees. Then silence. Only the noise the grass made as it rustled in the wind that gusted intermittently.

As they started towards the trees, there was more crashing noises as Billy came back out from under the trees.

"I missed it," he yelled.

"Missed what?" Jimmy snapped.

"A bloody big cat."

They stared at him as he took a couple of steps towards them.

"What happened to the Roos?"

"I never saw them. I saw this thing that wasn't a puma, but it was as big as one. It had teeth like a Sabre Tooth Tiger."

"Show me where it was," Anne said excitedly.

"Come on." Billy spun around and ran back towards the trees. Anne raced after him, clutching her camera.

"Shouldn't we be getting out of here?" Jimmy yelled uselessly at their backs. He turned questioningly to Big Bill who just shrugged as Anne followed Billy and disappeared under the dense tree cover.

The ground shook again, and the trees about them shuddered. As Anne followed Billy into the dense scrub beneath the trees, she felt a branch slash across her face, scratching her, but she didn't slow down. She kept right behind Billy.

"There," he said, stopping so suddenly Anne almost collided with him.

He pointed towards a low heavy branch. "It was sitting on that branch. It jumped off just as I shot at it."

He reached up towards the branch, pointed to a bit of split bark. "That's where the bullet hit."

"You would have missed it."

"I couldn't aim straight. The ground kept shaking."

He pointed to a scratched spot at the base of the tree trunk. "It landed there."

The Earth groaned deep down so they felt its vibrations shivering up their legs.

"We'd better go back," Anne said.

The tops of the trees above them whipped back and forth as the ground shook ever more violently. They emerged and started towards the vehicle where Jimmy and Big Bill were waiting for them.

"Come on," Jimmy yelled as they ran towards the vehicle.

The wind blasted them with a smell of sulphur, and suddenly Anne knew.

"We have to get down into that gorge," She yelled as they got closer.

"You're insane." Jimmy looked at her with astonishment.

"Listen to me." She sounded breathless, as if the air was too thick to breathe and run through at the same time. "There's a volcano back there where we were before, and it's about to explode."

"What volcano?" Jimmy asked fearfully.

"We were just there, where the smoke started coming out of the ground. If that volcano explodes there'll be a pyroclastic flow. That's a mixture of steam and sulphur, of pulverized rock and burning ash with lots of bigger lumps in it. It'll come rolling across the plain at six hundred kilometres per hour with a temperature of a thousand degrees."

"Shit! Then what are we waiting for?" Big Bill said. "Let's get the hell out of here."

"There's no way down," Jimmy said, reluctant to even think about going down into the gorge.

The ever-increasing wind gusts engulfed them in a bubble of foul-smelling hot air.

The ground wobbled beneath them making it hard to move without falling over. Their waiting vehicle shook.

That convinced them.

Coughing and struggling to breathe, they scrambled into the vehicle. Jimmy slammed it into gear and took them towards the gorge. Driving as fast as they could along its edge, they could see rocks bouncing up and down each time the ground shuddered. The wheels kept losing traction as the ground shook, causing the vehicle to slip and slide dangerously. Half of the sky behind them was black. Massive clouds of roiling ash and smoke pushed high up into the stratosphere. The Toyota shuddered violently and bounced from side to side, but Jimmy managed to maintain a reasonable speed. Everyone hung on desperately.

Ahead of them part of the edge crumpled, a huge section suddenly slipping away right in front of them.

Jimmy yelled. "I can't avoid it. We're too close."

"Don't try," Anne screamed at him. "Use it like ramp. Turn into it."

"It's coming," Big Bill yelled. He was looking behind them and could see a roiling black wall rushing towards them at incredible speed. "Go…"

The pyroclastic flow pushed a massive amount of air before it. This air hit the back of the vehicle as Jimmy turned towards the newly created ramp. It shoved them over the edge with a ferocity that stunned them. With all its wheels spinning the 4-wheel drive slipped down the ragged slope completely out of control. It slewed sideways, hit a large rock which was also sliding down the slope, rolled over onto its side. It continued to slide further down before it flipped over close to the flat bottom of the gorge Its momentum made it roll once more, finally, miraculously landing on all four wheels. They found themselves on a wide ledge several metres above the narrow river at the very bottom.

Without thinking, hoping it was still drivable, Jimmy dropped it into first gear and shoved the gas pedal down as hard as he could. It was drivable. With wheels spinning as they gained traction, he headed as fast as possible along the sidewall of the gorge to where there was an overhang of solid rock. They slammed to a stop under the overhang as far in as they could get.

The sound of the earth being rent, of rock splitting and wind roaring loud enough to burst ear drums was mind numbing. Anne held her hands over her ears, but still could not diminish it. Her very bones vibrated.

The moment they stopped under the overhang everything instantly went black as the wall of hot ash flew over the top of the gorge. Rocks pounded down like giant hailstones. They were beneath an avalanche. They hoped that the overhang above them wouldn't come crashing down to bury them. They could see nothing outside of the closed windows. The air became hotter and hotter. They were suffocating. Each gasped air that seemed devoid of oxygen, air that was almost too hot to breathe.

My lungs are boiling, Anne thought. She imagined them starting to cook like a piece of meat in an oven. *Don't panic. Breathe slowly.* She opened her eyes only then realizing she had squeezed them shut and saw dimly that Billy was struggling to breathe. She grabbed his arm. He turned to look at her, a deep fear in his eyes.

She mouthed the words "Don't panic. Breathe slowly," and he nodded his head.

Jimmy turned the air conditioning on full which helped them for a while as the temperature in the vehicle stabilized, but he couldn't keep it running for too long because it used up fuel they would need later if they were going to drive out of here.

It seemed like hours before the blackness became greyer as suspended ash settled. It filled the lower part of the gorge, completely burying the river. Being under a ledge had saved them. None of the hot ash fell on them, but it covered the ground they had driven along. As it got lighter the temperature also dropped. And Jimmy turned off the air conditioning and the motor. For a long while they could do nothing but stare out through the dirty windows at the grey ash that covered everything. Gusts of warm wind made flurries of ash rise, spin and disperse like miniature whirlwinds. It was a grey alien landscape as far as they could see.

"It looks like snow," Billy said wonderingly.

Only this snow was hot and dirty, and it suffocated everything.

Jimmy opened the driver's side door and tentatively sniffed the air. "It smells like rotten eggs," he said before stepping gingerly out. He looked up at the overhang that had protected them from the falling ash and wondered how strong it was. *Would it hold? Or would the weight of accumulated ash on top of it cause it to collapse?* Frightened that if he moved too abruptly or slammed the car door it could come down on top of them, he stood there unmoving.

The air was still hot, shimmering with the heat rising off the ash deeper down. But the worst of the heat had gone which encouraged them one by one to climb out of the battered vehicle. They stood staring at the grey wasteland before them. The air shimmered as heat radiating from the ash dissipated into the air above.

"This has not been one of my better days," Big Bill said.

"You've got a cut," Jimmy said to Anne.

"It happened back in the forest. But I'm going to have a big bruise here," she said, touching the side of her head where it had banged against the wall of the vehicle as they had rolled over on their way down into the deep gorge.

"What about you Billy?" Jimmy asked.

"I'm okay," the boy said. "A bit shook up. It was a good ride down though."

"Yeah, wasn't it?" Jimmy said.

Suddenly they all started laughing, the relief of having survived making them hysterical.

When the laughter finally died Big Bill walked out from under the ledge and back to the rubble-strewn ramp they had rolled down. Each footstep left a hole in the ash covering the track they had driven along. Looking at the steep angle of the slope, he shook his head. He couldn't believe they had driven down it, well, driven as well as rolled over to end up on their wheels. How they had managed to get under the ledge was a miracle. *There's no way we'll be able to get back up here*, he mumbled as he stared forlornly at the steepness of the slope.

"We'll have to go further down to find a way out," he told them when he returned.

Anne and Jimmy seemed exhausted, the shock of what could have happened to them only now sinking in. Billy climbed back into the vehicle to look for his rifle. He grabbed Anne's camera as well. He passed it to her. "Take some photos," he said. "Surely you'll want to remember this."

"What do you want the rifle for?" Jimmy asked. "There's nothing here to shoot." He waved his arms expansively to indicate the grey ash covered landscape. Everything as far as they could see was covered in layers of steaming grey ash.

"For a photo," Billy mumbled. He stood beside the battered Toyota, barely visible beneath the overhang that had protected them, and held the rifle diagonally across his chest in a defiant pose.

Still numb, Anne backed away from the overhang far enough to include some of the surrounding ash covered scenery as well as Billy cradling his rifle. He smiled for the camera. She couldn't help smiling herself at the irresponsibility of the young. She took several other shots of the surrounding area. Although she really didn't feel like it, she busied herself with composing good images in the camera, and pushed out of her mind all thoughts of what could have happened when they rolled down into the gully, as well as the more troubling concerns of how they were going to get back if they were truly in the past. It was something her mind couldn't comprehend so she blocked all thoughts of it.

Billy said cheerfully. "We should go look for a way out of here."

Without waiting for the others, he started walking along the bottom of the high cliff wall.

"Wait a bit," Anne called. "I'll come with you."

"I'll check the Toyota to see if it's still drivable.," Jimmy said. He figured it was better to be doing something positive rather than standing about doing nothing. Besides, doing something stopped him thinking about where they were, how in hell they had got there in the first place, and whether there was any possibility they could get back home.

"Don't go too far," Big Bill said.

"Don't worry about us," Billy said.

When Anne caught up to him, Billy had gone several hundred metres along the floor of the gully. He didn't stop but he acknowledged her arrival beside him with a slight nod of his head and a smile. He was worried but he would not admit that to any of them yet. They were the adults, they were the ones supposed to worry, not him. Stay cool, he whispered.

The still-warm grey ash covering everything in sight was infinitely depressing. The residual heat rising from the ash made walking difficult. They both stopped and Billy kicked up a cloud of powdery ash before he said: "We're not gonna get out of here, are we Professor?"

"What makes you say that Billy?"

"I mean…" He gestured vaguely towards the direction they come from. "How did we get here to begin with? And where is here?"

"I can't answer either of those questions Billy. I don't know. What I do know though, is that you should be asking when, not where are we."

"I'm not sure I understand."

"Does anything about this place look familiar? I don't mean this gorge we are in now. I mean the trees and the thick grass we saw before. And the atmosphere, it's tropical, or at the least sub-tropical. And what about those Roos we chased after? They were gigantic. Much bigger than anything we have today. I mean today, where we live in the time we come from, not now where we are. And that big cat you shot at; did you ever see anything like that before?"

"No." He shook his head. "But it's not possible to go back into the past."

"How do you know?"

"Those things only happen in movies or books. Not in reality."

They started walking again, further along the gorge. It seemed better to be walking than just standing. It gave them the illusion they were doing something positive.

"Did you know Billy that the last time a volcano erupted in this area was about two million years ago? And that was towards the end of twenty million years of volcanic eruptions that covered most of Victoria's western regions with thick layers of lava. Hundreds and hundreds of kilometres of it, all buried under layers of topsoil through weathering by wind and rain. Some of it had subsided and was under the sea for long enough for sedimentation to form sandstone before it was upthrust by volcanic eruptions and massive earthquakes to again be weathered by wind and rain into the landscape we know. There are national parks where you can see parts of this massive lava bed exposed, otherwise you wouldn't know it was there. Just how far back we are I don't know. I suspect closer to the end than the beginning because of the mega-fauna we saw, but there's no way to know."

"You've got to be kidding." He stared at Anne for a long moment studying the seriousness in her face. "You're not kidding, are you?"

"I'm not kidding," she said bluntly. "It's the only explanation. Have you ever heard of Chaos theory?"

"Yeah, but I don't know what it is…Something about a butterfly flapping its wings in China producing a hurricane in the Caribbean."

She had to smile at that, the same glib answer everyone gives. That and similar garbage you find on 'social media'.

"Chaos Theory is about the behavior of events governed by deterministic laws so unpredictable that events appear to be random. And yes, small events can have large consequences over a long period of time. I doubt that a butterfly flapping its wings in China, or any other place, would create enough of a disturbance in the air to cause a hurricane to form in the Caribbean. But it is possible, and that's the thing… Lots of things are possible when you have an infinity of consequences that can derive from any event that occurs anywhere in the world, at any time."

"Okay, that sort of makes sense. But how does that explain how we got here, if we really are in the past, like two million years back, as you say?"

"I can't really answer that. I'm guessing, supposing or extrapolating… There have been recent experiments which prove that time can be reflected from one moment to another," and she had a moment of clarity, an epiphany, as the word echoes formed in her consciousness, "time echoes exist. Time waves reflected would behave differently to spatial reflections. They can echo and reflect each other."

"You mean like a mirage?"

"Perhaps. That's a kind of special reflection. But no one knows yet much about time reflection, only that in a quantum universe it's possible. I think this is what we have here. If we were caught up in a time reflection, it could explain how we got here."

His eyes indicated he had no idea of what she was trying to explain. "You lost me."

Not certain she herself understood, she tried to clarify the idea in her mind. "Look," she said, "if you throw a stone into a still pond, after the splash it makes when it hits the water, ripples spread out in ever widening circles. Now imagine throwing another stone into the pond in a different spot. The ripples spreading from that second stone will bump into the ripples from the first stone and get jumbled together, overlapping and breaking the outward flow. I'm trying to image time ripples forming when a catastrophic event occurs spreading out into time forwards and backwards at the same time, just as its physical effects spread out, like waves shaking the ground, ash clouds spreading, pyroclastic flows. Maybe time is affected in the same way with a massive disturbance simultaneously spreading forward and backward through time, like ripples in a pond. If other catastrophic events happen close enough, in time rather than distance, maybe the ripples from each event will intersect, getting jumbled together. Anyone or anything caught in these jumbled points could inadvertently be shifted forwards or backwards in time."

Their voices sounded dead, with no echo off the ash-covered surrounds, and no sounds of any kind other than what they made as they kicked up clouds of the hot fine ash while they struggled to walk.

"You think that's what happened to us?"

"I can't think of any other explanation. It has been proved to happen at the quantum level in laboratory experiments, but on a bigger scale… I really don't know. No one knows. But it's the only thing I can come up with that might explain how we got here."

The ash had the same kind of consistency as fresh snow. Their feet sank into it, which made walking through it hard going. Some of the ash got into their shoes. It was still hot enough to make their feet feel as if they were burning. The fine ash still floating in the air as well as that which they inadvertently kicked up while struggling to move along the lower part of the gorge settled in their hair and stuck to their faces and clothes.

The difficulty of moving over the ash covered surface made them sweat so much their clothes were stuck to them. On top of that the ash turned everything they wore a dirty grey. They stopped and stared at each other; mud covered golems with eyes wide open.

"You look terrible," Billy said.

Anne smiled. "You don't look too good yourself," she replied.

"This is too hard. Maybe we should go back to the others."

"Look—" Anne pointed to a spot several hundred metres further along. "—It's not so steep there. Perhaps we can climb up to the rim. We'll get a better view from there anyway."

There was a broad ledge part way up where a clump stunted trees had struggled to grow. Anne imagined that these trees had been growing along the edge of the chasm on a part which had collapsed sometime earlier and settled part way down. They continued to grow like a miniature section of jungle inside the chasm, but like everything else, they were now covered with a heavy layer of ash. Unless it rained soon, they would stay smothered. Everything covered by ash would die if it wasn't already dead. Perhaps some things would become fossilized as the ash hardened into pumice over time.

"I still don't understand how we could get here," Billy said. "I mean we were just driving along, and then all of a sudden we are here in the middle of a damn volcanic eruption." He stared up the slope towards the small clump of trees. "Two million years in the past?"

"It does seem impossible, well, improbable perhaps. But I can't think of anything else to explain it. A volcanic eruption is not a small event," Anne said as she considered how they could have got here. "It could be something that has very large consequences."

Ash and loose gravel cascaded down into the gully as they clawed their way up to the ridge above. Something moved in amongst the stunted trees. Some of the ash fell off the branches. They kept losing their footing as they struggled to climb up the slippery slope that was deceptively steeper than it had first appeared. By the time they had reached the ridge with the stunted trees they were exhausted. The fine ash stuck to their perspiration-wet clothes giving them the appearance of strange beings newly created from primordial clay.

"I'm going to be stiff as anything, Anne said.

They sat down on the edge of the ledge to catch their breath, but the ash covering it was still too warm to sit on, so they stood up again. Rivulets of perspiration ran down their faces leaving flesh colored streaks in the ash that coated them all over. From their height above the gorge, they could see quite some distance both upstream and downstream. The small creek or river that had been there was buried under layers of grey ash. Anne wondered if it was still there underneath the ash or had it evaporated as it became buried? As far as she could see in either direction, the walls of the gorge were too steep to drive up unless they could find a spot where a partial collapse created a kind of ramp, like the one they had tumbled down into the gorge. Their only way out would have to be the way they came in. At least they could climb up and out even if they couldn't get the Toyota to drive up.

Finally, she attempted to answer the question Billy had implied before they started climbing up to the ridge. "It could be that the explosion which started this eruption sent huge ripples through time that echo across millions of years. Perhaps these ripples hit other time ripples coming from other catastrophic events further into the future and they bounce back and forth. I mean this is only a crazy guess. But what if catastrophic events can upset the flow of time? What if it causes ripples that bounce back and forth, that echo and reflect? Nobody has said that they understand time. Is it fixed? Or can it be affected in ways we can't understand or explain? Does it always move only in one direction? What if this isn't true and it behaves in ways that we simply can't explain?"

"Sound's crazy to me."

"Just go along with it for a minute. What if someone gets caught in one of these ripples and is shifted forward or backward through time? What if one of those ripples hits another ripple from another catastrophic event, and they both pause momentarily before moving through or around each other? If you happen to be caught at that moment you could get shifted to some other time, do you think that could be possible?"

"Or drive into it as we did?"

"Exactly. We could have driven into a time ripple or a reflection of a time past, and suddenly, here we are."

"I don't know. I guess it's possible. Anything is possible. Somehow, we got here from where we were, didn't we?"

"We certainly did. And if we don't find a way back, then this is where we'll stay."

Anne could feel her body getting stiffer by the minute. Her head where she had bumped it during that wild ride down into the gorge was throbbing. She felt an infinite lethargy seeping into her and wondered if she might have a concussion. Suddenly, because she was thinking about pain and concussion, her whole body ached so hard she almost fell over. She staggered, grabbed onto Billy for momentary support.

"Are you alright?" Billy asked.

"No. No I'm not. I think I may have torn a cartilage in my shoulder when we tumbled down the into the gorge."

If she raised her right arm too high a severe pain shot up into her neck and the back of her head.

"If we don't start moving soon, I won't be able to move at all."

In the clump of stunted trees, they had been heading towards, something moved causing a sudden fall of ash from branches higher up.

"There's something in there," Billy said softly. He pointed his rifle towards the trees.

Anne forced the pain washing through her shoulder and neck to go away. She focused on watching what Billy was doing and she felt the pain in her shoulder, neck and head recede to a dull ache. It would stay that way until she relaxed, then she was sure it would come flooding back, to overwhelm her completely.

Again, the tops of some of the small, stunted trees along the ridge moved abruptly, throwing a small amount of ash up into the air.

Billy stepped forward with the rifle pointing ahead of him.

"Be careful," Anne cautioned as Billy moved closer to the trees.

Billy ignored her advice. When he reached the edge of the trees, he shook the closest one as hard as possible. He wanted to knock the ash off it so he could see in under the canopy of leaves. It fell in clouds about him making him sneeze. There was a scrabbling sound moving away from him, more ash floating and settling. It sounded like something was being dragged along the ground. He waited until the ash had settled before he stepped in amongst the trees.

"Billy."

He didn't answer.

She was about to call out again when he answered. "It's all right. Just follow me in and wait till your eyes get used the dark."

Anne stepped slowly in under the trees and stood next to Billy. He pointed further in towards the darker part, where the stunted trees grew denser. "Can you see it?"

It took a few moments for her eyes to adjust to the low light level under the trees before she could see the creature's almost feline head, with its eyes unblinking, staring at them. Suddenly all her aches and pains vanished She couldn't believe that what she was looking at was real.

"Yes," she whispered. "It's beautiful."

"That's the big cat I saw," Billy said softly.

As they spoke the animal opened its mouth and hissed at them. Its most distinctive feature was the two elongated teeth that Anne knew were for slashing and tearing into the flesh of its prey. It didn't seem frightened, but it edged slightly away from them exposing its fawn and brown spotted side. A thick bushy tail twitched nervously. The fur under its neck and underbelly seemed almost creamy and was without spots. Billy edged a little closer. The animal raised itself up pushing with one of its powerful front legs. It snarled, exposing more large sharp teeth. Its other front leg hung uselessly. It was bigger than Anne had imagined, at least a metre and a half long, and when it reared up and snarled at them it must have been a metre tall.

She had seen many illustrations of what different scientists thought Thylacoleo would look like; some had stripes like a thylacine, others had spots and stripes or spots in rows like stripes, extrapolations from fossil or bone fragments found over the years, and although they all approximated the real thing, none of them looked like what she was seeing in front of her. She looked at its massive front legs and saw the opposing claw that obviously helped it to climb trees, and that like a cat's retractable claws, could be used for tearing into flesh to eviscerate its prey. She couldn't imagine it eating grass or fruit. When it opened wide its mouth she could see the sharp teeth, and with its two long razor-sharp fangs emerging from each side of its upper jaw, there was no question it was a carnivore. But what stunned her was its eyes. She looked into them and felt she was seeing something intelligent deep inside. Here was the largest marsupial carnivore that ever existed in Australia, an animal at the top of the food chain. It had nothing to fear from any other animal that existed alongside it, and it knew its place in its environment. It understood what it was. She had never seen that in an animal before. She felt it knew what had happened to it and what its fate would be. It was a revelation that stunned her.

"It's beautiful," she whispered.

"It's got a broken leg," Billy said softly. "Did I do that when I shot it?"

"You missed it — remember? You showed me where your bullet hit the branch. It must have been blown over the edge of the chasm by the pressure wave from the explosion. The same as we were."

"That's a relief. You think it broke its leg when it fell over the edge?"

"It's a long way down for any animal to fall, and there's no ramp here like we tumbled down. It's a straight drop down to this ledge."

"Yeah, you're right. This is where it broke its leg. And it crawled in here to hide."

"It's not a cat," Anne said after a while. A sense of wonder coloured her voice. "It looks more like a huge possum."

"With teeth like that?" Billy whispered. He didn't want to talk too loud in case the thing got frightened and attacked them. An animal cornered is dangerous, and this one looked more dangerous than anything he had ever seen before, even with a broken front leg. It had nowhere to go. But it was a beautiful animal, he had to admit that. "It's much bigger than I thought it would be."

"It's a marsupial lion. Thylacoleo Carnifex." Anne said. "It has to be." She studied every visible detail that she could see in the dim light beneath the ash-covered canopy of the trees. "I've seen their fossils, made sketches of them based on the bones we've found. But never could I ever have imagined I'd see one that's alive. These animals became extinct over twenty thousand years ago." She turned to Billy. "Is this what people see and think is a puma, or a mountain lion?"

"I don't know. I suppose so. Maybe animals like this are probably what have been grabbing the sheep."

"They must get caught up in the time ripples, just like we got caught; only they go forward to our time." Then she added, "and back to here, or people in our time would have shot one of them by now. It obviously doesn't happen often, but it must happen sometimes, or we wouldn't keep getting reports of big cats attacking sheep and other animals."

"And if they can go forward," Billy said excitedly, "then so can we."

And instantly Anne's eyes lit up. "That's it. That's what we've got to do."

"What?"

"We've got to find a ripple we can drive into," Anne said excitedly. "If these lions can go back and forth then the time ripples must be stable. At least for a while, I hope, because that may be the only way we can get back. Billy, we've got to go back to the volcano. That's the source of the disturbance that created the ripple which brought us here."

"What should we do about this lion?"

The trapped animal made a hissing sound in response to their excited voices.

That put a damper on her excitement as she thought about the animal. With a broken leg it would not survive and would die a slow death under the ash covered trees. There didn't seem to be much hope for it.

"It's got a broken leg. How long do you think it can survive like that?" She hesitated for a moment, then said, barely able to get the words out, "You'll have to shoot it."

"What?" Billy looked at her, dumbfounded.

"Didn't you want to shoot something big?"

He nodded, reluctant to admit to himself that it was what he had wanted to do.

"Didn't you try to shoot it before? Didn't you want to bring back a trophy?"

Billy hesitated. "That was different then."

"It's not going to run away, so it should be an easy shot," Anne said with a harshness she didn't feel. She was stunned momentarily at the way her voice sounded. The very thought of killing such a beautiful animal, extinct in her time, was anathema to her. She didn't want to do it any more than Billy did. But they couldn't leave a seriously injured animal to die a slow death, which would certainly be what happened if they left it there with its broken leg.

"Why don't we let it live out its life?" Billy said. He wasn't certain anymore about shooting a beautiful creature like this. Here was an animal whose whole species had died out or was about to die out and become extinct in the future, the future they come from — and the professor was asking him to shoot it. "It'll be extinct soon enough," Billy muttered. "All of them will"

"It's in agony Billy. It's got a broken leg. It can't survive. Don't you think it better to put it out of its misery rather than let it starve to death in agony?" She hated herself for saying such things, but it was the humane thing to do. After all, people do it all the time when they have pets or domestic animals that are too sick to be cured or too badly injured, they have them put down, put out of their misery. Why would this be any different? But somehow it seemed different.

Billy stared at the animal's sad brown eyes. It seemed to sense what was about to happen. It stood very still. Reluctantly Billy raised the rifle to his shoulder. He held it firmly and sighted along the barrel. His eyes looked deeply into the eyes of the lion. It wasn't frightened of him. These animals had never seen a human up close and had no fear of them. But in Billy's imagination he thought he could see in the animal's eyes an awareness of the fact it was going to die, either by the hand of the strange creatures in front of it, or as a result of the eruption and having a broken front leg.

His arm shook as he tried to hold the rifle steady. No. It's not fair, he thought. He couldn't do it. He let his arms and the rifle drop down.

"What's wrong?" Anne asked.

"I can't do it."

"Yes you can. You must." Then thinking perhaps Billy didn't want her to see how nervous or reluctant he was to do it she backed away. "I'll wait back there." She moved away until she was out from under the clump of trees.

She stood and looked back along the direction to where they had left Jimmy and Big Bill checking the Toyota.

Alone under the tree canopy, Billy once again raised the rifle and sighted along it. His own eyes expressed the sadness he felt as the enigmatic eyes of the lion looked deep into him. He knew it understood what he was about to do, understood its fate. It made a low mewling sound as if to say: it's all right. I understand. Do it please. And finally, Billy was able to do what he had to.

"Sorry," he mouthed silently.

He pulled the trigger.

The lion's head jerked slightly, then the animal fell over.

Billy turned and walked out from under the trees.

When Anne stood beside him, he snapped angrily at her, "Aren't you going to take a photo of it?"

She had completely forgotten she had her camera with her, hanging from a strap around her neck. It was very dark under the trees, but the camera had a pop-up flash that automatically activated if there wasn't enough light. She went reluctantly back in under the trees. Looking at the lifeless form awkwardly laying on the ash covered ground she found herself crying. It looked like a heap of fur lying there. A dead animal, like roadkill. She felt nauseous and backed away. No photograph would ever do it justice.

Emerging from under the trees she turned to Billy and said, "It's too dark under there, even with the flash." That was her excuse, rather than trying to explain how awful pictures of a dead animal would be. Why had she not thought to take a shot while it was still alive?

"We could drag it out into the open?" Billy suggested.

"I don't need to take a picture of it," she snapped back at him. "I'll never forget how it looked."

From their vantage point on the ledge, they could see a fair way along the gorge in the direction they had been trying to go. It got deeper with the walls steeper and closer together.

"There's no way out that way," Billy said. "I think the only way out is the way we came down."

"But the ramp is too steep." Jimmy said when Billy and Anne returned and told them there was no other way out of the gorge other than the rough ramp. The gorge gets narrower and deeper beyond where we went." Neither she nor Billy said anything about shooting the large catlike creature under the trees. The gunshot had been muffled by the dense ash covering everything and the others hadn't heard it.

"It's not any better the other direction either," Big Bill said. He had gone a few hundred metres past the slippage they had used as a ramp and found nothing but steep walls with sections that had collapsed, but nothing like the ramp they had come down. "This is the only way out of here."

While they stood at the base of the landslide that was the rough ramp they had tumbled down, and considered how they could use it to get out of the chasm, Anne told them her theory about the time ripples. Still coming to terms with the event that projected them into the gorge, they accepted without question the fact that they had to get back to the volcano so they could find their way back to their own time. But the immediate problem they faced appeared insurmountable.

"We'll never be able to drive up that ramp," Jimmy said.

"It's too steep for the Toyota," Anne said, "but not for us to climb out."

"You want to leave the vehicle here?" Jimmy was bewildered. He couldn't understand her suggesting he abandon his Toyota SUV. Doesn't she know how much these things cost?

"Look at it Dad," Billy said. "It's a wreck. What can you do with it?"

"The boy is right," Big Bill said.

"The sooner we get moving the better," Anne reminded them.

The sky had begun to get even darker as the heavy clouds collided with the smoke and ash rising from the volcano. Lightening flashed ominously as the clouds continued to spread, covering most of the sky.

"We're going to get rain," Anne said. "If it rains a lot and we are still in this gorge we could be in trouble."

"Maybe we can winch it up," Jimmy finally concluded while staring at the steepness of the slope. He did not want to leave his Toyota behind no matter how battered it was. Damn it! If it was drivable, he was going to drive it. Or die trying, he muttered.

"Okay," Big Bill finally agreed. "Let's give it a go. We don't have any other option."

Jimmy jumped into the driver's seat and started the engine. He eased the vehicle out from under the ledge and backed it slowly to the rubble that formed the ramp.

Big Bill and Billy were already scrambling up the steep slope. Small stones and gravel they dislodged rolled down behind them. At the top of the ramp, they found several large rocks sticking up out of the ground, one of which seemed firm enough to hold the weight of the vehicle.

At the bottom of the slope Jimmy had faced the Toyota towards the slope. Big Bill and Billy slithered back down to the vehicle dislodging another cascade of gravel and small stones.

Lightening flashed again, and a few heavy drops of hot rain smacked down, creating little explosive puffs when it punctured the ash covering the ground.

"I don't think you've got a long enough cable," Big Bill said as he studied the cable wound around the winch in the front of the vehicle. "You're gonna have to drive up the ramp a bit."

"What about that boulder we hit on the way down? Wrap the cable around that and I'll winch up towards it. If we wedge some rocks behind the back wheels, it might stop us sliding down long enough to undo the cable and get it up to the rocks over the top."

"Billy and I will get some rocks," Anne said. She slipped the camera strap over her head and put the camera down off to one side so it wouldn't get in the way while she carried the rocks.

Big Bill grabbed the hook on the end of the cable. Jimmy released the clutch mechanism so Big Bill could drag the cable out as he climbed towards the large boulder embedded a third of the way up the slope.

"Okay," he called out once he had wrapped the cable around the rock and secured it with the hook.

By this time Anne and Billy had each placed several rocks part way up the slope, ready to slip them behind the rear wheels when needed. They stood level with the rocks, but a couple of metres away to avoid any slippage if the weight of the vehicle caused the slope to start collapsing.

Jimmy engaged the winch mechanism. He slowly took up the strain until the cable was taut.

"Watch out in case it slips off," he called from the driver's seat. "It'll fly back and hit you."

Big Bill stood well away from the boulder. He waved Jimmy to start reeling in the cable.

Jimmy increased the revs to the engine. The winch began turning. Slowly the vehicle started to move up the slope. The boulder shifted slightly.

"It's gonna roll down on top of you. It's not gonna hold," Big Bill called.

"It's got to," Jimmy called out over the noise of the engine.

Bit by bit the vehicle moved up the slope, and bit by bit, the rock the cable was tied around shifted. When the Toyota had gone its own length, Jimmy stopped. "Get those rocks behind the back wheels," he yelled.

As soon as Anne and Billy got the rocks wedged hard against the wheels, he released the tension on the cable. The vehicle slipped back a little, but it held.

"Bill," Jimmy called out. "See if you can get the cable lower down around the boulder. If we keep going it looks like it will tip over. Lower down it might hold long enough to get us high enough to get the cable over the rim."

When the cable had been retied closer to the base of the rock they started again, slowly winding it in so it gradually dragged the vehicle higher.

"That'll do," Big Bill yelled.

Quickly Anne and Billy wedged more rocks as tightly as possible behind the rear wheels. As they moved up the slope heavy drops of rain fell again. Lightning flashed jagged streaks and thunder rumbled with the noise of a thousand drums beaten simultaneously: a prelude to the heavens opening up.

From higher up the slope they could see that the vehicle had dragged the big boulder downward while it had winched itself up, but they had come up a third of the distance to the top. Perhaps now the cable would reach over the rim so they could lock onto something solid and haul the vehicle up the rest of the way.

Big Bill undid the cable. The vehicle slipped a little, but the rocks wedged behind the back wheels held it in place.

"So far so good," Anne said.

Dragging the cable behind him, Big Bill clawed his way higher then went over the top. Anne and Billy followed him as fast as the crumbly slope allowed.

There were several large granite boulders not far from the lip of the gorge. They were a bit further across from directly above the vehicle, which was good because they would have to drag it slightly sideways to miss the boulder they had used, or the vehicle would jam up against it and stop. The cable wasn't long enough to wrap completely around the boulder back from the edge, but it had weathered and split with a long crack almost dividing it in half.

"If we wedge the hook in that crack, it might do the trick," Big Bill said.

"Can you get it in far enough to hold?" Billy asked.

"We'll pound it in with some rocks."

When they were ready Jimmy started to winch in the cable. The Toyota slipped sideways as it slowly moved up the slope. Sweat poured off Jimmy's face as he concentrated on keeping the winding in as smooth as possible. If the cable broke, they were finished. It inched past the boulder initially used, and Jimmy was able to see that he had dragged it down almost a metre while he had been winching the vehicle up. If they hadn't stopped when they did, the boulder would have come unstuck and rolled down on top of the vehicle and that would have been the end of it. And of me too, Jimmy thought as he gripped the steering wheel with hands gone numb.

The moment the front of the vehicle appeared at the edge of the gorge the three on top of the rim cheered. Sitting inside behind the steering wheel Jimmy smiled triumphantly. He didn't join in with the cheering. It isn't over yet. He had the engine running and the wheels slowly turning hoping to gain traction to take pressure off the winch. I've still got to get over the rim…

The edge started to crumple, but Jimmy had it in gear and all 4 wheels were turning, gripping, then slipping, and gripping again. For a moment he thought he had made it.

But the wheels spinning furiously only managed to loosen the edge instead of gripping it, enabling it to crumble more rapidly. Suddenly a broad swathe of the edge crumpled, and the vehicle dropped down, its entire weight hanging on the thin metal cable.

Jimmy's smile vanished, replaced with a grim glare. He had the engine screaming and the wheels spinning but there was nothing anymore for the wheels to grip. The vehicle was hanging vertically against a new steeper edge where the upper part of the ramp had been.

With a twang loud enough to be heard above the revving of the engine the cable splintered and unraveled, then snapped.

It seemed an eternity before the vehicle started to slide backwards. But once it began to move it slid rapidly down for several metres before it rolled over and bounced down the slope throwing up clouds of ash, bits of loose dirt, and small rocks.

"Jesus," Big bill yelled.

Anne and Billy stared, too stunned to move.

The vehicle slithered on its side for the last few metres before coming to a stop against a huge rock in the flatter part of the gorge.

"Dad," Billy called out, and suddenly he was over the side slithering down the slope in a cloud of rattling stones and loose dirt. He wanted to run down but he knew if he tried that he would tumble over and probably kill himself smashing into a rock. He slithered down sitting on his bum coming to a jarring stop when he hit the bottom.

Anne and Big Bill followed as quickly as they could. When they got to the bottom Billy had already climbed up onto the wrecked vehicle which was lying on its left side, trying to wrench open the driver's door that was now pointing up to the black sky.

"Dad's not moving," Billy said, "And I can't open the door."

"We've got to hurry, "Anne said.

There was an electric tingle in the air. She could hear the air sizzling, could feel the electricity carried by the moisture in the air. Her skin tingled. She thought it smelled like gunpowder did after firecrackers had exploded.

Big Bill and Billy were both pulling at the door. Finally, they managed to open it a crack. Anne climbed up onto the side of the vehicle and between the three of them they wrenched the door open enough for Billy to slip down into the vehicle.

"He's still breathing," Billy called back to them, the relief obvious in his voice.

"Can you lift him up so we can grab him?" Anne asked.

"As soon as I can undo his seat belt."

Suddenly it started raining, big drops smacking into them, washing the ash off their faces and clothes. It got heavier, bucketing down. There was a huge lightning flash, and the explosion of thunder around them almost burst their eardrums. A vicious wind gusted about them and made the rain lash them like the tip of a whip. Each of them felt residual electricity pass through them. They shuddered involuntarily. If any of them touched the metal of the vehicle sparks zapped from their fingers across to the metal.

Big Bill and Anne grasped Jimmy's arms as soon as they appeared in the doorway and dragged him up out of the vehicle. They held him while Billy climbed back out. Together they lowered him down the roof side of the vehicle to Billy who had jumped down ahead of them.

"We have to get out of here as soon as possible," Anne said.

"Shouldn't we see if he's all right first?" Billy asked.

"Let's get up the slope," Anne snapped impatiently. "This gorge is going to fill with water." She grabbed one of Jimmy's arms and held it around the back of her neck. She turned towards the slope they had slithered down and started moving towards it, forcing Billy to do the same. Big Bill went ahead to look for the easiest way up.

"There was a river in the gorge before it half filled with ash," Anne said as they started up the slope. "Where do you think that water has gone?"

"How would I know?" Billy yelled at her over the noise of the wind and lashing rain.

Their feet kept sliding as the loose rubble and ash slipped away beneath them. The heavy rain washed the ash down, making the slope muddy, slippery, and more treacherous than when it was loose and dry. But they had no option. It was their only way up out of the gorge.

For every step they took higher they slipped back part of it. Dragging Jimmy's inert weight didn't help, but between the two of them they managed to drag him all the way up the steeply angled slope. When they reached the top, and had climbed over, they were exhausted. Barely able to move, they flopped down and sat on the wet ground. The rain revived Jimmy and he sat between them shaking his head as if to clear it. There was a huge lump on the side of his skull, which made his head oddly shaped.

"We made it," Jimmy said.

"We made it alright Dad, but your beloved Toyota didn't."

"Oh Shit." Suddenly Jimmy realized that the big boulder he was staring at down in the gorge was his battered Toyota lying on its side. "Shit."

"What are we gonna do?"

"There's nothing we can do," Big Bill said.

The pounding rain washed rivulets of ash down the slope they had just climbed. It created muddy waterfalls that made the slope dangerous, pooling in holes along the floor of the gorge.

"There's no way we could climb up that slope now," Big Bill said. "I'm amazed we actually made it up at all."

The slope was far steeper now that before, with the rain having washed the looser part away near the top leaving several metres of scarping. Even as they watched, the very edge started to collapse as the pounding rain washed away the looser soil.

"We should move away from the edge," Big Bill said, "in case it collapses further. I don't want to end up down there again."

"At least I feel human again," Anne said, "now that the rain has washed the ash off me."

They got to their feet and holding each other for stability they moved back from the edge of the gorge.

"What happened to the water?" Billy asked, recalling what Anne had said as they struggled to get Jimmy out of the gorge.

"I think it got blocked upstream somewhere where the ash fall was heavier, otherwise it would not have got buried here."

"What does that mean?" Jimmy asked.

"If it's blocked upstream, how long do you think it will take to breach the ash barrier? The ash is soft... and with this rain to help it along."

"We've got to get the vehicle out." Jimmy mumbled.

"Forget it," Big Bill said. "There's no way."

"There's got to be a way," Jimmy said without conviction. He was exhausted. His head throbbed. The focus of his eyes kept blurring. He could barely stand without support. It was remarkable that he had survived the fall inside the Toyota.

He's probably concussed, Anne thought as they staggered well away from the edge. They stopped and looked back. The hopelessness of their situation was only now sinking in. They were stuck there, and they were on foot. They had no supplies other than what was in the wrecked vehicle, and at that moment none of them considered climbing down into the gorge, knowing that getting in and out of it was now impossible.

"What are we gonna do?" Billy asked.

Before anyone could answer or even consider possibilities, they heard the noise. It was like storm surf pounding a rocky headland or the roar of a huge waterfall, only this swollen river wasn't falling over a high cliff. It came roaring along the gorge as a grey churning wall of water several metres high pushing boulders and rocks and broken tree trunks ahead of it. It slammed into the wrecked vehicle, and bounced over it like it was a huge boulder in the way. The vehicle held underwater for a few seconds before it popped to the surface and was carried along for a moment before disappearing forever beneath the grey swirling chaos of the river.

The four of them stood there wet and forlorn; too worn out even to think. They stared at the swirling dirty water rushing along the gorge. They could see the softer edges of the gorge slipping and sliding down into that fast-moving river. Even the slippery ramp they had climbed up had disappeared into the raging river. They forced themselves to move. Dragging their feet, they started walking slowly in the direction they had driven to get where they were.

They did not look back.

"We have to go back closer to the volcano." Anne said after they had gone far enough that the rushing water in the gorge was barely audible way behind them.

They staggered erratically through heavy rain no longer warm, and they started to shiver.

Suddenly Jimmy stopped moving. "Why?" he asked, his voice flat. He felt that a part of himself had been lost when his Toyota vanished beneath the grey waters of the river in the gorge. He knew this was crazy and was probably the result of the massive bump that throbbed on the side of his head. That was the only hot part of his whole being. He touched the bump and felt the heat of it on his fingers. It seemed to be sucking all the heat out of his body. "I don't feel too good," he mumbled.

"You'll be all right," Anne said. "We have to keep moving though."

"Why should we?" Big Bill asked irritably. "There's nowhere we can go. We might as well stay here. The other group might come along and rescue us."

Anne snorted. She shook her head. "Fat chance of that," she said. "How do you know if they followed us through? Did you see any other vehicle behind us as we drove away from the volcano?"

No one said anything.

"Our only option is to go back to the point where we entered this time, this place."

"And just how is that going to help us?" Big Bill finally asked.

"It's where we got into this mess. I think it's also the only way we're going to get out. So, let's get moving."

She started walking towards the clump of trees where Billy had first seen the big Cat. They had to go around that to head back towards the volcano. Slowly, reluctantly at first, the others followed. Billy took his father's arm and urged him to walk while at the same time helping to support him.

Because of the rain they couldn't see the plumes of smoke and ash from the volcano, nor could they follow the tracks they had made in the lush grass coming this way in the first place. The ash and the rain had obliterated all of that. But now that the rain had compacted the ash it was easier to walk on. Underfoot it felt more like wet sand rather than soft snow.

"The volcano is the only place I can imagine where we'll find the time ripple that brought us here. If not that one, it may keep producing smaller ripples. We will have to go through one to get back, just as we did to get here," Anne told them after they had trudged through the sludge for some time.

"What if it takes us further back instead of into the future to our own time? Or perhaps to a different future time?"

"It's a chance we'll have to take," Anne said. "There must be a huge catastrophe in our future that's set up an enormous temporal barrier. All these ripples from events like this eruption here bounce forward, hit it and come back. I think we got caught in one coming back. We need to get into one going forward. Just like the lions must do when they appear in our time, then disappear before anyone can catch them."

"What lions?" Big Bill asked.

"The one's we've been looking for," Billy said.

"They do this to get our sheep?"

"No," Billy snapped in a surge of anger. He took a deep breath and feeling calmer said, "they get caught accidentally. They go forwards and back. To them a sheep is no different from any other game they might hunt. Maybe it's easier to catch. They don't know about the ripples. It just happens that the ripples pass through their hunting range."

"What if it doesn't work?" Jimmy asked. He pulled away from Billy and was now walking unaided. He seemed more in control of himself.

"It's all the same. If we don't try anything, we're stuck." Big bill said. "We might as well try the volcano. We don't have any other option. We might still be stuck here, but we have to try. Like Anne says, maybe that's the only place we could find a way back."

"And the sooner we look for it the better," Anne added.

They were all stiff from the battering and bruising their bodies had sustained, but walking seemed to ease the pain. The more they moved along the easier it became. Anne knew that if for whatever reason they stopped again, they would not be able to continue. They had no option but to keep moving. Although she felt terribly depressed, she encouraged them by leading the way and by trying to remain cheerful. She drew on reserves of energy she never knew she had. She didn't doubt for a moment that they would find their way back. The fact that they got here meant that there must be a way back. They had to keep moving or their bodies would simply give up.

"Come on," she said encouragingly. "We haven't got all day."

What had once been a lush grassy plain was now a dark grey expanse of wet partially compacted ash. Huge black clouds still roiled across the sky. Lightning flashed ominously, and thunder rolled across the plain in tidal waves of sound. The rain slowly eased. Finally, it stopped, but they still kept walking.

They had a long way to go.

It seemed like forever.

Their feet dragged, but they continued to struggle forward.

The light was much dimmer as the clouds above thickened. They had no idea where the sun was but assumed it must be late afternoon. The plume of rising black smoke and ash disappearing into the heavy cumulus clouds above it was visible now the rain had stopped. It was their target. It told them where the volcano was.

None of them spoke. It was too much effort. Even Anne's cheerfulness had vanished. She felt as dispirited as the others. All they could do to keep moving was to shift one foot forward, drag the other to meet it, step forward again, and again, never stopping. She knew that if for whatever reason they stopped, that would be the end of them.

More lightning flashed around them as they got closer to the valley where the volcano was erupting. Thunder rattled their bones. The ground shook softly beneath them: little shudders as if like a human it shivered when it was cold. It was probably caused by super-heated steam bubbling through the lava deep underground.

Finally, as they entered the valley leading to the ancient caldera they had driven into what seemed ages ago, patchy smoke from burning trees and shrubs whirled around them. Jimmy stopped, and they all stopped with him. They stood to one side of a slowly moving glistening ebony-black mass that filled the lower reaches of the caldera. The leading edge was about a metre thick, and as they watched, it cracked and split as it moved. A deep red glowed beneath the ebony, before darkening as it cooled. Small flames burned around the bottom of the leading edge as it slowly flowed over the once lush grass. Any bushes in its path instantly dried out and burst into flame as the lava touched them.

They felt the heat rising off it in waves. The air immediately in front of it shimmered with the heat, but further in where the surface had cooled more the air was clearer. They could see almost right across the ancient caldera and the whole basin was filled with cooling lava. Anne was grateful that there had not been a true explosion other than that small burst of ash and steam that had burst from it and pushed them over the edge of the chasm. What she could see was a slow steady eruption, and that was good. There were spots she could see where fresh lava welled up, deep red and glowing strong enough to be hard to look at as it spilled over in layer after layer of slowly moving molten rock. It seemed to darken rapidly as it cooled, but fresh layers flowed over it. It would flow down towards the plain they had recently traversed, down along the way they had taken to get back here. They were lucky they had got here before that happened or there would have been no way they could get close enough to the original site of the eruption.

"Just look at that," Billy yelled over the grinding and crackling noise the lava made as it moved inexorably forward. He turned to Anne. "You should take some pictures Professor."

"Shit," she said as she suddenly remembered: "I left the camera back where we tried to winch up out of the gorge."

"I don't think we can go back for it now," Jimmy said. He smiled. For all the effort it had taken him, and all of them to walk back to this point, he looked a lot better than he had back at the gorge. The bump on his head had receded and was nowhere near as large as it had been just after they had dragged him from the wrecked vehicle.

The lava moved inexorably towards them, its leading edge continuously splitting as fresh hot lava pushed through, cooling as it was exposed to the air and the rain which continued to fall in short splutters, then turning black like the rest. The air above the lava shimmered with the heat rising and expanding. Hot updraughts funneled the smoke from burning plant material up into the sky where it spread outwards. Gunpowder cracking sounds, the rumble of the lava moving, like the slowed down sound of a deep river, the whoosh of flames as nearby trees suddenly ignited filled the air.

"It's good to feel warm again," Jimmy said as he stood near the edge of the lava.

"Do you see anything like the mirage we drove through to get here?" Big Bill asked.

They almost had to shout to hear each other speak.

Anne shook her head. The whole idea was ridiculous, hopeless. It was too dark here for mirages, and besides the heavy smoke from the volcano as well as the burning scrub obscured the sun. She was beginning to doubt that coming here was a good idea.

Waves of heat enveloped them as the lava continued to creep closer.

"We can't stay here," Jimmy said.

"We have to get closer," Anne said.

"You're insane."

"It's the only way. Look—" There was excitement in her voice as she pointed across the lava filled caldera to where an apparent mirage shimmered with a tinge of semi-transparent green. She knew this was something other than a mirage. "That's it," she yelled animatedly. She gestured frantically towards it so the others could see where it was.

For a moment she imagined she saw the image of a 4-wheel drive vehicle shimmering deep in the greenness of the mirage... their vehicle, Jimmy's Toyota. Then it was gone and all she could see was a glistening highly reflective surface like that of a bubble. There were tears in her eyes. She blinked furiously, shaking her head to dispel them.

"We have to go through that," she said.

They all stared at her, looked at her as if she was mad.

"We have to..."

Smoke wafted around them and then cleared as another wave of heat pushed it upwards. The green shimmering bubble had disappeared.

"That's lava," Jimmy stated as if speaking to a child. "It's very hot. It's molten rock. It's not something you can walk across. If I had any brains, I would never have listened to you. We should have got as far away from this as possible, not..."

"It's back," Billy shouted.

Ripples of light seemed to be bubbling out of the centre of the caldera, forming bubbles that glistened, like the soap bubbles children blow for fun. The bubbles expanded rapidly. Some of them popped silently, vanishing in an instant. One or two persisted, ones without defined edges. They drifted across the top of the lava.

"That one," Anne pointed. "The one that looks green. We should go through that one."

"We can't walk over lava," Jimmy yelled.

"Yes you can," Anne snapped impatiently at him. "It's solid on the top where it's cooled. The rain has cooled it so it should be hard enough. The fresh lava flows underneath. If we stay on the areas that are rippled and cracked and not the real smooth places, we should be able to do it."

"You are crazy." Jimmy shook his head. "Shit I must be crazy even listening to you."

"Jimmy, it's our only chance," Big Bill said.

"We'll be here till we die," Billy said. "We have to do it Dad."

"Trust me," Anne said. "You can walk over it. Vulcanologists in Hawaii do it all the time when they take temperatures and samples of fresh lava."

"I'm not a damned vulcanologist."

"Dad…"

"All right," he said angrily. He needed the anger to make him do what as a rational person he would never consider. "Let's do it. Let's do it before I have too much time to think about it."

He looked for a spot that seemed black enough, solid enough to walk on.

"Come on," Anne said. "That mirage is moving away from us." And she stepped onto the black surface of the solidified lava.

"All right, all right," Jimmy snapped, still reluctant to go onto the lava.

"Do it," Big Bill yelled.

"What the hell," Jimmy said. He stepped tentatively onto the solidified lava.

They could smell the acrid stench of burning rubber. It overpowered the sulfurous smell coming from the volcano.

"I'm on fire." Jimmy shouted. He looked down at his rubber-soled boots. Smoke curled out from around his feet.

"Don't stop," Anne yelled. "Keep going before your boots burn away."

"I'm on fire too," Big Bill said as he ran across the hot black lava towards the strange shimmering green glow.

"Come on Dad," Billy encouraged. "That's the way."

What if it cracks and we sink in? Jimmy wondered, but he kept running, willing himself to keep moving, knowing now that if he stopped he would be finished.

A bubble of light burst next to them, momentarily blinding Jimmy. He flinched. His feet had taken on a life of their own, moving him on towards the rippling bubble of lightness that seemed to grow steadily in front of them. It slowly drifted away, and he began to panic. *What if it burst before we could reach it? We'd be stuck here. We'd burn up on top of the lava.* His heart raced so hard he thought it would burst.

They were so close now Anne could see trees and green grass through the glow of the light.

"That's the way," Anne yelled, "I can see trees and grass…" It was like looking at a blurred reflection in water. She couldn't focus on it because it kept shimmering. It was impossible that such a thing could be sitting on top of a field of fresh lava.

Suddenly there was a hideous scream to her left. She turned and saw Big Bill's foot had slipped in. The lava surface where he had been running must have been thinner and had cracked beneath his weight. His left foot had gone under into the lava.

"Go Jimmy," she yelled. "That's the one." She pointed at the shimmering bubble with the blurred trees. "I'll help Bill. I'm closer than you."

"I've got him," Billy called out.

"Be careful the lava's thin there."

Billy was dragging Big Bill away from the smooth shiny surface. She could see the lava glowing in the hole and the cracks where Big Bill's foot had gone into it. She grabbed his other arm and helped Billy drag him away from the broken surface. Intense heat wafted around them.

I'm all right," Big Bill said. "I can't feel anything." But they held him up as they struggled towards the shimmering bubble Jimmy had already entered, hoping it wouldn't suddenly pop and disappear like some of the other bubbles had. He hopped on his good foot as they dragged him across the thicker lava towards the glimmering haze.

For a moment, Anne thought they wouldn't make it. The glowing bubble of haze seemed to drift away from them as fast as they tried to move towards it.

"We're not gonna make it," Big Bill said despondently.

"Don't fucking say that" Anne snapped at him. "We can't give up now."

Suddenly the hazy bubble shifted direction and flowed towards them. It enveloped them and instantly they felt nauseous. Cold shivers ran down their spines. Billy vomited. Anne felt as if something had twisted her intestines, knotting them into hard lumps like you get with salmonella poisoning. Big Bill remained stony faced, eyes screwed shut.

They hit soft ground, stumbled, fell in a heap in a dry sandy creek bed.

There was a blessed silence only broken by the soft rustling of half-dead gum tree leaves as a drift of warm dry air wafted over the tops of the trees. Above them the sky was a steely grey blue with a long thin contrail left by a high-flying jet dividing it in half. The air smelled dusty, with a hint of eucalyptus.

"We did it," Billy shouted excitedly as he stood up. "We ran across lava. Who's going to believe that?" then suddenly quieter he said, "I don't even believe it myself."

"Well I bloody do," Big Bill said. "Look at my foot." He was sitting on the sandy ground where they had fallen as they emerged. "The nerves must be dead because I can't feel anything."

Anne looked around, "Where's Jimmy?" She couldn't see him anywhere. He had gone through only a moment before them. He should be there waiting for them.

Big Bill's left foot was raw and blistered to just above the ankle. The heavy boots he wore had saved his foot. It had only been immersed in the lava for a few seconds, which had been enough to burn away his boot, but they had managed to pull him out before more than peripheral damage had been done to his foot.

"You're in shock," Anne said quietly, turning back to him.

"Hey, a hoarse voice called out, "You made it." It was Jimmy. He was quite some distance further up into the valley they had once started to drive into. "I couldn't see you anywhere. I didn't think you'd made it back," he called out as he stumbled towards them. He looked as if he was about to collapse from exhaustion and Billy ran to him and grabbed him by the arm to hold him steady.

"Take it easy Dad, we all made it back."

Across the dry plain a line of dust could be seen rising as the other vehicle they started out with drove towards them.

Billy let go of his father and ran towards it waving his arms above his head., He yelled out "Over here, over here."

They must have seen him because the vehicle turned and came rapidly towards them. When it reached them, its three occupants tumbled out and stared at them in confusion.

"We had an accident," Billy said before they could say anything. "And Big Bill's hurt."

"What the hell happened?" One of them managed to ask. "How did you get here?"

"Where's your vehicle?" Another said. "We thought you went the other way."

They rushed across to where Big Bill was still sitting on the sandy ground with Jimmy and Anne standing next to him.

"We had an accident," Jimmy repeated, his voice flat, dead sounding.

"You look bloody awful," one of the newcomers commented.

"I bumped my head when we rolled over going down into a chasm."

"What the fuck are you talking about?"

"And I got my foot burned in the lava," Big Bill said. And suddenly realizing how ridiculous that sounded he started to laugh. His companions joined in, all of them hysterical, while the newcomers stared at them in bewilderment. Then the pain hit him, and he fell back. "Jesus," he moaned and stated shivering uncontrollably.

"What Lava?"

"What's he on about?"

"It's a concussion," Anne said, and when she saw them looking at the horrible burn done to his foot she added: "From the accident. He bumped his head. So did Jimmy. We need to get them both to a hospital."

"Jesus, professor, you don't look too good yourself."

"I'm all right."

"We'll get a tow truck to come out here and pick up your vehicle," one of them said. "Where'd you leave it?" They looked about, trying to see where Jimmy's wrecked Toyota was.

"Forget it," Jimmy said when he realized what they were talking about. "It's extinct."

The four of them burst into laughter again, but the others wouldn't leave it alone. They said they'd call for a tow truck to come and get the vehicle.

He couldn't tell them what had really happened, they wouldn't believe it. He had to tell them something realistic. "It blew up," he said. "That's how Big Bill got his foot burned."

"It blew up?"

"Yeah, we rolled over and as we were getting out it blew up." Even as he said it, he knew it sounded unbelievably stupid, but what else could he tell them. No one would believe what had really happened to them.

"And all this happened in the last half hour?"

"What do you mean 'the last half hour'?" Jimmy said. "We've been gone all day."

"We split up half an hour ago. You went off one way while we came this way, and now we find you here. How the fuck did you get here?"

Jimmy didn't know how to answer that. He looked around and realized the guys were right, it was still early morning. The sun had barely risen above the tree tops and long shadows still spread across the desiccated grass. The time ripple or reflection, whatever it was, had deposited them back in their own time, and only a half hour after they'd left, but in a different spot. *Those blasted ripples must drift around...*

One of the men from the other vehicle used a mobile phone to call the hospital to tell them they had someone with a badly burned foot and could they have an ambulance meet them along Far-creek Road. It would take a while for the ambulance to get there because it had to come from another larger town, fifty kilometres further along the highway. They sat Big Bill in the front of their vehicle where he could stretch his leg and burnt foot out under the dashboard. The others all squeezed into the back of the 4-wheel drive.

The driver drove the vehicle once around in a circle as if searching for their footprints which would show him the direction they had walked from their wrecked vehicle. There were none, other than what they had made in the sand around the point where they had been sitting. He headed back across the dusty plain towards the town.

They laughed hysterically and joked amongst themselves about the lava and pyroclastic flows and extinct lions all the way back into town.

No one ever found the wreckage of Jimmy's 'blown-up' Toyota although a short search had been conducted along the trail where he had supposedly gone, as well as around the spot where they had been found several kilometres away. There were no wheel tracks or footprints anywhere to indicate how they had gotten from one place to another.

None of those who had travelled in Jimmy's Toyota would ever say anything other than it had blown up and was beyond all hope of rebuilding, and no one should bother to look for it.

It was a mystery everyone would remember and talk about next year when once again they would have another puma hunt.

A Last Abstract Cry

I was over the fence and into the side street in a flash, fear giving me strength and speed I never knew I had.

Ear shattering metallic groans and squeals came from the monstrous structure behind me. Loose cables snapped taut with a twang. It should not have been possible, but it was moving. The ground shook as the structure tried to uproot itself.

I was sure it wanted to stop me.

I bolted along the side fence to the front street and almost slammed into the crowd that had gathered in the street to watch the groaning structure.

"You alright?" someone asked.

"You were in there for hours," another said.

I pushed and shoved my way through them. "Out of the way," I snarled at them. "Get away from here, all of you." I yelled as I shoved and pushed at those who tried to stop me.

Finally, I broke free of them and ran down the street. Several started to follow me.

One of them called out: "What about the artist?"

He was a famous painter of gigantic abstract pieces that sold for a fortune and were displayed in large public spaces, huge galleries, big bank foyers, and corporate boardrooms.

There was something about his work, a three dimensionality that if looked at carefully would draw your eye relentlessly into the painting, and you would be lost for hours contemplating — who knows? Everyone saw something different.

When I knocked on his front door, he called out for me to come in.

I pushed the door open and stepped into a mess. Bits of rusty metal, and parts of machines littered the passage. I stepped over coils of fencing wire.

"I'm in the kitchen," his husky voice called from beyond the end of the passage.

I glanced into what I assumed had been a living room to see every available surface covered with clocks and watches: hundreds, perhaps thousands of them in various stages of disassembly, many of them still working. The room was filled with a subdued susurrus as all the various ticking combined into a single blurred noise. All the rooms off the passageway were full of similar junk.

After stepping over what looked like an old vacuum cleaner and entering the kitchen there was no preamble. The artist simply stated, as if we were in the middle of a conversation, "I've gone beyond painting. I need to work with something more solid."

I nodded. The smell of burnt rubber and hot metal filled the air.

The artist had a pair of black tinted welding goggles in his hand as he gestured towards the back of the house. He threw them onto the table as if suddenly realizing he didn't need them anymore and didn't quite know where to put them.

"As soon as you told me your name over the phone I knew who you were," he said. "I've read some of your work. It's not bad. You seem to understand the artists you write about. That's why I said you could come over."

There was nothing to say to that so again I nodded.

"You want a coffee?"

"Thanks."

The kitchen was worse than I had imagined. Worse because he

obviously used it as a working area, unlike the other rooms I had passed which were simply somewhere to put all the stuff he collected until he was ready to use it.

The sink was fully of scabby dirty dishes, piled up and overflowing to one side. I grimaced when he grabbed a couple of grimy mugs and rinsed them under the tap. By the wall near the sink there was a rubbish bin jammed full of plastic bags and who knows what else. Stuff had fallen out of it onto the floor. Oddly enough it didn't smell, or at least it was covered by the recent welding smell. He pushed a button on an electric kettle to start it and shoved some things aside on the table to make a space to put down the mugs. As he did this something fell off the other end of the table. He spooned instant coffee into each mug. Turning aside he pulled open a cupboard door and rummaged about inside finally turning back with a small bowl of lumpy sugar. He dumped it on the table next to the mugs.

"Help yourself to the sugar," he said.

Sticking out from under the table were several wooden boxes stuffed with broken toasters and what looked like bits of old radios. On the table were more clocks, sticks of solder and a soldering iron. Right beside the table stood two dark metal bottles strapped together, an oxyacetylene kit. The welding gun and the hoses were wrapped around the top of the bottles. There were no chairs in the kitchen, nowhere to sit.

"Painting doesn't go far enough," he continued while we waited for the kettle to boil. "I want to do more than draw people's minds in. I want to entice them to walk into the reality of my work. I want them to see it from different angles. I want their perception of it to change as they see it from inside, or from underneath."

The kettle stopped boiling. He poured the steaming water into the mugs. I added lots of sugar to mine hoping it would cover the underlying taste of grime I was certain was there.

"I want to make things that move and metamorphose, so every time you look at it, it's different."

I cautiously sipped the coffee. It was undrinkable. It had an oily flavor beneath the added sweetness of all the sugar. I thought it was disgusting.

He gulped his with enthusiasm despite it being too hot to do more than sip it slowly.

Suddenly he slammed his mug down on the table and stepped back. "Come outside, I'll show you what I mean."

Happy to leave my barely touched coffee on the table I followed him outside.

His yard was full of complex abstract structures. Like his paintings had been, these metal pieces were very large and surrealistic. Alien was the word that popped into my mind. I thought of Escher, Dali, and other surrealist painters. If they had been sculptors and working with metal, their work might have looked like this. Trying to follow some of the shapes with my eyes left me feeling dizzy for a few moments. Whatever he had done in his earlier paintings to draw one's eye into the space, seemed far stronger here. I had to shut my eyes and shake my head to stop being drawn in.

"Why don't you go inside one of them?" he asked.

When I looked at him dubiously, he pushed me towards the largest of the structures.

"Go on," he insisted. "Go inside and see how your feelings alter as your perspective changes. Its essence is different from inside."

I was hesitant at first, but he pushed me towards an entrance, so I stepped in.

I wasn't moved or impressed at all. It looked different from inside, but I couldn't see what he was on about. Metal sculpture always leaves me cold. It is not the art form for twenty-first century. This was like a last abstract cry from a century now past, from a time not far beyond the Industrial revolution, a waste of time in my view. The art of the future will be in the mind, created by computers and electronic networks, an expansion of virtual reality. Computer games were getting closer to that every day.

I tried to tell him that when I emerged a few minutes later, but he dismissed me furiously.

"This is not sculpture," he yelled at me, and shoved his face so close I could smell his stale breath, "but living pieces that evolve and grow, that have their own agenda."

Flecks of spittle ejected as he yelled at me made me step back.

"It creates itself as much as I help create it." He said this a bit softer having seen my reaction. "Sometimes it even directs me…"

He was crazy. Sadly, that was my impression. He had obviously locked himself up in this house overflowing with mechanical and electronic junk for too long. He had not produced a painting for years, and many people in the art world thought he had died. He might as well have. No one would want the stuff he was building in the back yard.

"Whatever," I mumbled.

"Get out," he snarled. "Get back to your cosy art world and leave me do what I have to."

He followed me to the front door, slamming it behind me.

"Don't come back here again," I heard him yell from behind the closed door.

So much for the interview! I would write something for the magazine along the lines of eccentric old artist gives up painting to go backwards. I would suggest as a joke, that anyone with old metal, mechanical or electronic junk leave it on his front lawn as a donation to his cause instead of dumping it at the tip. I made a point of stressing that it didn't matter what it was, he would be sure to find it useful.

The joke backfired. A few months later my editor wanted me do another interview with him. I was reluctant to return, but you do what you must in order to keep your job.

When he opened the front door, the old artist was happy to see me. He was effusive with thanks for the help and publicity I had given him.

"People came from everywhere," he said as he led me inside. We negotiated the clutter and eventually found our way into the back yard. All the while he had kept talking. "They gave me wonderful stuff, little electric motors, switches, videos, cameras, old computers and motherboards, thousands of them. They couldn't sell them for anything and rather than throw them away they gave them to me. Nearly everything worked so I could use it right away."

There was no backyard anymore. The whole space had been taken over by a huge monstrous integrated assembly. It was like a huge crazy machine, a machine that has no purpose but has lots of moving and shifting parts, which do nothing sensible other than move. Part of the construction even covered the rear of the house. I looked up at it and saw parts of it shifting slightly as if it was rearranging itself. It gave me the creeps.

"What is it?" I asked.

He seemed momentarily confused, as if it had not occurred to him to think of it as any particular thing. I could see he hadn't been looking after himself. His hair was longer and now mostly white. His face was etched with deep lines and his pallor was as grey as the sky above. With dark shadows under his eyes, he looked sick, as if he was wasting away. His enormous construction had sucked everything out of him.

"It's very big," I said.

"It gets bigger every day."

"You keep adding to it?"

"I change or add to it as the mood takes me. Day or night, it doesn't matter. Sometimes when I come out in the mornings it's different from the way I left it the night before. Sometimes it's bigger over here," he gestured towards the back of the house, "and sometimes it's moved over there. It changes by itself."

"How can that be?"

"It creates itself. When I'm not there it goes on without me."

"It goes on without you?" I didn't know what to say.

"Yeah, like things appear out of nowhere to became part of its structure…"

Now I knew he was crazy. He wasn't making any sense.

"…like little machines that look like spiders or beetles. They just keep appearing. I never made them. I couldn't make anything like that. They scavenge for stuff and it's those things that keep changing the way everything looks. Keep adding… building, constructing… I hardly have anything to do with it anymore."

But whatever it was he was doing; he had certainly created an incredible landmark. People everywhere talked about it. They often came by to stop and look. Visitors and tourists were sent to see it. Some of them even went inside, walked or climbed about to look at it from different angles and perspectives, just as the old artist wanted. Most of them came out shaking their heads; upset over something none of them could define. When asked if they would go in for another look, they all said they would never do that again.

That's why I was there. My editors wanted me to have a look to see if I could make some sense of it for the magazine.

"Can I go through it?"

"Of course," he said, suddenly animated. I guess he wanted some kind of approval for what he was doing, and the magazine I worked for would give him that. It was a prestigious magazine in the Art World, and we had done stories on him in the past, but that had been a long time ago. Most of our readers had forgotten who he was. He pointed toward what appeared as an opening to a tunnel into the structure. "Come this way," he said, taking me by the arm to guide me towards it.

But up close to it, I felt uneasy about entering such a huge structure. It was dark in there, not much light penetrated through the shifting metal and plastic constructions overhead. The sky being sombre, and grey didn't help the mood either. The narrow entrance he led me to seemed dark and menacing. I could see nothing inside but dark shadows, some of which shifted intermittently. I hesitated.

"There's nothing to be afraid of," the artist said reassuringly. "I go in there all the time."

I gave him a pointed look, squared my shoulders, then stepped into the structure. The tunnel I saw ahead was surrounded by wire coils, which quivered as I passed. I could hear a deep and unnerving hum that didn't seem to have a specific point of origin. I had not been aware of that sound before stepping into the structure.

"Go on," the artists said from behind me.

I walked forward and into the tunnel that twisted and coiled back on itself, thinking the artist was right behind me to explain what he had created, but he wasn't. he had left me on my own.

Within moments I lost my orientation. There were sections that seemed to shift slightly as I walked towards them, yet on closer examination they were solid and unmoving.

Was that an optical illusion? The artist was good at things like that. It was one of the reasons his paintings had been famous. Certain shapes could make you feel disorientated, while others could, by making your mind's eye twist back on itself, create a feeling of nausea.

I heard skittering noises and spun around. Everything was still, but it looked different. Had it changed just then? My heart gave a nasty flutter as I realized the tunnel I had just walked along was no longer there. It had changed!

There was a clanking noise off to one side. I jerked around feeling fear insinuate itself along my spine. There was the tunnel! It had been there all the time; I had simply been looking in the wrong direction. At that point I decided I no longer wanted to be inside the bowels of this damned thing anymore. I raced back down the tunnel and out into the yard.

I had come out a different way to the way I had gone in. I was on the other side of the structure. I couldn't have gone that far. I had only taken a few steps, yet here I was well away from where I had entered. A deep feeling of unease twisted in my gut as the structure in front of me quivered. The opening I had just exited through suddenly closed.

The artist was nowhere to be seen. He was probably inside the damned thing, having gone or been directed in a different way to the one I was following. I called out to him but got no response, so I left.

I wanted nothing more to do with it or with him. I told myself once I was safely outside in the street that, I will never go back inside that thing again.

Back at the office I wrote a short piece describing the structure as a tourist attraction. I didn't know what else to say about it. If I said anything about what I had experienced my editor would think I was crazy.

Nevertheless, I was intrigued, and often drove past to see how the tower, as nearly everyone called it, was progressing. As far as I could see it stood on what appeared to be four or six solid sections, which supported the ever-growing height and weight of the Gothic structure towering several stories above the original house. It seemed to have swallowed the house as not much of that building could be seen. The tower was visible from quite some distance away and always drew a crowd of onlookers hoping to catch a glimpse of the artist at work. Sometimes they would see an emaciated figure high in the structure, moving about, hammering, welding, and changing things. At night, sometimes a strange glow emanated from inside the tower, but it never lasted long, and not many people saw it. The sounds constantly emanating from the tower indicated that construction of some kind was continuously happening, even at night. Did the artists never sleep?

By the end of the second year the tower had totally subsumed the house. No longer was it visible. It most likely didn't exist anymore, having been cannibalized to become an integral part of the tower itself. No one ventured inside the structure anymore either; it had become too monstrous, but they were still fascinated enough to come and watch the thing grow, this wonder of human creation.

There was no end of speculation upon what it was, what might be its purpose, and what force drove the artist to create such an incredible thing. No one considered that the emaciated artist could not actually be constructing this monstrosity. But it was obvious to me, thinking about the last time I had seen him, that he was incapable of doing anything other than perhaps giving directions to those hideous little robot machines.

But where had they come from if he hadn't made them? I remembered he told me they kept appearing out of nowhere. He thought at first the construction itself was making them, but there were too many; they had to have come from somewhere else.

"Where do you think they come from?" I asked him.

"I have no idea," he whispered hoarsely.

Was it still his creation or had the machines taken over? I kept thinking that every time I passed by the ever-growing tower.

Almost three years to the day I had first spoken to him, I happened to be there in the crowd the afternoon the artist emerged for the last time. He was wild-eyed and disheveled. He trailed a long line of wires behind him. I couldn't see if he was holding them in his hand or if they were tied around his waist.

I was shocked by his condition. His scraggly long hair, totally white, emphasized how gaunt his face was. His skin seemed translucent, and I imagined I could see the pallid colour of his skull showing through the paleness of his face. If he hadn't been clothed in filthy rags, I was sure I would see his skeleton through the thinness of his skin. It made me utterly sad to see him like that.

He must have seen me in the crowd. He pointed to me and when I nodded, he waved me over. Reluctantly I went to him. There was a feral glint in eyes that somehow seemed too large to fit into his skull.

"It's nearly finished," he told me, his voice weak and husky from disuse.

"What is it?" I had to ask.

There was absolute silence from the crowd.

"My life's work," he whispered to me.

He looked past me and suddenly realized how many people there were in the street. His eyes closed and he backed away.

"Wait," I said, but he turned and scuttled back into the protective depths under his monstrous tower.

"Did you see the way he looked?" a man beside me and asked.

"He'll die in there," another said.

"You should go in there and get him," the man next to me said.

"Don't look at me," I said as nearly everyone was staring at me, waiting for some kind of response.

"He seemed to know you."

"I've spoken to him a few times, that's all."

Silence again. They were scared, not one of them daring enough to venture in there after the artist. I knew exactly how they felt because I had been in there more than once and knew how weird it was. I imagined it would be much worse now.

They kept staring at me as if I knew what to do.

Suddenly I heard my voice, and I was shocked to hear it say of its own volition: "All right. I'll go in and get him."

Damn, why did I say that? I don't want to go in there again.

Those nearest me nodded encouragingly, compelling me to move. I stepped onto the last part of the front lawn that was not covered by that monstrous structure. I stared up at it and shuddered. It had grown so huge and complex, so grotesque it seemed to have taken on a life of its own. I was certain that it was aware I was about to enter it, that it waited in anticipation. Would it consider me an invader? Or would it let me enter as it once had?

What's the matter with me? It's only something someone built; nothing more than a weird gigantic machine; metal and plastic, electronic and clockwork. It doesn't really do anything.

There's nothing to be frightened of I tried to reassure myself.

The tower quivered in anticipation as I very reluctantly walked towards it.

I could not get rid of the feeling that it was watching me, waiting for me to come in.

I remembered clearly how disoriented I felt the last time I went in, and it was much smaller then.

I stopped at the base of the tower and looked up. It was like looking up at the steeple of Cathedral. It struck me then that this was perhaps the artist's homage to God. It was his greatest and final creation. 'My Life's work', he had said. All of it, all his thoughts, his abstractions and concepts, all combined into the one immense piece of work. No wonder it appeared unnerving.

I walked along the perimeter and called out to the artist. There was no answer. Nor did I expect one; I was looking for a way to put off entering the construction, but with everyone in the street watching I felt I had no choice but to go in, though calling out to the artist and waiting for an answer delayed that inevitable action.

I passed a narrow gap between two supports then stopped. It seemed like a good spot to enter, not a big entrance but a way of sneaking in surreptitiously.

I squeezed in, and once past the supports there was a small space about the size of a shower stall. I was no longer standing on the ground, but on a metal plate, which as I looked down, turned. I spun around quickly in the opposite direction, ready to jump back out through the narrow gap I had come in, but it was gone.

My heart started to beat frantically. I was strapped. I spun around looking for a way out, then I saw another gap had opened to reveal a thin tunnel leading slightly upwards into the bowels of the structure. I was being invited in.

Taking several deep breaths, I tried to calm myself, to slow down my heartbeat. I don't know how long I stood there staring into that tunnel, but eventually I had to move. I stepped slowly forward and discovered a maze of tunnels and pathways writhing and twisting through the structure as far as I could see. In the gloom I caught a momentary glimpse of a white shape as it flitted across the end of the tunnel ahead. *That's him!* What else could it be other than the artist running madly about inside the monster he had created? I called to him, but he was gone. Perhaps he had not heard me.

There were soft noises all around me as I moved cautiously forward through the tunnel; whirring noises like an old tape deck makes when the tape is on fast rewind, soft hisses, and faint clanking noises. Behind me a metal door slid shut with a solid thump. Startled, I turned back only to see the small room I had been in closed off. My heart started its frantic beat again and I stood frozen trying to calm down once more. The structure definitely wanted me inside and that scared me. My only hope was to go further into the thing to find a way out.

I should never have come in. I knew that, but it was too late to change my mind. I had to go further in and find the artist, to find him and drag him out of the structure. I would make him show me the way out.

I passed several black and white televisions that were flickering with static. That explained the hissing I could hear. Whatever I touched, metal or plastic, was warm and carried a soft fine vibration. An occasional static zap convinced me that the whole structure was connected to a power source. The artist had probably tapped into the street power. As unnerved as I was, I had to admire the old artist's genius. Whatever this was, it was a magnificent achievement. No one else had ever created anything remotely like it before.

As I moved upwards along the tunnel several small video cameras tracked me. Then I saw him again. He was high up in the structure, a wraith-like figure hovering within a mass of coiling wires and cables. *How could he have gotten so high up?* It was only a few seconds ago when I had glimpsed him in this very tunnel.

He looked terrified. I could see his mouth moving but could not hear his words over the ambient noise all around me. I started to climb higher to get closer to him, but he shook his head violently from side to side. He screamed one word, which I did hear. "NO!" Then he vanished, like the image on a video screen that had been switched off.

There was no way I was going to get him out. He was a captive of the thing he had created, an integral part of its structure. I couldn't imagine how he could have achieved that. He knew he was doomed, which was why he had tried to warn me to leave, to get out of the thing. It hit me then; if I didn't get out right away, I too would become trapped and wired in just like the old artist.

Almost as if the structure knew what I was thinking, the moment I took a tentative step forward knotted wires shot across the tunnel both in front and behind me. I was trapped. The wires quivered with tension. I couldn't go forwards or backward. I looked up and realized if I could jump high enough to grab a support, I could haul myself up.

Taking a deep breath, I leaped up and grabbed a crossbeam. It was one hell of an effort, I don't work out, spending too much time in front of a computer, but fear gave me extra strength and I managed to pull myself up enough to squeeze into another tunnel that seemed more solid than where I had been. The only problem was that it was narrow and not very high. I was forced to scramble along hunched over.

I passed video screens at random spots along the tunnel. Each one showed a different part of the structure. I didn't want to stop but I couldn't resist the temptation to look.

One screen showed several self-propelled machines, mindless robots doing spot welding. Did the old artist make these things? *If he didn't, as he had claimed, then where did they come from? Another dimension, another time, a parallel universe?*

As the robot machines came closer to the camera's point of view, I saw them much more clearly. I shuddered involuntarily. They looked like a cross between a giant cockroach and a summer beetle. They looked alien, something not of this Earth. This was not something the artist could have made. These were not machines you could buy at a hardware store. Only another machine could have devised something like that. Another screen showed little machines that looked more like black spiders. Skittering noises somewhere above me reminded me that I had to keep moving or I would never find a way out. A cloud of small spider-like things dropped down into the space where I had been standing a second after I moved forward. They ran about in circles seemingly at a loss to work out why their target wasn't there. I tried to move further along the low tunnel with as little noise as possible.

In another screen I passed I saw a cockroach machine examining a part of the structure with extended feelers. Two more cockroaches trundled up to it and extended long feelers. The moment they touched the examined spot sparks flew out and the screen degenerated into static. I ran on and pulled up at another screen facing me at a junction. The artist's emaciated face stared out at me. I was horrified to see twisted wires that looked like dreadlocks growing out of his head. They were just like the wires that had tried to trap me in the lower-level tunnel.

"Get out now," his scratchy voice emanated from a tiny speaker at the base of the screen. "You will be absorbed… I'm finished and they'll want someone new, a fresh brain…"

Before I could move his face disappeared to be replaced by a moving view of the tunnel I had just come along. It was a wide-angle view that showed a silhouetted figure against a bright screen. It was me. As I watched momentarily unable to move the figure became larger and clearer as whatever was coming along the tunnel behind me got closer.

I didn't look back. I turned and shuffled away from it as fast as the low tunnel to the left allowed.

There were screens everywhere with words scrolling down them too fast to read. There were scrabbling sounds in the tunnel behind me. Still hunched over I forced myself to go faster. The height of the tunnel started to change. The top got lower, and it started to narrow. The skittering of the spider machines I had seen in one of the monitors, like those that had dropped down but missed me, was directly above me. They didn't need to run along the tunnels. They could run through the whole structure in any direction they wanted, they were that tiny. I tried not to think about what they would do if they found me and dropped on top of me. The louder scrabbling noise in the tunnel behind me was closer than ever.

There were loose cables in the tunnel, and they started to wrap around my feet just as I reached the end of the tunnel. It finished not at a wall but at a gap that went all the way down to the ground.

The cables flexed like snakes. I pulled my feet free only to have the cables try snarling them again. I was stunned at how high I was in the structure. I didn't remember going upwards, but somehow, I was at least fifteen metres above the ground. The gap was a little over a metre and the wall across from me was a kind of grid that reached all the way to the ground.

I can climb down it.

But as I reached across and touched the grid, a burning sensation shot up my arm. I snatched my hand away. The grid was electrified.

The thing in the tunnel behind me was closer than ever, and in the corner of my eye I glimpsed a dark spidery machine scuttle down the wall beside me. It was larger than the ones that had tried to drop on top of me.

My shoes were rubber soled so the current in the grid wouldn't earth, but I still couldn't touch the metal with my bare hands. Frantically I pulled my sweater off and wrapped it around my hands. I let myself fall forward until I could grab the metal grid.

The spider thing leaped off the wall onto my leg.

I screamed. The weight of my body dragged my feet free of entangling cables. The spider thing fell off.

A faint voice somewhere above said, "Wait…"

Was that the old artist, or was that the machine trying to talk to me? The voice had sounded different.

I wasn't waiting for anyone, or anything. Terror and gravity gave me an athleticism I never knew I had. I scuttled down the grid as fast as I would have fallen. I hit the bottom with a crunch hard enough to jar my bones from my feet to my head.

Here the structure was solid and unmoving. These were the foundations that supported the whole monstrous construction. Yet solid as they were, the metal still quivered as I desperately squeezed past between the grid and the foundations of the structure above looking for the way out. God only knew what was happening above.

I saw a hole beside one of the many supports. I dropped to my hands and knees to crawl though. Next to the hole was a half-buried small black and white TV. Suddenly it started flickering. The face of the artist appeared, wires still growing out of his tangled hair. His eyes seemed all white, blind, yet staring at me. He was saying something, but no sound came from the set. The image broke into jagged lines for a second, and then cleared again. The artist was still staring at me. His eyes cleared and I was sure he could see me. He mouthed a few words, slowly, clearly enunciating them so I could lip read.

"It…must…be…" then a tinny sound emanated from the set and his voice said, "stopped…I don't know what I did, but I opened a path to another dimension, and these things came through… you have to stop…" His face spasmed, his eyes turned white.

The image zapped into jagged lines, which suddenly shrunk to a tiny glowing white spot in the centre of the screen.

Did they kill him? Or had they just cut the power to this old TV?

I wasn't going to try and find out. Something moved in the metal near me.

I bumped my head as I turned away from a dark flitting shadow. Little things crawled across my hands. I pulled them away from the ground but one of the things clung tight with tiny pincers. I stared at it incomprehensibly before I realized what it was.

It was a tiny scavenging machine, a miniature robot, and it was carrying a rusty screw. The structure was sending them out to gather material. That was how it kept growing. It no longer needed what people brought it. I ripped the thing off my hand and threw it to the ground. It ran around in a small circle before joining a line of other similar creatures entering the structure.

Suddenly I felt the weight of the whole structure crushing me. I couldn't breathe. Something fell onto my leg near the ankle, and I shook it violently trying to dislodge whatever it was. For some reason it had latched onto my shoe, which came off in the struggle to free myself from it.

In desperation I dived through the hole and rolled across a narrow strip of ground between the structure and the original side fence separating the artist's property from the street. The ground shook beneath me. A dark shape blocked the hole I had just exited.

The whole structure seemed to be reshaping itself, as if struggling to free itself of the ground, to come alive. Perhaps it had absorbed the soul of the artist. Maybe it had downloaded his essential thoughts, the core of his being. Whatever was happening was unprecedented. The artist had given a metal and electronic inanimate monster a semblance of life, and it had taken him over.

Would this monster survive the death of the artist? His mind was the source of its anima. Could the tortured writhing inside the structure be a reaction to the death of the artist rather than the birth throes of a new kind of being? The structure must have killed him when it finished downloading his mind. *Am I looking at both the monster's simultaneous birth and its death?* I wasn't going to hang around to see.

Something fell into the gap between the structure and the fence. Buzzing and clacking, it scuttled towards me.

I was over the fence in a flash, running towards the restless crowd that had moved further away when they saw the structure writing and twisting. Metal squeals and deep groans emanated from it, further enhancing the crowd's desire to move back.

None of them tried to stop me as I shoved through.

Several trailed along behind me for a short distance then stopped and turned back to stare at the thing that was newly born while perhaps simultaneously dying.

Something glowed inside the structure as it moved more violently. One of the supports emerged from the ground and it wobbled precariously, before regaining a semblance of balance. The glow disappeared and the tower became still, although metallic groans and screeches still radiated out intermittently from inside the monstrous structure. There was still something happening inside it, so it wasn't completely dead.

With my last glimpse of the tower I saw a dark shadow flowing out from under the property fence. It was black and looked shiny like oil. *That's not oil! That's millions of nano machines.*

I cried out to those around me as I pushed through, "get away from here, all of you..." But they were too interested in looking at the tower which was now still again.

I heard someone behind me, someone a bit closer, yell out in surprise. "Hey look at that. It bit me."

"What is it?"

"Some kind of tiny beetle."

I ran as fast as I could and never looked back.

People behind me started screaming.

A Beach Too Far

It was turning out to be much hotter than he had expected, but it was too late now; he was already well beyond the point where he could turn back. He would run out of fuel if he did that. He had to keep going. The car radio suddenly spluttered back to life. It had gone off a couple of times as he got further away from the last 'civilized' town. Radio reception this far away was erratic at best, and as for mobile reception; it simply didn't exist.

… and now for the afternoon weather report: Conditions will remain the same until the late afternoon when a cool change is expected. The temperature should remain in the high thirties until then. Strong wind warnings are…

The voice cut out as he leaned forward and switched off the radio. He didn't need the weather forecast to tell him it was hot. He could see the heat shimmering on the road ahead, the mirages of water over the road receding as he moved towards them. Dust blew across the road from his left, blasting the car like wind driven rain. Only there was no rain here, just wind gusting strong enough to blow fine sand from the tops of one dune to another as they continuously shifted inland. The road wound between a field of dunes and wind periodically blew layers of shifting sand over it, causing the road in some places to disappear.

He glanced at the car's temperature gauge and saw that it was dangerously close to the red.

Damned air conditioning, he muttered. **Uses up too much power. Doesn't work properly anyway.**

The air blowing from the vents could hardly be called cool, let alone cold, but it did evaporate the sweat forming on his face.

Needs re-gassing. *You should switch it on from time to time in the winter,* that's what they say. **But who the hell puts their air conditioning on in the winter?** He asked himself.

Coming out on the winding road between the sand dunes he entered an area where half-dead Ti-trees still survived on both sides of the road. Between the Ti-trees as they flashed past his right side, he caught occasional glimpses of the ocean sparkling as the afternoon sun glanced off it, but he was too far away from it to catch the fresh smell of sea water. All he got was the dusty dryness of fine sand continually whipped up and swirled as it was blown intermittently by the gusty wind.

Glancing inland he saw several tall concrete silos, faded and weathered, long abandoned when the farmers left years ago as their land dried up. In the far distance ahead of him he could see a giant sand hill jutting up above the greyish green of the Ti-trees. Sand blew like a haze off the top of it. He could see it drift down, showering the trees. It would eventually bury them as more sand moved up from the beach to replace that lost from the top of the hill.

The road curved inland in order to get around the bigger sand hills, and here, sand blew continuously across the road. He had to slow down to maintain traction. He had come too far to turn back, and it was in that moment that he realized he'd made a mistake wanting to drive along this old road beside the coast.

The tyres on his old car were getting bald. He should have replaced them months ago, but money was the problem there. He relied on a pension, barely enough to survive on these days, and the credit on his cards was at the maximum limit. He would have to make do with the car the way it was until things picked up.

Once he lost sight of the beach, the car seemed to get even

hotter. Sweat trickled down his neck, his chest. The air in the car seemed so hot he could hardly breathe.

Bloody heater must be on, he mumbled and reached forward to check if he'd accidentally turned it on when he switched on the air-con.

The green light over the AC button was glowing so the useless air conditioning was still on.

I'm getting too old for this.

How many times had he told himself that?

How often did he ignore his own advice?

I should have known better than to drive along this old coastal road.

Nostalgia for the past is all well and good, but sometimes past memories should be left in the past. The world was very different now, with rising sea levels ever increasing, with fierce storms and longer heat waves, year after year.

This coast where he used to holiday with his parents when he was child, and where he and his late wife had made many trips, had long been abandoned. The small towns snuggled in tiny inlets where they had often stopped had been left to rot and fall apart long before they vanished into the rising seas, the cliffs along much of the coast had eroded and fallen into the encroaching ocean making the coast different, yet strangely enough it still looked much the same.

Driving along he began to wonder if it was the same road or if it was a new road that had been built further inland from the coast road he once knew to allow for erosion of the famous sandstone cliffs, and subsequently abandoned as the relentless sea ate into the coast faster than expected.

I could have picked a better day though. Christ it's hot, he said above the noise of the struggling engine.

His mouth hung open, and he was panting like a dog. He couldn't seem to get enough oxygen into his lungs. A dull shadow moved across in front of his eyes and suddenly he couldn't see the road. He blinked furiously, wiped a sweaty hand across his face, then stared ahead at the shimmering road. His breath came faster, and his lungs hurt. He felt as if something was burning them inside.

The road curved back towards the distant ocean, and he decided that when he got closer, he would stop. Pain shot across his chest and across his back between the shoulder blades.

I'm having a heart attack, he thought, on the verge of panic. He couldn't breathe except for tiny shallow breaths like a reverse cough.

He leaned forward across the steering wheel and his foot pressed harder on the gas pedal. The old car rattled as it surged forward. The engine protested.

Must stop.

Dark splotches obscured his vision, but past the edges he could see the blue of the sea.

Must stop now.

His foot felt like it was encased in lead. He managed to drag it off the gas pedal to put on the brake. The car started to slow even though he'd put no pressure on the brake pedal. It hit a thick sandy patch across the road and slowed even more. Coming out of the sand it slipped sideways, and instead of turning into the skid, he gripped the steering wheel so tight his knuckles turned white. The car started a slow spin before the back wheels hit the edge of another sand drift. The front of the car slewed back to face the direction of the movement and it ran off the road, coming to an abrupt stop as the nose buried itself in a low sand dune two car-lengths off the road.

The driver jerked forward barely restrained by the seat belt and bashed his head against the steering wheel. The engine stalled. The driver's side door flew open and hot salty air filled the vehicle.

His breathing eased. Paradoxically because he bashed his forehead when the car slammed into the sand dune, the splotches before his eyes cleared. He could see perfectly. The pain in his chest had gone, but he had an enormous headache. He could feel a lump forming on his forehead where it had hit the steering wheel.

He fumbled to release the seat-belt buckle and almost fell out of the car when it gave way. Hanging onto the open driver's door for support he managed to haul himself to his feet and stood there bemused. The metal of the engine pinged. The heat had been too much for his old car.

He shook his head, as if that would clear the headache. He touched his forehead and felt an enormous lump. He found his breathing had eased and it was no longer a struggle for each breath as it had been in the car.

On legs slightly wobbly he walked around behind the car. His feet sunk into soft sand. There was no apparent damage to the car that he could see, but there was no way he could get it back onto the road the way the front was buried so deep into the sand. The skid marks he'd left in the sand over the road were already disappearing as wind-blown fine sand trickled over them. He would have to wait until someone came along so he could get a lift into the next town, the last town left along the coast road, or back to where he'd been before, where he could organize a tow truck to come back and drag the car out.

He had been driving for several hours and had not seen another vehicle along the road, or passed anyone, so he resigned himself to having a long wait before there was a chance someone would come along and see his wrecked car.

There was a packet of Aspirin in the glove box, so he got this out and took two tablets, washing them down with slightly warm water from an old Thermos flask he kept filled in case of emergencies. He had never used it and the water tasted bitter, slightly metallic. *How long has that been there?* He was about to tip the water out but thought better of it. It was the only water he had, and he might need it. *Who knows how long I could be here?*

He stood beside the car and waited, then he walked to the roadside and waited a bit longer. The only movement he could see was the shimmering hot air above the surface of the road and the fine drifting sand that rippled as the wind kept blowing across it.

Where's this cool change they promised?

With the new maglev freeways running inland, hardly anyone used the old roads anymore. *I could be here for bloody hours before anyone, if anyone, comes along. It could be days even,* and the thought upset him.

He couldn't wait here. It was too hot, and there was nowhere he could find a shady spot to sit in.

But someone knew he had come this way. He had asked at the service station in the last town that still sat close to the sea, what the old coast road was like.

"It's still good, but nobody used it anymore," he was told. The attendant looked at him askance when he told him he was going to go that way.

"I like to look at the ocean," he said. "It brings back memories. My wife and I used to holiday along here years ago."

"Must have been a long time ago mate. All those coastal towns are gone, except for one; swallowed by the sea. You're lucky there's still a road there. You should tell the coppers you're going along that road."

"Why?"

"Anyone going along that road tells them. If you have a breakdown, no one will know because hardly anyone uses it. If they know you're going that way, they'll call ahead to tell someone in the last town's service station to expect you. It's a fair distance and you'll have to fill up when you get there before you can come back. There's nowhere to go beyond there. And if you don't turn up, then they will go looking for you. Okay?"

"Okay, I'll do that."

It was too hot to wait beside the road, and sitting in the car was not possible. The temperature inside had risen enormously. He couldn't touch the roof without burning his fingers. Even with the driver's side door open he could feel the heat wafting out. The sand he was standing on, unless it was shaded under a scrawny bush-like Ti-tree, was hot enough for him to feel though the soles of his shoes. There was nowhere to sit under a tree, they were all stunted, with branches close to the sand beneath them. His only option was to find a path down to the beach where he could cool off at the water's edge.

It can't be that far away. He could smell a hint of salty air as wind gusts off the water blew inland. He had seen it clearly as he drove along, less than a kilometre off to his right, so all he needed to do was find a way through the scrubby trees and there it would be.

He had a towel in the car, and he took this out and draped it over his head and shoulders to keep the sun from burning the back of his neck and his balding head. He sprinkled a bit of water from the Thermos over the towel and the dry wind evaporating it cooled him slightly. He started walking through the sand dunes stabilized by the Ti-trees towards the distant ocean.

There used to be holiday towns along this southern coast. He used to come here every summer when he was a kid, but the rising sea swamped the towns and the people fled inland. New beaches formed as old sandstone cliffs crumbled and collapsed into pounding waves. The shape of the country changed, and people abandoned the coast, preferring to live in climate-controlled cloisters far inland. All around the country it was the same as luxury homes fell into the encroaching sea.

The few towns left along this new coast, like the one he had left behind, where he had told the police he was going on to the end of the road, to the last town, were partially populated by hardy types who still preferred a natural environment to an artificial one: people who had lived there for several generations whose roots went way back, and who under no circumstances could be convinced to leave what was their life, behind. They would eke out a living no matter how hard it was.

In one town, squatters had moved in and taken over most of the abandoned places. They treated anyone coming into 'their' town with suspicion that sometimes erupted into violent confrontations. The few people who had need to travel this coast road never stopped, if possible, in this squatter town, but drove on through. He had passed that town and hadn't stopped there. He had been seen though. Furtive faces behind shrouded windows had been obvious even to him as he drove slowly along the main road through the town. He couldn't imagine people living in buildings so dilapidated they almost appeared to be collapsing.

His shoes kept filling with sand, so he took them off. He managed a few paces before the sand was too hot to walk on without burning his feet, forcing him to put the shoes back on again. He stopped every few minutes to sip some bitter water from his Thermos, and to empty more sand from his shoes. Each time he reached the top of a rise he stared at the distant ocean and wondered why it wasn't getting any closer. The sight of the water, the sound of the waves on the beach and the odd breath of cooler sea air revitalized his spirit and kept him going. The road and his abandoned car had long vanished behind him.

I must be getting closer, he said into the hot air.

He had used all the water from the Thermos and left it where he last stopped to shake the sand from his shoes. His pace had slowed because his feet were blistering. The sand was still too hot to walk on without shoes. Slowly shuffling up and over another rise he felt momentarily dizzy as he reached to top. It was like he was going to fall. The sand shifted slightly under his feet. He staggered forward into air that was much cooler and sighed with relief. The track was wider too, more delineated and clearer to see. The sound of the waves was much louder, and the fresh smell of the sea air was delicious. He stopped to take in a few deep breaths, to give himself a moment to rest. Looking about he saw the Ti-trees were much greener and taller than the desiccated ones back closer to the road by his crashed car. They looked much more alive. *Must be because they're closer to the beach and can get more moisture,* he thought.

Looking above the trees he was stunned to see the sun was almost in front of him. When he had left the car, it had been behind.

Have I gone the wrong way? He couldn't recall turning or doubling back. The track zigzagging through the trees had been in one direction only, and it must be right because he could hear the waves on the beach quite loudly. It was not too far ahead. *But how come the sun is in the wrong place?* The other thing that seemed odd was he had the impression it was early morning. *That can't be.* It had been mid-afternoon when he abandoned his car to walk the kilometre through the sand dunes and Ti-trees to the beach. For an older man it was hard walking through sand dunes. His legs ached, particularly his calf muscles. His lungs burned, his throat was dry, but the sound of the waves breaking on the beach filled his ears. The fresh sea air began to invigorate him.

He staggered up to the crest of the last sand dune and there before him was the wonderful, sparkling blue water of the ocean. His shoes fell off as he ran awkwardly down the gentle sandy slope onto the firmer sand of the beach. He didn't stop until he reached the edge and the ripples rolling around his feet cooled the burning but stung where the blisters had formed. He jumped and splashed as the water brought life back to him.

The sound of laughter, of kids yelling and calling to each other, permeated his whole being as he ran along the wet sand and happily splashed in the shallow water.

The towel flew off his head and fell to the damp sand behind. A cool breeze caressed his face. A sudden iciness enveloped his feet and calves. He stopped and looked down. Seawater swirled about his feet, further cooling. He had gone further out into the water without realizing it. The water was quite cold once you got into a deeper section. He took a deep breath and flung himself forward, splashed into the waves and went under. A delicious coldness enveloped him. He opened his mouth and let the saltiness of the water swirl around in his mouth. He even swallowed a tiny bit. He bobbed back up, spat out the sea water and took a deep breath of cool air and floated on his back.

What a wonderful feeling it is to float, to be shoved about by the waves.

He relished the water as a wave rolled over his face and body. His clothes became heavier as they absorbed water and he started to sink so he stood up and shook the water from his face. He stared back at the beach and was amazed to see children running along the sand, yelling and laughing with joy, just as he and his brothers had done when they were little. There were umbrellas, and towels. People with glistening bodies lay in the sun, people everywhere. No one cared about the ozone layer or skin cancer when he was a kid.

Ball games were being played with young men leaping into the air and flexing their muscles attempting to attract the attention of nubile females who studiously ignored them. Other children were building sandcastles by the water's edge and several older obese people were sitting in the warmer water where it lapped against the beach.

Standing in thigh-deep water he stared at the people on the beach. There had been nobody there when he ran down across the beach and into the water.

Where did all these people come from? There must be a car park nearby and a path through the Ti-trees and the dunes. **How come I didn't see that?** He said aloud but the waves crashing on the beach drowned his words.

He let himself fall backwards into the water. A wave whooshed over the top of his head and pushed him toward the beach. He rolled over and swam a few strokes until his hands touched bottom, then stood up and walked towards a kid who was digging a hole in the wet sand in front of him.

It was just beyond where the waves reached, and the sand was still wet and firm. The tide was going out. The hole kept filling with water, and the kid kept emptying it with a bucket.

"Why don't you dig the hole a bit further up so it won't keep filling with water?" He asked the kid.

"Because this is where I want to make the hole."

The kid looked up and stared at the stranger. A look of surprise crossed his face.

"Why have you been swimming with your clothes on? Don't you have a swimsuit?"

He couldn't answer the boy as a memory long forgotten surfaced. *It can't be,* he thought. *It's impossible.*

He stood immobile as his thoughts swirled. He kept staring at the boy. A young man rushed over and rudely shoved him away. "What are you crazy or something?" The man yelled at him.

He was about to apologize, but the words stuck in his throat as he recognized him. He felt as if a heavy blow had struck him in the chest. He staggered backwards, almost falling over as his feet dug into sloppy wet sand.

"Go on, get the fuck out of here," the man yelled. He stood between the young boy digging the hole which had now filled with water, and the old man in his sea drenched clothes.

He turned and half-ran, half-staggered along the wet sand. Tears ran down his face. Behind him he could hear the man scolding the young boy, his angry voice blending into the hubbub of the beach as he ran further away from them.

He didn't need to hear the voice though; he remembered what his father had said the day the strange old man dressed in wet clothes had staggered out of the surf.

"Didn't I tell you never to talk to strangers, to people like that," the young man told the boy as he had pointed at the old man in his wet clothes running along the beach, "They do nasty things to kids." He remembered his father telling him. "They trick you by being nice, then they take you away from your family and do horrible things."

He remembered his father stood there for a long time staring at the dwindling figure of the old man until he was so far down the beach, he disappeared in the haze blown off the surf by the wind which had changed from hot offshore to cool onshore.

"Something strange about that old man, though," my father had mumbled finally before ordering me to pack up because we were going home. It was too cold to stay on the beach once the wind changed and the temperature dropped.

The old man stumbled to a stop because he could go no further. He was out of breath. Exhausted. He could barely lift his feet. A touch of cold air behind him made him shiver. He turned around to see if he could see himself on the beach. He remembered that day so clearly now. How the stranger had looked so distraught, and pathetic standing there in his wet clothes staring at his father as if he had seen a ghost.

But the beach was empty. There was not a soul anywhere to be seen.

He walked back following his footprints which were dissolving into the wet sand to the spot where he had come out of the water. There were no other marks on the beach, but this was the spot because his own track showing where he came down from the dune to enter the water was clearly visible. All along the beach it was pristine, and the only noise was the hot wind blowing off the dunes. No cool change.

He sat down by the water's edge and let the sea swirl about his blistered feet. He deliberately kept his mind blank. He didn't want to think about what he had experienced, because to think about it was to contemplate the possibility that he was going mad. It certainly didn't feel that way. *But what other explanation is there?*

He sat for a long-time cooling himself by the water's edge. The sun was again behind him behind the dunes and the Ti-trees lowering to become swollen and orange. Finally, as the heat of the day diminished, he stood up and moved about to ease the stiffness.

He ached all over from the long walk through the dunes, let alone from his run along the beach. He didn't even want to think about having to walk back, though he knew he had to, or nobody would know where he was.

I should have stayed by the car. That's the advice they always give you: when you're in trouble, stay by the car. But sometimes, staying by the car will kill you, especially when it is so hot. In this case with the beach nearby it was only sensible to go there and cool off instead of waiting in the heat.

He turned slowly around studying the beach and the dunes.

They all look the same, these beaches. Yet it's different. This beach wasn't here when I was a kid.

He shook his head and blinked as the setting sun sparkled and reflected off the water running up onto the sand. There were two black spots far in the distance and he thought his eyes were playing up again. They had emerged from what looked like wind-blown spray that drifted over the beach from breaking waves. He shook his head, but the spots didn't go away. His eyes were fine.

The spots got bigger, and he could hear engines, like wild lawn mowers revving in anticipation of cutting broad swathes through the grass. The spots resolved into two shapes, and he knew what they were. *Beach Buggies!* They came tearing along the harder sand towards him.

He hadn't seen a beach buggy for years. They had long been banned for the damage they did to the environment. Churning up the sand, ripping out delicate roots from fragile grasses that struggled to grow in the dunes. And the precious fuel they used; you couldn't buy that anymore.

He didn't care though. Illegal or not, he would get them to give him a lift back to his car. He really didn't want to walk all that way through the dunes again.

He started waving to make sure they would see him. They swerved towards him, their huge wheels throwing up great gouts of sand. He thought he could hear the wild laughter of the boys driving them.

Suddenly he realized they weren't going to stop.

One of them swerved up towards the dunes. The other barreled right at him. Panic struck him and he jumped back out of the way. The driver yelled and screamed at him but the roar of the motor drowned his words. His feet stuck in the wet sand, and he felt himself falling backwards.

His mind shifted as he back-pedaled.

Unbelievably, he was the driver, suddenly aware that he was about to run over some stupid old bastard who had appeared from nowhere and was standing right in front of him waving frantically. He spun the steering wheel as fast as he could, and the big front wheels turned. Sand sprayed up and splattered the old bastard as if it had been fired from a shotgun. As he flashed past, he saw the old man staggering backwards until his feet hit the wet sand and he fell backwards into the water.

"Bloody serves you right," he yelled as he revved the engine to gain traction and tore up towards the sand dune where his mate had gone. "What the fuck are you doing here anyway?"

He glanced back but the beach was deserted again. Before he had time to think about it, he shot off the top of the dune and was airborne for a moment before the big front wheels came down and bit into the sand.

"What a ride," he yelled raucously as he chased after his friend.

The old man stood up and the beach was silent. Water dripped off him and he shivered.

There was not a mark on the sand where the beach buggies had gone. It was as if they'd become airborne at the top of the dune and never landed again. They simply vanished. The tracks in the sand where they had travelled along the beach were fading rapidly and within minutes there was no mark in the sand to show they had even been there.

What the fuck is going on? he yelled at the empty beach.

That was me. I remember the beach buggies and how we used to race along the beach. Jesus! I don't remember almost running over some old man.

He stood there a long time. He ran his hand over where his forehead had hit the steering wheel when the car ran off the road, but the lump was gone. It felt tender to touch and he was sure there was a huge bruise forming. He tried to tell himself that the bump had rattled his brain, was making him see things that had happened in his past, but none of it made any sense. It had all seemed so very real. It couldn't just be imagination or memories surfacing. There had to be some other explanation.

The air was still hot, but now it felt pleasant. His head started to ache again. The wind stopped as the sun lowered itself beyond the Ti-trees and tendrils of cooler air moved in off the ocean. He started to walk back towards the dunes and almost fell over as a sharp pain pierced his head. As he moved around and eased the stiffness in his legs the pain abated, but a dull throbbing persisted.

I should never have left the car to come down to this weird beach.

He looked for his shoes but couldn't find them anywhere. His clothes had dried, but the salt made them stiff. The sand was no longer hot to walk on, so he turned and started to follow his footsteps through the dunes. There would be at least an hour of twilight so he would have no trouble finding his way back if he followed the tracks he made earlier.

As the sound of the beach receded and the silence of the dunes surrounded him, he almost felt happy. Though his head still ached, most of the stiffness had gone, and he strolled along almost as if he were a youth again. He didn't notice when his footprints from earlier on disappeared and the path through the trees seemed wider, more delineated than before. He had often walked through scrub covered dunes like this when he was young and holidayed with his parents down along this coast, and later when he was a teenager, he and his mates spent time here. They were the best days…

Most of the coastal towns were long gone, swallowed by the sea years ago when the West-Antarctic ice shelf broke away allowing massive glaciers to flow into the ocean raising sea levels around the world, forcing the abandonment of major coastal cities as well as thousands of small towns, villages, and settlements along the coastal fringes of every continent… and these were not the same dunes. They couldn't be. They constantly changed as the wind sculpted them. Yet there was something about them…if he stopped and listened.

He could swear he heard voices.

No, I'm being silly. He started walking again, then stopped suddenly because he heard something.

A girl's soft laughter.

A young male voice said: "Let's put the towel here."

"No. It's too close to the path," the girl said. "Someone will see us."

"Okay, through there then."

There was the sound of sand swishing as the couple went further into the dunes, further way from the path where the old man stood.

He pushed his way through the scrubby bushes and stared at the spot they had vacated. Suddenly, he remembered how he had followed her into the dunes. He remembered now with a deep feeling of sadness for a time long past how she had initiated him into the world of grownups, how she taught him that evening what a wonderful thing sex was, and that whenever they were together, they could never get enough of it.

He could hear them laughing in the distance and as their voices faded, he smiled wistfully. He never saw her again after that summer holiday, and could not remember her face, but he remembered what she taught him, and was forever grateful to her.

"Thank you," he whispered into the darkening shadows along the path.

It was getting steadily darker as he walked back along the track towards his car. Behind him, the sky was red, with high tufts of pink cloud stretched across it. Ahead, it was turning deep purple, and the first stars were flickering.

It was getting hard to see the path.

A kind of a mist had settled down between some of the dunes. As he came over one, he saw a light ahead.

Ah… Someone has found my car.

He stumbled towards the light feeling a deep sense of relief.

It made sense to shine a light so he could see where the car was.

They must have figured I went to the beach to cool off.

Certainly, they would have seen his footprints leading away from the car. Then again maybe the wind had blown enough sand over to cover them, and they wouldn't know which way he had gone. But he felt good knowing his rescuers were there and he hurried towards them.

He went down between the dunes. The light was behind the large dune ahead of him as he staggered out of the mist in the hollow and scrabbled up the side of the dune. He didn't remember the dune being this high before, but he was a lot more tired now and maybe it only seemed higher. He could see the light glowing behind the top of it.

When he reached the top and looked over, he couldn't see anything. The light was blinding.

"Over here," he called. "Here I am." He waved his arms above his head thinking that with such a bright light they would surely see him. There was no response, but the sound of the sea was much louder and could have drowned his rescuer's voices.

He staggered towards the light and suddenly found himself on rocky ground.

What is this? I don't remember rocky ground. It was all sand beside the car.

He started to panic. He stopped. He spun around and looked behind, but it was completely black. The light had blinded him. He could see nothing. He could hardly see the ground he was standing on. It too was black. But he could feel it. Hard and stony, with lots of sharp pebbles that dug into his feet. He could barely walk on it.

"Hey. Is anyone there?"

Calling out was useless since his voice was drowned out by massive pounding waves that were so close, they seemed to be underneath him. He was blinded by the brightness of the light and could see nothing but darkness around him. Waves of salty air and sea spray accosted him, so he started walking towards the light, limping as stones dug into his feet.

The light filled his eyes. His head was filling up with it, swelling like a balloon. He heard a tremendous roaring noise. His feet had gone numb, and he could no longer feel them. He floated on the noise, drifted closer to the light.

Suddenly the light was above him, and he found himself walking on smooth concrete towards a rounded concrete wall. It was a lighthouse that towered above him. And the roaring was the sound the great breakers behind him made as they pounded the rocky base of the cliff above which the lighthouse stood shining its unblinking beacon out to sea.

He was stunned. He stood beneath the light and stared out over the angry sea, massive waves highlighted by the brilliant cone of light shining above them.

What happened to the sand dunes?

There was no one in the lighthouse. He knew that. All of them around the coast had been automated a century ago.

Then he remembered that one night when the sea moved in, the cliff beneath it collapsed and the lighthouse had disappeared into the darkness. One day it was there as solid as granite, and the next it was gone, vanished without a trace. And the cliffs had looked the same, yet different. There was no stopping the sea.

Then what the hell was it doing here now?

He leant against the wall of the lighthouse and felt it quivering. Spray whipped over the top of the cliff by the wind drenched him and he started to shiver uncontrollably. The ground beneath him shook. It shook, he thought, in unison with the pounding waves. *This isn't good.*

He went around the base of the lighthouse, away from the pounding sea, and followed the path that led away from the structure. He had barely gone a hundred metres along the path when he felt a deep groaning noise. A sound so low he could not actually hear it, but he felt it through the ground. It vibrated up through his feet and into his bones.

"Fuck," he yelled as the ground shook violently, almost throwing him off his feet.

He ran like mad, away from the lighthouse and the cliffs it stood on.

There was a tremendous splitting noise, like the sound of a piece of wood being slowly torn in half combined with enormous deep groans of pain. He stopped and turned to see the ground around the lighthouse slowly open and fall away. The lighthouse started to go down like it was descending on a lift. Then suddenly it toppled forward, and the light snapped down towards the water and vanished.

The sudden blackness was filled with roaring and deep thunderous roars and groans as many undermined cliff-faces all along the coast followed the lighthouse into the water. The sea had reclaimed more land.

Staggering and stumbling, he went as fast as his exhausted body would allow and only stopped when he found he was on a long stretch of highway. His heart pounded. His head still ached. He slowly turned around in a complete circle and found he was on the coast road he had earlier driven along. In the moonlight he could see the sand dunes between the road and the distant sea, and there in a dark hollow was his car.

He collapsed rather than sat down by the edge of the road and tried to take stock of what had happened to him. He tried to convince himself that it must have been a dream, or a near death experience. But his exhausted and blistered body left no doubt it had been real.

Some kind of time warp perhaps? A lot of strange things have been happening along this coast over the last forty years. People in the last town had said things sometimes appear out of nowhere along that road, and then disappear again, like a mirage. You see it, but when you get too close it's not there.

He sighed. **That's wishful thinking**, he mumbled.

Perhaps it all happened in my mind, he thought, *while I stumbled through the sand dunes.*

He tried to stand up and found he couldn't move.

Shit. **I've got to walk back,** he said out loud to encourage himself. **Get yourself together.**

Again, he tried to move, and this time he succeeded. He dragged himself to his feet, slowly, with his whole body shaking in protest.

I'll have to rest a bit first, he finally decided. *It's not so hot now. Maybe I'll just sleep in the car. I can walk back in the morning before it gets too hot again.*

It took him longer than he would have thought to go the few metres from the road to the car. It was a wonderful relief to sit down on a soft seat, to relax...

He didn't remember falling asleep.

They found him the next morning.

The senior policeman from the town he had left, had telephoned through to the last town left along the road to inquire about another unrelated matter, and in passing mentioned the old man taking a nostalgic trip along the old coast road. When he was told the man had not arrived, he just shook his head, and said to his junior; "We'd better go look for him. I'll bet he's stuck in a sand dune."

"What'd I tell you?" The policeman said when he saw the old man's car half buried in the sand off the side of the road.

"Looks like he skidded and ran off the road. That fine sand can be as slippery as ice on a road."

They found him slumped in the front seat unconscious. His breathing was labored but his heartbeat was strong.

"These old turbines give off gas. If he had all the windows locked and the air conditioning on, he probably would have got enough fumes into the cabin to make him dizzy. I guess that's why he ran off the road."

"Poor Devil. He should have made sure he had his seat belt on though. He must have knocked himself out when he hit his head on the dash. Look at that bruise."

"Jesus, look at his feet," the younger policeman said as they pulled the old man from the car. "How do reckon that happened?"

"Who knows?"

"I don't see his shoes anywhere. Can you see them?"

The two of them made a quick search around the car but couldn't see any shoes.

"Enough mucking about. Let's get him back to town before it starts getting too hot."

The next day when his rescuers visited him in the hospital and asked him what had happened, he thanked them for rescuing him. But he had nothing to say about his experiences on the beach. He was sure no one would believe him anyway.

"When you get out, we'll organize to bring your car back," the senior policeman said.

"I won't need it," the old man said. "I'll be taking the Maglev inland. I won't be going anywhere near the coast again."

"Perhaps that's for the best," the junior policeman said.

They never found out what happened to his shoes, nor why his clothes were so crumpled and full of dried salt, and they didn't bother getting a tow truck to bring back the car. If the old man didn't want it, no one else would either. It was a relic of a time past, and best left where it was. In any case it would soon be swallowed by the encroaching sand as the coastline continued to shift and change.

Into Darkness

The seven men were not wearing their uniforms, but wore clothes typically used by the locals, yet their demeanor told anyone who saw them that they were special forces or at the least had been highly trained. With backpacks weighing them down, they stood in silence to pay their respects to the dead woman who sat as immobile as stone on an old wooden bench. Her eyes were open but were as blank as white marbles. Her whole body was white with streaks of grey marbling the skin that was visible. She looked like a marble statue.

None of them approached too close because their Geiger counters registered a higher-than-normal radiation count, which explained why her body was not touched by ravenous insects and crows. Anything that got near her died.

"Bastards…" one of them mumbled, expressing what they all thought about who or what had done this atrocity.

Behind the woman's body, from the charred ruins of what was once a house, thinning smoke drifted up to swirl loosely in a breeze that was becoming restive, hardly staining the sky as the last of it dissipated.

"How long ago do you think this happened Sarge?" One of the men beside him asked.

"Yesterday maybe, but more than likely this morning. Four or five hours ago, I'd say."

Beside the frozen woman, a tiny ash covered body lay on its side in a scorched cradle. The men backed away slowly, seemingly unable to take their eyes off the two dead bodies.

This wasn't the first lot of bodies they'd seen, scorched, burnt, turned to ash or something that resembled waxy marble, with the immediate surrounds radioactive and dangerous. Over the last several weeks they'd searched for the home base of the aliens that had appeared out of nowhere to wreak destruction on this beautiful country. Every village, settlement, farmhouse, or property in this part of the country had been destroyed, along with all its occupants. Only brief glimpses of the super-fast jets they used screaming across the sky had been seen. No one had yet seen what these beings looked like. No one knew what weapons they used to destroy buildings and people, but whatever they used it was horrifyingly effective. They appeared suddenly in isolated places across Southeast Asia, seemingly out of thin air, or glowing patches of sky, or out of storm clouds; they appeared, wreaked havoc, and disappeared before anyone could react.

The world was going through a strange cycle, with the magnetic poles wandering and wobbling as if about to flip and reverse polarity, with patches of sky glowing like flickering flashlights, people complaining about things appearing and disappearing, of farm animals eviscerated, and now these alien ships flashing across the sky burning up buildings and killing people and animals with fierce glowing lights the moment they appeared. Was this the beginning of an alien invasion? So far this was the only country where they had appeared. How long would it take before they started to spread out to other parts of the world?

They had to be stopped. But how can you stop something you only see a few moments before a devastating attack occurs? Something that screamed down out of the sky in vehicles that defied our ability to see them or stop them? They came at speeds we couldn't match, with the ability to change or reverse direction instantly. Like what we used to call UFOs. They were there and then gone before the sound of them coming arrived. Fucking impossible, Sarge thought.

"This is the closest we've come so far," Sarge said. He turned away from the dead woman and looked towards a mountain range a few kilometres away. The tops of the mountains were covered with dark roiling clouds, promising a storm. The clouds flickered with glowing light. All the reports they'd been able to collect seem to indicate that these alien ships came out of these mountains, and that's where they were headed, to search for a possible base, if one existed.

"That's where we have to go." He pointed towards the mountains, "The old farmer told us those things come from the valley his people used to live in up there in the mountains."

"That's better than staying here," the big heavy-set man next to him said. He held up his radiation monitor to remind them of the level they were being exposed to.

"Right on Dom," Sarge replied. He tapped him on the shoulder. "Let's get out of here." He immediately started walking across the open rice fields that had been partially drained in preparation for harvesting. The others followed trampling the rice into mushy lumps as they worked their way across, heading towards the cloud covered mountains.

They studied the narrow canyon before them and saw an obvious path leading up along one side of a sheer rock-face. The roar of the river emerging from the canyon, rushing and splashing over and around boulders drowned out any possible conversation, so Sarge simply pointed towards the path and started towards it.

The slash in the sheer rock-face in front of them was narrow enough to be invisible from a distance, but up close it appeared as if the rock face of the mountain had split in half, separating the two sides of the mountain with a narrow canyon barely one hundred metres across at the bottom though it was much wider the higher up it went. The top was obscured by roiling clouds as updraughts raised warmer air which rapidly cooled and condensed into heavy clouds. The canyon was recent, geologically, with bare rock slippery to walk on, though there had been time enough for soil to gather, plants to develop and a narrow rushing river fed by constant rain higher up in the mountains to course through it.

The old farmer they'd spoken to days earlier had said it was the mountain pass that his people had used to come down out of these mountains. They came through a tunnel under a part of the mountain and along this pass into the plains below; to find fertile land where they happily settled, because their once beautiful, secluded valley was being destroyed. Where they originally had come from was lost in stories forgotten for too long. But they had been happy there in their isolation until one night a weird electrical storm filled the valley with glowing clouds of electricity out of which came a dozen or more strange flying machines. He also said that creatures had come out of the machines, killing anyone who went near them. He saw them seeding the river with vicious eels, and doing something that killed or replaced the grass near the flat land by the river with something weird. The sun became blocked with unremitting storm clouds that never seemed to go away.

"We couldn't stay there," the old farmer said. "Those few of us who had escaped being massacred had no choice but to leave. When we found the way through, we had to carve out the path along the side of the cliff so we could get down onto the plains. There was no other way to get down. We used axes and shovels, knives, whatever we had that could be used to chip away the rock."

Sarge stared at him with astonishment. They chipped a path along the side of the mountain!

"It took a long time, and we lost a few men who fell into the chasm, but we did it. Ten years ago. We had lived there for centuries before being forced to leave. Now that those things are emerging and killing everyone down on the open plains, we will have to move again," he said, "at least the younger ones. I'm too old to do it now. I'll stay and await my fate, whatever that might be."

That was the first clue to the possible location of the aliens attacking and killing everything in the area.

"We'll stop them," Sarge told the old farmer. "Our job is to find where they come from, and when we do that," he added with confidence, "we'll get rid of them."

The old man smiled knowingly but remained silent. The brava-do of the young never ceased to amuse him.

The track the men followed had been wide enough at first, but as they got higher up on one side of the sheer cliff face, it be-came narrower the further in and the higher they went. They had to slow down, make sure every step was firm, that they balanced properly. To fall off the ledge and down into the chasm would kill them. Even falling straight into the rushing water of the river would kill them. It smashed into rocks and bounced over obstacles as it roared along the narrow valley floor before spreading out into a slower wider stream across the rice plains they had left behind them. Wet sound waves rose above spray and mist, making their voices flat.

"Are you sure this is the way?" Dom asked Sarge, who was lead-ing them.

"Did you see any other paths to follow?"

"No."

"Then it has to be the way."

At this point they were almost two hundred metres above the bottom of the chasm. Light slanting down sparkled on the rip-pling water of the narrow river below. Closer to the river below the rocks were moss covered and looked soft, but if you slipped and fell, that would be the end of you. The rocks under the thin layer of moss were as hard as the rock-face against which they leaned against.

The men had their backs to the sheer rock wall of the cliff and were stepping cautiously sideways to move along it. Their back-packs had become a problem and they had taken them off and were holding them in one hand, close against their sides, drag-ging them along as they shuffled sideways along the narrow ledge. To continue wearing them would have unbalanced them, causing them to topple off the ledge and fall into the deadly chasm be-low. If they leaned forward and looked down, they would see their feet almost hanging over the edge of the ledge that was 'the path' they inched along; 'the path' the old man's tribe had laboriously chipped out of the rock-face so to escape the invaders destroying their valley.

None of them looked down for fear of falling. It was slow going; first moving one foot sideways until a firm spot was felt, then moving the other foot to the spot vacated by the first as they shifted weight from the right to the left leg. Each person paused after each step with their backs pressed hard against the sheer cliff wall. The harder they pressed against the rock face, the safer they felt.

"Even a mountain goat couldn't negotiate this path," the man next after Dom muttered.

"The old man said it was narrow," Sarge said, once again marveling at how the old man's men had been able to hack this path along the side of the chasm wall. They would have followed natural ridges and cracks chipping away... No matter how hard he tried, he couldn't visualize them doing it.

"How much narrower can it get?" Dom asked. "We're already moving sideways. Jesus!"

"We can't go back," Sarge said, suddenly brought back to the reality of their precarious situation.

"Why not? This is no good here."

"There is no other way. This is the only path. We've got a mission to do, to find where those things are coming from, to stop them. That's exactly what we're going to do."

"Mierda," a voice further back called out as several stones were dislodged. The noise they made rattling down the side of the chasm diminished rapidly as the stones hit the moss-covered rocks below before bouncing into the rushing water.

"Be careful back there Jose," Sarge yelled.

"I'm okay Sarge," Jose responded. He remained still for a moment to allow his heart rate to settle.

Taking a deep breath, Sarge shuffled further along the ledge, edging slowly around a slight bulge. Dom followed, and behind him each one in line did the same, with cautious shuffling steps.

From the other side of the chasm, the seven men would seem like a row of ants crawling along a thin line etched into the sheer side of the split mountain's face. From further away, they would not even be visible against the magnitude of the sheer rock face.

Dom slowly followed Sarge around the bulge only to see the path further ahead become even narrower. He suddenly doubted that he would be able to edge along it even going sideways. He was the biggest and bulkiest of the team members and though this was often an advantage, right now it wasn't. But what seemed worse, it appeared to end against a large bulging section of rock face.

"Are you sure this where the old man said the tunnel was?" Dom asked. "It doesn't look like there's anything there."

"It's what he said. It's hidden behind or is beside that great rock."

"I can't see anything beyond there. It looks like the path just stops." Dom was becoming more concerned the longer he looked at it. "We might have to go back and find another way."

The man at the end of the line, out of sight of Sarge and Dom because the rest were on the ledge behind the bulge, yelled out, "Will you two arseholes stop talking and keep moving." Everyone had stopped while Sarge and Dom studied the rock at the end of the narrow ledge. "My legs ache too much to stand still."

"Yeah, hang on a minute Sandy," Dom called in response. His back was pressed firmly against the sheer cliff face but looking down he saw that his toes were hanging over the edge of the ledge. Beneath them, empty space and the glistening roiling water of the river below. *Shit, if it gets any narrower, we're all fucked.*

"Don't look down," Sarge said, "let's keep moving. Somewhere there," he nodded his head in the direction of the large rock where the ledge terminated, "is the cave the old man told us about. It's only a slit in the rock, he said… you won't see it until you're right in front of it."

"Yeah, I remember him saying that."

The rock jutted out from the otherwise flat cliff face blocking any further extension of the ledge, if it extended beyond that point. There was no way they would get around it.

"It has to be there," Sarge said, hiding a hint of desperation under the false confidence he exuded. The ledge appeared to end about ten metres ahead, right against the jagged rock that would be impossible to go around.

The old man was wrong. There's no way around that.

"What's up?" Sandy, the man behind Dom, asked as he negotiated his way around the bulge.

"Looks like a fucking dead end," Dom said.

"We might as well jump off and be done with it," Sandy suggested, almost cheerfully. Being slender he had no trouble standing on the ledge or moving along the narrow path, but he was aware that Dom could be concerned. He was sideways on the ledge with his back hard against the rock-face, almost as if he was stuck to it.

"That's not funny," Dom snapped back at him.

Ben, the next in line after Sandy, edged around the bulge, stopped and looked beyond the men in front of him to see the path and the ledge they were on ending against an impassable section of rock jutting out over the chasm below. "Is that the end of it?"

"Sure looks like it," Sandy said.

"Didn't the old man say we had to go right to the end before you would see it?" Dom reminded them.

"Right, he did. So, let's keep moving," Sarge said and started his sideways shuffle again.

Suddenly the screaming whine of an alien aircraft drowned out the noise of the rushing water deep in the chasm. They froze against the side of the cliff, trying to become a part of the rock face, hoping their ragged clothes would blend in against the rock-face camouflaging them. They were completely exposed. The alien aircraft came tearing up the chasm flying about the same height as the ledge they were standing on. It flashed past them in the blink of an eye barely a few metres away, buffeting them with a fierce back draft as it tore past. It suddenly changed direction and went up vertically, disappearing into the lowering clouds above the narrow chasm.

"Fuck, that was close. Do you think it saw us?" Dom said. With his back stuck to the rock-face, his left-hand fingers gripped a narrow crack in the rock so hard they'd turned white, while right hand still had hold of his backpack resting on the ledge. He knew his grip of the crack in the rock had saved him from being blown off by the back draft. It was the first time on this mission he had felt scared.

"Who knows? But we can't stay here. If it comes back again it will see us." Sarge said and started to shuffle forward again. As he continued along the ledge to the bulging rock that blocked it, he saw a narrow cleft in the rock face against it.

"It's here," he called out, his relief obvious. His legs quivered with small spasms as he stopped in front of the dark crack in the rock-face. The ledge was wider here in front of the opening. The opening itself was barely wide enough to allow someone of his size to pass through. "It's just like the old man said," he yelled encouragingly to the rest of the team. "You only see it when you are right in front of it."

The crack opening into the mountain was narrow at the top but widened lower down. He couldn't see how far it extended because it was pitch-black inside. It was exactly as the old man had described. With his eyes adjusted to the brightness outside, he wouldn't know what was inside until he went in. He pushed his backpack through the opening and eased into the gap behind it. Crouching down he shoved the backpack forward. Beyond the narrow opening the cave widened out and he moved in with no more trouble. He put his backpack to one side to allow room for Dom to follow.

"I won't fit," Dom said the moment he saw how narrow the entrance was.

"Come on," Sarge called from inside the cave. "You don't have a choice. You can't go back."

He knew that. The others were still shuffling along the ledge towards the cleft in the cliff.

As Dom pushed his backpack through the narrow opening and he felt Sarge grab it and pull it further in to make room for him to squeeze through the opening.

The others behind him had stopped. They had to wait for him to go through before they could move forward. Dom knew that they were exhausted, and their legs were probably quivering and aching as were his, and if he didn't hurry up one of them might lose balance and fall off the ledge.

"What the fuck are you doing?" the man nearest him on the ledge asked.

"I'm going... Just give me a moment."

Crouching down, Dom turned and moved sideways into the widest part of the opening. He couldn't go straight in like Sarge had. He would have to go sideways. He exhaled so his chest would collapse a bit and eased himself into the opening. The rough edges of the opening scratched across his back and chest as he pushed into the gap until he got stuck. He realized he would have to get lower, down onto his back perhaps and wriggle in like a snake. But before he could try this, he felt Sarge grab his arm and start pulling to help him worm his way through. I can't get stuck, he told himself. Or we're all fucked. He was desperate to take a breath, but if he did that his chest would expand and he'd never get through. He forced out whatever remaining air was in his lungs allowing his chest to collapse a tiny bit more and pushed as hard as he could. Sarge pulling on his arm and dragging him forward was the clincher. Without that he would not have got through the opening.

He collapsed, gasping and wheezing once he was through.

"I told you you're too bloody fat," Sarge said.

"It's all muscle," Dom mumbled without taking offence. He was gasping and trying to breathe again while sitting on the floor of a large cave. The entrance was now clear for the others to come in.

Within no time, they made their way in off the narrow ledge outside and were sitting or standing, looking around at the size of the cave hidden behind the cliff face. There was enough light coming through the narrow opening to allow them to see. They also saw, at the opposite side of the cave from the entrance, a much darker opening.

"That must be the tunnel through to the valley on the other side," Jose said.

"Just like the old farmer said,' Sarge commented.

With their eyes adjusting to the darkness, it was clear there was no other way to go.

"Okay, now that you've all had a rest, we should get a move on," Sarge said.

They groaned, grumbled and cursed, got their torches out, picked up their backpacks, slung them over their shoulders and stood ready to follow Sarge.

"That's the spirit."

Flashing their torches about to gain an idea of the size of the cave, Jose shuddered when he saw the ceiling above them covered with writhing bats, disturbed by the sudden brightness of the torches. They squealed in protest. Some let go and fluttered towards the entrance, but discovering it was too bright, returned to their perches upside down on the ceiling.

"I hate those things," Jose said.

There are probably worse things in here than bats," Sarge said, shining his torch on the floor further away from the entrance. They saw cockroaches and centipedes wriggling furiously to escape the light shining on them, burying themselves in loose bat shit.

"This place creeps me out," Dom said.

"Follow me," Sarge commanded as he strode confidently towards the dark hole delineating the tunnel. He wanted to keep them moving so none of them had time to dwell on where they were or what they might encounter in the tunnel through the mountain.

Each of them had strapped their torch to their shoulder so it always pointed forward and slightly down, leaving their hands free in case they needed to use a weapon, or more likely, to steady themselves so they wouldn't stumble and fall.

The tunnel was an inverted V shape several metres wide at the bottom but narrow at the top several metres above them. The path they walked along was firm enough, composed of gravel, stones and earth that had been compacted over the years. The rock sides were covered with mosses and hardy fungus. There were no stalactites or stalagmites so it was obvious that water running through this crack hadn't happened much at all, but there must have been enough water drain in from time to time or mosses and fungus wouldn't grow. Fortunately for Jose, once they had gone a short distance along the tunnel there were no more bats; they obviously preferred to stay in the cave near the entrance.

At first, they walked warily, alert for any possible attack from wild animals, but after half an hour, they relaxed and strode along with ease. After several hours they slowed down to a rough shuffle. After the climb along the side of the cliff to find the opening into this tunnel they were exhausted. Hardly saying a word to anyone, they stopped when Sarge stopped and dropped his backpack onto the ground. He sat down next to it. They did the same, too tired to move one step more.

Within a minute of sitting down next to his backpack, Sarge leaned across onto it, to rest his head, and fell asleep. Dom reached over and switched off his torch.

"We'll have to switch off the torches while we sleep, or there'll be no power in them when we wake up." And saying that Dom switched his own off.

"I don't like the idea of being in the dark," Sandy said.

"What's wrong with you?" Dom asked. "Do you sleep with the light on at home, or in the barracks?"

"Just saying… What if there's a cave in?"

"Just go to sleep."

The others, too exhausted to make any comments shuffled about trying to find more comfortable positions, and one by one the torches were switched off, leaving them in total darkness.

"First one who wakes, switch on your torch and wake the rest of us, okay? Dom asked.

"Yeah," and "we'll do that," were the mumbled replies, before silence settled over them.

Sandy woke up feeling as if he was buried by falling rocks. His scream woke the others, and they fumbled helplessly in the total darkness until one of them found his torch and switched it on. With light to see they calmed down.

"Did you feel that?" Sandy asked.

"Feel what?" Sarge said.

"An earthquake. I thought we were having an earthquake. The ground trembled."

"You must have been dreaming," Dom said.

"Maybe you felt someone farting," another joked.

"No. Look around. It's dusty," Sandy said, then added, "There was no dust in the air before." He shone his torch along the tunnel to highlight drifting dust particles.

Others did the same and saw the torch beams delineated by a mist of floating dust. It hardly moved, the air was so still, but as each of them stood up they disturbed the fine floating particles which swirled about as they moved through it.

"Maybe you're right," Sarge said. "Now that we're all awake, we should get moving."

This was followed by groans and grumbles as they fiddled with their backpacks.

"I gotta take a piss," one of them said.

"Do it. Everyone if you need to. Do it now and then we can move on. We don't want to be in here if there is another earthquake." Sarge turned his back on them so he could piss against the rock wall. Like a pack of dogs leaving a scent marker, he thought as he zipped up afterwards. "We ready to go now?"

There was an affirmative chorus.

They continued their trek on into the darkness, their feeble torch beams showing them the way.

It seemed like forever as they shuffled along surrounded by darkness and the ever-present fear that the tunnel could collapse and bury them. To conserve the torch batteries, they only used one at a time, switching to another when the light from the one used started to dim. That way, they hoped to make the torches last until they had got to the other side, which everyone hoped wouldn't take much longer.

Finally, when they were beginning to think they would be trapped underground forever, they saw a dim light ahead.

"That's gotta be the other end," Sandy exclaimed.

"Thank Christ."

"About fucking time."

"I wouldn't get too excited yet," Sarge added as they picked up the pace.

After a moment it almost became a rush to see who could get to the opening first.

They stumbled out of a narrow split in the jagged rock face and stood looking down across a grassy valley. It was darker than they expected. A dim glow in the clouds on the other side of the valley hinted at an imminent sunset. The feeble light left exposed a broad plain with waist high grass quivering as if being caressed by a slight breeze, but they could feel no breeze at all. Dark heavy clouds, almost black in some places, filled the valley obscuring the sky above. The air was dank, replete with moisture. A few heavy drops of rain spattered off the rocky ground near the opening to the tunnel. They heard the hissing of heavy rain falling further up the valley. The clouds vibrated with dim flashes of lightning somewhere deep inside followed by a groaning rumble of thunder a moment later.

The tall grass quivered as if in anticipation of receiving rain. The hiss of rain further along the valley became louder as the falling rain moved towards their position.

"I don't like this place one bit," Jose said softly. He stepped towards to the edge of the grass. Something slithered away, and he jumped back, startled.

"What kind of place is this?" Sandy asked. He pulled out a satellite phone from his backpack and switched it on. "There's no reception in here," he said after staring at a blank screen.

"Maybe we're too close to the mountains. Might be better further in," Sarge suggested.

"It's the cloud cover. It's too heavy and full of electrical disturbances." And to emphasize his comment a stronger flash of lightning lit the interior of the clouds. Almost instantly loud rumbling thunder pummeled them. The satellite phone buzzed as static electricity coursed through it. The air around them sizzled. Sandy almost dropped the phone before he could switch it off. "Shit!"

"Can you at least get a position, so we know exactly where we are?"

"Nothing's coming through those clouds smothering us."

"Fuck."

"Yeah," Dom said. "I agree."

Their voices were muffled, flat, drowned by the heavy humidity in the air.

"We should move forward," Sarge said, almost reluctantly. "We need to find a place to camp, and some water. I'm all out."

"Me too," one of the others said.

"Why don't we camp just inside the tunnel?" Byron, the one who always seemed to find himself at the end of the line asked. "It's late. We should wait until tomorrow before going on."

"What about Sarge?" Byron's mate George asked. "We could set up here and wait until morning."

"No. We'll head across to the centre of the valley, see what's there. The sooner we know what we're up against the better."

Without waiting to see if they agreed with him, Sarge stepped into the long grass, pushed it aside squashing it beneath his heavy boots. His feet squelched in the moist ground. Something unseen slithered away as he moved forward.

"Was that a snake?" Dom, right behind him, asked.

Neither of them saw anything, but they heard it and hesitated.

"I hate snakes," Sarge said, but pushed on regardless.

"I got water in my boots," Dom said as he squelched along behind Sarge.

Reluctantly, the others followed one by one.

"Do you think there might be leeches in this sludge," Sandy asked. He was close behind Dom. "I can't stand leeches," he added but no took any notice.

They pushed and sloshed forward through grass that seemed to get thicker and more rubbery as they got further away from the rock face.

"Come on guys, don't dawdle,' Sarge yelled out, but his voice was flat and didn't carry far in the heavy air. He didn't look back to see how they were doing. His entire focus was on moving forward through the rubbery thick grass. It never dawned on him that it didn't feel like grass, even when it seemed to be wrapping itself around his feet. He ripped through it, tearing roots and stalks out of the soggy ground, clearing a path that made it easier for those following behind. He didn't notice the waist-high grass on either side of him shaking and twisting, leaning towards him. After about five hundred metres, with legs aching, and with lungs having difficulty breathing in the heavy wet air, he heard running water ahead somewhere and that encouraged him to keep moving. He forced himself to push harder, to move a little faster, and as he got closer to the sound of the running water, the grass finally thinned and became easier to get through.

"Can you slow down a bit?" the man at the end of the line called out. "I can't get enough air in. It's like I'm trying to breathe underwater." He stumbled as hit feet seemed to stick in the sludge the men ahead had churned up.

George, the man immediately in front of him stopped to help while the others forged ahead.

"Come on Byron," he said encouragingly, as he grabbed his arm to steady him. "We're almost there."

Far above the clouds that filled the hidden valley keeping it in semi darkness, the sun had passed beyond the mountain range and was about to set. Deepening shadows filled the valley with gloom.

Sarge surged ahead, pushing aside and squashing the thick grass making a path for the others to follow. The sound of running water was much louder. It got darker and with no moon or stars to lighten the coming night because of the heavy clouds he was desperate to find somewhere free of the grass and the slush beneath his feet where they could set up camp for the night.

Emerging finally from the waist high rubbery grass, he stumbled over a few rocks, and staggered forward before he found himself standing on flat cracked layers of basalt devoid of grass. He was breathing hard, but this calmed as he waited for the others to join him on the wide rocky shelf next to a narrow river. The running water was a welcome sound.

"This'll do," he yelled exultantly as the others one by one stumbled out of the grass and onto the flat basalt surface. "We'll set up here for the night." He dropped his backpack onto the ground and strolled over towards the creek that ran beside the rock shelf he stood on. He stared down into water that was as black as an octopus' ink, with no light from above to reflect off its surface. It was wider than he expected, and the water was flat and smooth. The sound of running water he'd heard had been from where the river dropped over a rocky obstruction to a lower level. He wondered briefly if this river somehow went down under the mountain to become the fast-moving river in the canyon they came up on the other side of the mountain. It had to go somewhere, if this was an enclosed valley.

Staring at the water while the other men emerged from the grass to drop their packs on the flat basalt surface, he saw brief flashes of bio-luminescence beneath its surface. He started to bend down, to sweep his hand through the water, to scoop up a little to see if it was fresh enough to drink when he saw the bio-luminescent flashes zigzag across the smooth water beneath the surface straight towards him. He caught a glimpse of a hideous face with a mouth full of sharp teeth that glowed briefly as, whatever it was, shot towards him leaving a trail of phosphorescent flashes that almost instantly faded into the blackness of the water.

He jumped up and staggered back, stumbling. Dom caught him, preventing him from falling over backwards.

"What happened?"

"I saw something in the water." And when Dom gave him that look, he added, "Something came at me. Bloody fast. I don't know what it was."

"Can we find our way back to the cave," Dom asked, "If we can't stay here that is?"

"Sure. We just follow our tracks. We should be able to see them in the dark."

"I don't think so," Byron, the last man to arrive said. "Have a look back there."

They all turned to look.

The grass was undulating and heaving on both sides of the path they had smashed through it. The stalks they had broken and trodden down into mush were swelling and starting to rise up, quivering as if to shake off whatever had squashed them. Stunned, they watched as the track they had made through the grass to get where they stood on the hard rocky surface disappeared. The undulations ceased and the grass stood tall, quivering slightly. It was as if they had never pushed their way through it.

It looks thicker now, Sarge thought, or am I imagining that?

"Fuck," George, standing beside Byron blurted. "What is this place? That's not fucking grass, is it?"

"What else could it be?" Sandy asked.

"I don't know, "George said. "It's not like any fucking grass I've ever seen."

"Forget about the grass," Sarge said. He shook his head to clear his thoughts. "Set up the tents. We'll stay here for the night. It's too late to look for another spot."

Large drops of rain splattered the ground about them as darker clouds descended from above.

"It looks like we're in for some heavy rain. I certainly don't want to be looking for a place to set up camp while it's pouring down. So, let's do it now."

"We should have stayed back by the tunnel entrance," Byron mumbled, as he dropped his backpack onto the rocky ground. He kicked aside a few loose rocks to clear a space for his tent.

With practiced ease, each one opened their backpacks, extracted a one-man tent and had it set up in no time. When the rain came pounding down, they were all out of it and dry inside their small tents.

Darkness enveloped them as the heavy impenetrable rainclouds sank lower into the valley. The sun far above had set beyond the mountains containing this small valley, and where the camp was, it was as dark there as it had been inside the tunnel through the mountain. The only light was from intermittent flashes of phosphorescence in the water, or flat lightning in the heavy clouds above. The rain had come and gone, but as exhausted as they were, none of them could get to sleep. The total absence of light was more terrifying than the darkness itself, and it was made worse by the continuing flashes of lightening that lit the clouds enough to not allow their eyes to adjust to the darkness. They heard slithering sounds coming from the nearby grass, and series of splashing noises in the water beside the flat rocky surface where they'd erected their tents.

Sarge sat inside his tent, listening to the unnerving sounds outside, and horrible visions of slimy things slithering towards them in the darkness filled his head; visions of hideous snake things with no need to see, that could sense their prey by smell, and the vibrations it made as it moved.

He shook his head to clear his mind. Get a hold of yourself… and just as he finally started to relax…

A gurgling cream filled the night. Sarge leaped up, almost knocking his stent apart in his haste to get out, to see what made that noise. He spun around but could see nothing in the darkness apart from flashes of light in the water of the creek.

"What the fuck!" Dom was standing beside him, his torch lighting up a mass of black slimy eels wriggling around one of the tents. More were sliding up out of the water. The others were out of their tents, kicking away the slippery creatures that came too close. Everyone was yelling and kicking at the eels.

All; except one. One tent vibrated and shook violently as the person inside struggled with the black slimy eels that surrounded his tent. They were slithering into his tent which convulsed and shuddered.

"Byron!" Sandy yelled out as she shone his torch towards the tent swarming with eels.

"That's his tent," Dom said as he also shone his torch on the violently shaking tent. Monstrous eels slipped in and out of the opening.

"Fucking Hell!" one of them yelled.

They ran to the tent, pushing and kicking the massive eels away. Some turned and snapped at them, needle sharp teeth glistening in the torchlight. Other slithered away and flopped back into the water. They didn't like the light. As the torches shone on them, they writhed and twisted around each other attempting to escape.

Dom was the first at Byron's tent and he ripped open the entrance flap to shine his torch in.

The others, right beside and behind him, caught him as she staggered back in horror.

Muffled gurgling sounds came from Byron as he struggled to escape from the massive slimy creatures writhing all over him. There was one massive one wrapped around his throat, and it was disappearing down inside his mouth, suffocating him.

"Fuck!" exploded from Sarge. It was involuntary.

The men pulled and kicked at the eels all over Byron. With all their torches shining on them, they rapidly disengaged and slithered back towards the drop into the creek. The water splashed loudly as most of them fell into it. Further along, away from the torch light, others were sliding up onto the bank, emerging from the water.

"Get them off him," Dom yelled. He reached forward and tried to grab the eel that was entering through Byron's mouth but couldn't pull it out. He couldn't even get a proper grip on it. It was too slimy. "No, No, No," he yelled as he struggled to get the eel out of his friend's mouth, but inexorably it kept sliding in further. It was too slippery to get a grip on.

Sarge grabbed him, pulled him away.

"It's too late." Sarge said. "He's dead. Leave him."

"We can't just leave him there."

"He's not moving. He's dead, and that fucking thing is inside him."

"We have to help…"

"There's nothing we can do," Sarge said as he dragged Dom forcibly away from the tent.

The other men had retreated some distance away from the Byron's tent.

As they moved away, the eels started to come back out of the water again, sliding up over the edge of the embankment and slithering towards the body in the half-demolished tent. It only took a few minutes for the body to be covered again with the writing black slimy eel-things.

"We can't stay here," Sandy said. "Or we're all dead."

They were clustered together well away from Byron's body, staring in horror at the writhing mass covering Byron's body. More eels were coming out of the water, and these headed towards them instead of going towards Byron's tent. This time the torchlights didn't faze them. They had hardly any strength, the batteries in all the torches were almost depleted after their use in the tunnel. A couple of the torches started flickering as their batteries failed, so they were switched off.

"We've gotta get the fuck out of here," Byron's friend George said.

Some of the eels slid into the next tent in the line. They soon emerged and joined the others slithering towards the group standing as far away from them as they could get.

They shone their weak torchlight on the grass with the forlorn hope that the path they had made through it might still be visible. It wasn't. It stood tall, quivered slightly. They could not see one broken blade or any flattened areas that would indicate the path they'd made though it when they left the cleft in the side of the mountain.

"Which way do we go?" Dom asked. Desperately.

Looking at the unbroken grass, Sarge said, "How the fuck would I know?" This was the first time ever that he was so unsure he didn't know what to do. It was not a feeling he liked. He glanced back towards the creek, a bit beyond where they'd set up their one-man tents, then pointed in a direction directly away from the area. "That way…" It was as good as any other direction. At least it was away from the creek. There was no way they could stay there with those vicious eels coming at them.

They again shone their weakened torches on the field of tall thick grass, leaving the area behind them in darkness. Almost immediately, they heard more splashing in the water and louder slithering sounds as more eels coming up out of the water joined the ones wriggling across the hard ground towards them. Within a moment several eels had started writhing around their legs.

"Fuck this," One of them yelled and kicked furiously to dislodge the eels.

"Let's get out of here," Sarge yelled, finally galvanized into moving as he felt an eel slide around his feet. He kicked it away.

"The tents…" Dom started to say.

"Leave them." Sarge ordered. "Leave everything. Grab a knife or a machete so we can cut through the grass but leave everything else." He pulled a long blade from a scabbard strapped to his belt, bent down and hacked off the head of an eel about to wrap itself around his feet. "Let's go," he yelled. "Let's get the fuck out of here."

Grabbing a few knives, they left everything else and ran towards the long quivering grass which welcomed them by trying to wrap itself around their legs. As they pushed into it, swathes of it were ripped up and left lying in the mushy soil underneath their feet.

"Make sure you don't trip or fall over," Sarge yelled as he pushed his way into it.

"I took a compass bearing just after we got here," Sandy said and held it up so Sarge could see its fluorescent dial. He pointed the direction they needed to take to get back to the opening of the tunnel through the mountain. He gave the compass to Sarge. "Take this and use it for the direction."

"We can't stop," Sarge yelled out as he slashed his way into the grass. He didn't have to add, 'or they'll get us' because everyone thought the same. He heard the others yelling and cursing as they too slashed their way through the grass behind him. They all went into the boggy grass at different points but after a few metres the ones who were a bit slower than Sarge and Dom edged their way into already cut path the two ahead were creating.

Would the eels come into the grass after them? Or was the grass something else that would get them? Sarge slashed away with more fury than he thought he could muster opening a broad path the others could follow. Dom was slightly behind him to the right side, hacking and slashing with equal fury.

The further they got away from the camp into the field the

harder it became to push through it. The grass seemed to resist them. It had a much firmer grip in the damp soil underneath and couldn't be torn out and pushed away as easily as it had before. It was much thicker and rubbery than they remembered, and if they stopped to catch their breath, they could feel the stalks beginning to wrap around their legs and their waists, which spurred them on to greater effort. They hacked it away with the knives and machetes they carried. It was the only way to get through it. A thick sticky sap oozed out of the cuts. Each time they cut it, a soft hissing sound emanated from the surrounding grass, which on either side of them writhed furiously.

"Don't get that sticky shit on you," Sarge yelled out after slashing a particularly thick stalk that resembled an octopus tentacle more than it did a thick stalk of grass. It wriggled as it fell to the ground, and quickly burrowed into the soft damp soil. What the fuck have we got ourselves into?

Sarge, and Dom, and Sandy forged ahead, slashing and cutting their way through.

Behind them, the last man in the line, George, tripped and fell as his feet were suddenly entwined. He landed on his face and oozing sap burned into his skin. He yelled and tried to stand up, but more strands of grass and roots wrapped around his forearms preventing him from standing. Blinded by the acidic sap he called out, "Help me," but those ahead ignored him, or they didn't hear him as they continued to slash and cut their way through the much taller, thicker, more resistant grass.

They screamed, shouted, and cursed as they forced their way forward in the direction they hoped would get them back to the edge of the cliff and the entrance to the tunnel, their only way out of this cursed valley. Their torches were useless, the batteries having given out. The only way Sarge knew which way they were going was after every few cuts he would check the glowing compass bearing to make certain he was leading them in the right direction.

They continued to hack and slice, becoming weaker by the minute. But they couldn't stop. The moment they did that the grass would trap them. Wrap them up, cocoon them, and God knows what would happen after that.

This isn't fucking grass. It's a field of tentacles. Like a million octopuses trying to grab us. And with that thought Sarge hacked away at it with renewed fury. Dom moved alongside of him and with a nod of encouragement cut into the grass with equal fury, cutting a wide path for those behind to follow.

"Come on," Sarge yelled out. "Don't let this shit stop you."

The grass grew back almost as quick as they could cut it. The others behind hardly heard Sarge because the heaviness and dampness of the air swallowed his and their own voices. Combined with the hissing and the noise the grass made while twisting and writhing rendered their voices inaudible to each other, each trapped in their own space, hacking and cutting, as the grass sprung up in front of them, while at the same time the grass behind writhed and entangled their feet. It seemed to be possessed of a conscious malevolence that was incomprehensible to them. This terrified them, giving them extra strength, enabling them to cut and slash their way with renewed vigor.

Another tripped and fell, sprawled on his face. Before he could call out, roots swarmed up from the moist soil entering his mouth and nostrils to smother him. He struggled weakly for a moment before succumbing to unconsciousness. He was left behind as those in front entirely focused on hacking their way to freedom were unaware that he had fallen.

It seemed like forever, but as the ground beneath their feet hardened, they knew they were close to the edge of the field and the rocky base of the mountain. The grass thinned, stopped grabbing at them and they moved easier. They found themselves staggering along the rocky ledges at the base of the mountain where nothing could grow. Four stopped and stood on the grass-less rocky ledge not far from the opening to the tunnel, momentarily holding each other to stop falling over, Sarge, Dom, Sandy and Jose. Their legs shook and they struggled to get their breath.

Shining his feeble torch back along the path they had cut, Sarge looked for the stragglers, George and Ben, but they didn't appear. As he waited anxiously to see if they would appear – they should have been right behind him – the grass was rapidly growing back, filling the path they'd hacked out with new shoots. It looked like the whole soggy ground was moving as roots wriggled up out of the earth only to bend over and reenter. New shoots would start coming up from the exposed root, thickening and twisting as they grew upwards.

"Come on guys," Sarge mumbled, but he knew they weren't going to make it.

"The tunnel's up here," Sandy called out. He'd gone ahead to look for it.

Sarge didn't hear him. He still stared at the re-growing grass, hoping the stragglers would make it through. But there was no sign of them. The grass further in had completely grown back, and their torches were too weak to throw any light into the darkness beyond a few metres.

"We should stay the night inside the tunnel," Dom said. "It's not safe out here."

Sarge said nothing, but he let Dom lead him away, and the four of them entered the cleft in the side of the mountain that led into the tunnel. A few metres inside the entrance they collapsed rather than sat down, totally exhausted. For a few moments each of them shivered uncontrollably as they struggled to process what they'd been though. When their bodies had calmed down and they were able to think the first one to say anything was Sarge. "Maybe this place is some kind of alien nursery," he said.

"Maybe it's their food supply," Dom said.

"Who the fuck knows?" Jose mumbled.

They all stared towards the entrance of the cave but couldn't see anything outside because it was as dark there as it was inside the cave and the beginning of the tunnel. They hoped nothing would crawl in to attack them.

"Do you think when it's light, we can go back and get our stuff?" Sandy asked.

"I'm not going back out there again," Sarge said, "no fucking way. You can go if you want, but I won't. I'd start heading back through the tunnel right now, only I'm too fucking exhausted to even think about it."

There was immediate murmured assent, after which they fell silent, each individually enveloped in their own misery.

A loud humming noise woke them. It was dawn and the heavier clouds that filled the valley had risen enough to allow enough daylight into the valley to brighten its lush landscape, highlighting the intense greenness of the strange grass. Without a word they crowded around the entrance to the cave so they could see what was making the humming noise.

A dark smudge appeared within the clouds before it emerged and solidified into one of the pursuit planes that had been hunting them on the other side of the mountain. It came straight down to settle on four struts on the rocky ground beside where they had pitched their small tents.

"You still want to go and get your stuff? Sarge asked Sandy.

Two dark figures emerged from underneath the vehicle and floated down to the ground underneath. They were indistinct, wearing black uniforms that hid any physical features. They were bipedal and had two arms that seemed very flexible, as if they were jointless. Their heads were covered with helmets that reflected the light like a black mirror.

"They're not walking, Dom noted. "They seem to float along."

The two aliens stopped and looked around, as if searching for the missing occupants of the tents.

"Be quiet," Sarge said.

"They couldn't possible hear us from way over there," Dom whispered.

The two aliens floated across to the end tent which Byron had been in when he was attacked by those ferocious eel things.

A second ship floated down out of the clouds above the valley and settled beside the first. Two more dark figures floated down out of the ship to join the two beside the tents.

"I'll bet they're wondering how we got into their hidden valley," Dom said softly.

The aliens examined each tent, and then moved towards the

edge of the grass and looked about as if searching for evidence of how the men who erected the tents had got there.

"Shit, they'll come looking for us when they see the path we made to get here."

One of the aliens moved into the grass close to the edge of the rocky flat area and stopped. The others joined him.

"That stuff's already regenerated," Sarge said. "There's no way they can see which way we came or went. They'll think the grass, whatever it is, got all of us. Or if not the grass, the eel things."

"You wouldn't know anyone had even been here," Jose said, "except that we left our tents and equipment there by the creek."

They watched as the aliens moved back towards the water's edge where they stopped. Several large eels slithered up out of the water and started writhing around the legs of the aliens. As the four men watched from the safety of the tunnel entrance, hundreds of the eels emerged from the water and started writing around the four alien beings who remained immobile, and unperturbed by their writhing visitors and the sparks of light that emanated from their sinuous bodies.

"What are they doing?" Sandy whispered.

"Maybe they're communicating with each other," Jose suggested.

"How would we know?" Sarge said.

Suddenly the eels dropped off the four aliens and slithered back into the water.

Once again, the alien figures turned towards the grass and stared across it as if trying to see where the occupants of the tents had gone.

Involuntarily the four men inside the tunnel entrance moved further back into the darker recesses of the tunnel.

"We should go now," Sarge said, "as soon as our eyes can adjust to the darkness. "If they come over here, they'll find us."

"I'll fucking kill them if they come here," Dom snarled. His hand went to the long knife resting in its scabbard attached to his belt.

"I have no doubt you'd try," Sarge said. "But I don't want to lose anyone else. So that's not going to happen. Come on, let's get away from here."

Enough light filtered into the tunnel through the narrow entrance which enabled them to walk a fair way back into the tunnel, where they paused for a while to allow their eyes to adjust to the darkness. None of them wanted to walk through the tunnel again, but they had no choice; there was no other way they could go. They had left their torches back in the tents, and this worried them at first, as each thought of stumbling along in total darkness, as good as blind. But as their eyes adjusted, they discerned a faint glow coming from some parts of the rocky sides of the tunnel. It was enough to allow them to proceed without stumbling or feeling their way as they thought they would have had to do.

"We know where their base is now," Sarge said as they started on the long trek back through the tunnel, "or at least where they're coming from. When we get back…"

"If we get back," Sandy muttered to himself rather than the others.

"When we get back," Sarge repeated affirmatively, "We'll be able to tell the Air-force where to drop bombs. A few incendiary clusters would do…"

"A couple of tactical nukes," Dom interrupted, "should give those bastards something to think about."

"Wipe out the whole valley. Kill every fucking thing in it," Jose said, grimacing with pain as he remembered the horrible deaths his teammates had endured. He was glad it was dark and the others couldn't see the tears welling up in his eyes.

With renewed energy the four remaining picked up the pace, marching doggedly into the darkness of the tunnel, heading towards the light they knew would greet them at the other end.

Anomalies

EYRESEA

1...

The water heaved.

It rolled aside, parting as if cut with a knife from underneath, and a monstrous scaly head reared up, rivulets of water cascading from it. A huge mouth opened; a guttural hiss exploded from it like a deep disappointed sigh. It knew it had missed its prey, but none the less it snapped at the retreating figure of the boy.

Billy was stunned at how lax he had been.

Sitting by the water's edge at his favourite fishing spot, he was distracted by a small dark shape that gradually resolved itself from the glowing distant haze into boat. It was coming from the north.

No one comes from that direction, he thought. It's too hot and dangerous.

Squinting to bring it into focus, he saw sails flapping loosely in the quiet breeze that ruffled the sea's surface. The boat took a long time to become more than a small dot near the horizon.

He assumed it was heading towards Eyresea — where else would it go? They had not had any visitors for a long time. Outside news was always welcome, and perhaps it could be carrying something interesting to trade with them, but coming from the north was unexpected.

He didn't want to admit to himself that he was feeling excited. His father had gone to the north years ago and had never returned. Perhaps these people might know something about what happened to him. But he deliberately pushed that thought down; he didn't want to get his hopes up.

Billy's favourite fishing spot was partly shaded by she-oaks growing close to the water's edge. A short stretch of red sand separated the trees and the rough grass growing beneath them from the water which at that spot dropped down into deeper hole where larger fish often congregated. He almost always caught something there. But this morning he had barely thrown in his line when he spotted the small dot on the northern horizon emerge from the glowing mist to resolve into the shape of a boat. Taken by the unexpectedness of it he did not see the dark shape beneath the surface gliding silently towards him.

But because he was young and lithe and could react quickly, when the monster burst from the water Billy instantly dropped his fishing line and leaped back out of the way.

"Ha!" He yelled at it. "You're not fast enough to catch me."

He jumped up and down well out of reach of the giant crocodile's snapping jaws yelling obscenities at it more as a way of chiding himself for having been inattentive rather than being angry at the croc. It was only being itself, always hunting to fill an insatiable appetite.

"Don't go away. Stay there… we're coming back to get you."

The monstrous crocodile hissed at him.

Billy caught a whiff of its foul breath before its jaws snapped shut and it sank beneath the surface, drifting back from the edge, sinking so only its eyes, nostrils and a small part of its head remained above the surface. Eyes unblinking, it stared at him for a long minute before submerging. The water rippled, the grass growing in the shallow depths shifted and heaved as the crocodile settled in to wait and watch. The water and the grass soon became still, and you wouldn't know there was a huge crocodile lurking there, waiting…

I've never seen one that big before, Billy thought as he watched where it had disappeared. After a few minutes the top of its head reappeared in the waterlogged grass, its eyes, and nostrils remaining above water. The rest of its huge body remained invisible beneath the surface.

It was too big to rush out of the water to chase him which is why he hadn't run further away. Even though its powerful tail could propel it out of the water, once on land these big old ones were sluggish, their enormous weight slowing them down to a rapid waddle. A juvenile crocodile would have been out of the water in a flash and after him so fast he would not have got away.

There were more crocodiles coming down from the north every year, finding plenty of room to hunt though not a lot of food in Eyresea other than flocks of pelicans, silver gulls and other wading birds that easily escaped a hunting croc. Of the land birds, the cockatoos, galahs, budgerigars and finches that flocked in their thousands along the shores of the sea, crocks couldn't get near them. Occasionally they got lucky with water birds like waders and herons, pelicans, seagulls and magpie geese which they sometimes caught feeding in the grass along the water's edge. Most other wading and sea birds flew off the moment the water near them became disturbed. The invading crocs managed though, by catching some of the larger fish, birds too slow to take off in time, and wild boars, kangaroos or other animals that came close to the water's edge in the evenings. Because the water was salty, as sea water always is, these larger land animals rarely came to the water's edge to drink; they came to cool off after a hot day.

In the water you wouldn't have a chance. Once those jaws full of foul-smelling teeth locked on, you were rolled over and dragged under with your back snapped and held under until you drowned. You would then be wedged somewhere the croc considered a safe place for storage of food, and it would wait until the natural decaying processes tenderized you to a degree it considered soft enough to eat. Crocodiles don't chew their food; they swallow huge chunks. Anything large it catches and drowns will be wedged somewhere to allow rotting to set in before it tears off chunks to swallow.

Billy grabbed a rock and pitched it at the monster's head partially hidden in the waterlogged grass. The water rippled as the croc moved into deeper water, a dark indistinct smudge against the bottom. It was waiting in case the boy was silly enough to come back to the water's edge again. But unlike some other grazing animals where out of sight was out of mind, and almost immediately they would forget the danger and venture back to the water's edge, Billy knew better. He knew it would lie in wait for hours if necessary, and that it would remain in this area until it was either killed or forced out by younger crocs coming down out of rivers and swamps further north.

He wouldn't risk retrieving his fishing rod where he dropped it. It was too close to the edge. He would come back later for it. In the meantime, he would go back and tell everyone about this monster. A hunting party would quickly be organized. A big crocodile was a valuable commodity, supplying the people of Eyresea with skin for jackets and boots and belts to trade with visitors from the south, or to take south themselves when they needed to trade for other essentials. It would also supply them with lots of meat that they would either salt or freeze for future use.

"Hang around you big bastard," Billy yelled at the indistinct shape lurking beneath the surface.

He tossed another stone into the water, a last gesture of defiance, then turned and walked briskly up the path leading over the low hill at the back of the peninsula jutting out onto the water. The town, Eyresea, where he lived, was on the other side facing the stretch of the sea that extended southwards towards the narrow channel between two mountain ranges, that opened into the Great Southern Ocean.

From the top of the low hill, he barely glanced at the flat land shimmering as the sun bounced off the sand and rock and saltbush scrub. Once well away from the inland sea it was still a barren land even though the sea had been full and brimming with life before he was born. He couldn't imagine how it must have looked when it was empty, dry, glaring white, sparkling as the sun glistened off salt plains stretching to infinity. It would have hurt your eyes to look at it, burnt a spot into your retina if you stared too long. He never believed it had been that way. It was always a sea, even before his father was born, and his grandfather before that, although the elders still tell stories from ancient times insisting it had once been a massive salt plain.

After years of successive droughts and dry seasons when the giant lake, *Kati Thanda*, was a salt plain used for testing super-fast rocket cars to set land speed records, it started to fill with water that attracted millions of land birds as well as sea birds to breed and feed along its shores. Fish and prawns and crabs and crustaceans appeared out of nowhere to give life to that vast lake. These were rare events celebrated across the country, bringing thousands of tourists to see this temporary but remarkable inland sea. As the century neared its end and global warming began changing the climate, the periods of being filled came more frequently and eventually, when the West Antarctic ice shelf slid into the sea and raised its levels, the lake filled permanently as coastal cities drowned, becoming uninhabitable. This worldwide flooding was exacerbated when the Doomsday Glacier— Antarctica's Thwaites Glacier —rapidly melted and retreated raising sea levels roughly another two metres worldwide.

The effects of anthropogenic climate change continued with ice shelfs worldwide sliding into the oceans creating an enormous rise to sea levels. The great Salt Lake, *Kati Thanda*, filled from the north as well as from the south, the sea coming up through narrow gaps the government of those times created with a series of small low-yield atomic bombs to clear a path between mountain ranges.

Looking down from Space it would appear the continent was divided into two parts. The two thirds west of the new inland sea appeared mostly uninhabitable except along the far western coast, while the one third to the east of the new sea was greener, less desert like, with smudges of pollution surrounding many settled areas. The great Southern Ocean through the newly created narrow channel, flowed into that ancient dry lake —that was several metres below sea level— from the south, while far to the north, a much wider area of permanently drowned swamps and rivers once called 'The Gulf Country' allowed the tropical waters of the

Arafura Sea to infiltrate southwards into the lake, turning it into an inland sea dividing the continent.

The desert areas close to the edge of the new inland sea became green and lush with plants never seen before as well as a huge variety of wild animals, birds and reptiles. But it would take many centuries for the land further from the sea that was desert for hundreds of thousands of years to become green again. Vast areas of desert still existed especially on the western two thirds of the continent.

Now that ancient lake was like an ocean that stretched as far away to the north as you could see, with greenish blue water capped with tiny white tops even though there was almost no wind blowing over the waves. The tide rose and fell twice a day because it was connected to the sea in the south where the vast world ocean had risen high enough to create new bays and inlets extending far inland drowning cities and country towns, and in the far north through vast river flats and swamps that once flooded during wet seasons but now remained permanently flooded.

The northern waters were brackish and murky, hidden by haze resulting from high humidity and severe heat that prevented anyone from exploring it. If they didn't turn back to escape the enervating heat, it would kill them.

Years before, Billy's father had gone that way, to explore the north. He never returned. Billy had come to terms with losing his father, and after his mother died from an illness they couldn't cure, he had lived with his uncle. He didn't think about this anymore but staring at the glowing haze obscuring the horizon far to the north and seeing in the distance a boat coming from that direction, involuntarily brought back memories of his father.

For a moment he wondered if his father could possibly be returning, a forlorn hope he immediately submerged. It had been too many years.

The boat that had stolen his attention was still a fair way out and would take a while to get to the village; plenty of time for him to get back.

In the distance against the edge of the sea that curved around the long peninsular he could see the dark mottled patch surrounded by the green of the shade trees that protected his town from the fierce inland sun, and he hurried towards it.

News of the boat coming had spread around the town and there was an air of excitement as Billy ran along the short main street towards the open plaza in front of the long and short jetties where the fishing boats tied up. There were people standing along the foreshore watching, speculating about who could be on that boat and how it could be coming from the north. No one ever went north; it was too hot. They always worried about the heat barrier and whether it could come closer to them one day but to date it remained where it was making passage to the more tropical regions impossible. When Billy got to the main jetty it was crowded at the end where the view was the same as from the foreshore, but some people thought they could see better from the end of the jetty.

A stocky solid man with a weather-beaten face standing in a flat-bottomed skiff called to him as he arrived. "There's a boat coming, Billy."

"I saw it from the other side."

"It's been a while since we've had visitors come by sea. Everyone's excited."

"Yeah." Billy stopped beside his uncle who tied up his small boat and climbed up onto the old wooden planks of the jetty. He hauled up a bag of prawns he'd netted.

"There's not much wind so I guess it's a slow haul,' his uncle said, squinting as he looked towards the slowly moving yacht in the distance. It was hard to see against the general glow far in the background. "Should be a while before they get here."

"There's a big croc out there where I usually sit to catch fish," Billy said once his uncle was standing beside him.

"How big?"

"Big! Believe me, it's the biggest I've ever seen."

His uncle smiled. He knew how teenagers like to exaggerate, always telling tall tales, and Billy was no different, which was perfectly normal in a boy his age.

"How Big?' he asked again.

"It came out of the water," Billy said seriously. "Tried to grab me… Believe me it's a monster."

His uncle looked at him thoughtfully for a moment but said nothing. He waited for Billy to continue.

Billy was reluctant to admit that he had not been careful. Everyone knew that not being careful could get you killed, so instead he finished with: "It was too heavy to chase me, so it just sat by the water's edge for a moment before sliding back in."

Now his uncle was interested. Catching crocks was bonus for everyone. The meat was good to eat, better than fish, and would go a long way. And the skin was worth a lot. Properly preserved and tanned there was always a ready market for the leather produced. A big croc was a bonus.

"How big did you say it was?"

"Its jaws were this long." Billy spread his arms wide to indicate the length.

His uncle snorted. "Now you're exaggerating."

"No, it's true. It's the biggest croc I've ever seen. Smart too, I'd say. It just slid back into the water and sat there for a long time waiting for me to come back to the water's edge."

"You can find the spot again?"

"Of course, the exact spot. I left my rod there, right where it came out after me, so I could find it again."

More likely dropped it when you ran, his uncle thought.

"Good Lad," he said. "We'll go after it this evening. It won't go too far if it thinks it's found a good hunting ground." He held up the bag of prawns he'd caught. "Let me take these to the freezer. I'll be back in a minute. Should be a while yet before that boat gets here."

They both walked to the end of the jetty and joined those already there to look at the distant sailboat slowly getting larger as it came closer. The whole population had come to the foreshore once word of a strange boat had spread. A group of kids ran along the narrow beach, yelling and gesticulating, while others stood quietly waiting. There was anticipation in the air. It had been a long time since they'd last had seaborne visitors and everyone looked forward to meeting and gossiping with the newcomers.

The boat, a dull grey colour, was much closer now and they could see it was bigger than expected. There were two people on the deck, hard to discern clearly because of the background glow silhouetting them, but as the yacht slowly came closer Billy's uncle suddenly felt relief wash over him. A girl was steering while the man with her was reefing in the mainsail, leaving only a smaller sail to help maintain their forward momentum.

It was the girl steering that allayed his fears.

He had worried at first that there may have been a hidden crew on board, and who knew what intentions strangers could have. Two years ago, they'd had a regrettable visit with a bunch of wild men, pirates in a raiding party from the west swarmed off a ramshackle hulk which had sneaked in at night hoping to catch the townsfolk by surprise. They had come from the southwest side of the channel open to the Southern Ocean. They found unexpected resistance, and quickly retreated, not to be seen since. Word had come to them that pirate raids on shipping further south had recently increased, so any unknown boat approaching was a worry. It also explained why they hadn't seen any boats from the south for the last few years. Pirates would have attacked them in the narrows they had to pass through to get here.

But this yacht was coming from the north.

No one ever came from that direction. The far north was too hot to be inhabited by anything but reptiles and birds. There were big crocs in the swamps and rivers along with other marine life, while on land, there were giant goannas, snakes, lizards, with vicious cassowaries being the worst of the birds.

I've got to ask how they survived up there.

Once the yacht's mainsail was reefed in and tied securely the man turned and waved at them.

Everybody waved back excitedly.

2...

Leaving the flooded city behind, Joe had no regrets. He hoped that the young policewoman who had saved his life would recover from her gunshot wounds, they had been worse than his— a skull fracture and several cracked ribs —but he knew she was in good hands with the Chinese doctors in the rooftop community.

They sailed out through the much-wider heads of the bay and turned east. The ocean water along this southern part of the coast was calm with huge swells which to Joe felt comfortable. It was good to be out of the city and away from all the shit going on there; free, with nothing but wind and waves and the odd sea bird to keep them company. He was thankful that it wasn't too windy or stormy as it often was, and that they had caught the outgoing tide. If the tide had been coming in, he would not have been able to sail against the inrush of the sea. He was not that good a sailor yet and would have had to use the auxiliary motor. He didn't want to use it unless there was no choice. With everything collapsing, with rampant looting, there was no guarantee they would find fuel for the motor no matter where they went. Fuel was one of the first things people took with them when they abandoned the flooded coastal cities. And since the few refineries left in the country were close to the coast, they were now completely underwater. There wasn't going to be any more 'fossil' fuels other that what had been stored, and only if it had been stored someplace where the rising sea had not affected it. Wherever it was, it wouldn't last long anyway.

What a fucked up world we've got, and there's no one to blame but ourselves, he thought as he made sure to keep the coastline in sight about a kilometre off his port side.

He had never sailed a yacht of any size out in the open ocean. He was familiar with using runabouts and small motorboats—

and had even done some sailing for fun with sea scouts —but he'd never sailed a yacht of this size. He was thankful that whoever had done the rigging after Mary's husband Harold was taken to the hospital, had kept it to a basic Bermuda sloop rather than the more complicated gaff rigging. He was confident he would soon learn how to handle it if they could have good weather for a while. This part of the coast between the mainland and Tasmania was notorious for bad weather and icy storms blowing up from Antarctica, but for the moment the weather was fine, and the sea relatively calm with large rolling swells helping to push them along. It felt good to be free of the land with a soft wind and sea air driving the yacht smoothly along.

The rolling and pitching didn't bother him much, but Helen was not faring well. As far as he knew, she had never been on a boat of any kind during her fifteen years of life, apart from a short trip with him a few weeks back to see the building where her father had been murdered, and that five minute trip across to the about-to-be-demolished apartment building didn't count.

They were travelling parallel to the coast and the waves, while pushing them along, also hit them partly side on, causing an uneven sideways rolling motion combined with the forward up and down movement as they rode over the swells and troughs.

While Mary stayed below decks, Helen had come up so she could breathe fresh air in the hope it would help her not become seasick, but to no avail; she leaned over the side rail and vomited.

Pale and forlorn, she turned and looked at Joe in the cockpit standing behind the huge steering wheel making sure they maintained an easterly heading. She tried to smile but didn't quite make it.

"Is it going to be like this all the time?" She managed to ask in between retching and coughing. Nothing came out. She had already vomited the entire contents of her stomach.

"No," he said and smiled encouragingly at her. "It'll get much worse."

She leaned awkwardly back against the side of the hatch. "I'll never survive," she groaned.

"I'm joking. When we get further away from the coast, out into the open ocean heading north, it'll be much smoother. Once you get your sea-legs, you'll be fine."

She started retching and heaving again, but nothing came up.

Joe fixed the steering wheel, tying it with a short rope to keep the heading, and went to help her. She was standing halfway out of the hatch leading below deck. She had her head lifted high and her eyes closed.

"Open your eyes and look in the direction we are going. That'll give you a fixed point of reference. If you look at the sea and how it moves, you'll only feel worse."

He took hold of her shoulders from behind and turned her to face forward towards the bow.

"Try and keep your knees flexible so they can bend as the boat moves beneath you, and don't hang onto the rail too tight. Let your arms be flexible. Basically, you stand relaxed and vertical while you let the boat move around you. Your knees and elbows absorb the boat's movement. If you can do that the seasickness will diminish."

"I'll try," she mumbled.

"That's a good girl," Joe said.

"Is everything okay up there?" Mary called from below decks.

"Nothing to worry about," Joe replied. "Helen's just getting used to the boat's movement. "She'll be fine in no time."

"That's what you think," Helen croaked, pushing her dark hair away from her face so the salty sea air could blow across it. She took a deep breath and let it out with a sigh.

"I'll make us a cup of tea then," Mary said from below. "That should help."

Helen looked at Joe and rolled her eyes. She had regained some colour in her face and had stopped feeling nauseous now that she was allowing her knee and elbow joints absorb the movement of the boat.

"Why is it that old people always think a cup of tea makes everything better, Uncle Joe?"

"Who are you calling old?" Mary retorted from the cabin below.

Joe chuckled. "Well, doesn't it?" he asked her, referring to the tea.

"You've got to be kidding."

"See, you're feeling better already."

Helen called him Uncle Joe when she was little; but had forgotten about him since he had not been there as she grew older until her father's tragic death reunited them. He wasn't a blood relative. He had been her father's best friend until they had a falling out and did not see or contact each other for over five years. For him to reappear in her life when she found out her father had been murdered was a blessing. She had no one else, and while her part of the city suburbs was not inundated when the sea initially came up, it was a battle to survive. Without her father, she would have ended in an institution, or with the remnants of the city's suburban population who were being relocated to work camps inland where new towns and accommodations were being constructed. Anyone over the age of ten ended up in a work camp; especially if they were on their own as Helen was.

Joe helped her after her father was murdered and thrown off the top of an apartment block due to be demolished and dropped into the sea, a futile attempt to form a protecting reef against damage the rising sea could do. He'd rescued her from the gang that controlled the partially submerged city, and together with Mary, whom she regarded as a kind grandmother, they managed to escape the worst of the unfolding violence. She tried not to imagine what horrible things could still be happening in the city they had left behind them. Anywhere they went, would have to be better.

Many people refused to leave the city even though it was permanently flooded— too many, according to the provisional government. To protect the centre of the city from the rising sea, buildings on the ocean-side outskirts were forcibly evacuated and demolished, forming reefs the rising sea could batter instead of buildings further in the city. It was a forlorn hope that the water would recede; it would continue to rise, and there was nothing anyone could do about that.

Further efforts to move people out were not as successful as authorities wanted. Hardcore groups refused to move, barricading themselves inside taller buildings where they tried to make the best of living with the rising sea inundating the lower parts of their buildings. They refused to move inland to become forced labour building the new enclaves. They preferred to stay where they were, to make the best of it no matter how difficult. And they were succeeding to a degree, with communities in various buildings becoming interconnected via bridges over rooftops, as well as by boats in city streets turned into canals. Those who preferred to stay on the water in boats, built floating jetties and piers to which they moored. They went fishing and traded their catches with the communities growing fresh fruit and vegetables on many rooftops across the flooded city as a subsistence economy rapidly evolved.

Criminal gangs took over distribution of government supplies to those who couldn't produce or obtain their own food. Always ready to take advantage of any situation, corrupt government officials became involved with the criminal gangs and profited at the expense of those ordinary stalwarts who refused to leave their homes and apartments, who thought they could survive the rising seas and adapt to living in a permanently flooded city.

Helen's father was a police detective who refused to become part of a criminal enterprise in collaboration with corrupt government officials who wanted to use a frightening means of getting people to evacuate the city. He threatened to expose them, so they eliminated him. Joe was at that time recording the disastrous effects of climate change around the world and the sudden rising of sea levels. He was there when Helen's father was thrown off the top of a building about to be demolished.

Stunned to discover who the victim thrown off the building was, he immediately went to help Helen sort out the problems caused by her father's murder and became involved in confrontations with police as well as the paramilitary initially attempting to bring some kind of order to the city, and the criminal gang that ruled most of the city. This led to his own boat being destroyed in an attempt on his life, Helen being kidnapped, and him partnering with Mary whose late husband Harold had built the yacht to escape the flooding he knew was coming. Barely surviving after rescuing Helen and getting the local fishermen to storm the gang's building, he left the city with Mary and Helen on the yacht Mary's husband had built. Most of the fishermen and those who had managed to survive on small boats and barges moored around the outskirts of the flooded city also left after the riots in search of a better place to live. The doomed city, now nothing more than a series of connected vertical islands thrusting up from an all enclosing sea, was left to those few who controlled the rooftops and the gardens they had constructed there.

Moving closer to shore when it became darker, Joe was cautious of hidden reefs, areas that had once been small rocky outcrops that were now submerged below the surface after the sea level came up. There were many of these outcrops where abalone divers once worked. It they struck one of these hidden outcrops they would be in serious trouble. He didn't want to be sailing at night, at least not until he was well away from the coast and heading north. Spotting a narrow river mouth, he edged the yacht towards it, and started lowering the mainsail. They drifted slowly into the river mouth and by the time they dropped anchor it was already dark.

"We'll stay here for the night," he told Mary and Helen. "I don't like the idea of sailing at night so close to shore."

"Thank God for that," Helen said. "It'll be nice to have no movement for a while."

"There's always movement if you are on a boat."

"You know what I mean. This is nothing compared to what I felt out there."

Mary said, "I suppose we should think about what to eat tonight."

"Do you have any fishing gear on board? Did Harold fish at all?"

"Harold was never a fisherman, but there are some hand lines he stored away before the flood came. I'll see if I can find them."

"It would be nice to start living off the sea and the land with what we can catch or hunt and save our stores for more difficult times. A fresh fish or two would be good."

After eating the fish Joe caught, they turned off all the lights in the boat to conserve battery power and settled down for the night. A few hours later he sat up suddenly, startled by distant sounds he was sure were gunshots. Going quietly up on deck he looked out to sea. Light from a full moon glistened on the waves silhouetting two small boats about half a kilometre offshore. He heard indistinct yelling and another gunshot, followed by a splash. Then it was silent, with nothing more than the sound of waves breaking on a beach around from the river opening, and soft waves lapping against the hull of the yacht.

"What's going on?" a soft voice behind him said, making him jump.

"Don't sneak up on me like that."

"Sorry," Helen whispered. "I heard you getting up."

"There's a couple of boats out there. I heard shouting and came up to have a look."

The faint rumble of motors came across the water as the two boats started to move away further along the coast. After a few minutes both boats disappeared, heading in the same direction they would be going the next morning.

"What do you think happened?" Helen asked.

"I've no idea."

He didn't tell her that someone had been shot and dumped overboard after an altercation amongst those on board both boats.

"We'll have to be very careful about where we go and what we do if we see other people in boats. We would be a good target for any opportunistic person we come across. This is a good looking vessel and to anyone seeing it with only one guy, an old woman and a young girl on board, they would think it was an easy target. It's very dangerous out there now."

"They'd be wrong then, wouldn't they?" Helen said with certainty, adding, "I'm not that young."

"You have more confidence than I have."

Joe couldn't help smiling at how good Helen's positivity made him feel.

"Come on," he said. "Let's go back down and get some more sleep. Try not to wake up Mary while you're at it."

"She was snoring like a log when I came up. She won't even know we were up here."

At the crack of dawn, they left the safety of the river mouth and within an hour passed the southernmost point of the Australian mainland. They headed further east before turning north. Out here the swells were huge, and the yacht sailed up and over each one as it came on them. Not so much side movement this time, but more up and down as they undulated across the surface of the vast ocean surrounding Australia.

The wind was fresh and filled the sails making them taut. The yacht sailed beautifully, swooshing through the water.

"Look at that," Joe called out as both Helen and Mary joined him in the cockpit.

"Dolphins," Helen exclaimed.

Three dolphins surfed in front of the bow wave the yacht created, periodically leaping out of the water with cascades of sparkling droplets falling off them. A flock of sea birds followed. Several swooped down to snatch a small fish disturbed by the yacht's wake while others floated in the air behind, waiting their turn to dive on an unsuspecting fish.

"What a fabulous day," Mary said. "It makes you forget all the horrible things that are happening around the world."

"Yeah, out here you do tend to forget. I want to be well offshore as we go north to avoid getting anywhere near the major coastal cities or any of those useless wind-farms along the coast." He imagined most of them had been blown or knocked over during the storms as the sea level came up, but they would constitute a dangerous obstacle course to any ships or small boats sailing along the coast where they'd been established.

He was also thinking of the shooting incident that had woken him during the night, and the chaos that would be happening in

Sydney with houses falling into the sea as the waves sucked away the land beneath them and drowned its northern beaches, pushing the coastline inland. Inside the Harbour it would not be initially as catastrophic as in Melbourne, with lots of dwellings on high rocky promontories safe from rising waters. But like every other coastal city around the world disasters would be unfolding as services failed and people started to panic. Supermarkets and pharmacies would be stripped. There would be brawls in the streets as desperate mobs grabbed whatever they could from shops no matter the usefulness of items needing power. And then what will they do when nothing's left to steal? We're better off out here...

"We're too good a target for people desperate for supplies, or anything that takes their fancy," he continued. "If we stay far enough offshore, hopefully no one will see us as we head north."

"And do you have any idea where we are going?" Mary asked.

"Not really. There are plenty of islands along the Great Barrier Reef far enough offshore that could be suitable until things settle down. After that, I have no idea... Once we're somewhere safe, there'll be plenty of time to think about it."

"Why are we going north?" Helen asked.

"Because it's too bloody cold down south," Mary answered her.

Joe laughed briefly, adding, "and there's nothing down south anyway."

His focus had been on getting as far away as possible to be safe. It hadn't occurred to him to think about where they would go. Heading north was only logical. "I'm sorry Mary, I should have asked you where you wanted to go."

"Somewhere warm," Mary affirmed.

Mid-afternoon he checked their position with the GPS and decided they'd sailed far enough east. He changed course to a north easterly direction to run parallel to the coast. They couldn't see it because they were about 100 kilometres out to sea. The only way he had any idea of where they were was by checking Global Positioning. At least the satellites in space were functioning. If he had to calculate their position the old fashioned way, he couldn't do it, even if there were log-tables and a sextant on board. He didn't know how to use them. Using the compass was fine for direction, and with Global Positioning, he knew exactly where they were in relation to the coast.

He set a line with several baited hooks to trail behind them in the hope of catching pelagic fish, but not one appeared or even attempted to take the bait. He gave up trying after a while having decided the rise in the sea level must have changed where fish could be found. He suspected the ocean was now like a desert with vast areas affected by the rising waters, changing water temperature, and differences in salinity forcing the fish to move elsewhere. He hoped the dolphins and their giant cousins would be able to find enough food to survive, or the world would be a poorer place without them skylarking in the oceans. He wondered briefly where the fishing fleet would have gone, because obviously they needed to catch fish to survive. By the time he'd recovered enough after the riot he'd instigated with the fishermen from the floating city, they'd all gone. There were hardly any boats left amongst the floating piers and jetties when Mary, Helen, and he had departed.

He set the self-steering and joined the other two for an early evening meal.

"I love the sound of the waves swooshing by as we sail through them," Helen said.

She was sipping a cup of tea. Mary was checking the pot simmering on the induction stove in the galley. A delicious smell of chicken stew filled the cabin.

"It didn't take you long to get over the sea sickness," Joe said.

"I'm good now. Like you said, be flexible and let the boat move around you. It seems very natural."

"It is, when you get used to it."

"Dinner is ready," Mary interjected. "I'll start serving now."

Once dinner was over Joe said, "The weather's still good so I think we should keep sailing through the night; get as far north as we can before we are forced to seek shelter somewhere along the coast."

"Sounds like a plan," Helen said.

"Are you going to stay awake all night?" Mary asked.

"No. I was thinking I might take a nap for a couple of hours first. If you," and he looked at Helen, "could keep watch while I'm asleep, that would be good."

"What do I do?"

"Nothing really. I've set the self-steering, so we're good for the moment. We're far enough offshore that it's unlikely we'll encounter other ships, certainly not smaller boats this far out. The big cargo ships have stopped sailing as each country has had to deal with the rising sea and severe flooding. Port facilities are all underwater and useless. Everything's disrupted, so we should be safe enough out here. Follow me and I'll show you what the compass reading shows and how the self-steering works."

On deck in the cockpit, which was the control centre of the yacht, Joe explained what he thought Helen needed to know.

"If anything happens, or changes, you come and wake me immediately, Okay?"

"Like what?"

"Like if the wind changes, or you see a boat approaching, or if it gets rougher, which means we must change how the sails are set… Stuff like that. Anything you're not sure of or worried about, come and get me."

"I can do that," Helen said with confidence and a big smile. "Yeah."

Joe told Mary the same things and then lay down in the bunk in the aft quarters allocated to him. He was asleep before he even knew it.

3...

He awoke the instant he rolled out of the bunk and slammed onto the floor.

"Shit!"

The yacht heaved over sideways and shuddering as the rail along the port side hit the water. He heard the sails flapping wildly. He felt the yacht twist underneath him.

Mary was holding on to the side of her bunk. Shaking as the yacht shuddered around her, she called out, "What's going on Joe?"

"Helen," Joe screamed out as he got himself up and staggered up the several steps through the hatchway up into the cockpit. He'd forgotten to tell her to clip herself to a side rail in case the yacht did something strange which could cast her overboard. If she went over, they would never find her. The yacht, continuing to shudder slowly righted itself as he grabbed the rails on either side of the short staircase.

"I'm okay," he heard Helen yell as his head popped up above the cabin top. He could see her hanging on tightly to the big steering wheel. Her face appeared bleached white in the moonlight. "I didn't have time to call out."

Suddenly the yacht rose up while he was halfway out of the cabin. It was like being in a fast lift racing to the top of a monstrous skyscraper. His stomach dropped. He almost collapsed onto his knees.

What the fuck! The sea around them glittered with phosphorescence, brilliant white, sparkling, foaming with billions of tiny bubbles. A glance upwards showed the sky far to the south filled with burning meteor fragments. They vanished almost before he had time to register seeing them. His stomach sank as they continued to rise. A wall of phosphorescent water, bright enough to drown the light from the stars, extended on either side of them as far as he could see. The upward movement ceased, and the yacht rocked and shuddered as the sea around them twisted, swirled, bubbled and boiled.

It's a fucking tsunami!

The sea rolled away underneath them while the yacht shook ferociously.

"Don't let go whatever you do," Joe told her.

"I'm tied on. I'm okay."

"Good, I'll make sure Mary's okay, then I'll come back up."

He dropped back down into the cabin and found Mary was still hanging on tightly to the edge of her bunk. He could feel them rapidly sinking as the wave passed beneath. The movement down was not as severe as the upward movement had been but was still rapid enough to be disconcerting as they swiftly dropped, sliding down the back of the giant wave.

"What just happened Joe?"

"I saw something crashing into the sea way to the south, but that couldn't have done this. I think a large part of the Antarctic Ice Shelf just collapsed into the sea. With millions of tons of ice suddenly slamming into it, a giant tsunami is what you get." He shook his head in disbelief. "We were lucky we were far enough offshore. It passed under us as a huge flat wave. Anywhere along the east coast on our side of the Pacific and along the west coast of the Americas on the other side will be hit with the biggest tsunami ever…"

"That's not good," Mary mumbled.

"No. It's not. Let me help you get back into your bunk."

"No, I'll stay up. I don't think I'll be able to go back to sleep."

Joe suddenly remembered the night the wave had engulfed the already flooded city barely a year ago. He'd been lucky to see it in time to quickly turn his runabout into the oncoming wall of water, to ride up over it. It was the same night he saw this very yacht sail past him down a main city street with Mary's late husband Harold manning the tiller. That image would stay in his mind forever. But that wave was nothing compared to this, only a few metres high at the most. He couldn't help thinking about his friends left in the city; would they survive? Hopefully the taller buildings they occupied would withstand the onslaught of this giant tsunami. But there was nothing he could do. Nothing anyone could do. Once it retreated there wouldn't be much left wherever it hit.

The yacht shivered and shook.

The sea rolled away underneath them, heading north and smashing into the coastline along the whole length of Australia's east coast.

Out at sea the tsunami was a flat wave travelling around 500 miles per hour. It passed underneath them in seconds, that seemed like an eternity, lifting them up, then allowing the yacht to slide down the back of the massive wave as it passed underneath them. But close inshore where the seabed became shallow the water was restricted. A giant wave began to build up towering higher and higher as the sea rushed towards the shore. It hit the entire east coast. Slicing into it, smashing everything constructed along the shoreline still standing after the initial sea rise, then bouncing back out to sea carrying with it the rubble and flotsam of towns and cities, trees, bushes, animals and those people who had still been living along the coastal fringes. All gone, the land stripped bare as far inland as the range of mountains along the entire east coast; everything sucked out into the ocean, and when the sea settled after a succession of smaller waves no less damaging followed the big tsunami, a new coastline with a new ocean level had been achieved. And that was only the start. As more ice covering land melted and found its way to the sea, the level would keep rising and the continents would be reshaped. The ice age from which humans had emerged was truly over, and a much warmer period would ensue for the next 100,000 years until a new tipping point arrived allowing another ice age to begin.

Joe reduced the amount of sail carried because a gusty wind started blowing the moment the flat tsunami had passed beneath them. He sent Helen back down into the cabin to keep Mary company while he steered the yacht on a more easterly course. The yacht cut through waves that were choppier than before and there was some bouncing up and down. *Harold did a great job when he built this boat,* Joe thought with admiration. It rode smoothly and comfortably and didn't bounce like his runabout would have done, but then his runabout would never have been able to get this far out to sea in the first place.

He wanted to be further out now than he'd originally planned so they wouldn't encounter the rubbish sucked into the ocean by the retreating tsunami after it had smashed into the coast and bounced back into the ocean, or worse, the bodies of those killed and drowned by the giant wave and the lesser ones that followed. We don't need to see that; he thought as he focused on steering due east. He was certain the islands they had been contemplating as a refuge would either be underwater now that the sea level had risen again, or at the worst, stripped bare after the wave had passed over them.

Putting aside any thoughts of what they might find as they went further north his only concern was to keep going. In the morning, they would consider their options. They had enough supplies to stay out at sea for several months if necessary.

After that… *Who knows?*

Dawn revealed the ocean choppy and disturbed with white-caps grey and muddy looking. He spotted dark lumps in the water which he thought could be tree trunks, and that surprised him considering how far out they were from the coast.

The yacht rode smoothly through the uneven, choppy water which overlaid larger rolling swells underneath it. The troughs between the massive swells were so dark they appeared black. Not even the rising sun could penetrate to the depths beneath. The propellers of the two wind turbines on top of the canopy covering the cockpit spun furiously as they generated electricity to be stored in the batteries.

They were well offshore, moving northeast again with only a small foresail pulling them along. Heavy dark cloud on the horizon ahead as well as port-side where the mainland was indicated a massive storm brewing. He was hoping they would get far enough north before the storm coming from the west hit them. There was no way to avoid it other than to run before it.

Leaving the self-steering to control the course, he went below to join Mary and Helen.

"You both look pretty good," he commented.

"We're getting used to it," Helen said.

"Is there a storm building?" Mary asked.

"Looks like it. Sea's choppy."

"I thought so. I remember how it felt the night Harold and I left. It was worse than this."

"It's going to get worse. I'm not sure we can outrun it. You'll have to tie yourselves to something otherwise you could get thrown around. And whatever you do, don't come up on deck without wearing a harness and latching onto the rail along the cabin roof. If you get blown or washed overboard there's no way to turn around and rescue you."

To emphasize his words, the yacht suddenly heaved sideways, rolling perhaps thirty degrees before righting itself. A rogue wave had hit side-on pushing into and under them. They heard the wind suddenly whistling louder in the rigging above the deck. Everything on the table, their cups of tea and the toast Mary had made, slid off crashing onto the floor. The two women were thrown out of their seats to land on top of their breakfast.

As they picked themselves up the yacht settled back into a more even movement, though it wasn't as smooth as before.

"It's come up quicker than I thought," Joe said. He grabbed two short lengths of cable and clipped them to his belt and the harness he was wearing. "I'd better go back up and make sure we keep running with the wind behind us. Strap your harnesses on now and latch yourselves to one of the bench tops, so you won't get thrown around. If it gets really bad, strap yourselves into your bunks."

Back in the cockpit he clipped both cables to opposite side rails so whichever way he was thrown either cable would prevent him from going overboard if a large wave engulfed them.

The storm came up fast. Ripping across the ocean's surface, blowing the tops off choppy waves and blasting salt spray at the yacht. It stung like needles as it hit his hands and face, the only parts exposed to the elements. He changed course to run with the wind behind. The sideways rolling diminished, and they mostly had to contend with big waves rolling past raising them up and down as each wave went by underneath them from stern to bow.

The wind strengthened, screaming in the rigging and pushing against the bare mast, making the two small wind turbines spin so fast Joe thought they would tear apart. He reefed in the foresail so it wouldn't be ripped to pieces by the increasing ferocity of the wind. The yacht surged through the water almost keeping up with the waves as they rolled by underneath them. Oddly, the movement of the yacht up and down lessened and the massive swells rolled beneath them with a much smoother movement. The swells had become huge, towering above the yacht as the waves rolled by and they sank down into the troughs, before rising as the following wave lifted them and rolled beneath.

They had been going too fast before, cutting through the waves with water washing viciously across the deck. The yacht had shuddered each time it cut through a wave, as spray exploded over them. Though he wore protective gear, Joe felt like a waterlogged rat on a sinking ship. But now that he had the yacht running with bare masts and only one tiny foresail for stability, they were moving more in tune with the way the waves moved. If the wind increased and pushed them forward even faster, he would drop a sea anchor over the stern to slow them down, to keep in tune with the wind and the movement of the swells it generated.

Luckily, the storm passed them, tearing on ahead, leaving the swells to slowly diminish in height and width and the movement of the yacht to become less violent. The screaming of the wind in the rigging also disappeared as the sea quickly returned to a more normal state.

The wind was still blowing, though not as fiercely as moments before so Joe ran a smaller sail up. It billowed and filled with air, allowing the yacht to make its way forward smoothly. He reset the self-steering and the course back to northeast, following the path of the storm now way ahead of them. Beyond that he could see a line of towering clouds filling the sky from the wave-tops all the way up for thousands of metres. Billowing, rising, towering cloud heads, brilliant white at the top but so dark as to be almost black underneath where they sat just above the sea's surface. The cloud barrier stretched from west to east as far as he could see, the Zone of Convergence?

It shouldn't be this far south, he thought as he stared at it.

He'd flown through the Zone of Convergence years before when going to New Guinea at the start of a wet season, and there was no way he was going to try and sail beneath that towering wall of storm clouds. Normally it never came as far south as the Tropic of Capricorn, and that was still a long way north of where they were. He couldn't stop staring at it. The threat it represented was frightening.

He changed course and headed due north which in a couple of hours would bring them closer to the coast instead of running parallel to it.

"Is everything alright?" Mary had popped her head up out of the cabin door. "I felt the boat turn." She took a deep breath of salty air and let it out with a sigh.

"It's fine. The storm's gone, but I'm a bit worried about what's ahead."

Mary stood up higher so she could look over the top of the cabin towards the direction they were travelling. "I don't like the look of those clouds."

"Me either. I'm taking us in closer to the coast where we can find a safe place to anchor in case we get hit with another squall."

Looking back Joe saw a squall rapidly forming with dark clouds swirling furiously to create the beginnings of a waterspout. It seemed to be racing towards them. The waves around the yacht again became choppy and confused… Like they don't know what to do, which way to move, he thought. This is not a good place to be…

"The sooner we can get back to the coast where we can wait out the storms, the better," he said to Mary.

"There's another one," Mary said, pointing to the east, well out on their starboard side where heavy clouds swirling down out of a darkening mass of cloud above created a long thin waterspout.

"They're all around us," Joe confirmed.

The waterspouts and squalls were caused by the constant amount of air rushing towards the massive wall of clouds still far ahead of them to the north which darkened by the minute while sporadically being lit with stroboscopic flashes of lightning. The thunder produced was nothing more than a deep rumble when it got to them, after being broken up by turbulent winds and waterspouts.

The yacht heaved and lurched as the waves around them kept changing direction. The sail snapped and shook, whipped by variable gusts of wind.

"I've never seen anything like this before," he said to Mary before she dropped back down into the cabin.

He decided to pull down the sail and run towards the coast using the motor. Even though it used precious fuel they wouldn't be able to replace, it would give better control to the yacht as they tried to evade the worst of the oncoming squalls.

With the yacht thrown about by constantly changing wind directions and broken waves it was a struggle not to be seasick. Joe had no time to think about how Helen and Mary were doing below decks, he had to focus entirely on avoiding the many vicious waterspouts that randomly rose up to merge with the swirling black cloud tubes descending from above. The yacht was pushed and shoved by the waves, turned and tipped over almost to the point of capsizing. Caught momentarily in a furious gust of wind it was twisted in a complete circle as a tight waterspout formed next to it. Joe struggled furiously to get the boat away from the aerial whirlpool as wild spray ripped off wave-tops swirled up into the air around them. If he hadn't been using the motor, he would never have succeeded.

Finally clear of the waterspouts, and completely exhausted from his efforts to maintain control of the yacht, he could see the darker shadow of the coastline ahead of them emerging as the sea closer to shore calmed. Relieved, he motored towards the coast while further out to sea the waterspouts and storms rushed northwards.

It looked unfamiliar, but that was to be expected after the tsunami. There weren't many trees and most of the land at the water's edge was naked, rocky, stripped of trees and anything else that was there. Tonnes of debris in the water forced him to slow to a speed not much more than controlled drifting to push a way through thousands of floating tree trunks, branches and other debris being washed back and forth. He didn't look too hard, but he was sure he hadn't seen any bodies in with the debris which he assumed was because this part of the country was uninhabited despite the many towns once located along the coast. He didn't want to think about how many of those towns close to beaches in Bays and inlets had been washed away with all inhabitants... His entire focus concentrated on searching for a suitable inlet where they could safely anchor for the night.

It took a while to find a place where they would be protected by hills on both sides where the land had been high enough to have been safe from the devastation of the tsunami. There were still trees on the higher ground. Cautiously entering the inlet, he had to move close to one side to find a spot shallow enough to drop anchor. The inlet had been scoured by the tsunami and all the accumulated soft sand and mud that builds up in a tidal inlet had been sucked out leaving it too deep for their short anchor chain, but he didn't want to anchor too close to the edge in case they became stranded when the tide went out. It took a while, dragging the anchor over smooth bare rock before he found a spot where it caught and held. Satisfied they would be safe for the oncoming night; he went below and after assuring Helen and Mary that they were in a safe spot; he fell into an exhausted sleep.

He was not aware that the yacht had been seen entering the inlet by an observer on top of the hill on the far side from where they had anchored.

4...

A thump against the side of the boat woke him. He thought it must be debris being washed in and was about to go back to sleep when another thump occurred followed by a scrape. Something was being dragged against the side of the yacht. He felt a slight rocking motion different from the movement created by the flow of water in the inlet.

Someone had climbed on board.

He was instantly wide awake.

A pale light from the sun about to rise came in through the starboard portholes pushing away the darkness of the night. He leaped up and went into the main cabin. Mary and Helen had also been woken by the thump and the scrape against the side of the hull. Mary watched as Helen was about to open the hatch so she could step up and see what the cause was. There were scraping sounds against the side of the hull and another thump.

"I don't like the sound of that," Mary whispered.

"Me either," Joe said softly.

Helen pushed open the hatch and stepped up so she could see the stern where the noise had come from and was stunned to see a heavily bearded man with wild hair hanging across his shoulders climbing on board, while another unshaven skinnier man was standing in something she couldn't see and was holding tight against the rail along that side of the deck. The intruder saw her the moment her head appeared in the hatchway, so there was no point in being quiet anymore.

"Uncle Joe..." Helen said.

"I'm right here." He stepped onto the first step in the hatchway.

"Hello beautiful," the stranger said. "What are you doing here?"

Helen quickly moved up and aside to wait beside the hatchway allowing room for Joe to emerge.

He stood beside Helen.

A slight mist floated above the still water of the inlet. The sun was just peeking above the horizon far out to sea.

"We saw you come in last night," the man said, looking at Joe. "Thought we might pay you a visit."

"So you sneak up on us hoping we would be asleep?"

Through the corner of his eye Joe noticed several dinghies with two men in each paddling furiously to get close to them. They were halfway across the inlet having come from the far side.

"We were wondering if you had anything that could be useful to us."

Joe came up out of the hatchway and stepped towards the stranger. His equally scruffy partner was still hanging on to the railing so their dinghy wouldn't drift away with the tide starting to run out.

It was obvious that the man wanted to keep them talking until his mates in the other dinghies arrived. Joe wasn't going to let that happen.

"We don't have anything on board that you can have." Joe said as he took another step towards the stranger.

Suddenly the man pulled out a long curved knife, like the type used for boning out a leg of lamb in a butcher shop. He waved it threateningly. He held it as if he was going the thrust the blade into something.

"I think we'll have a look when my friends get here." The man said ominously.

"You think that knife will help you?" Joe asked while taking another step towards him.

The man couldn't retreat, because he was hard against the railing at the stern. He slashed back and forth with the knife to show Joe he meant business. He grimaced, but his eyes gave away that he hadn't expected to be challenged.

"If you don't want to get cut, you'll stay back," he said menacingly. Voices called out from a wild bunch of men paddling the dinghies crossing the inlet. The bearded man turned his head a fraction to see how close his friends were. They were still too far away to be of any help, but the instant he looked aside Joe closed the gap between them.

Suddenly realizing Joe was too close, the man lunged with the knife to stick it into Joe's abdomen; a panicked move because his threat hadn't worked. His attack was unbalanced as the boat rocked when he lunged forward to thrust with the knife. In the restricted deck space close to the stern there was only room enough for Joe to twist slightly to avoid the knife thrust. He deflected the man's arm, without trying to take away the knife. Continuing his forward movement, he slammed into the bearded stranger who couldn't move back, being trapped against the rail across the stern. The man flipped backwards over the railing into water. He went under with a gurgled yell and a huge splash, disappearing for a moment before resurfacing flailing wildly, spluttering and yelling for help.

The man standing in the dinghy beside the yacht immediately let go and went to the rescue of his friend. The other wild men crossing the inlet started yelling furiously as they paddled desperately to get closer. They were now only metres away. They all had knives or machetes and if they managed to get to the yacht Joe knew he would be in trouble. Obviously, they didn't have guns, or they would already be shooting at him. There was no time to haul in the anchor.

"Helen, do you know how to start the motor?"

"Yes."

"Do it now."

The men yelling and paddling the dinghies were almost there, their yelled threats, deafening.

Joe raced to the side of the cabin where a small axe was strapped.

The first of the dinghies reached them and the lead man leaned forward stretching out to grab hold of the rail beside the stern.

Joe grabbed the axe, pulled it free, and tore past the cabin to the bow where he chopped the cable connected to the anchor chain. The cable immediately disappeared over the side as the yacht pushed by the outgoing tide moved towards into deeper water. It started to turn as the outflowing water pushed it towards the inlet's opening to the sea.

The motor roared to life with a rumble beneath the deck.

Good girl, Joe thought, racing back to the cockpit. He bypassed it and kicked the man who had grabbed the rail in the face, knocking him back over where he fell into the dinghy and onto the man who was attempting to follow him.

He then jumped into the cockpit and grabbed the wheel turning the yacht towards the centre of the outgoing flow of water. He gunned the motor and the sudden surge of water from the propellers pushed the first dinghy away. The second dinghy had been just a metre behind with one of its occupants reaching forward ready to grab the side rail when the yacht surged forward. There was no way they could paddle fast enough to catch the yacht with its motor running. Their screams and yells of frustration faded rapidly as the yacht headed towards the inlet opening and the sea beyond.

"That was close," Helen said.

Their last glimpse of the would-be attackers was of the paddling men hauling their waterlogged mate back up into his dinghy, before they disappeared as the yacht rounded the taller headland and headed out into the open sea.

"We'll need to be a lot more careful about where we stop in future," Joe said as Mary joined them. "There'll be lots of places like this where desperate people will be struggling to survive."

"Perhaps we should have given them some supplies," Mary said hesitantly.

"And what good would that have done?"

"I don't know… It just seems mean not to help when we could have."

"If he hadn't threatened me with a knife…"

"But he did," Helen said. "He tried to kill you."

"Well, what's done is done," Mary said with acceptance.

And they motored out, slowing down enough to avoid floating debris again being carried out by the outgoing tide. The sun was now well above the horizon, beaming from a mostly clear sky. The massive wall of storm clouds and waterspouts they had encountered the day before causing them to seek refuge in the inlet had vanished overnight moving further north towards the equator. He feared they would encounter them again if they continued to travel too far north but for the moment everything was good. He let out a sigh of relief once they'd left the coastal inlet behind.

Once far enough out where there was no debris, Joe killed the motor, hauled up the mainsail, set a course towards the northeast, connected the self-steering and went down into the main cabin to have the breakfast Mary was preparing.

They sailed northeast for many days without seeing anyone else, which was a relief. Joe was reluctant to encounter anyone until they had a better idea of who and what had survived the tsunami, and there would be survivors, he had no doubt.

The days became warmer as they entered sub-tropical waters. The sea had a different hue and sparkle where the sun reflected off the surface. It seemed more transparent than the sea further south. He couldn't help smiling. The actual air smelled different as well. He thought he could smell a hint of tropical fruit.

When the first island indicating the southernmost regions of the Great Barrier Reef appeared on the horizon, Helen could hardly contain her excitement, exuberantly jumping up and down and waving her arms at her first glimpse of the distant island.

"Is that an island? Can we stop there?"

"We'll have a look at it," Joe said.

"I'm sick of seeing nothing but endless ocean…"

Mary smiled as she saw the island, a distant smudge with a few clouds hovering above marking its position. She was relieved to know land wasn't far away. As much as she loved being on the yacht, and living on it because it was her home after all, she thought it would be nice for a change to walk on dry land, on something solid that wasn't constantly moving.

"Do you think there'll be people there?" Helen asked.

"I don't think so," Joe said. "Most of these smaller islands are uninhabited. But we'll find out soon enough."

"I can't wait," Helen said. She made her way forward, easily passing the cabin to sit cross-legged on the deck in front of it where she had an unrestricted view ahead.

With a steady breeze to help them, they didn't take long to get close enough to see the island's jagged outline.

"It's barren," Mary, standing beside him in the cockpit said. "I don't see any trees or greenery."

"Maybe they're on the other side where we can't see them," Joe said. "It shouldn't take long before we get there."

When they got much closer it was obvious that there was nothing at all on the island. There was no soil, no sandy beaches, no bushes, no palm trees, nothing green at all, nothing but dark rock alternating with bleached sandstone or coral that had been calcified into stone. The tsunami had raced over it as it moved north and stripped the island down to its rocky base.

Beyond it, they could see other rocky outcrops indicating nearby islands, and as they passed between them, they saw the same thing; every low lying island had been stripped bare, leaving nothing but the underlying rock or coral base. There was not a hint of anything green anywhere.

Helen, her disappointment clear, went down into the cabin without a word.

"I'll see if she's okay," Mary said.

"Leave her, she'll be fine. After her excitement of seeing our first island only to find it totally barren… it's understandable she's upset. I feel a bit that way myself."

"What are we going to do?" Mary asked, her voice flat.

"Keep going," Joe responded encouragingly. "There are bigger islands further north, big enough to have survived the ravages of the tsunami. I'm sure we'll find somewhere soon enough."

"I was looking forward to strolling about on dry land…" Mary said wistfully.

And a bigger island loomed on the horizon a few days later. Tall, of volcanic origin, a central cone towered high enough to have low lying clouds surrounding its peak. The tallest cone was covered with jungle, a beautiful green sight, while a secondary cone was also covered with bushes, small trees with scattered palms. The lower slopes and the edges of the island where it reached the sea's surface had been stripped bare of plant life leaving a scoured surface of hard rock. There were no beaches, although Joe thought there probably had been pure white coral sand beaches surrounding the island before the tsunami hit it and left the sea level higher after it had passed. The line of demarcation was a stark reminder of how the force of the tsunami thousands of miles away from Antarctica where it had originated, was still able to do considerable damage.

"Now that looks promising," Mary said as they got close enough to see details.

"I like it," Helen said.

They were standing with Joe in the cockpit as the yacht gently sailed towards the island. To their starboard they could discern a thin dark shadow beneath an extended layer of scattered cloud suggesting the mainland was not that far away.

Joe looked for a safe place to anchor. The water beneath them was still too deep, especially since they'd lost their main anchor and a good length of cable. The smaller spare anchor could only be used in shallow water. The side of the island they were approaching was tumbling rock right to the water's edge, a series of broken cliff faces where the swells rolling along smashed into and rebounded from them.

"There's probably a harbour around the other side," Joe said, "Facing the mainland."

"I can't wait to get there," Mary said.

The more they saw of the island as they sailed around it, the more they liked it. After weeks at sea that seemed endless, it was a relief to see green trees and vegetation on an island big enough and high enough to have survived the tsunami.

"That's a sight for sore eyes," Mary said as she imagined walking through the rich green bushland.

"There are some people up there," Helen said."

"Where," Joe asked.

"Up there where the tree line begins, making their way across the rocks." She waved at them, but they didn't respond.

"I see them, Joe said. "They seem to be keeping pace with us."

Helen waved again. And again, they didn't respond. Instead,

they disappeared into the trees. "They're not very friendly," she said.

"Would you be, if you had a nice safe place and saw strangers approaching?"

"Yeah, I would. I'd be happy to see someone new, especially after what's happened."

"Not everyone's like you Helen. There'll be others on the island, and they've gone to tell them they saw us approaching. They were probably lookouts. I'm not sure we'll be welcome."

"Why not?"

"They would have limited resources they won't want to share with strangers. They don't know who we are or what our intentions might be. If I was in their situation, I'd be wary. But let's wait and see when we get around to the other side and find a place to anchor."

"Joe's right," Mary added. "Remember what happened the other day when we anchored in the inlet to avoid the storm."

"Surely not everyone's like that," Helen said.

"I say we assume everyone we encounter is like that, or worse, and act with caution until we know otherwise."

"You're a pessimist," she said petulantly, "A spoilsport."

"In this world, a pessimist is likely to live longer than an optimist," Joe said, but he tempered his words with a smile.

They rounded a short promontory and entered a wide bay. The wind on this lee side of the island had dropped and the sail hung loose. The yacht lost some momentum but continued to drift towards where a few moribund fishing boats were tied to a pole stuck between several rocks close to the water's edge. There were several people standing beside where the ropes from the boats were tied. Two of them held what looked like rifles. Another held something cone shaped in his hand.

"We have a reception committee," Joe stated.

The man with the cone shaped object brought it up to his mouth; it was a megaphone, and his voice came across to them loud and clear.

"Please leave. You are not welcome here."

The yacht continued to drift towards the men waiting beside the fishing boats. Suddenly one of the other men raised his rifle and fired a shot at the yacht. He wasn't aiming at its occupants, but at the hull which was metal. The sound of the shot wasn't loud; more like a soft cough, but the ringing clang as the bullet fired hit near the bow and ricocheted into the water was loud enough to get the message across.

"We don't want to shoot anyone," the voice from the megaphone said. *"But we will if we have to."*

Joe spun the wheel and the yacht slowly started to turn. *That means they'll shoot all of us and take whatever is on board,* he thought. At least they're not too desperate yet. Give it another month and they might not be so friendly.

The sail shifted position and grabbed more air. Perhaps it wasn't quick enough or perhaps they didn't see it at first, but another shot rang out as the bullet again ricocheted off the metal hull and into the water.

"What are they going to do when they run out of bullets?" Mary said to Joe as he worked on turning to yacht back out to sea.

"We wish you well, and bon voyage," the voice said as soon as it was obvious the yacht was turning away and heading back out to sea.

You too, Joe thought, raising his left arm in a back-handed goodbye wave.

5...

"Things are not looking good," Mary commented later over a shared cup of tea in the main cabin. With no islands showing on the charts Joe felt safe to let the yacht steer itself while they considered future possibilities.

Helen preferred to sit back and sip her tea.

"They're only going to get worse," Joe admitted. "That was probably the friendliest rejection we'll ever see. We won't get any warning next time." He stood up and after a cursory glance around the cabin he continued. "Sooner, rather than later, we'll run out of supplies. At least we have a means of desalinating seawater, so that's not a problem. But there aren't many fish around. Lines I've been trailing off the stern haven't caught anything. The change in water temperature and the destruction of shallow habitats after the tsunami is the likely cause. It means soon we are going to need new supplies and to do that we will have to go ashore somewhere."

"There's no flour left so I can't make fresh bread anymore." Mary said.

"Forget about fresh bread," Joe said. "To get ingredients for that we'll need to find a store somewhere that might have supplies, and there's fat chance of that. The same goes for canned food and any other type of dried food like beans and rice. Stores everywhere would have been looted and emptied long ago. If there's any farming going on they won't supply local towns let alone cities. They'll keep it for themselves and their own community. Any habitable occupied islands we come across will not make us welcome. They'll want to conserve whatever they have for themselves. Anyone we encounter will not part with anything unless we can trade them something they may need for it. Do we have anything we can trade if this possibility arises?"

"Nothing," Mary said emphatically. "We soon won't have

enough of what we need ourselves, let alone anything we can trade."

"Maybe we should have gone inland instead of sailing off on our own," Helen said tentatively. She didn't really believe it, but she felt she had to say something.

Both Mary and Joe looked at her in silence, while the sound of the water passing along the sides of the hull filled the cabin with a reassuring soft hiss. It was a relaxing sound that most of the time none of them noticed but was always there in the background as the yacht sailed through calm waters.

"That would not have been a good idea," Mary said after a pause.

"Absolutely not," Joe agreed. "We are better off, leaving as we did. Sure, we have some problems, but we are better here than we would have been in the work camps. Like those who stayed on the rooftops in the flooded cities, I'll bet they are better off than the poor bastards forced to live in labour camps inland."

Having finished his tea, he added, "I think I'll change course and head closer to the coast. If we can find a river or an inlet, an estuary we can enter, we might have better luck with catching fish."

But they didn't get a chance to go far before the sky started flashing with bursts of stroboscopic light. Out of a clear sky, silent exploding bursts of intense light popped into existence and lingered like giant bubbles. They drifted haphazardly down to hover over the water's surface. At first Joe managed to avoid them since they weren't too large, but as more appeared, they became larger. Several floated down ahead of them one after the other, forcing him to take sudden evasive action to steer around them.

It's like they are targeting us, trying to capture us as we move forward...

"What's going on?" Mary asked as she came up to join him on deck. Helen was with her.

The sea had flattened as if something invisible but heavy pressed down upon the surface. There were hardly any swells, even though a steady breeze filled the sails giving them some forward momentum.

"It's like those light bubbles have flattened the water," Joe said. I've never seen anything like that before."

The smaller bubbles were so intense it hurt to look at them, but they were easily avoided.

Their skin prickled, stung in many spots with tiny bursts of electricity. The air around them sizzled. The humid air close to the sea's surface glowed in patches with entrained static electricity. Far above, the sky, still blue, flickered with intense bursts of light.

"What happens if we run into one of them?" Mary asked.

"I'm scared," Helen said.

"Can we turn and go back out to sea?" Mary asked.

"That's not an option." Joe responded. "Look behind."

Looking back Helen saw that some of the bubbles had bumped into each other, merging into larger masses of glowing light. Further behind, there seemed to be a wall of glowing bubbles rolling towards them. Some of the bubbles bounced off each other while others merged with flashes of blinding light to form much larger glowing balls. Where the glowing globes kissed the water's surface, it bubbled furiously giving off steam that roiled and twisted upwards before dissolving into the air above. The air around them was filled with the sizzling hiss of electrical discharges. As far as they could see in every direction, glowing globes of brilliant light bounced and merged into larger clumps with electrical discharges zapping between them as they joined to become massive balls of intense light.

The larger some of them got, the clearer they became, and Joe thought as he stared into the nearest large sphere of light that he could see a different landscape through the light, a different sea, a different shoreline, but it vanished the moment he saw it, behind layers of flashing electrical discharges. He kept trying to steer the yacht around them, but it became more difficult as the glowing bubbles continuously merged into much larger ones almost as soon as they formed. They were surrounded with no path open to clear water...

"I don't feel so good," Helen said.

"Look out," Mary screamed.

A huge ball of light exploded into existence directly in front of them. It rolled towards them. Thin fingers of lightning flowed from the expanding bubble to lick the top of the yacht's mast. Joe tried to turn aside, but the instant he touched the steering wheel he felt a thump in his heart. His hands were stuck to the steering wheel and his arms vibrated violently as static electricity zapped along his arms. Helen shuddered and shook as you would if you received an electrical shock from a faulty appliance. The three of them instantly felt dizzy as the sphere of light rolled over enveloping the yacht. Mary fell to her knees, shaking and vomiting. Helen collapsed. Joe's mind went blank momentarily. He couldn't breathe.

Whether the yacht sailed into it, or it rolled over and engulfed the yacht, the result was the same: instant disorientation for the three of them, moments of unconsciousness, violent shuddering as if some force was trying to remove their bones by shaking and rattling their bodies.

Joe thought he heard Helen screaming, but maybe it was he himself who screamed.

Suddenly it was over as fast as it had occurred, and they were on their knees, having vomited. Their clothes were stuck to them, and they sweated profusely. The cockpit was a mess and would have to be hosed down.

It was extremely hot, and struggling to breathe, what air they managed to suck in seemed to burn its way into their lungs.

Looking up Joe saw the sky was clear, deep blue, with not a glowing bubble in sight anywhere. The yacht seemed to be drifting along in a relatively smooth sea. Behind them, the horizon was obscured by a brilliantly glowing haze. The sun above burned with an intensity he hadn't felt before. Too bloody hot, he thought, humid, which was unexpected. Sweat beaded his skin and ran off in rivulets with every movement he made. Gasping because the air seemed too thick to breathe, he struggled to stand. Mary was having difficulty with her breathing, and he immediately helped her to sit on the edge of the cockpit. Once Mary was seated, he turned to assist Helen, but she was already on her feet.

"Are you okay?" He asked them.

They both looked pale.

"I think I'm all right," Helen said.

Mary's eyes were glazed and distant. She kept taking short gasping raspy breaths; obviously struggling to breathe properly.

"We should get Mary into her bunk where she can rest," Joe said.

With Joe lifting Mary, he and Helen managed to get her below deck and onto her bunk where she could rest comfortably. He switched on a tiny fan that blew warm air towards her creating a sluggish breeze. It didn't evaporate the perspiration that made her bare skin glisten, but after a moment her breathing improved. She smiled at them.

"I think I might have had a heart attack," she whispered, unable to get any strength into her voice.

Joe remembered the thump he felt in his heart as the glowing sphere engulfed them. He thought it had stopped beating for a moment before he'd blanked out... and woke to find himself on hands and knees vomiting in the cockpit. Mary was older than he was, and it would have affected her much more. He had taken her for granted since she always seemed fit and active, but suddenly, after whatever had just happened, she looked ancient and frail. He'd never asked her how old she was but had assumed she was in her late-seventies or perhaps touching eighty.

"I'll get some water to rinse your mouth." But before he could move Helen was beside him with a glass of tepid water.

"I'll give her the water," Helen said.

"Okay, make sure you drink some as well, we're dehydrated. I'll go back up on deck and clean up the mess we made in the cockpit, and then try and figure out where we are."

The compass indicated they were heading south. We must have got turned around, he thought. The last time he'd looked at the compass they'd been heading northeast, back towards the coast. He checked the GPS, but it was inactive. It was powered up but not receiving any signals.

He had no idea where they were. The sky to the south was clear and bright, while behind them it was a glowing haze. He assumed that was the remnants of the light spheres they had encountered so he decided to let the yacht continue sailing south, away from them. It was very hot and humid— nothing like it had been before they'd been engulfed by the weird electrical storms —and he figured the further south they went the more bearable the temperature would become, so he left the yacht to itself. A patchy breeze kept it moving southwards.

The sea around had a different colour, murky and greenish rather than deep blue and clear. It must be a lot shallower here, he thought, closer to land.

He stared around but saw no signs of land on the horizon, nothing but water and small choppy waves as far as he could see in every direction.

We'll just keep going south, away from the heat. Sooner or later, we'll see land and figure out where we are.

What he couldn't understand how they had managed to turn around to be heading south instead of north. Even though he'd been on his knees and vomiting, there had been no indication of the yacht turning. No matter how sick he'd been he would have felt it. Unless it had happened while we'd been momentarily unconscious…

The glowing haze behind them to the north stretched from horizon to horizon, east to west and from the surface up until it merged without demarcation into the sky. It was nothing like the Zone of Convergence that indicated a line of tropical storms extending around the globe above the equatorial regions, and which moved north or south of the equator depending on the Earth's axial tilt and whether it was summer or winter in one hemisphere or the other. This was something different. The sluggish wind was also blowing away from that glowing haze too, rather than towards it which was unexpected. But I'm not complaining. The sooner we get away from that the better.

He looked at his hands and saw burns where he had gripped the steering wheel. And having looked at them, he suddenly felt the pain the burns were inflicting. Making sure the yacht was unlikely to bump into anything— the sea was empty as far as she could see —he dropped back down into the cabin where he knew Mary had a medicine chest. There would surely be something to put on burns in there.

"Do you know where we are?" Helen asked the moment he dropped into cabin.

"No. The GPS is not receiving. I can't get a fix. Nothing else is working. No radar, no depth sounder, probably shorted out. But I reckon the sea here is shallow, nothing like where we were before we got zapped in that sphere of light." He nodded towards Mary. "How is she?"

"She's sleeping, and her breathing seems more normal now."

He found a burn cream in the medicine chest and rubbed it into his hands, and immediately the burning sting dissipated. That's good stuff. Feeling better he smiled at Helen. "You know, I think we somehow got shifted to another place. The air smells different, not like it does out at sea."

"That doesn't make any sense," Helen said.

"I know. Go up and have a look. See what you think."

He followed her up on deck and they contemplated the greenish sea over which they were sailing.

"It does look different." Helen agreed.

"That's exactly what I mean. We were sailing in a deep ocean before we were swamped by those glowing light bubbles, and now we're in a shallow sea. Judging by the smell in the air and the colour of the water we should be near the coast, which I can't explain because moments before we were miles out to sea."

"I don't see any coastline."

"But you can smell land. The only explanation that makes any kind of sense is that somehow were shifted from one location to another, and here we are."

"How is that possible?"

He shrugged. He had no answer to that.

They hardly seemed to move through the water, but they must have been making headway because the glowing haze extending from the sea's surface up so high as to disappear imperceptibly into the sky itself appeared much further away. The air wasn't as stifling either. It was still hot, but without the humidity he'd felt earlier. It was easier to breathe. He checked the compass, and they were still headed south. The wind came in small fluttery gusts that intermittently filled the sails, and that kept the yacht moving.

He sat down in the cockpit and contemplated the horizon ahead while the yacht steered itself. He didn't know how long he sat there thinking about what had happened to them when he became aware that ahead was the green and brownish smudge of a coastline. At first, he thought it might be an island, but as they got closer, he realized it was a peninsula extending into the sea from a more distant coastline off their port-side.

"Hey," he called out, and Helen popped her up through the hatchway. "There's land ahead."

She immediately came up to join him in the cockpit.

"You can't see much yet," he said.

"Do you think we'll find anyone here?"

"No idea yet. It'll be a couple of hours before we get close enough to see anything."

"I'll go down and tell Mary," Helen said, barely able to keep her apprehension at bay as she remembered their last couple of encounters. What will happen this time?

"How's she doing?"

"She's awake. She took a bit longer to recover than we did."

A moment later, after dropping down into the cabin she popped her head back up through the hatch and said, "Mary's made us a cup of tea. You should join us."

"That's good." Joe said and smiled broadly. "I'll be right there."

He'd been worried about Mary. Whatever it was that shifted them here, it had affected her much worse, probably because of her age. Now he felt as if a weight burdening him had lifted, and with a spring in his step he went to the hatch and dropped down into the cabin.

6...

Sailing towards the western side of the promontory Joe saw clusters of houses stretching back from the water's edge onto gently rising tree covered hills. The buildings looked solid, as if built from stone, but rendered and painted bright colours. Their roofs glistened as the hot sun was reflected off pale coloured tiles giving the place a cheerful ambiance. Many houses had small dish antennae pointing directly upwards. Off to one side beyond the houses and well away from the shoreline was a solid boxlike building with a large dish antenna pointing directly upwards next to it. To him, it appeared incongruous, much too large, in relation to the general appearance of the houses he could see but then he thought it may be part of a radio telescope array. He recalled there were many radio telescopes being set up across the inland, which were linked to a similar array in Africa, giving a much enhanced detailed view of the cosmos, with a 'lens' the width of the Earth's diameter. He couldn't recall if it had been finished and operational before the James Webb telescope sent into orbit overshadowed it with the glorious images it attained for astronomers to study.

Three short jetties extended out from an open space, a plaza of sorts, and surprisingly, a crowd of people were waving. Some were on the jetties, but most were by the shore fronting the town plaza. Children ran about on the sandy beach in front of the plaza playing games.

Well, that's different. He hadn't expected a reception like this. Being suspicious, he was wary. The buildings he saw fronting an open space were well-kept and the jetties didn't appear dilapidated.

There's something odd here, he thought as they got closer.

Concerns aside, he reefed in the mainsail and while Helen was manning the steering, keeping them aimed towards the longest of the jetties. He involuntarily found himself waving to the people on the jetty and smiling. There was not a hint of animosity. The feeling emanating from them was excitement. They were obviously happy to see a boat arriving.

"They seem like a nice bunch," Helen said cautiously.

"I don't see any guns." Joe noted.

"That's good, isn't it?"

"It's better than what happened the last time."

Mary joined them. She didn't want to miss anything.

When they were closer to the crowded jetty, Joe took over the steering. "Helen, chuck a rope from the bow to them when we get a bit closer. They can pull us in while I furl the short sail."

Helen raced to the bow where a thick rope was coiled around a stanchion. She unwound it and stood quietly waiting until the yacht drifted close enough for her to throw it over to the people waiting on the end of the jetty. The kids on the beach had stopped running about and stood watching the yacht's arrival.

With the bow approaching two metres from the jetty, Helen threw the rope to the group waiting.

"I've got it," the boy who grabbed it called out. He immediately started pulling the bow of the yacht closer before he wrapped the rope around one of several poles along the side of the jetty. While he was doing this, Joe threw another rope from where it was curled up on the deck behind the cockpit across to the men waiting. One of the men grabbed it and he pulled the stern of the yacht towards the jetty before firmly tying the rope around another pole. The side of the yacht gently bumped against the padded edge of the jetty before its movement settled and it became relatively still.

"Welcome," said the man who had tied the second rope. He was smiling broadly. He leaned forward to offer a hand to Joe so he could climb up out of the yacht and onto the jetty. "It's been a long time since we've had visitors." He held his hand out to help Mary climb up onto the jetty. Helen stepped onto the jetty by herself.

"We're happy to be here," Joe replied cautiously.

"My name's George," the stocky man said. He was well-muscled and obviously strong. His hair was thinning on top and had been cut short. "And that's my nephew Billy talking to your girl there."

Let him think she's my daughter, Joe thought. He didn't want to give these oddly cheerful people too much information until he had a better idea of who they were. But more important, he wanted to know where they were. He was still wondering about the shift from a temperate deep ocean to this shallow hot coastal sea; how could it have happened, and why? *Perhaps these people could explain…*

Mary didn't say anything apart from hello to those who greeted her. Her legs felt weak, almost as if they weren't strong enough to support her. She grabbed Joe's arm and held on. She felt light-headed, still a bit weak and didn't want to embarrass them or herself by stumbling and falling. It felt strange because the surface she stood on wasn't moving. *This will take a while to get used to*, she thought. After all the time she'd spent living on the yacht Harold had constructed in their front yard, it felt awkward to be standing on something solid, unmoving.

"I'm Mary," was all she said when Joe introduced her to George.

George said, "Let's go ashore where we can be more comfortable."

As they started to follow George along the jetty to the shore and the plaza, she tightened her grip on Joe's arm. Joe patted her hand to reassure her. "You'll get used to it," he said softly. "By the time we get to the end of the jetty and onto dry land you'll be back to normal."

With George leading the way, they walked along the jetty towards the open space where other people, not as many as before, were standing, waiting to see the visitors up close. The others who had been out on the pier followed behind them. Kids, having already lost interest with the newcomers and the novelty of their arrival, ran away along the beach doing whatever it was that kids always did by the seaside. The crowd that had filled the square began to dissipate leaving only the more curious still hanging around.

Joe walked slowly, supporting Mary.

Once off the jetty, he looked around and smiled at the obvious curiosity of the townsfolk as many wandered out along the jetty to have a look at the strange yacht moored at the end of it. Helen had gone ahead with Billy, and they were waiting for them beside a large tree casting shade over a concrete picnic table and chairs. There were several of these along the foreshore fronting the open space. A small number of people waited silently near the table as Joe and Mary arrived to sit there. They were all anxious to hear whatever the newcomers had to tell them.

"I feel much better now," Mary said when she sat down at the table. Joe sat beside her.

A woman came out from a nearby house carrying a tray with mugs and a large pot, spoons and a bowl of sugar, which she placed on the table. She smiled at Mary and said, "I imagine a nice cup of tea wouldn't go astray."

"Sorry we don't have any milk," George said as he sat down opposite them.

"That's fine.," Joe said.

The woman started to fill the mugs with the pungent dark tea, after which she sat beside George.

"We haven't seen milk for a long time," Mary said feeling comfortable with the prospect of a cup of tea.

After stirring sugar into his tea, George looked directly at Joe. "Where have you come from?" He asked bluntly.

That's a bit hard to explain, Joe thought.

"Nobody has ever come here from the north." George said when Joe didn't immediately respond. "It's uninhabitable. It's too hot and humid there. The wet-bulb temperature exceeds 35. Mammals, especially humans, can't sweat to regulate body temperature and they begin to cook. Reptiles and Birds have a higher tolerance and can survive, but humans can't."

"Ah, that's why it was so bloody hot," Joe said. "We could hardly breathe, but what was worse was the nausea and vomiting until we managed to get out of it."

"You were lucky, but what I should ask is how could you be there in the first place? You would have had to sail past us to get further north and we never saw any boats, let alone yours, going north. We haven't seen any boats for over a year, and when we do, they come from the south. They never go beyond us because there is nothing there but the hot zone, and it seems to be slowly extending. It's a lot closer now than it used to be." He let that thought fade before adding. "Boats used to come more often..."

"What kind of boats?" Mary asked, not to be left out of the conversation.

"Trading boats. People wanting to trade for things we have that they don't. In exchange we get things we need as well as updates on what's happening in other places." Switching back to his previous line of thought, he turned back to Joe and said, "to see you coming from the north; well, we would have thought that was impossible, but here you are."

"Have you ever seen glowing bubbles of light descending from the sky?" Joe asked.

Looking blank, George shook his head.

"They were all around us," Joe said. "We were sailing north along the coast, well offshore to avoid the flotsam and rubbish washed out to sea by the tsunami when we got caught in a storm with waterspouts forming everywhere around us, and when they stopped, these glowing bubbles, like massive ball lightning, started floating down or forming everywhere as far as we could see. We tried to avoid them."

He paused when he saw George and the tea lady looking at them as if they didn't understand a word he was saying.

"Hang on," George said to break the moment of silence. "What coast?"

"The east coast. We came out of Melbourne, what was left of it, sailed east and then north parallel to the coast. What coast did you think I meant?"

George didn't answer. He could hardly believe it. But seeing the strangers' yacht up close convinced him that they were telling the truth. No one had made or seen a boat like that, made from metal, since the world flooded, and every major coastal city was abandoned —*How long ago was that?* He shook his head, not willing to accept what he was thinking. What ultimately convinced him more than anything else was the condition of the newness of the yacht; it was not a rusted hulk. He had heard of other people mysteriously appearing out of nowhere but thought they were stories people liked to tell each other and not real events, but now he was beginning to believe they were true.

Feeling uncomfortable with no response from George and the others across the table who continued to stare at them, Joe continued, "When Antarctica's ice started melting the sea flooded the cities and they started to fall apart, the government did things to force people to accede to its demands Things got bad. People were forcibly removed and sent inland to work camps to build new enclaves. Those who refused to leave barricaded themselves in the top levels of still-standing buildings, but eventually I think they would have had no choice but to abandon everything and head inland too. We decided going to sea was a better option for us and we left in Mary's yacht. A lot of fishermen living in a floating enclave beside the city also left."

George and his companion looked at each other, frowned with disbelief, before turning back. "And this... happened when?" George asked.

"No more than a couple of months ago." Joe said. "We were sailing up the east coast looking for a warmer, safer place to stay when a large chunk of the Antarctic ice shelf broke off and crashed into sea. It created a huge tsunami that destroyed what was left of everything along the coast."

"The east coast is a long way from here," George said, not ready to believe what Joe was telling him. "Around two thousand kilometres... I don't know exactly... It changed a lot after that tsunami brought a huge rise in sea levels." He looked intensely at Joe, and then Mary before adding, "That tsunami was a terminal event..."

"What?" That explosion of one word cut George off mid-sentence. *What terminal event?* Now Joe and Mary stared at George and the villagers crowded respectfully around the table listening with intense interest. Lost for words trying to comprehend how they could have been sailing in the deep ocean then suddenly be somewhere else thousands of kilometres away sailing in a different direction, Joe and Mary stared at George. *What the hell is he saying?*

"We are located at the southern end of what was once called Lake Eyre, or *Kati Thanda*." George explained. "It's now an inland sea, like the old explorers of this country imagined was there, but all they ever found was an enormous dry Salt Lake. Sometimes it filled with water after tropical storms in the north flooded rivers that ran south into it, bringing it to life, then it would dry up again for years. But that's ancient history. It's always been an inland sea since before I was born. —He paused a moment to let that sink in— As you said, the sea came up and flooded the world when the ice cap melted and slid off into the ocean... That was more than a thousand years ago."

Joe and Mary stared uncomprehendingly at George. Their tea untouched rapidly cooled. *That can't be right... More than a thousand years... Ancient history...*

"The founders of this town established a small settlement on this promontory, a couple of hundred years after that catastrophe. They couldn't stand the enclaves and struck out on their own. Joined by few other like-minded individuals they ventured further inland in search of the mythical sea the old explorers believed had to be there, and this time it was. We live in a very different country. The risen sea has eaten into it, eroded it, extending inland, and in many places well inland of what was once the coast."

He stopped to take a sip of his now cooled tea while he thought of what to say next, giving his visitors time to absorb what he'd said. They looked stunned.

"This sea here connects to the ocean to the south, but not to the north. That way is impassable. It's too hot; a barrier that goes right around the world separating the northern from the southern hemisphere and no one can go through it. And that's a good thing because the northern hemisphere practically destroyed itself with paranoid nations thinking they were being attacked by other equally paranoid nations, unleashing missiles and atomic bombs upon each other. Those that weren't immediately destroyed regressed into small groups and tribes fighting each other over scarce resources. Radiation fallout killed a lot. Animals, plants, whatever the rising seas and tsunamis didn't get, they themselves destroyed.

Ancient bacteria released as the permafrost melted finished almost all the rest with diseases that modern humans had no immunity to. We can't be sure there were any survivors, but I doubt if there were. There has never been any contact with anyone on the other side of the heat barrier. We were lucky in the southern hemisphere; with a lot less people and smaller continental areas affected. Even so, the times were horrific until things settled down."

"We can vouch for that." Joe said finally. "We were there, and we saw what happened. It's not something I'd want to go through again. We left because things were not getting any better. And we weren't the only ones. Somewhere out there," and he indicated vaguely towards the east, "there's a community of fishermen, a floating enclave…" and then he thought, *ah shit, that was a long time ago…* He stopped trying to wonder what might have happened to them, and of the ones who stayed behind living on the rooftops of the sunken city. He looked at George, waiting for further explanation.

"There are satellites that still function in orbit which we can use to see what the northern hemisphere looks like today. Historical records and images from the time of the extinction events have been downloaded and are accessible. Billions of people died," George said. "Two thirds of the world's population lived in the northern hemisphere and most if not all of them were wiped out. There may be some small groups surviving in remote mountainous areas, but no one knows for sure. Everyone has studied what happened in school and there are researchers still trying to put together the whole story. They'd be very interested in talking to you because you were actual witnesses to real events that are only history to us."

"I would give that a miss for the time being," Joe said, "at least until I have a clearer picture of what the world is like now." He didn't wish to be unfriendly or uncooperative, but after what they'd been through, it was too soon to be talking to others about it.

"It was a long time ago," George said. "There's no hurry. What used to be major cities across Europe, North America, and North Africa are nothing more than radioactive ruins and wastelands."

"More than a thousand years ago?" Mary muttered, struggling to accept the possibility they were in a future time, not their own. She was remembering the initial flood, the death of her husband Harold, and how she met Joe and Helen, and the collapse of the society she grew up in. She found difficulty comprehending the idea that what they had experienced so recently was a thousand years in the past. *It's not possible...*

George nodded affirmatively, allowing them to consider it.

"No wonder I feel so old," Mary said finally.

George couldn't help smiling at Mary's little joke.

After a minute or two, Joe shook his head to clear it. "Ancient history," he said softly because to say it out loud made it seem too real. *More than a thousand years ago...*

"You look stunned," George finally said.

"Wouldn't you be? We were there, right in the middle of what you call 'ancient history'. For us it's only a few months ago, not a thousand years. I find it hard to accept."

"But it's the truth. How you got here is what we find hard to accept."

They were interrupted as Helen and Billy ran up to the table where they were seated.

"Billy tells me there's a giant croc nearby and you are going to capture it later today," she said, hardly able to contain her excitement.

"That's right," Billy added. "Would you like to come with us?"

"You might find it interesting," George added, relieved that the subject had been changed. "We can't leave a big croc anywhere nearby. It's an apex predator; too bloody dangerous. There are kids that play along the beaches and swim in the sea, and fishermen that wade into the shallows to net prawns and fish. We don't want anyone becoming a victim of a croc attack."

"Okay," Joe said. "I'm with you."

"Not me," Mary said. "I'm too old for that kind of excitement."

"What are you going to do when you catch it?" Joe asked. "Relocate it?"

"No way. We don't have the means and if we did, where would

we take it? It would only return after a few days or weeks depending on how far away we could take it. No, we'll catch and kill it. We use the meat, and we can tan the skin and sell it or swap it for stuff we need when an occasional trader comes up from down south."

"How often does that happen?"

"What? Killing crocs, or trading the skins?"

"A trader coming up from down south."

"The last time was a bit over a year ago, so we are overdue for a visit. A few years back we had a bunch of bandits come in and try to take over the village. We soon got that sorted, but normally, roughly once a year we would see a trading boat come up from the south where there are more enclaves and settlements."

Joe lapsed into silence. They got that sorted... He wondered what George meant by that. He remembered reading something a couple of years ago, *Fuck, more than a thousand years ago if this was true,* about gravity waves from a collision of massive black holes not long after the universe began, that travelled for billions of years before reaching us and being detectable, gravity waves that disrupted the fabric of space, causing splits and shifts in space and time. These waves had been detected along with echoes in time that although momentary were hard to define. He'd read about it online. *Perhaps as the gravity waves passed through our solar system, they caused disruptions to the earth itself, creating unprecedented volcanic activity, earthquakes and tsunamis, causing glaciers to shatter and melt, along with the ice shelves in Greenland, Patagonia, and Antarctica to slide down into the sea. Maybe these gravity waves had more to do with it than the much talked-about global warming that everyone thought was the cause. But a thousand years ago?* He still couldn't wrap his mind around that. Perhaps the world has settled down and is more stable now. Suddenly a thought pooped up; *Is there is a way back?*

"Do you think there's a way back?" Mary asked almost echoing Joe's ultimate thought.

"Why would you want to go back?" George asked, surprised at the question.

"I don't know. I mean, it was our time…"

"A time of chaos and death, disruption and destruction; no one would want to go back to that… Would they? How would you do it anyway?"

"I don't know, "Joe said. "Sail back the way we came and see if we can find some of those glowing balls of light and energy that had surrounded us before we were engulfed and ended up here. Like, do it in reverse."

"If you go back into the hot zone, you may not find what you are looking for before the heat and humidity kills you. No one has ever gone there and come back out."

"My father did that years ago when I was very young," Billy said. "He went exploring to the north."

"And never came back." George added.

"I don't want to go back into that," Mary said. "I had trouble breathing until we came out of it."

Remembering how he had been affected by the transition, Joe also thought he would not want to do it again. Not voluntarily… *but maybe it was not so much the transition but where they found themselves afterwards, the hot zone… There could be other places not so dangerous where it may be possible… Then he immediately thought, even if we could go back, would it be such a good idea? Would we survive? We only experienced the beginning of the bad times. And what if you can't go back, only forwards? Would it be better or worse than where we are now?* He was not sure he would be willing to find out, at least not yet.

He looked around the at the people listening to their story, and beyond them at the houses fronting the town square, all so neat and tidy, so well looked after… *We should consider ourselves lucky to be here…*

"I'm happy to stay here," Helen said affirmatively.

But for Joe, the thought that it may be possible to return to their own time lingered in the back of his mind.

7...

As the sun dropped below the horizon, Billy led them to where he'd encountered the big crocodile. It was a small inlet leading to a narrow channel in which water could run down the odd times it rained, but at that moment it was dry. Grass grew in the channel extending into the water mixing with reeds growing in the shallows at the edge. Some of the reeds were quashed flat.

"That's where it was hiding," he told George who held a coil of rope with a lasso in one hand. "You can see my fishing rod on the sand where I dropped it."

Billy was about to start forward to retrieve the fishing rod, but George put a hand on his shoulder to stop him. "I wouldn't do that," he said. "It's probably lurking right there at the edge. Let's put the bait down to entice it to come out of the water so we can grab it."

There were five townsfolk as well as Joe, Helen and Billy. They had travelled on a flatbed battery operated work truck out from the back of the town over the sand dunes behind this part of the peninsula to the spot where Billy had been fishing. Behind the cabin in front was a strong metal arm used as a small crane for lifting things onto the flatbed. The vehicle had wide independently operated tracked wheels that reminded Joe of the Mars rovers he had seen in documentaries; an all-terrain vehicle that could go almost anywhere. At the site, they left the vehicle behind a ridge, so it was hidden from the water, and followed Billy down to the spot where he'd dropped his fishing rod as he'd jumped back out of the way.

Joe and Helen accompanying Billy, being observers rather than participants, kept away from the hunting group so they wouldn't be a hindrance.

One of the other men also carried a lasso, while another had slung across his shoulder a bag containing half of a wild boar carcass to use as bait.

Both George and the other man carrying a lasso opened the nooses and laid them over each other in the centre of the channel two metres up from the water's edge, then two of the men went up the far side of the channel uncoiling the rope behind them. George uncoiled his rope back along the side where Joe and Helen stood beside Billy. The man with the bag slung over his shoulder dropped it on the ground, opened it, lifted the end exposing the carcass of a recently caught wild boar. Extracting the carcass, he went almost to the water's edge and laid it on the ground for a moment while remaining alert to any movement from the crocodile. He then dragged the carcass away from the water and back up into gully leaving a thin trail of blood and gore along the grassy surface until he reached the lassos. He placed the carcass inside the lassos, then came back to join George. He brought the empty bag with him. All of this they did quietly, not wanting to attract the attention of the crocodile before they were ready.

"Now we wait," George said.

"This is the boring part," Billy whispered to Helen. They had moved well back from the hunting party.

Deep shadows were forming inside the narrow channel. The air was warm and sultry, but being so far inland it would soon cool off as the night progressed.

With everybody hidden behind the ridges on each side of the gully they settled down for a long wait for the crocodile to emerge to take the bait.

It darkened rapidly and millions of stars appeared. Joe was amazed at how many he could see. It had never been this clear as far back as he could remember. But that was a thousand years ago... He still found it hard to accept they were in a different time and place. Those rising seas stopped industrial pollution dead along with the civilization that created it, and after so much time the atmosphere had cleansed itself. He was jerked out of his thoughts by splashing in the water.

Something moved in the reeds by the edge, then it stopped and all they could hear was the soft movement of grass behind them being ruffled by a tepid breeze. Then there were more splashes, and startlingly loud, a heavy exhalation of air like a soft explosion that was suddenly cut off. In the moment of silence that followed, no one moved or said anything. The slightest sound could startle the croc causing it to retreat.

They waited… hardly daring to breathe.

More heavy exhalations were followed by wet slithering as the heavy crocodile dragged itself up out of the water to follow the blood trail towards the carcass that irresistibly tempted it.

George lifted his head but could hardly see anything in the darkness of the channel. As his eyes adjusted, he saw fragmented reflections off parts of the crocodile's wet scaly body moving towards the bait. There was enough bright starlight for them to see it now as it moved up into the shallow gully. There was no stopping it.

"It's almost there," George whispered to Joe.

It took another minute, but suddenly the bait was obscured as the crocodile opened its mouth and grabbed the carcass. There was a wet squelching noise as the carcass was crushed in its powerful jaws.

"Now," George called out as he stood up and flipped the rope to bring the noose over the crocodile's snout. The man on the other side did the same and they both pulled hard to close the nooses and keep the crocodile's mouth partially shut. It had the carcass half in and half out of its mouth. Joe grabbed the rope as well to help George keep tension on it. Those on the other side did the same.

The crocodile's tail lashed viciously from side to side. It lifted its head and shook it but couldn't release the nooses wrapped tightly around its snout. The carcass flapped from side to side.

"Don't let go," George yelled.

"We got it," came a voice from the other side.

The crocodile lurched backwards down the gully towards the water, but the men held on even though they were almost pulled over. They dug their feet into the ground, holding onto the ropes with all their strength. The crocodile twisted and shook its head. It couldn't roll over because it was out of the water. It shook violently.

The monstrous crocodile dug its front feet in and pushed itself backwards dragging the men trying to hold it over the top of ridges on either side.

"Billy," George yelled desperately, "Get that bag over its head."

Billy rushed forward and dropped the bag the carcass had been in over the crocodile's head and almost immediately it stopped moving, unable to see what was attacking it. The men still held on tight with the ropes, maintaining tension. Billy quickly came back and grabbed a long black tube-like device left on the ground where they'd been waiting. Moving quickly to the crocodile he leaned forward and pressed the end against the monster's skull. There was sizzling zap, and a bright spark of electrical discharge caused the monster to shiver and shake violently for a few seconds before becoming still.

"Wow, that was something," Joe said. He exhaled loudly, letting go of the rope.

"It's not dead yet," George said. "Hang onto the rope and keep it taut while I finish it off." He passed the rope back to Joe who did as he was asked.

George pulled out something that looked like wide chisel. It was the size of a garden hoe blade. Its sharp edge glistened in the starlight. The blunt end finished with a thicker flattened area. Billy handed George a heavy duty hammer which had been on the ground next to the electrical prod used to stun the creature. George made his way cautiously towards the huge crocodile. He nudged its side with his foot, and when it didn't move, he immediately straddled the creature behind its head, placing the extra wide chisel blade at a spot between the back of the head and the start of the neck. He brought the hammer up high and smashed it down onto the flat top of the chisel. He repeated the blow again driving the blade further down into the crocodile to sever its spinal cord.

George leaped off as the monster shivered violently before becoming still again.

"Now it's dead," he said as he stood up.

One of the men backed the flatbed vehicle towards the top of the channel. He fixed a rope to the winch that worked from the small crane at the rear of the cabin. The other end he brought forward and wrapped it as best he could around both front legs as well as wrapping it around the head of the monster croc. With the end of the flatbed tilted down so it touched the ground, he used the winch to drag the monster up the short distance of the channel to the back of the flatbed where it was easily pulled onto it. They threw ropes over it and tied them to both sides. The flatbed was leveled again, and the man jumped into the driver's seat.

"How big is it?" Helen asked. She moved closer to look at it.

"About six metres," George told her.

"I had no idea they could get that big," she said, eyes wide as she looked at its enormous head still with a half swallowed carcass dangling from its mouth. She shuddered as she imagined the horror of being in the water and having a monster like that latch onto her.

"They can get bigger, but this is the biggest we've caught. We never used to see them this size."

The flatbed lurched. And Helen jumped back involuntarily as the driver started the engine.

"We'll walk back," George said, "unless either of you," and he looked at Joe and Helen, "want to ride back sitting on top of the croc."

"I'm good," Joe said.

"I'm not getting on there with that thing," Helen said.

Turning towards the vehicle George yelled out "Take it away."

The flatbed seemed to have trouble getting traction with the weight of the crocodile on board, but after a few wheel spins, with sand spurting out backwards, the tracks grabbed, and the vehicle started moving slowly away. The group followed, walking in the tracks left by the flatbed.

Sitting in the cabin of the yacht with Joe, Mary and Helen, George said over a nightcap before returning to the village, "you're not the first people to mysteriously arrive, although you're the first we've seen here."

After a moment of silence, Joe said, "that's why you didn't seem too surprised when I told where we'd come from."

"We're not totally isolated from everywhere else, though it might seem so at first. We prefer to be out here on our own, less chance of problems occurring, and we are self-sufficient. But we are in regular contact with other communities around the country, at least the parts where people can live. Over the last ten or so years there have been reports of groups of people or of individuals suddenly appearing, all of whom claim to have been in that same place, or near enough to it, at a time when the floods took place and society collapsed as cities were abandoned."

"But people disappearing mysteriously or appearing out of nowhere is not something new." Joe stated. "There are, or were, historical records going back centuries of mysterious disappearances or appearances. And relative to my time, ships with hundreds of passengers, and flights of aeroplanes mysteriously vanished never to be seen again in the Caribbean Sea, in a place called the Bermuda Triangle. It happened elsewhere as well, but the Bermuda Triangle disappearances are the most famous. There were strange gravity readings there which no one has been able to explain. It's not something new. The Bermuda Triangle disappearances never reappeared, and if a shift in time was responsible, then they were shifted way back into the past before there were inhabitants in those places, or there would have been records or folktales… some kind of indication, but there was nothing. Maybe they were shifted into future, like us, and have yet to appear. Or perhaps even into another alternate reality."

"That's a bit far-fetched…"

"Is it?" Joe interrupted. "Is it any more far-fetched than us arriving here the way we did? And what about animals? In my time there were periodically reports of big cat-like animals appearing and attacking farmer's sheep or other domestic animals in remote country areas, but they always disappeared before anyone could get a good look at them. Hunting parties searched for them, but none were ever found."

George didn't know what to say to that.

Joe continued; "my job at the time was to report on worsening global climate events and the way people were affected around the world, but when the whole world suddenly became a disaster zone, all that went out the window… everything fell apart. It came down to every individual trying to survive on their own." He stopped to gather his thoughts. There had been far too many things happening for him to think of them in any coherent order. Finally, after the silence had dragged on for almost a minute, he said, "I was lucky to have met Mary whose late husband constructed this yacht, and with Helen, we managed to get away when we encountered a massive tsunami followed by the weirdest storms and ended up here."

"No," Mary said. "I was lucky that Joe and Helen came along. I would never have managed without them. They saved my life."

"Let's say we saved each other and leave it at that," Joe said, turning towards Mary and giving her a reassuring smile.

George nodded. "From our perspective what you survived was the tipping point where everything had been building up with slowly increasing pressure on the environment in different but interconnecting ways. There were tsunamis caused by kilometres thick ice sheets sliding off major continents into the sea instantly raising levels hundreds of metres. There were volcanoes spewing lava and noxious gases into the air because the land shifted and bounced back up when the enormous pressure the kilometres thick ice shelves had created was released.."

I'm glad we missed those… Joe thought.

"What caused it is still debated, but what everyone agrees on is that there is only so much strain and tension you can put on a system before it collapses, and we, our ancestors I should say, did that with pollution and environmental destruction to the point of creating what can only be called a partial extinction event. People knew it was coming, but ignored it, or didn't want to believe it. 'Too hard to solve', they proclaimed, leaving it for the next generation. But problems of this magnitude don't go away, they only get worse."

He paused to gather his thoughts, to take a deep breath.

"And it's not over yet. The planet is still warming and the hot zone traversing the entire world along the equator is expanding to the north and the south. It may take a few centuries more before we are forced to move further south to the only continent left that will still be habitable, Antarctica, but it's inevitable. Teams are down there exploring possibilities, but it's a barren inhospitable place. We were lucky we didn't have the population densities of the northern hemisphere where all of them were wiped out. Here in the southern half of the world, over half the population died during that first year, if not from the violence of the destruction, then from fighting each other for limited resources. The survivors moved inland, either forcibly or by their own choice, but there was little option to stay where they were even if it hadn't been destroyed. But that didn't stop additional increases in deaths from a flesh eating bacterium that bred in warmer waters brought on by less salinity in the oceans. At least half the surviving population died from this horrifying bacterium, as well as other large viruses released into the environment from melting permafrost that humanity had no immunity to. It took over a hundred years before things stabilized. If what you went through was the start of that extinction event, it was also a reminder that it's not over, and humanity, what's left of us now, may still not survive in the long run. History of previous extinction events tells us they were truly catastrophic. So far, we have survived. The northern hemisphere didn't as far as we can tell, and maybe the same fate awaits us here in the south. The odd appearance from time to time of people like yourselves is an anomaly, reminding us that whatever is happening is still going on."

Suddenly he stopped, almost breathless from talking non-stop. He stood up, smiled ruefully.

"It's certainly been an interesting day," Joe said.

"It's late. I should get back and leave you to rest."

8...

The sun was barely above the horizon with long shadows still stretching across the land when Billy strolled along the jetty towards the yacht moored there. The coldness of the inland night was giving way to the Sun's promise of hot day. A dry wind stirred up by the warming land ruffled the treetops.

Billy hadn't slept much during the night; the excitement of strangers arriving, and the crocodile hunt filling his head with thoughts and dreams and remembrances of his father having gone off in search of— who knows what? —to never return. He found it amazing that these visitors had lived in the times he'd only heard stories about. Thinking about what they had gone through to get here was unimaginable. *How could it have been possible?*

Then the idea that perhaps if they left, when they left, because he was sure they wouldn't want to stay here for too long, would it be possible to go with them? He wanted to see more of the world, but deep down he wanted to look for his father. Although living with his uncle was fine, he did miss his father. If he had somehow gone into the past like the visitors had come into the future, why had he not come back? *Did he not want to come back? Was he still alive somewhere? Some-when? In the future? If it's getting worse every year the future may have killed him, and he'll never come back.* He desperately needed answers, and with the arrival of these strangers, perhaps now he had a way to find some.

Leaning against a bollard at the end of the jetty he studied the moored yacht. It was the best looking boat he'd ever seen, better than any of the boats that sometimes came from the south to trade and sell stuff they couldn't make for themselves. None of those boats were made of metal like this one, which made it easier to believe it had come from a past time when technology was different to what they had today. He found it impossible to imagine what the world had been like before the termination event, but these people had lived in that world, had come through the destruction of everything they knew, and were here now. They could tell him what it was like.

Lost in his thoughts, he didn't see Helen pop up through the hatch, but she saw him.

"Hey," she called softly, "are you spying on us?"

"Sorry, I was lost in thought." He blushed unexpectedly, momentarily embarrassed that his face had gone red. "I couldn't sleep."

"Me either." She stepped up onto the deck, jumped across the slight gap between the jetty and the yacht to stand beside him.

Suddenly neither of them knew what to say to each other. They stood silently together and watched the sun rise. As soon as it got above the tree tops Helen could feel its heat burning into her skin and thought she'd have to ask Mary if there was any sunscreen on board.

"Is it always this hot here?"

"This isn't hot," Billy said, "it's always like this. It's cold at night though."

"I noticed that."

"But hot is where you came from. Nobody goes that way because the further north you go the more unbearable it becomes. It'll kill you. They tell me the whole world is hotter than it used to be."

"They always say that don't they? Back where, or should I say when, I came from they used to say we were coming out of an ice age, when half the planet was frozen."

"Frozen…the planet? I can't picture it."

"We were taught that the whole of human civilization only occurred after the ice retreated, that it would get hotter for a few thousand years before cooling off again into another ice age. But we changed that, didn't we? With mountains of industrial waste and millions of tonnes of carbon dioxide pumped into the air, we started a runaway greenhouse affect and another ice age will never happen."

"I don't know if that's good or bad," Billy said, "or even true.

The world is the way it is whether we like it or not."

On the beach well away from the jetty a couple of men appeared carrying nets. They put them into a wooden dinghy and pushed it into the water. They both jumped in and started rowing way from the shore. A couple of kids ran across the square and disappeared up a narrow street. Other people appeared and started to set up stalls in the square.

"It's market day," Billy said. "Farmers bring in their produce to trade with each other."

"So not everyone lives in town."

"That's right. Local farmers bring fresh fruit and vegetables once a week to trade for fish or meat. A lot of them will go home today with salted crocodile."

"From the one you caught last night?" She was surprised.

"It's already been butchered, with some salted for immediate use and the rest frozen for later."

As they were talking, they walked back along the jetty to the square to watch the farmers setting up the stalls. More kids appeared and went up the same narrow street where the others had gone, but with a lot less enthusiasm.

Helen nodded towards the kids and Billy explained, "They're off to school."

Helen found herself smiling at the thought of kids going to school. Some things never change.

"They do a couple of hours every morning," Billy said. "It's too hot later in the day to bother."

As they walked into the town square Helen smelt an invigorating freshness in the air. She took several deep breaths exhaling loudly after each one. It almost made her feel dizzy. She could smell the fresh fruit and vegetables that people were putting on display on fold-able tables under awnings to keep the rising sun off them. This surprised her momentarily because she'd never smelt fresh fruit and vegetables back in her own time, even in open markets: the air, she guessed, had been too full of other smells from traffic and industry and all that civilized stuff. She remembered the sky was never blue and clear like here. It was tinged with grey or brownish overlays from chemicals blasted into the air by industry and the exhausts of motor vehicles that clogged city streets with endless traffic jams.

"This has got to be the best time of the day," she commented.

"Once the sun gets higher and the dry wind starts it's not as nice," Billy said. "I always get up early, before sunrise, to enjoy the quietness and the coolness."

"You guys don't know how lucky you are," Helen said. "It's beautiful here."

That left Billy at a loss for words. He couldn't make a comparison because he'd never known anything else. This was the way the world was, as far as he knew.

"I guess so," he mumbled.

Helen strode towards a stall displaying heaps of green and yellow melons stacked high, only stopped from rolling off by a narrow frame around the edge of the bench. The aroma emanating from them made her mouth water.

"I should get some of these to take back to the boat." She said to the woman behind the counter. "They smell delicious."

"And what do you have to trade for them?" the woman asked.

Helen was taken aback, not knowing how to answer.

"You have to exchange something for them," Billy explained as he came up beside her. "Perhaps you have something she wants in exchange for the melons."

"Not that I can think of."

"Perhaps something off the boat?" the woman behind the stall suggested.

"You'd have to ask Joe or Mary about that," Helen said cautiously. She turned to Billy. "You don't use money, or something like that?"

She suddenly realized that money, if they had any, would be worthless if they were really in the future. It was a stupid question. Money from her time, even back when they left the city was redundant with the ever increasing use of electronic payments often forced upon those who didn't really want it, and after the catastrophe, it had disappeared completely. Trading something someone else might need for something you needed had already started. She should have realized it would be the same here. She started to move away from the stall.

"Hey, take one," the woman behind the stall said, "as a gift."

Helen turned back to see the woman smiling, holding a melon out towards her. She hesitated.

"It's alright," Billy said. He took the melon the woman proffered and handed it to Helen who was not sure whether she should accept it, but the delicious smell of the melon in her hands was too much to resist.

"Thank you," she mumbled and smiled at the woman who beamed back.

The square was filling with people bringing things to trade or setting up stalls of various sizes with items to exchange. With Billy beside her, she quickly walked back to the boat at the end of the jetty. At least they would have a delicious melon to eat for breakfast. It would be a lovely change from the preserved fruit they had in their almost empty pantry.

Joe woke to the sound of voices on the deck above where his bunk was located. The yacht rocked gently as the two conversing moved along the deck. He recognized Helen's voice and assumed, with a smile, that the person with her must be Billy. As he pulled on a T-shirt and a pair of shorts, he became aware of other voices, distant enough that they blended into a general hubbub of soft sound. Something's going on in the square. He stepped into the galley so see Mary was already awake, preparing cups of tea accompanied with toast. It smelt delicious.

"I didn't want to wake you," Mary said when she saw him. "You looked as if you needed a good sleep."

"Yeah. The last few days have been a bit tough." Stepping to the bench he said, "You look like you could do with some more sleep yourself."

Mary gave him a sad smile. "I'll be okay. I can't seem to sleep more than a couple of hours at a time these last few weeks, and coming through that storm or whatever it was, hasn't helped..."

"That was something we won't forget." He put his arm around her shoulders and gave her a hug. "Let me help with the toast," he said, then added, "I didn't know we had any bread left. Did you make that last night?"

"No. One of the ladies gave it to me while you were out hunting the crocodile."

"It smells really good." He was already salivating as he drew in a deep breath filled with the aroma of fresh bread toasting.

"This smells good too," Helen stated as she dropped through the hatch into the main cabin beside the galley. She held out a large rock melon. "A lady at the market just gave it to me. We can have it for breakfast."

That explains the distant voices he had tuned out once he started moving about.

Billy dropped into the cabin to stand beside Helen. "Today is a market day," he said. "It happens twice a week. People come in from outlying areas to exchange or swap their produce for stuff they don't have or can't produce. But more than that, it's a chance for everyone to catch up and gossip. And guess what event they are all talking about?"

"Our arrival?" Joe suggested.

"Spot on," Billy said. "Don't be surprised if a lot of people come out to have a closer look and a bit of a chat."

"That's fine by me," Joe said, although he sounded reluctant.

"Me too," Mary added. "I hope they don't expect me to answer questions. I 'm still a bit too tired to do that."

"You just relax and take it easy," Helen said. "Uncle Joe and I can do that."

"Maybe," Joe said. He didn't feel like answering questions having too many of his own he wanted answered, but these people were kind, and certainly friendly and he would do his best to reciprocate.

Helen placed the melon on the table and cut it into eight slices, two for each of them. With the toast done and spread with jam from the last jar in their pantry, and fresh black tea, they tucked into the breakfast with hardly a word other than a mumble of pleasure or a happy smile as they each tasted the fresh melon followed by the toasted bread and jam.

Sitting back as he sipped his tea, it was Billy who asked the question that had been on Joe's mind without him being aware of it.

"Where are you planning on going when you leave here?"

He was unable to come up with an answer not being something he had yet considered— We've only just got here, for Christ's sake. —but having had the question put to him, he realized it was time to consider it.

"I thought we might stay for a while," Mary preempted him. "We're a bit weary of travelling for the moment. A good rest is what we need. We've run out of supplies and could do with replenishing the pantry before we consider going anywhere else."

"Besides," Joe added, "we have no idea where to go from here. Whether we try and find a way back to our own time or stay here and explore a bit… we haven't thought about it, let alone discussed it."

"I think we need to find out what it's like here before deciding anything," Helen suggested.

"Why do you ask Billy?" Joe said.

Suddenly nervous, Billy said, "I thought I might ask if I could come with you. I'd like to see what it's like away from Eyresea which is what this place is unofficially called."

"Does it have an official name? Mary asked.

"It's registered as S15. S for settlement."

"That's a stupid name," Helen said. "I like Eyresea better."

"Me too," said Mary.

"Why would you want to come with us?" Joe asked.

"Like I said…"

"Not that. What's the real reason?"

Billy hesitated before answering. He blushed and looked aside as he tried to find a way to say it. He finally blurted out, "I want look for my father."

"What makes you think that if you came with us, we might be able to find him?"

"I don't know. I just hope it could be possible. I really miss him…"

Joe glanced towards Helen, whose eyes were fixed on Billy. He saw in her face that she understood how Billy felt. She'd lost her father not so long back— he'd been murdered and thrown off a building —and she missed him. But she'd had closure with the body being recovered and cremated and they had scattered his ashes at sea. Billy had no such thing. His father had simply disappeared sailing to the north. *Was he still alive somewhere as Billy hoped? Or was he dead, somewhere nobody would ever find him?*

"He led an exploration trip four years ago," Billy said, "and never came back. None of them did."

"Maybe he was lost at sea," Joe said. "But what if he encountered a storm like we did? If he was shifted into the past somewhere, or into the future like us, we'll never find him. Have you thought of that? The world is very large and chances of finding any individual anywhere are worse than impossible."

"But that's my hope, after hearing how you got here," Billy said softly. "That if you were thinking of going back by sailing into one of those storms, back to your time, we might find him there."

"I'm not going into one of those storms again," Mary said emphatically. "It damn near killed me. You can go but I will stay here. I'm sure I could find something useful to do in town, if they'd have me."

"Billy, we've only just got here." Joe said. "We're going to need time to rest, time to replenish our supplies, and before we even consider going anywhere, we need to find out more about what it's like here." Turning to Mary he added, "It's your yacht. I wouldn't consider going anywhere without you."

"But when you do," Billy asked, "Can I come with you?"

He saw Helen nodding in agreement. She liked the idea.

Helen could do with someone her own age for company. He'd already decided to allow Billy to join them.

"We'd have to talk to your Uncle George about that…" Joe said with a hint of reluctance, "Let's leave it for the time being, okay?"

Billy couldn't stop smiling. "Yes," he said, "Okay."

Later, while Mary went ashore knowing she could swap a jar of her precious powdered freeze-dried coffee for much needed fresh fruit and vegetables, and while Helen had disappeared somewhere with Billy, Joe ran into George in the middle of the crowded plaza. "Just the person I want to see," he said as he greeted him.

"What's on your mind?"

"Diesel," Joe said. When George appeared perplexed, he added, "Diesel fuel. I was wondering if we could top up our tank with some. We used more than I expected as we tried to avoid the worst of the storm that brought us here."

"Ah…" George exclaimed as he realized what Joe was referring to. "There isn't any. No one uses hydrocarbon fuels anymore. They no longer exist. People finally realized a good part of the catastrophe that almost wiped us out was excessive use of hydrocarbon fuels and ceased their manufacture. It was too late; the damage had been done. We still suffer the consequences today. Bees, butterflies, and other pollinating insects vanished. If it wasn't excessive use of insecticides, the hotter temperatures killed them, which makes growing food difficult. On a small scale like we have here, crops are hand pollinated, and that's enough for a town this size. It's much harder to do on a large scale though. The planet is a lot warmer than it used to be, and there are many parts that will remain uninhabitable and unstable for a long time yet."

Joe wasn't surprised. Back in his time the signs of a massive impending disaster were everywhere— he'd been reporting on some of them for a major news channel —but it was ignored. No one was willing to do anything about it. Everyone thought it would be fixed by future generations… Well, it wasn't, and now the whole world is fucked.

"Everything runs on electricity," George continued, "either broadcast, or generated from solar arrays and modular nuclear plants. They gave up on wind power… too unreliable. Those monstrous turbines scattered across the country did nothing but ruin the environment. They barely lasted a few years before they fused, burnt out, fell over or were blown down in severe storms that also destroyed many of the solar farms. All that money wasted on pipe-dreams of idiotic politicians. The turbines offshore along the coast were washed away by tsunamis." He paused to clarify his thoughts, adding, "The storms raged on and off for two hundred years before the climate stabilized into what we have now."

Again, Joe was reminded that no matter how normal everything appeared, it was another time, a thousand years after the one he'd been born into, and he still had to come to terms with it.

"We don't have nuclear here, but we do get solar and broadcast power in abundance." As he said this, George pointed vaguely towards the sun which glared down upon them. "Come, I'll show you."

Joe allowed George to lead him through the people milling in the plaza. Beyond the edge of the crowded plaza, he gestured towards the large dish pointing up into the sky.

"There are several satellites put up by the South Americans in geosynchronous orbits that receive power from the sun, convert it to electromagnetic waves which are broadcast down to earth. Dishes, like the one here, receive and convert it into electricity to be used directly day and night by those connected to the system. Those using solar power have batteries for storage and use at night. Solar is basically backup if the orbiting power sats go offline."

"Has that ever happened?"

"No, not in my lifetime. But you never know… There's a lot of old shit still orbiting up there and sometimes those in lower orbits decay and crash into each other before falling to Earth."

"But you do have vegetable oils…" Joe started to say, bringing the conversation back to his immediate problem.

"Of course. olive oil, rape seed oil, canola… There are many different oils used in cooking, and for lubricating machinery, but not fuel oils. Everything runs on electric power."

"Perhaps I could use refined vegetable oil." Joe said hesitantly. "It wouldn't run very efficiently, but it would work."

"Why bother. We can change your motor to an electric one. With a small receiving dish, and an inverter, you could have all the power you need day and night."

Why would they do that? What would they want from us in return?

"It would be an interesting challenge, but I'm sure we can do it. You know, I've never seen a hydrocarbon fueled engine before."

Joe didn't know what to say. He would of course speak to Mary about it because it was her yacht. The idea of a silent electric motor sounded good. He tried to picture electric boats, electric planes, cars, trucks, tractors, everything… but found it difficult. They were experimenting with this before the disaster hit, and he remembered they even had small planes in limited numbers. But batteries were the problem, with some exploding and burning furiously when being recharged. Sometimes they exploded spontaneously. He remembered that happening on a plane full of passengers that luckily was near an airport and could make an emergency landing. No one was injured but the plane was a write-off. They also restricted how much power could be used. Planes and trucks required a lot of power all the time and could only be used for short spells before needing to be recharged, but continuous broadcast power beamed down from orbit was never ending. It changed everything. All you needed was an appropriate receiver and inverter.

"I'll organize it tomorrow," George said before Joe had time to even think of something to say. "Might take a couple of days though, depending on what needs modifying."

"What do we have that we can give them in exchange for that?" Mary asked Joe when he told her.

"Nothing. Money's no good, not that we've got much of that."

"So why would they go to the trouble of changing the motor, and converting everything to running on broadcast power? Our solar cells, the wind generator and battery are good enough for the stove and the navigation aids we use."

Joe shrugged. "You can't run a big motor on battery power for any length of time…but continuous broadcast power, that's different. Maybe they just want to be nice— but he thought nobody does stuff like that without recompense of some kind —I think it's a good idea. The motor's useless without fuel, and there's hardly any left in the tank. Once that's gone, it's a dead weight. They'll upgrade our solar power and rewire everything to be more efficient too, so we might as well let them do it."

"I suppose so," Mary reluctantly acquiesced.

With George accompanying them to make sure the new motor functioned as it was supposed to, Joe and Mary cruised out several kilometres into the long strait that extended to the great Southern Ocean. There was an even swell and the yacht travelled smoothly with its new engine silently running while its sails remained furled. The only sound accompanying them was the swish of water along the sides of the hull as the yacht sliced through the gentle swells, and the squawk of seagulls that followed their wake hoping to catch fish or shrimp disturbed by their passing.

"I must say it runs far better than I expected."

George smiled.

"It seems strange to be moving so fast without the rumble of the original engine underfoot."

George looked puzzled, and Joe explained, "When it was running you could feel its vibrations through the deck. To be moving without any sound or vibrations will take getting used to."

"I like it," Mary said. "So quiet, so peaceful."

"We fitted a bigger engine than you probably need for a boat this size. I always say it's better to have something in reserve... You never know when you might need it. At the moment it's running on half power, so there's plenty in reserve."

They stood in the cockpit and listened and all they heard was the soft slosh of water slicing along the hull, the splash the bow made as it cut into an oncoming swell, the gentle gurgle of water as it flowed away behind the propellers beneath the stern.

"You won't need to use the sails anymore," George said.

"Oh yes we will," Joe said. "This is a sloop, a classic sailing boat. The sails make it what it is, and once we're out in the open ocean where there are real seas to contend with, we'll still need the sails."

"It doesn't matter where you are," George said. "Broadcast power is everywhere."

"Have you ever been out on the open ocean?" Joe asked.

"No,"

"Then you have no idea. This sea here might be salty and is sea water as far as that goes, but it's nothing more than a big lake. I can smell the dry land and the desert around us. It might even get choppy if it gets too windy, but it's not the ocean where there are thousands of kilometres in every direction with nothing but water. The ocean is an enormous space for wind to build up waves. And believe me it can be wild at times. There can be waves three times the height of the mast on this sloop. One after another, they never stop coming. A motor, any kind of motor, is good for cruising inland, up rivers, across lakes like this one as big as it is, or in passages between clusters of islands close inshore to a coast, but out on the open ocean a sailing sloop comes into its own. It was designed and built for that... We'll keep the sails, and we'll use them when we really are out on the open sea."

"But we do appreciate your efforts and have no way to thank you for what you've done," Mary, ever the diplomat, said.

"Would you like to take the wheel and run us back to the village?" Joe asked.

George smiled. "Yes, I would."

Joe moved aside to let George take control. He took the sloop in a wide circle finishing on a heading back towards the distant promontory where Eyresea was located.

The sun sparkled on the waves splashing fragments of light across the yacht as it moved swiftly through the water on its return.

9...

There were three men waiting for them when they walked off the jetty into the square. A small crowd had gathered around the perimeter of the square, quietly watching. The three waiting in the middle of the town square wore dark uniforms festooned with a variety of weapons, and their heads were covered with a helmet not unlike a motorcycle helmet. They had dark visors covering their faces.

Joe stared at them, noting their stances and the way the held themselves. It seemed to him that they had no fear of anything, that they expected the local townsfolk to kowtow to them. *Arrogant bastards*, he thought. He glanced at George, who the instant he'd seen them waiting, had hesitated, broken his stride, almost stumbling before regaining composure to continue walking as before.

"Who are they?" Joe asked.

"Enforcers," George said softly, and when Joe looked puzzled, he explained, "Government police. We haven't seen then around here for years. I don't like it one bit."

More like military than police, Joe decided. "What do you think they want?"

There was obviously more to this world than he had imagined.

"They probably want to have a talk to you about how you got here," George said apologetically.

"How the fuck did they know we were here?"

"Your arrival would have been detected via satellite monitoring. They 're always watching."

Watching for what? "And what if I don't want to talk to them?"

"You don't have a choice."

"We'll see about that."

As they stepped off the wooden jetty and entered the square Joe glanced towards the people watching from the edges to see if he could see Helen and Billy, but they were not visible. *Billy's a smart kid; he's probably keeping Helen out of sight. He'd know who these arseholes are.*

Joe put his hand on George's arm and said, "Stop here."

George hesitated but stopped when Joe stopped. "They expect us to walk up to them," he mumbled.

"They can come to us. If they want to talk to me, I'll wait here."

"Not a good idea…"

"Relax. Let's see how this plays out." And saying that, Joe moved slightly ahead and away from George so there was a space between them. If anything was to happen, he didn't want George to be hurt. He smiled and looked directly towards the three dark suited men, waiting for them to react.

When it became obvious to the three waiting men that Joe was not coming to them, they looked at each other, glanced around to see where the locals were, looked back at Joe, then started walking towards him. They spaced themselves out as they walked and when they had reached him, they stopped each about a metre distant from him, partially surrounding him. This they did with not a word spoken between them that Joe could hear. He had no doubt they communicated with each other via radio, but their voices didn't sound outside their helmets.

He waited, maintaining a relaxed posture, saying nothing. A hint of a smile still lingered on his face.

The man on his left placed his right hand on a truncheon strapped to his belt while the man on his right had a hand on the butt of a holstered pistol. The man in the middle spread his arms wide, a gesture not unlike someone expecting to receive a hug. A friendly gesture. "You need to come with us," he said.

"I don't talk to people who keep their faces obscured," Joe said.

The three men stiffened. People normally complied with what they demanded.

Silence. The soft murmur of waves washing the beach filled the air.

Not a sound emanated from any of those watching from the

edges of the square. George shook his head slightly but didn't move from where he was standing.

"Okay," the man in the centre said. He raised one hand to the side of his visor and lifted it to expose his face. It looked pale and hard against the black of his helmet. His eyes glittered as if light bounced of facets of a lens. "Is that better?"

"Yes. What do you want?"

"You need to come with us."

"Why?"

"Because you don't belong here."

"What does that mean? That I don't belong here in this town, or that I don't belong here in the world?" As he said this, he glanced to his left to see that man's grip tightening on the truncheon, preparing to draw it and strike.

"Both. That's why we need to talk to you. To you and your companions." The man in the centre said trying to keep Joe's attention on him.

After a deliberate pause while he studied the three men Joe said, "We don't need to do anything."

The moment he'd finished the man on his left drew and raised his truncheon to strike Joe. That was a mistake.

Instantly Joe moved inside the strike almost before it began, slipping forward with his left foot he extended his left arm to slightly deflect the down-coming strike, and wrapped his arm around the attacker's right arm to lock the elbow.

A sudden upward jerk with Joe's left arm snapped hard against the man's elbow. The truncheon fell to the ground. The man's scream of pain was blotted out as Joe took another small step with his right foot blocking the man's front leg so he couldn't step back and smashed a flat palm against the man's visor. He went down in a heap as Joe released him. The other two were momentarily stunned that Joe had moved so quickly and unexpectedly. Before the man in the centre could move, Joe lashed out with a snap kick to the side of that man's knee, and he too went down to the ground being unable to stand with damaged ligaments. The third man had drawn his pistol, but Joe slapped it aside as he moved in, grabbed the man's head and twisted it, so this man too went down in a heap. He didn't move when he hit the ground. The man in the centre, despite his damaged knee, had managed to draw his pistol and was bringing it up to aim at Joe, but George stepped in and took it off him, then offered it butt first to Joe.

"Thanks," Joe said. He took the pistol.

"It won't do you any good," The man on the ground in the centre said through a grimace of pain.

"They're coded to each individual's fingerprints and DNA," George said.

"I see." Joe turned, walked a couple of steps back towards the jetty and threw the pistol out into the water before returning to the men on the ground. "You need to take your two associates and get them to a hospital," he told the man in the centre.

George helped the man to stand. He could barely balance as his damaged knee wouldn't support him. The man with the injured elbow struggled to his feet, his injured arm dangling by his side. He moved to help his companion with the injured knee. He didn't think of drawing his pistol, after seeing what Joe had done. They both looked down at the third man who lay unmoving on the ground. He was still breathing.

"I'll get some townsfolk to help get him to the aircar," George said. He waved and gestured to those watching and several men reluctantly came forward to help lift and carry the third injured man. They followed the two injured enforcers supporting each other as they struggled to hobble to their aircar and helped the seriously injured man into it.

It was only then that Joe noticed the aircar parked off to one side of the square under a shade tree. It was dark, almost black and blended into the shadows beneath the tree. He watched silently as the townsfolk loaded the unconscious man into the rear of the vehicle, after which the other two struggled to get into the front seats. The car moved from under the tree and spread insect-like wings out before it lifted above the surface, blowing small clouds of dust about.

When it had taken off and was headed southeast over the desert beyond the town, Joe let out a sigh of relief.

"Why am I not surprised at what you just did?" George asked rhetorically as they watched the aircar disappear into the distance. Once it had vanished from sight he said, "That won't be the end of it. They'll send another lot to come and get you."

"Why? Why are we important to them? And who the fuck are they anyway?"

"You're an anomaly, that's why. You don't belong here. How you got here is what they want to know,"

"What good will that do them? I've no idea how we got here."

"But they think you do. And no doubt they think if they could get that knowledge from you, they could replicate it, and use it for their benefit. They control the whole country, what's left of it, from one central location. Used to be the old capitol of the country."

"Canberra?"

"Canbra. That's it. You know the place?"

"I've been there… a long time ago. Still full of arseholes by the look of it."

"You're right about that. They're desperate to find a better place to move to. To move everyone to. The way you arrived gives them hope that there is a way out."

"There is no way out. You live with the world the way it is. You adapt, you go on, you survive; or you don't."

"But they don't think like that. Everyone works for them. Even towns like this, of which there are a few scattered around the country trying to be independent of their centralized system, eventually need them for the technology they can supply. We wouldn't survive without that."

"Yes, you would. It wouldn't be comfortable, but humans are innovative and have survived without technological stuff for thousands of years and managed to build viable civilizations. If you have to, you will. It may be inevitable."

People emerged from where they'd been watching what unfolded in the square. Mary had been watching from the yacht and she came and stood beside Joe. Seeing how quickly he'd handled those three men brought back memories of the time she'd been a captive on her yacht and how Joe had taken out the gang members responsible before releasing her and going on to rescue Helen. Unlike these three, those men didn't survive.

"I'm not so sure I like this place so much after all," she said.

"I think we should get ready to leave. I'd hate to bring more trouble down on the people of this town." Joe said to Mary as she stood beside him.

Suddenly Helen who had been watching from the sidelines along with half the townsfolk was by their side, an anxious look on her face. "What the hell was that all about?"

Billy was with her, looking at Joe with respect. Most of the other townsfolk held back, willing to listen but not to ask questions.

"Wherever you go they'll follow you. They will be monitoring you by satellite so you can't hide," George said.

"I won't try to hide. I'll talk to them, but on my terms. I will not let them drag me in like a criminal to be interrogated. Next time it happens, I won't be so lenient."

"Ah, yeah... I imagine they'll be a lot more careful the next time they approach you." There was a degree of respect in George's voice. He had been as stunned as the three policemen at Joe's ability to take them down in a few seconds.

Mary gave Joe a slight nudge with her elbow to let him know she understood exactly what he meant. Joe looked at her and smiled.

Truth was, he hadn't been trying to impress anyone, he'd simply reacted to the situation as it unfolded, using a minimum of force to subdue them without doing undue damage, although he may have gone a bit far with the third man. Wearing that helmet had made it hard to determine exactly how far to twist the head without breaking or dislocating bones in his neck. He hoped that the man would recover, and that no serious damage had been done. Still, he tried to draw a gun on me, Joe rationalized, and that justified the action he'd taken.

"We should arrange what supplies we can and leave as soon as possible so there'll be no reason for them to come here and bother you if they can track us and see that we've gone."

"Where would you go? You know you can't go north."

"I thought we might return to the city we came from, to see if there's anything left after all these years. We can get there by following the way to the open ocean and then travel along the coast..." He turned to Mary. "If that's okay with you?"

She looked bemused for a second. It was nice of Joe to ask her. She was content on the yacht— it was after all her home —and happy to leave decisions like that to him.

"I doubt there's much left of it after a thousand years." George said.

"Maybe, but I'd like to know what happened to the people who stayed behind. At least it's a goal to work towards."

"A thousand years ago...?"

"Yeah, I keep forgetting." He shook his head as if to clear it of accumulated rubble.

"Unfortunately," Mary said, "We don't have any way we can pay you."

"I wouldn't worry about that," George said. "We have more than enough to help friends in need."

Billy had moved closer to Joe, and he gently tapped Joe's arm. "What about me?" He asked softly.

Joe looked at George, caught his eye, and asked, "Has Billy spoken to you about coming with us? I was going to talk to you about it. I know it's a bit sudden, our imminent departure, but I do think it's better for all if we move on sooner than later."

"He mentioned it, and I've thought about it. I don't think he'll ever find his father if something like what happened to you happened to him, but it's time he went out into the wider world. Everyone needs the opportunity to discover themselves as they experience the world around them. It would help him in ways we can't imagine. I have every confidence he'll be in safe hands if he goes with you."

Billy's face lit up. "Yes!" He whispered.

Joe could see Helen smiling too.

"Are you willing to take him with you?" George asked.

"He'll be fine. We'll need someone who knows this world to

help us, and you needn't worry, we'll look after him."

"You will return and bring him back at some stage?"

"Of course. We would love to come back. You've been very kind to us…"

"Then it's settled. Let's see about what supplies we can give you for your voyage." Then almost as an afterthought, he dug into his pocket and found a translucent card. He handed it to Joe. "You'll need this as well. I took the liberty of loading enough credits on it so you have a way of paying for things you might need."

Reflexively Joe accepted the card offered. "I don't know what to say…"

"Don't say anything. It can't be traced back to me or anyone here. If you need to buy something, supplies, whatever, use it." He reached out and grasped Joe's shoulder, gave it a squeeze, let go and walked away.

10...

"We're not going north, are we?" Billy asked, his disappointment showing.

Eyresea and the peninsula was nothing more than a slight smudge against the horizon behind them. The sea sparkled with sunlight glistening off the tops of small swells that rolled by them. A steady breeze filled the mainsail and the yacht cruised smoothly through the water. Several gulls and other unidentified sea birds hovered above the wake behind the yacht.

When Joe didn't answer he said, "Why aren't you using the motor?"

Joe smiled as he answered. "Because I prefer to use the sails whenever I can to improve my ability as a sailor, and not rely on a motor to power us."

Seeing Billy's puzzled expression he added, "I once had a runabout, a small motor powered vessel, before I met Mary and her yacht. I'd never used a sailing boat until three months ago. I'm still learning... The more practice I get, the better."

"But broadcast power is free, and always there."

Thinking of it in terms of solar power, Joe said, "What about when it's cloudy or when the sun isn't shining?"

"Makes no difference," Billy stated. "Broadcast power is like radio waves. It passes though cloud layers, buildings too, and is broadcast at night as well. The sun in space never sets and the geosynchronous satellites are always in the sun, always broadcasting. There's no shortage of power."

Joe had no answer to that. Broadcast power in his time was an improbable dream. He had yet to accept the reality of it. Like setting up a colony on Mars to guarantee human survivors. He wondered when that had happened; had the tsunami and subsequent rise in sea levels delayed that possibility or initiated its eventual success? George told him colonies on the Moon and Mars had been established by the South Americans with launch facilities in Northern Argentina shared with Brazil, and they were actively sending people there. But his mind still saw it as a dream, not a reality.

Helen, after lounging on the deck space in front of the cabin joined them in the cockpit. "Why do you want to go north?" she asked Billy. "We were nowhere near that wall of shimmering heat, yet it was so hot we could hardly breathe. If we hadn't headed south, it would have killed us. Is it because your father went that way and never came back?"

Billy nodded.

"So," Joe said, "either of two things happened to him."

Billy looked expectantly at Joe.

"One, he died from heat exposure," Joe said bluntly, almost harshly, but added "Like George said, when the wet-bulb temperature is more than 35 degrees, humans and most mammals begin to cook as their organs heat up and the body can't be cooled. I wouldn't wish that on my worst enemy."

Billy nodded.

"And?" Helen said.

"The second possibility is your father was dragged into one of those weird electrical storms that we encountered which shifted us through time to here and now. He may still be alive somewhere, —and Joe saw hope flicker across Billy's face— but not in this time, or he would have come back. Perhaps he's in the past somewhere, or worse still, in the future, who knows how many years ahead… If he went into the past, he would know what was ahead and perhaps could have left a message for you."

"There were no messages of any kind." Billy said sadly.

The three of them stood silently for a few moments, allowing the sounds of the water slicing past the yacht to fill the emptiness. Billy looked back along the wake the yacht left but there was no sign anymore of Eyresea and the peninsula it nestled into. Turning back to Joe he asked, "Does that mean he didn't go into the past?"

"Based on what happened to us… We were shifted a thousand

years into the future. Maybe these time shifts only work one way."

"You think he's in the future? And that's why he couldn't send a message?"

"There's no way to know unless we encounter another storm like the one which brought us here and go through it to see where it takes us. That's not something I want to do again."

"Me either," Helen agreed.

"I don't think there is a way back," Joe said. "People who disappeared never came back. We would have heard about it if they did." And to change the subject, "Let's just enjoy the day. The weather is not always so benign."

"It's nearly always like this," Billy assured them.

Joe smiled. "Wait till we got further south and into the real ocean."

"Yeah," Helen chuckled, "just wait and see."

Two days later the strait they sailed through began to narrow. The shadow of land on both sides, West as well as East was becoming more prominent. On the western side smudges of red and deep ochre indicated a low lying mountain range stretching to the far west. On the eastern side there was nothing remarkable, just more sand dunes and scattered dark rusty stones. No trees. But sometimes, when it wasn't so hazy with dust in the air Joe thought he saw an occasional flash of sunlight off a metal surface a few hundred metres in the air.

"We're being followed," he said to Billy beside him in the cockpit learning to keep the yacht on steady course. "There's an aircar keeping pace with us."

Looking in the direction Joe indicated, Billy also saw a brief flash of sunlight reflected off the glassine screen of a flying vehicle. "Yeah, that's an aircar," he affirmed. It was flying parallel to the coastline, drifting along, keeping pace with them.

"Do they think we can't see them?" Joe asked.

"They don't care if we see them," Billy said. "They won't fly out over the water. They'll keep pace with us that's all."

"Why wont they go over water?"

"It affects their ability to receive power. I don't know… upsets the supply through reflection or something. Causes feedback that shorts out the engine and they crash."

"But I can use the engine in this boat without feedback occurring.?"

"It's different, being on the water and receiving. In the air they also get reflection up off the water as well as direct receiving… I don't know how it works but it sets up some kind of resonance that stuffs up their electronics, so they don't fly over large bodies of water."

"That's interesting. If we stay far enough out to sea, they can't follow us and won't know where we are?"

"Not exactly. Satellite monitoring can find us, but the satellites are not always overhead like the power satellites. They travel in low orbit around the earth several times each day and night so there are times when they cannot observe us."

"So, we can give them the slip and hide, or change course when they can't see us and not be where they expect to see us when the satellite passes over again."

"I suppose… But what good will that do? There's nowhere to hide out here."

"I'm not trying to hide. I was just thinking though…"

"You can see them at night," Billy said, "like faint fast moving stars travelling across the sky. I'll show you later. Once it's gone over you have an hour before it comes back for another pass."

They fell silent, enjoying the wind gently blowing, filling the sails, powering the yacht, while listening to the rush of water past the hull as it cleanly sliced through the waves, and the cries of sea birds hovering and floating in the air above their wake.

The next morning it was clear they were entering a strait. The land on either side, to west as well as east, kept getting closer. Ahead they could see the space they had to travel through ominously narrowing.

"It's quite narrow where we go through," Billy explained as Joe studied the distant converging cliff faces with binoculars.

"You've been here before?" Joe asked.

"No. We learnt about it in school. There was a low lying part of a mountain range blocking the rising sea. The government sent a team to blast an opening through the range with small nuclear explosions to connect the lake to the Southern Ocean."

"What about radiation?" Helen, who had joined them looked worried.

"That was six hundred years ago. There's no radiation now. Wasn't any after a few months."

"That's a relief," Helen said with a big smile.

"They did that so you could access the ocean?" Joe asked.

"Well, yes. There were plans for settlements on the western side, and they needed to bring ships and supplies in, but authorities had problems with rebellious people who claimed possession of the land on the west side, so it didn't go ahead."

They fell silent for a few moments as the yacht sailed steadily forward. Ahead Joe could see the sides of the low-lying mountains were suddenly much closer than before. Jagged rocky scarps which on inspection through binoculars confirmed they had been fused, no doubt from the nuclear explosions that Billy talked about. Weathering had started eroding them. Cracks had gathered dust and soil giving sparse vegetation a chance to take hold in some places. Most of the scarps though were bare rock, deep red or dark brown depending on the angle you looked at them. In some places there were hints of purple in the shadows. Seen against the deep blue of the ocean water the place had a serene beauty that Joe imagined had been in existence for millions of years.

As they approached the narrowest section, the sea in the 'canyon' was obviously disturbed with strong currents swirling through it as the tide was running out. Waves were choppy and wind in the canyon was confusing, not flowing smoothly along the stretch but bouncing off the side walls and twisting back on itself. He was not a good enough sailor to even consider sailing through that. Running on the engine was the sensible option. But he was having second thoughts when he saw how disturbed the water ahead was in the narrowest part of the canyon. He should have anchored before entering the canyon and waited for the tide to change. They could then easily travel through while the water remained calm for an hour or so before it flowed back with the incoming tide. *Too late now...*

Joe with Billy's help quickly reefed in the sails.

Can't turn back now, Joe affirmed as the yacht was shoved and pushed with great force.

"We'll run through with the motor. It will give us better control than the sails. The bloody wind is all over the place, and there's no room to tack."

As with all narrow straits connected to the ocean, whenever the tide was coming in or going out, the narrowness restricted the flow of water, and it would build up on one side and rush through the narrow section towards the lower level on the other side. The water would roar over the shallow area, humping and splashing, churned into foaming waves that swirled and twisted with incredible force, smashing into the sides of the canyon before bouncing back into the middle where the flow was faster and stronger. Looking down at the water flowing through the narrowest section an observer would have thought it was a massive waterfall, only instead of being vertical and flowing down, it was horizontal and flowing out.

With Helen standing beside him looking worried, he said, "Strap yourself to the rail here so you won't get thrown overboard." He called out to Billy who was on the fore-deck in front of the cabin having finished storing the reefed sail in its locker to do the same.

The yacht lurched upwards a metre before dropping back down again as the water beneath them humped over a rocky ledge on the shallow bottom of the canyon. Billy was flung up into the air as the yacht leaned sideways underneath him. When he landed, he fell awkwardly and slid towards the starboard rail, which he immediately grabbed. He clipped his harness to the side rail, before standing again one hand on the rail to steady himself. "I'm okay," he called out over the roar of the rushing water around them.

The yacht lurched to the side as the flowing water moved around another obstruction beneath them. The yacht shuddered and vibrated, dropped briefly before being slammed up again. There was a crash inside the cabin as things fell over.

I hope Mary's okay, Joe thought, gripping the steering wheel so hard his hands turned white.

He was about to ask Helen to go down and see how Mary was when the yacht again lurched sideways. Billy was flung over the side rail. Being strapped on he didn't completely enter the water. His legs were under, and white foam splashed around him as he was dragged through the water beside the yacht. He was still clinging to the rail as well as being held by the cable strapped to it, but he didn't have enough strength to pull himself back in. It was hard enough to keep his head and chest above the rushing water.

Joe instantly let go of the steering, unclipped his harness and reattached it to the rail on the starboard side. "Hang on Billy," he yelled. "I'm coming."

Helen grabbed the steering wheel and did her best to keep the yacht steady as Joe made his way forward to where Billy was desperately clinging to the rail. A second later, at Billy's side, he grabbed him with both hands, hauling the frightened young lad back on board. They both hunched down and hung on as the yacht almost spun around before straightening itself in preparation to ride over the massively corrugated water ahead.

Neither of them said a word until they were back in the cockpit and strapped in.

"I'll go down and see if Mary's okay," Helen said.

"Be careful."

She nodded, unclipped her harness and took the two steps to the hatch where she grabbed it firmly before allowing herself to drop down into the cabin. "There's a bit of mess here to clean up," she yelled out over the noise of the rushing water. "But Mary's okay."

Joe relaxed. *Good*, he thought, *now I can focus on steering through this crap.* He increased power to the motor and felt the yacht respond. No longer pushed by the rapidly flowing water, it cut through it. That's better.

Ahead, the water was less chaotic. There were no more whirlpools, only a series of humps as the water flowed over underwater ridges. *Looks like we're through the worst of it.* The yacht would ride over and through that with ease. With the motor powering them he had control again. They were traveling slightly faster than the fierce flowing water, no longer being pushed and shoved, no longer a piece of flotsam at the mercy of rushing water.

"That was some ride," Billy exclaimed as the yacht steadied.

They were through the narrowest portion with both sides retreating to become distant shorelines again. The current rapidly diminished as it had a wide area to spread into. Joe relaxed, letting the tension he'd accumulated dissipate. Ahead, off to the east a brief flash of sunlight caught his attention. *Those bastards are still up there watching us.*

"You should have told me how rough it gets," Joe said, "I would have waited for the tide to change before entering,"

"I had no idea. I've never been here before."

When he saw how upset Billy looked, he smiled and clapped him on the back. "It's okay Billy, don't worry about it."

"It could have been a disaster."

"But we got through it. When we come back, we'll be a lot smarter. We'll wait for still water in between tide changes."

He smiled at Billy and after pause said, "It was one hell of a ride though, wasn't it?"

11...

"I hate to say it," Mary said as she sipped a cup of tea with Joe in the main cabin while Helen and Billy were up on deck sailing the yacht, "I'm getting too old to be of any use. You should have left me back there."

"You can't be serious. This is your home."

"I know. And I love it. But look at me. I haven't been the same since we came through that anomaly. It sucked the energy out of me. I'm exhausted. I'm an impediment..."

"Don't say that."

"What's going to happen when we hit bad weather? And we will, there's no question about that when we get down into the open ocean again."

"Harold built a magnificent boat. There won't be a problem with bad weather."

Mary smiled briefly at the mention of her late husband, who had never lived to see how well his creation performed at sea.

"I'm too frail to be of any use Joe, you should have left me behind."

Joe shook his head. There was no point arguing with her. She was right. She was frail and looking... almost ancient. He hadn't noticed before, there had always been too much happening, but now that they were sitting quietly...

Mary stood up and even though the yacht was quite stable, with the narrow stretch of wild water well behind them, she made sure she was holding onto something as she stepped into the galley.

Joe studied her as she took each step. Her frailty had come on rapidly. She hadn't been like that before they came through the storms that shifted them into this future. He remembered how she seemed to have had a heart attack after they found themselves vomiting while on hands and knees in the aftermath of the storm.

It was bad enough for himself and Helen, but Mary being much older... He'd thought for a moment she was going to die. The week they'd spent in Eyresea where Billy lived brought some colour and strength back, but she had moved carefully and slowly since then. It was also evident that she had lost weight, was thinner than he'd remembered. She certainly looked frail. Although they were not related and had only known each other a short time he'd come to regard her as he did his late mother, and he was worried.

He would never leave her behind, and she'd not suggested it before. Had she done so he would have argued the chances of them returning were remote, and he certainly wouldn't leave her there with that a possibility. This was her home. It wouldn't be the same without her on board.

Regarding Billy, he had an unmentioned understanding with George that the likelihood of them returning would be remote at best, and that Billy would have to make his own way in the world, just as his father had done before him. But he'd promised to return, and if it was at all possible, he would keep that promise.

"Hey Joe," Billy yelled out from above, "Get up here quick."

Joe leaped to his feet and with a glance towards Mary indicating she should remain calm, he launched himself up through the hatch and onto the deck beside Helen and Billy who were staring and pointing towards a large ungainly boat coming towards them from the west.

There were people running around on the fore-deck doing something with what looked like a canon.

"Who are they?" Joe asked.

"Pirates," Billy said. "People from the west. Wild people,"

"I suppose they think we are a juicy target," Joe said.

"They think anyone is juicy target," Billy said. "They are why we don't get many boats coming through into the sea like we used to."

"Helen," Joe said turning towards her, "Can you go down and get the rifle please."

She disappeared instantly, to return a moment later with said rifle. "It's loaded, but there's not a lot of extra ammunition."

"I know. But I only need one or two shots." He checked to see if the safety was on and released it.

From the approaching craft there was a puff of smoke, followed by the sound of an explosive charge detonating and a crude harpoon shot out of the canon trailing a long cable. Accompanied by wild yelling and gesticulating, the vessel that fired it continued to come closer.

Joe felt an impulse to laugh but resisted the temptation. Flying in an arc towards them was what looked like a long metal lance with a barb on one side, a primitive harpoon. The cable connected to it was obviously going to be used to drag them towards the raiders or to pull the two boats together so they could board the captured vessel.

"Steer away from them," he told Billy who immediately complied.

The harpoon instead of landing on the deck as it would have had they kept to the course and not changed, hit the side of their yacht with a loud clang and a scraping noise before it dropped into water rushing past their hull.

"That's enough provocation for me to fire back at them."

Joe raised the rifle and took careful aim at the man who had fired the canon. The men around the canon were staring at them in surprise. They had expected the lance to penetrate the hull so they could drag the boats together. They had not expected it to bounce off and fall into the water. The weight of it dragging through the water slowed them down, causing their boat to founder and twist.

"They must have thought we had a wooden hull," Joe said.

He squeezed the trigger.

The sound of the shot was muffled by the water rushing past the hull.

The man behind the canon yelled, jerked backwards and crashed onto the deck of the attacking boat. Those around him immediately froze, then in confusion dragged their fallen comrade away from the bow of the boat.

There was no need for another shot. Joe passed the rifle back to Helen. "We won't need it again."

"Did you kill him?" Helen asked.

"No. Shot him in the leg. A warning to leave us alone."

They watched the pirate boat grow smaller as they surged away from it. The last thing he saw was the men hauling back on board the harpoon they'd fired, before their boat turned away and headed back towards the western shore.

Billy had a broad grin across his face. "That'll teach them," he said out loud.

Mary appeared in the hatchway. "What happened? There was one heck of loud noise. Did something crash into us?"

"Those bastards retreating fired a lance at us. It bounced off the hull." Joe said.

"I'll check it out," Billy said and immediately ran towards the bow. Holding onto the rail he leaned over and studied the spot where the lance had hit them. "There's a bit of a dint and a long scratch," he called back over his shoulder. "No other damage that I can see."

"See, everything's fine," Joe assured Mary. "We'll paint over it later when we find a spot to stay awhile."

"I guess that's our excitement for today," Helen said. She held up the rifle. "I'll put this away now."

Sitting at anchor in a secluded bay on the eastern side of the straight, Joe, Mary Helen and Billy were on the fore-deck relaxing after their evening meal, while the boat rocked gently in the soft waves washing ashore. The night was flawless. The moon had yet to rise, and the sky was resplendent with so many stars brilliantly shining Joe couldn't help the feeling of amazement that flooded his being. Back in his time less than half of these stars had been visible due to pollutants in the air. With that gone for a thousand years, the sky was again looking as it had when primitive humans first looked up and wondered. And as the Earth turned, he saw the beginnings of the Milky Way reaching above the horizon, *the edge of our galaxy,* a view nothing short of astonishing. He was also aware of the bright redness of Mars, and not far from it a brilliant star that didn't twinkle so it must have been a planet. *Jupiter? Or*

Saturn? Then his eye was caught by a small star moving across the sky. He hadn't noticed it at first because he was so taken by the grandeur of the night sky, but once he caught it moving, he followed it with his eyes as it moved across the sky.

"That's one of the satellites," Billy said. He was pointing up to it.

"Seems too bright..."

"It's in a low orbit. It takes around thirty-five minutes to go over. And an hour or thereabouts before we will see it return."

"What about the International Space Station? Is that still up there? It should be brighter than that."

"It's not up there."

"Was it decommissioned?"

"As far as I know, from history lessons, it fell out of orbit around the time we were hit with gravity waves. No one on board survived. It broke up in the upper atmosphere and the pieces that didn't burn up on re-entry ended up in the remote southern Pacific."

"And the Chinese space station?"

"Same thing. Knocked out of orbit and burnt up in the atmosphere, like almost all the near Earth orbit satellites. They suffered the same fate."

And suddenly the memory of the moment he'd seen what he thought was a meteor shower the night the Tsunami rolled by underneath them hit him— *That was it, that was the space station coming down!*

"What is it?" Mary asked when Joe had been silent and staring up at the sky for a while.

"Nothing. I was remembering something." He turned to Billy and asked, "Who put up the power satellites?"

"Brazil and Argentina. They're the only two places with the resources to get us back into space, even if it's only power satellites and smaller earth monitoring satellites to keep an eye on developing deterioration of weather as global warming continues. There's no one in the northern hemisphere, what's left of it, capable of doing anything like that. Australia and the southern part of Africa have evolved other technologies, but getting into space wasn't the way they decided to go."

"And what about the satellites you say the enforcers here use to monitor the population?"

"They paid the Argentinians to launch them, as far as I know."

"So, there is contact between South America, and us. What about southern Africa?"

"No one knows what's happening there."

"And is the weather getting worse?" Mary asked.

"Not that you'd notice. But over time it will get hotter and the uninhabitable zone around the equator will widen. There are plans to move to Antarctica, which is now free of ice for the most part."

"Can everybody move there?"

"Yeah, essentially the world population in the southern hemisphere isn't that large anymore. There's plenty of room. But who would want to go there? The land is barren with only wild grasses and scrub growing. Lots of sea birds though. There are no trees… I mean it was covered in ice for millions of years. There's hardly been any time for anything to grow or evolve there. We're better off here where we are."

He stopped for a moment, uncertain whether he believed that or not, finally deciding that he didn't believe it after all, but he also didn't want to go to Antarctica.

"The South Americans are focusing on getting back into space and re-establishing a colony on the Moon and doing the same on Mars," he continued. "They're not interested in Antarctica. They see it as a short term solution. The long term one is to reestablish humanity on another planet, and Mars is the only possibility we have."

"Why is that?" Helen asked.

"Because Mars is not unlike Earth only colder and drier. Earth will keep warming, maybe too much for humans to stay here, maybe not. No one knows for sure. But they want to have the option of being able to survive off Earth, to become an interplanetary species."

"Ah Billy, all that sounds fine," Joe said. "As far as I can remember, it seems nothing in that regard has changed. The players are different. We had gone back to the Moon and established a base there, and private space companies were developing rockets to take colonists to Mars to establish an off planet foothold in case a disaster befell us on Earth. Unfortunately, the disaster happened before they could do it. There was a base on the Moon, but no one had gone to Mars."

"It's being done now," Billy said. "There is a Moon colony, and soon Mars too will have people living there. It's all very exciting…"

"Would you consider going to Mars?" Helen asked Billy.

"I don't know… It might be the only long term solution."

"And on that note," Joe said, standing up, "I think I'll get some sleep. I'm exhausted after that ride through the straight. I want to be fresh for whatever the day brings tomorrow."

"Me too," Mary said. "Could you help me stand up Joe? I'm a bit wobbly."

He took hold of Mary's arm and helped her to stand. He felt the thinness of the flesh on her arm and the bone beneath it. "Be careful," he said as he held her and guided her along the side of the cabin to the cockpit and the hatch leading down into the main cabin.

"Thank you," she said softly.

Down below decks she said, "I don't think I'll last much longer Joe."

"What are you talking about?"

"I haven't been the same since we came through that anomaly. I keep getting palpitations and the sensation I'm going to collapse or faint. I get dizzy too, and to be honest, I don't think I have much time left."

"Don't talk like that. You'll be fine. You're taking a bit longer to adjust than the rest of us, that's all." But he was still shocked at the reaffirmation that Mary had aged, had become so frail over such a short period of time. He looked into her eyes and saw sadness there, an infinite sadness.

"No that's not it. I know. I can feel it in my bones." She put her free hand on her chest. "And here in my heart. My days are numbered Joe. Promise me you'll take care of the yacht and look after Helen, and Billy too, once I've gone."

Joe stared at her. He didn't know what to say.

"Promise me," Mary implored.

"Yes, I promise," he said hesitantly.

She smiled at him. "Now I can rest easy. Goodnight Joe."

"Goodnight Mary."

12...

"Hello," a voice called, "Can I come on board?"

Standing by the stove in the galley waiting for the kettle to boil for his first cup of tea for the day, Joe looked up startled by the unexpectedness of the voice outside. It was early, the sun barely up. They'd anchored in a remote bay with little but rocky desert extending inland; there should not have been anyone around.

Cautiously he opened the hatch and looked out. Beside the cockpit holding onto the rail was a young man. He had a rope in the other hand, ready to tie his small inflatable boat to the yacht so it wouldn't drift away.

"Hello there," he said with smile lighting up his face.

"Good morning," Joe said. "What is it you want?"

"I've been following you since you left the settlement…"

"Ah, you're one of the people in the aircar that's been trailing along behind us." Joe interrupted the young man. "I see you're not wearing a black uniform," he said while coming up out of the hatch onto the deck.

"I'm not one of the enforcers. I'm merely an observer, and the only one in the aircar."

"Okay, in that case you can come on board. Tie your boat to the rail."

As the young man did that, Joe came across and offered the visitor a hand to get on board. "I was just making a cup of tea. Would you like one?"

"Yes, that would be nice," he said with a cheerful smile as he clambered awkwardly over the rail to finish standing on the deck. The yacht rocked gently from side to side for a few moments from the effort the young man made as he climbed on board.

"Where's your aircar?" Joe asked. He looked across the small empty beach towards ridges covered with sparse scrub extending away from the shore.

"It's behind those bushes on the ridge overlooking the beach. I didn't want to frighten you by landing on the beach."

Joe looked at him curiously, as if trying to see into him, to determine the visitor's motives for having followed them since they'd left Billy's hometown.

"What's going on?" Helen asked. She had partially emerged from the hatch to have look. "I heard talking." She rubbed her face to clear the cobwebs from her mind. She had just woken up.

"We have a visitor," Joe said. "He's joining us for a cup of tea."

"Lovely," she said, and disappeared back down into the cabin.

"After you." Joe said. He indicated that the visitor should go down into main cabin.

Following him down, Joe found everyone in the galley waiting for them. Mary was seated at the table, Billy stood beside Helen who was by then pouring hot water into a pot for the tea to steep.

Billy studied the visitor. "I've seen you before," he said.

"Yes," the young man replied. "My name's Aaron, and you've seen me in town as I come from time to time to deliver technical stuff that's needed to keep things operational. We haven't met officially, but I know who you are."

Billy nodded.

Aaron looked around the interior of the yacht with curiosity. "I've never seen a boat like this before."

"They don't make them like this anymore," Joe said.

Mary chuckled, nodding in agreement.

While Aaron looked puzzled, Helen nudged him, moving him towards the small table. "Take a seat," she said, "While I pour the tea."

Suddenly, Aaron felt nervous, sitting across from Mary who watched him without blinking. Joe stood beside him while on the other side were Helen and Billy, whom he knew from various visits to Eyresea. He was the son of the man who had disappeared years before, and his uncle was the one in charge, an unofficial mayor, or spokesperson. The others were total strangers who didn't seem to fit. Perhaps they came from the northern hemisphere. That could explain the oddness of the boat they were using which seemed primitive, yet modern at the same time. It was certainly very good. He had no doubt of that after seeing it sail through the rapids of the tide change. Most people would have waited for the calm in between tide changes, but they didn't. Very few boats could have survived that cascade of tumbling swirling water. Perhaps there are still people living in the northern half of the world, although everyone believes it isn't possible. But if so, how did they get here? His understanding was that no one could survive the hot zone, let alone travel through it to the other side. He didn't know what to think and was regretting having made himself known. He'd also heard about what Joe did to the three enforcers who'd gone there to interview these strangers in their usual inimitable manner. The news of it had spread like wildfire through the capitol. No one had ever done that before. He smiled inwardly at the fact that the controllers were nervous. And having Joe standing there beside him only added to his own nervousness.

He couldn't stop his hand shaking slightly as he raised the cup of tea to sip it.

Seeing that, Joe moved a step away from him, allowing him some 'breathing space'.

"Relax Aaron," he said. "If you're not a threat to us, nothing will happen."

"Oh, I'm not a threat. I'm merely an observer."

Mary asked, "And what exactly is it you observe?"

He put his cup down. Now he was nervous again and wished he hadn't decided to visit the boat anchored in the small cove, but his curiosity had got the better of him. He couldn't resist a closer look at this strange but obviously efficient boat.

At a loss momentarily he mumbled, "strange phenomena."

"Like the sudden appearance of people out of nowhere?" Mary asked pointedly.

"Yes, there were rumors a group of people, had appeared out of nowhere, at sea, in a boat. That was unusual. Usually these appearances are on land, and never involve more than two people, mostly only one, and they are not common these days, although they were several years ago. When I heard that a team of enforcers were headed to Eyresea," he nodded towards Billy, "I had to come and see for myself."

"And what about people disappearing instead of appearing?" Billy asked, "Like my father."

"That doesn't seem to happen much anymore. I heard about your father. That was a long time ago when things like that were more common."

Mary looked at Joe and he imagined that she was thinking, there's not going to be a way back. They were stuck here and would have to make the best of it. He was thinking the very same thing. Except they had come through in the edge of the turbulent hot zone, so maybe there was still a possibility of a return, or a shift further into the future if they went into the hot zone. He refused to think about it for the moment, with their recent experience still too fresh in his mind to contemplate repeating it for a dubious outcome. All it might do was kill them.

"Why do the controllers want to talk to us?" Joe asked.

"Because you're the only people who arrived in a boat, and because of that, they think you have a way of controlling it, the shift from one place to another, that you can use the boat to travel through..."

"Time? They think we have a time machine?" Joe interrupted him. He chuckled at the thought of it. "Now that would be something wouldn't it?"

"If it's true, they need to know because it gives them a better option than migrating to Antarctica. Their problem is what will happen years later when it becomes too hot to live in Antarctica? Where can they go then? That's why they want to talk to you. They're desperate, and they think you have a solution, that somehow you have control of...."

"They're out of their minds," Joe said bluntly. "We don't have answers. We don't know what happened or how we got here. We're as much the victims of these transitions or time shifts or whatever they are, as any of those who've disappeared or suddenly appeared out of nowhere. We can't help them."

"They won't accept that."

"I don't care what they won't accept. We can't help them. That's all there is to it."

"I would be very careful," Aaron warned. "Enforcers can be nasty at times."

"Don't worry about us," Joe said with more confidence than he felt. "We want answers too, and if we don't find them here, then maybe we'll head south to Antarctica… Don't know yet."

"I think I'd better get going. I'm only supposed to observe, not to talk with you," Aaron said. "Just be careful. They can be dangerous."

"Thanks for the warning," Mary said.

They watched silently as Aaron rowed his inflatable dinghy back to shore where he deflated it, folded it, and carrying it, disappeared behind the ridge where he'd left his aircar. They waited until the aircar rose up and headed away towards the east before getting ready to leave.

Joe hauled up the anchor, unfurled the sails with Billy's help and got underway. He had no idea where they were headed, but that didn't matter. Going somewhere, anywhere, gave them something to do, with the subconscious feeling that they had a goal they were working towards. Joe couldn't see them fitting into this new world, but eventually they would have to, because he was certain there was no way back. There was only forward into this world, or forward into an unknown future if they encountered another anomaly.

A steady breeze blew across the water, so Joe decided to use the sails and not the new electric motor. He suspected it gave off traceable signals. He thought using the sails would in effect render the yacht invisible, except to satellites that could watch from above, but they were not always overhead. If they changed course after a satellite had passed over, they could be in a different place than expected when it comes over the next time, causing the monitors to take longer to find them, confusing them as to the course they were travelling, making their destination unpredictable. *The more unpredictable we can be, the better.* He smiled mischievously.

Their destination was unpredictable anyway because they had no idea where they were going.

"Do you know when the satellite watching us passes overhead?" Joe asked Billy.

"Not right now, but if we look tonight, we can see what time it's visible to us. It's usually overhead for around thirty-five minutes, then it takes an hour to continue its orbit before reappearing. Once we get the times at night, we'll know the times during the day when we can't see it."

"How good are the cameras on those things?"

"They can zoom in close enough to see the expressions on our faces."

"That good?"

"Yeah, high resolution. Enough to count the wrinkles on your forehead."

"I hadn't imaged that."

"If you are basing your perception on what you saw while you were with us, you need to remember Eyresea is atypical. We opted to live a quiet, old-fashioned lifestyle where we don't rely too much on modern technology. It could fail at any time for many reasons, and if you rely too much on it, you're in trouble. It has failed in the past when there have been violent sunspot outbursts, causing complete blackouts. Fortunately, those outbursts didn't last long and we managed with batteries and regular solar panels."

Joe had been wondering about the electric motor that was installed, where it had come from. There had not been any indication that it could be manufactured in Eyresea that he was aware of, although the town did have sophisticated technology, it was basically an agricultural and fishing town.

"Technology underpins Eyresea, keeps it running," Billy continued. "Without it, we'd be like those primitive tribes out west."

"Like the pirates we encountered?"

"Yeah, or worse."

Joe felt silent for a moment. He enjoyed the soft breeze blowing over his face as they sailed at an angle to the wind. The sails were full, taught, drawing the yacht forward at a good speed. The sea bubbled behind in their wake attracting gulls and larger birds to hover over them or to hang back aft hoping to catch a morsel disturbed by their passing through the water. Joe smiled when a lone dolphin leapt out of the water ahead of their bow. The first one he'd seen since being here. *It's good to see dolphins again. Well, one anyway.* There must be others nearby. It was a good sign. The dolphin accompanied them for a few minutes before veering off and heading away.

"Billy, take the wheel and keep us heading south." He indicated the compass reading. "Stay on that heading okay."

"Got it," Billy said cheerfully.

"I'll send Helen up to keep you company."

When he was alone with Mary, he asked, "Are you okay? You look... a bit pale."

She gave him a small smile. "I'm okay. But I feel washed out."

"Perhaps you should lie down."

"No. I feel better sitting here."

"Do you want to come up on deck? Get some fresh air? It's a nice day."

"I'm okay Joe. Don't worry. The thought of going up on deck right now makes me feel..." She couldn't think of a suitable word. "I'll just sit here for a while."

A week ago, she was fine, but suddenly... she looks so fragile. How come I hadn't noticed before? We're together all the time, it should have been obvious.

Sometimes you don't see what's in front of you. Small changes not noticed accumulate, and suddenly for some reason you see the result, and it shocks you.

"Is there something else you're worried about?" Mary asked after Joe had been staring at her for almost a minute.

He shook his head. "No, I was lost in thought. If it's okay with you, I'll sit here and keep you company. The kids can look after things above for the time being."

"That would be nice."

13...

They sailed south towards the great expanse of ocean that encircles the bottom half of the world surrounding Antarctica. Here seas can be ferociously huge because of the vast distances wind can travel and move the water without being interrupted by land. But Joe's intention was not to go too far south into that great ocean; but to stay close to land, and so he kept in sight the coastline that bordered the southeastern half of the continent.

The narrow gulf leading towards the great Southern Ocean was wide enough at this point that the western lands on their starboard side were below the horizon and invisible, while on their port side, he kept the eastern lands about a kilometre away, so they were always visible. He didn't have charts, or satellite positioning. He was no good at dead reckoning, and in any case, there were no manual instruments or logarithmic tables on board that could be used to calculate their position. When Harold built this yacht, he intended to rely on GPS positioning. He was not to know that in the future this navigation aid wouldn't be available. He could never have foreseen how bad the catastrophe that ruined the world he knew would play out. Nor could anybody at that time have imagined the possibility of being shifted forward in time. But here they were, and they were out of their depth, with no idea of where to go or what they might do. But at the very least moving on, surviving, sailing along this new coastline gave them the impression they were doing something, even if it didn't amount to much.

Well, they did have something to do; they were helping Billy search for his father, with little hope of ever finding him, since he disappeared years before, but at least it was a motive. An excuse to explore some of this world in which they found themselves.

The sea was relatively calm with gentle rolling swells. Billy stood on the bow excited to see two dolphins intermittently leaping out of the water creating cascades of spray. Helen was steering from the cockpit. A plethora of sea birds followed in their wake as well as circling overhead. Fish schooling leapt out of the water to escape the dolphins and the birds that attacked them. Helen loved watching the cormorants continually diving down into the water to disappear underneath for a few moments before reappearing with a glittering fish in their beaks, as they flew back up into the air. Looking over the side, glittering silver flashes sped past the yacht as schools of sardines swam past them. The school of fish moved away, accompanied by the diving cormorants and the leaping dolphins.

What a beautiful day, Joe thought as he helped Mary come up out of the main cabin so she could sit in the cockpit with them. It's too good to be cooped up down there.

They sat quietly together while Helen steered the yacht.

For a long time, no one said anything, it was too good a day to spoil it with inconsequential conversation.

Sailing wide around an area of reefs with small islets scattered amongst them, Joe wondered whether that was once the city of Adelaide. Even if the whole city hadn't been drowned, a thousand years of waves and storms smashing into the buildings would have reduced them to rubble and sand with nothing left. He also wondered about Melbourne and the people he'd left there when they sailed out into Bass Strait and headed east and then north in search of a more comfortable place to live. It too would be nothing more than rubble, hills that were islands surrounded by the sea that had eaten far into the land. Don't even think about it. That was a thousand years ago, there can't possibly be anything left.

"Hey, what are you thinking?" Mary asked softly. Sitting beside Joe in the cockpit, she gave him a slight nudge with her elbow.

"Nothing really," he said, turning towards her.

"Come on, I know that look. Harold used to get lost like that when he was thinking about what he had to do next while building the boat. You were far away…"

"You're right. I was thinking about the people we left behind, wondering what happened to them. I still can't believe that what was a couple of months ago for us is more than a thousand years ago. How long did they stay there on the tops of those buildings before the sea continued to erode them away, and where did they go then? Did the tsunami a few weeks after we left damage the buildings enough to force them to leave sooner than expected? Or did they stay on for years? Eventually the sea would cause the remaining buildings to collapse and there would be nothing there now but reefs and islands of rubble. I keep wondering what they would have done."

"And that young policewoman, whose life you saved?"

"Actually, she saved mine but was seriously wounded. I liked her."

"I know. She would have been okay, I think," Mary said. She gently squeezed Joe's arm, a feather-like touch of sympathy.

"I like to think so, but we'll never know."

Billy suddenly stood in front of them. "What are you too oldies talking about?"

"Who are you calling old?" Mary responded with a wide smile.

"Just saying… If you look ahead, you'll see there's a large boat coming."

"Shit." Joe exclaimed. He stood up and looked ahead over the cabin top. And in the distance coming from the east was something that looked like an old time navy patrol boat. If they stayed on the same course, it would intersect them probably within half an hour.

"Should we change course and try to outrun them?" Billy asked.

"No," Joe frowned. "It's obviously more powerful than us. I doubt we'd be able to outrun them. We should heave to and wait for them."

He stepped took over the tiller control from Helen who had been maintaining their course. He turned the yacht slightly, so the wind spilled from the sails. They flapped uselessly and the yacht immediately lost forward momentum and started to drift.

"Billy," he said, "Let's haul in the sails and wait for them to come to us."

By the time they'd furled the sails and tied them neatly the patrol boat was a lot closer. Several figures on deck moved about in preparation for when the two boats came together. Joe also noted there were several gun posts fore and aft and wondered why such a patrol boat needed to be heavily armed. One crewman was sitting behind one of the forward gun posts, and as Joe watched the gun swiveled towards them.

"There's a lot of guns on that boat," Joe commented.

"Not a good sign," Mary said.

Helen was extremely nervous, and to reassure her Joe put his arm around her shoulders and gave her a brief hug. "Relax Helen, if they were going to shoot at us, they would have already done so."

She gave him a nervous smile.

"They probably do this with every encounter, not knowing how someone will react to being stopped at sea. It's good policy to be ready for anything."

"Yeah," Billy added. "They're always on the lookout for pirates and marauders."

The patrol boat was only a few hundred metres away and slowing down to match their drift speed.

"How come you never mentioned that before?" Joe asked.

"Never occurred to me. Everybody knows…"

"We didn't know," Joe snapped and then immediately regretted his harsh tone.

The yacht started to bounce up and down as the patrol boat made a circle on their port side, turning to run parallel with them. It disturbed the flow of waves, making them monetarily short and choppy. Barely two metres separated the two boats.

"At least their guns are no longer pointing at us," Mary said.

"I suppose they don't see us as a threat anymore," Joe said.

"Ahoy there," a voice from the patrol boat called out. "We're going to throw you a cable to tie onto the bow so we can tow you back to port."

"What? They don't say hello?" Mary said. "Maybe we should throw the cable overboard."

"I doubt that would be good idea," Joe said. He called out to the man on the patrol who was holding a coiled cable, ready to throw it across to them. "We can follow you."

"Better if we tow you," the man replied. "We know the reefs and spots where you might have problems."

They obviously don't want to take the chance we might make run for it. Wouldn't do us any good anyway…

"Okay," Joe yelled across the gap between them. The patrol boat had already shown it was much faster than them. "Toss the cable over."

The man with the cable complied and Billy snatched it when it hit the deck. He ran forward and tied the cable to a stanchion by the bowsprit.

"I'm scared," Helen said.

"Me too," Mary admitted.

"It'll be okay," Joe said. "Let them tow us to their base. Then we'll find out what they want. They came out here to intercept us. They're not looking for pirates."

"You're not worried?" Mary asked.

"I am, but the only way to learn anything is to go with them. Let them think we're frightened and don't want to cause problems. Sooner or later an opportunity will allow us to escape."

The patrol boat moved ahead of them. The tow rope tied to their bow extended across the water to the stern of the patrol boat. It was unreeling and lying flat on the waves until the patrol boat was around fifty metres ahead when suddenly it bounced up out of the water becoming taut. Droplets sparkling in the sun fell off the cable. Their yacht lurched forward, paused, then surged forward smoothly as the patrol boat made headway at a speed faster than they could have sailed. Joe felt the forward surge of the yacht beneath his feet and was glad they hadn't contemplated outrunning them.

Helen and Mary looked at him with an expression that implied, *what do we do now?* Billy joined them having made sure the cable wouldn't come undone.

"I guess we sit back and enjoy the ride," Joe replied to their unspoken question.

14...

The patrol boat towed them for almost an hour before it turned into a wide bay, the entrance to another flooded inland area. The sea had come up through the wetlands that surrounded the mouth of the Murray River and had extended far inland into what was once a barren area. They passed other boats as they were towed further into the huge bay extending way beyond them, big enough to be another inland sea.

The harbour and port they entered was not large, but it was bustling with fishing boats and small trading vessels entering or leaving in a constant stream of maritime traffic. On shore, they saw small trucks and other vehicles loaded with goods either leaving to take them elsewhere, while other trucks arrived with goods to be unloaded and stowed on board small trading boats. In some parts closer to shore, the remnants of drowned buildings protruded above the surface. Floating jetties had been built out to some of them. The town that extended back from the waterfront appeared heavy and solid, the buildings made of stone, with only a few rendered and painted bright colours. Many of the buildings were dome shaped, like beehives which Joe thought was an odd style of construction.

"Seems a busy place," Joe said to the others in the cockpit with him as he watched the activity around the myriad piers and jetties.

"Yeah, this is where the occasional trader came from when they brought stuff to us," Billy said. "I never thought it would be such a busy place."

"I suppose they trade stuff around the coast to the east. That's where the bulk of the population used to be before the waters came up. If they moved somewhere inland, they would still have access to bays and new harbours for coastal trading," Joe surmised. "I don't see any big cranes like we used to have for loading and unloading container ships, so I'm guessing there isn't much international trading anymore."

Billy gave Joe an odd look, wondering what a container ship was. He said nothing though, more interested in all the activity around the harbour. This was the first time he'd ever seen a bustling port, and he was impressed. For Mary, Joe and Helen, this seaside conglomeration of domed and flat roofed stone buildings was nothing more than a medium-sized seaside town, only gloomier in appearance to what they were used to from their own time.

The patrol boat towed them past a series of smaller bays where stone buildings came down to the seashore and where there were plenty of small boats that looked like fishing boats. They entered a larger bay that seemed more of a commercial port, with boats large enough to be called ships docked at several piers, but the patrol boat bypassed this as well and headed towards an adjacent secluded area where there were twin piers. No boats were moored there although there was room for several to be accommodated.

On shore fronting the twin piers there were three grey bluestone buildings that had seen better days surrounding a small square. To Joe, they appeared recently abandoned. He guessed this patrol boat and the few sailors operating it to be the remnants of a greater force now gone. There was a high fence around the outskirts of the buildings separating them from other buildings and activities around them that gave life to the city by the sea.

"I don't like the look of this place," Joe said.

Mary agreed. "It looks depressing."

"Reminds me of a prison." He expected to see people doing things, but there seemed to be no activity at all. "It looks deserted."

"That's not good, is it?" Billy asked.

"No." Joe said. Not good!

Within moments of entering this secluded harbour space, the patrol boat slowed, bringing them close to one of the twin piers. It made a wide turn so its bow pointed out towards the open harbour. As their yacht drifted towards the pier a sailor ran along it and indicated that they should tie up to a large stanchion and release the tow rope. Joe went forward and released the tow rope which was quickly retrieved by the patrol boat crewmen. He threw a smaller rope across to the waiting sailor who immediately tied it to a stanchion. As he was doing this, the patrol boat moved forward to execute a wide turn finally coming in behind them and tying to the wharf. The captain of the patrol boat strode along the pier towards them. He was followed by two other men who carried electronic weapons in a relaxed but ready manner. None of them appeared threatening, but Joe knew that was an illusion. There was a stiffness to the way they moved and the stoniness of the two men's faces indicated an underlying tension which contrasted to the relaxed manner of the captain who sported a broad welcoming smile. The sailor who had thrown them the rope stood by their stern. Joe tossed him a stern rope which he grabbed and secured to another stanchion.

The captain stopped by the stern where Joe waited. When the yacht was finally secured fore and aft, he asked if he could come aboard.

"Of course," Joe responded affably.

Mary glared at the stranger but was ignored. He only had eyes and attention for Joe whom he assumed was the captain or the person in charge.

"Welcome," he said once on board. "Welcome to our city by the sea."

He expected Joe to say something, but when Joe only smiled and nodded, he went on. "I'm happy you allowed us to tow you in… It was the sensible thing to do."

What choice did we have? "Yes, and what is it exactly that you want with us?" Joe asked.

"Um, well," he stumbled over the words, not used to people demanding answers from him. It was usually the other way around. "We were told you might be unfamiliar with our country…"

That gives nothing away while pretending to be friendly. "Told by whom?" Joe asked.

"Doesn't matter." But seeing Joe wouldn't accept that answer he fumbled to explain. "People who noted your sudden arrival. They… thought you might need some… assistance."

Which again, says nothing. "That's bullshit. We were sailing along nicely until you showed up. We don't need any assistance thank you."

And the captain was no longer smiling. "I obey orders. We were told to go bring you in. I don't ask why. I just do it."

"And now that we allowed you to bring us in, now what?"

Momentarily confused, the captain gave Joe an odd look. "You didn't have a choice," he stated.

Joe smiled briefly. "Yeah, sure," he said enigmatically.

"You come with me. There is a video link to the capitol in the barracks. The others can stay here. Someone will come along to examine your boat shortly."

"No, they won't." Joe stated emphatically.

"What!" The captain straightened his posture and glared at Joe.

"You don't send anyone to examine our yacht."

"It is an unusual…"

"And that's your excuse? Did whoever give you orders to get us also demand you examine our boat? Did they say why?"

"Look, I have no idea about any of this. I just do…"

"What I'm told. You already said that." He noted the two crewmen with their weapons moved position carefully so, if necessary, they each had a clear shot at Joe without hitting their captain. *This isn't going the way they expected,* he thought and smiled inwardly.

He wasn't the least worried they would shoot him. They wanted answers and shooting him would not achieve that.

With a nod of his head towards the two armed men, Joe looked directly at the captain and asked, "do you think two teenagers and an elderly woman are such a threat they need to be guarded?"

"Not at all," the captain said too quickly. He took a quick furtive glance to see where his men were. "They're to stop curiosity seekers from getting too close."

"So we're not prisoners?"

"Of course not."

"I don't believe you." Joe looked straight into the captain's eyes. "I have as many questions for them as they do for me, so I'll talk to your superiors. But only if you don't bother my family."

"Your family? I thought the young man was from…"

"My family. He's a part of it."

Joe moved towards the captain who stumbled a step backwards. One of the armed men on the pier raised his weapon, but let it drop when Joe passed the captain without touching him, jumping onto the pier while the captain stood red-faced and embarrassed in front of his men. Turning to look back at the captain still standing on the deck of the yacht, Joe asked in a commanding voice, "Are you coming?"

The captain stepped off the yacht onto the pier, and ignoring Joe, strode vigorously along it towards the barracks around the square. Joe was right behind him. The two armed men moved away a short distance from the yacht but not being ordered to leave, remained on watch.

"Well, what do we do now?" Mary asked Billy and Helen.

It was rhetorical because they knew the answer: wait until Joe gets back.

The three of them watched silently as Joe followed the captain. They watched them enter the nearest building closest to the pier.

"I'd like to have a look at this 'city by the sea'," Billy said. "I've never seen any other town or city other than Eyresea."

"Really?" Helen was taken aback. What she saw was nothing more than a run-down seaside town. She'd lived her younger life in a huge city before it had been destroyed by the rising seas, and even afterwards for a while. She wasn't particularly interested in this grimy small town. It was not somewhere she wanted to stay for any length of time. She preferred Eyresea, where Billy lived. Though smaller, it had character and a laid-back ambiance. This place reminded her of a preindustrial centre that had big ideas on what it was and with aspirations to what it could become.

But for Billy, who had never seen another town other than his own, it was an eye-opener. He'd never seen so many people, so many boats of all shapes and sizes, so much activity in one place. "Do you think the guards would let us leave so we can visit the town?"

"I don't think so."

"They look bored," Billy noted. "They're not even watching us."

"Yes," Mary said, "but I'll bet if you took a step off the yacht, they'll be right onto you." Studying them, noting how unhappy they appeared to be with guard duty. She said, "I've got an idea."

The two looked at her expectantly.

"Why don't you go forward where you can sit down on the deck hidden from the guards by the cabin? Billy, you could pretend to be checking the sails, to see they are properly tied. If the guards think you are doing some work on the yacht they probably won't be interested."

"And?" Helen asked.

"The forward sail locker is hidden from their view by the cabin. Inside the locker there is an inflatable dinghy. If you can get that out without them taking notice you can drop it over the side. It has a gas bottle which inflates it so all you need to do is hit the release and the dinghy will inflate before it hits the water. Make sure you hold of the rope connected to it, so it doesn't float away before you get into it."

"That's brilliant." Billy said enthusiastically.

"There's also a paddle with it. If you can slip over the side and into the dinghy without any noise, they won't notice, won't even see you if you keep low enough for the cabin to hide you. And for a few hundred metres, the boat will also hide you as you paddle out. They most likely won't see you until you get well away, if they bother to look in that direction."

"I like that idea," Helen said.

"Me too," Billy agreed.

"There's lots of other small boats out there too. They might not notice us once we get out far enough," Helen said.

"Let's do it." Billy enthused.

"I'll keep an eye on the guards, and let you know if they get curious." Mary said. She felt their excitement wash over her and couldn't help smiling. For the first time in several days, she felt good.

"Are the guards watching?" Billy asked Helen.

Crouched down, he was opening the sail locker.

"No. They're chatting and laughing. They're not even looking this way."

"Good." Kneeling on the deck in front of the cabin he reached in and took hold of the folded rubberized dinghy, pulled it out onto the deck beside the sail locker. There was a nylon rope coiled and tied next to a built-in gas cylinder. He undid the tie so the rope became loose, and he carefully wrapped the end of it around his wrist so he could maintain a grip. He looked up questioningly at Helen.

"They're still not looking this way."

He nodded and slid the folded dinghy across the deck and under the side rail. It would have been better to stand up and drop it over the side, but the guards would see him do that. Shoving it through under the rail, he hit the inflate button as he finally pushed it through. It dropped down and made several popping noises as it inflated in an instant. The noise it made inflating, and the splash as it hit the water seemed incredibly loud.

"Shit," he mumbled.

"They're looking this way," Helen said. "They must have heard something."

One of them took a step towards the yacht. Helen tensed.

From the cockpit near the stern, Mary called to the guards. "Is everything okay?"

They looked at her briefly, said nothing, but waited a moment to see if any more unusual noises would occur before they returned to leaning against a row of stanchions and resumed whatever they'd been talking about. Mary let out a sigh of relief.

Helen relaxed. She hadn't realized she'd been holding her breath.

Billy had slid across the deck, squeezed under the rail and was over the side and standing in the dinghy holding it close to the side of the yacht where it couldn't be seen by the guards. "Make sure you grab the paddle before you come," he said in a whisper to Helen.

Helen reached into the open sail locker, found the paddle,

slipped it across the deck to Billy, then sat down in front of the cabin. From his low position, with his head a fraction above the deck, Billy could see Mary in the cockpit. She was using her left hand, behind her back and invisible to the guards, to indicate they should paddle away.

"Come on,' he whispered to Helen. "Slide across and under the rail. I'll make sure you don't fall into the water."

Once Helen joined him, Billy used the paddle to push them away from the side of the yacht. He quietly paddled away in a line that the yacht would cover so they couldn't be seen. They could go a couple of hundred metres before becoming visible, and Billy was hoping that it would be far enough for the guards to assume they were just a couple paddling past on their way from one side of the harbour to another taking advantage to get a glimpse of the strange yacht that had been towed in.

In the cockpit, Mary relaxed and decided she would go below and make herself a cup of tea. The guards, involved in their conversation, took no notice of her as she went below. *The youngsters need some time together, to stretch their legs, see a bit of the world.* She knew Joe would be pissed off when he came back, but she could live with that.

"It's all good," she said to herself as she sat down in the galley and waited for the kettle to boil.

A slight current pushed their inflatable dinghy towards the direction they wanted to go, so minimal effort was needed to help control their drift towards the more populated side of the harbour. There had been no calls from the guards, so Billy and Helen relaxed as they drifted closer to where much activity surrounded two large boats. Many smaller craft were on the water and anyone searching for a particular boat would be hard pressed to pick an individual one out amongst hundreds of fishing boats, sail boats, dinghies, and runabouts that all seemed to move about randomly.

"Well, we did it," Helen said, exhaling a deep sigh of relief.

Billy hadn't realized how tense he'd been, but now that they were in amongst a plethora of other small craft, and out of sight of the guards by their yacht he finally allowed his tension to drain away.

Getting closer, they saw supplies were being unloaded from the trucks and taken on board the two larger boats— *small ships* he decided —moored one behind the other on a longer pier. There was no activity around any of the fishing and other work boats moored alongside the other jetties, it was concentrated on the two larger boats.

"It looks like they're preparing for a long voyage," Billy observed. "I wonder where they're going."

"We can ask, once we get ashore," Helen said.

They paddled to a beach several hundred metres from the docks where activity around the two larger boats was ongoing and pulled the dinghy high up onto the sand. They dragged it towards a row of scrubby trees where the sand finished. Billy pushed it under the trees, obscuring it from any passerby who might happen along the beach. He tied it to the base of one of the trees to discourage anyone from taking it away if it was discovered. He walked out onto the sand and scuffed away the tracks left where they dragged the dinghy across the sand. They both then walked casually along the beach, staying close to the trees.

The trees finally dwindled to a few stunted specimens before giving way to a bituminous road leading into a wide square from where many piers and jetties extended over the water. Several trucks were lined up with their drivers clustered near the first in the row, chatting and smoking. They took no notice of Helen and Billy as they wandered along the road into the square— just another couple coming to see what was going on. Beyond the cluster of drivers, a group of workers were carrying cartons and cases from one truck up a gangplank onto the nearest boat and stacking them on the deck. On board, others were taking these and disappearing with them below decks. Across the square scattered groups of onlookers watched with interest.

Nodding towards the groups across the square, Billy suggested, "Let's wander over to there to find out what's happening."

"You don't know where they're going?" An onlooker responded to Billy's question with eyes full of suspicion. He stared at Billy but became disarmed when Billy smiled back at him.

"We've been away for a while," Helen quickly interjected. "We've only just got back."

The speaker turned his attention to her for a moment, wondering where her odd accent came from. Finally, he said, "They're off to Antarctica. You know how barren it is…" Helen and Billy nodded knowingly. "The idea is to seed it with plants and bushes to help create a better environment for when we start moving down there."

"And that's what they're loading?"

"No. The plants and seeds are already loaded on the slave boat. This one's taking on supplies for the people going down there. They'll be travelling on this one. The slave boat follows in its wake."

Both boats were festooned with receiving dishes for broadcast power as well as connecting the two electronically together so both ships would be controlled from the manned one. Billy hadn't heard of that being done before; there being no need for anything like that in Eyresea.

"It's a pretty rough crossing to Antarctica," Billy said as a means of eliciting more information. "I don't think I'd like to do that."

"They've done it several times. There are survey teams down there working on locations for settlements. Been there a few years now. Trouble is everything's shipped down. There's nothing there, apart from wild grass that grew after the ice melted."

"But that was years ago," Billy said acting as if he was ignorant of that fact.

"Yeah, well it takes centuries for barren land like that to become livable. These expeditions are helping it along so we can move there when it starts getting too hot here."

Terraforming it… Billy had learnt about this in school.

"Would you go?" Helen asked.

"Not right now," the man said, "but when it gets too hot here, we won't have much choice. We'll have to go."

"How far off do you reckon that's likely to be?" Billy asked.

Again, the man looked at Billy with an odd expression, before answering. "Baa… Not in my lifetime, I hope. But I'd rather go there than the Moon or Mars. At least there's air you can breathe in Antarctica. It could get worse quicker than expected, but we've made a start, and that's good."

The man turned away in response to something another person said, ignoring them. Helen and Billy took this moment to quietly drift away. They didn't want to make anyone suspicious by asking too many questions about things supposedly everyone knew. The man had been starting to look at them suspiciously.

Passing between clumps of people they moved away from the piers and the activity everyone watched and were thinking about going into the town itself when a contingent of six black clad enforcers moved out of one street and into the square where they split into two groups of three and started urging the groups of onlookers to disperse.

"Shit," Billy uttered on seeing these unidentified helmeted men enter the square which was rapidly emptying as a result.

"We'd better move on," Helen said nervously. "If they see us, they'll know we don't belong here."

Tagging behind a group heading towards the road where the trucks were lined up, Billy hoped the enforcers hadn't noticed them. Are they looking for us? He wondered. Have they discovered us missing? Do they always disperse crowds they think might cause problems?

The group they were with spread out along the road leading away from the square, Billy and Helen, out of sight with the waiting trucks between them and the square, moved casually down onto the beach. Staying close to the edge where the trees overhung the sand, they made their way back to where they'd left the dinghy hidden under the trees. Glancing back, and seeing no one else on the beach, they slipped in under cover of the trees.

"We'll wait until the square is emptied and the enforcers leave, before we risk getting the dinghy back into the water."

"Do you think they were looking for us?" Helen asked.

"Maybe they went onto the yacht and found we weren't there."

"Oh Shit. Now I'm worried about Mary."

"I shouldn't have said that. Sorry. I don't think they'd do anything to her."

"She's an old lady," Helen said, attempting to reassure herself. "What would they gain?"

"They don't care." Billy said, again without thinking. "If they decide she knows something they'll try and get it out of her…"

"We've got to go back, right away," Helen insisted.

"No. They'll see us. We should wait here for a while… At least until the enforcers leave."

Before either of them could say or do anything else, one group of three enforcers strolled down onto the sand close to the water's edge where they stood looking out to sea. One of the men left the other two and walked along the beach towards the spot where they'd dragged the dinghy up onto the sand. He passed the spot, saw nothing in the way of tracks or disturbed sand and stood there for a few minutes.

Good thing I scuffed away the tracks, Billy thought.

He could feel Helen gripping his arm. *There's going to be a big bruise there…* She hardly dared to breathe as she watched from under the tree cover. It seemed like an hour before the lone enforcer walked back to the other two —it had only been a few minutes— and the three of them left the beach, heading back towards the town square.

"We'll have to wait a bit to make sure they've gone…" Helen whispered as the tension in her slipped away.

Billy sighed with relief. "As soon as the sun sets," he murmured, "we'll head back."

"That's at least a couple of hours off yet…"

"What else can we do?"

15...

The room they entered was abandoned. Following the captain inside Joe wondered about the vacant desks with papers scattered across them, filing cabinets with drawers partially opened, blank computers screens, and chairs pushed aside. He imagined people had grabbed what they thought was relevant before rushing off... *to where? What's going on here?* He stopped to look around as the captain who without taking the slightest notice of the room's disarray, went through another door.

"Are you with me?"

"Yeah, right behind you," Joe responded.

Beyond the other door was a small office with a desk with several chairs placed about the room. On one wall was a large monitor. The captain went straight to the monitor and switched it on.

"Where is everyone?" Joe asked.

"There are two teams down by the docks making sure people don't cause any problems."

"What do you mean...problems?"

"Not everyone wants to go to Antarctica, but some are needed for essential work there whether they like it or not, so they are going."

"And your people are there to make sure there aren't any problems?"

"That's right."

Jagged slashes of color ripped across the monitor screen.

"And the people that worked in here?"

"Already on board."

"On board what?"

"Ships leaving. Two heading for Antarctica, one with equipment and supplies, the other for us and those selected for the first colony. There are ships leaving from all the ports. We're supposed to accompany them. This will be ongoing for weeks, maybe months."

So, it's happening right now.

The captain sounded disgruntled, and Joe wondered if all his men felt the same. *How many were willing to head off to Antarctica? Would they be leaving their families behind?*

"Isn't it a bit premature? I was under the impression it would take many years to 'terraform' Antarctica to be suitable for habitation."

"Someone's got to be the first," the captain snapped back. He forced himself to relax before adding, "It's been going on for a while and some places are suitable now. My unit is one ordered to accompany the first group from here. The rest of the population will be ferried down there once suitable habitats have been set up." He paused, looked across to Joe, said as if it had just occurred to him, "It could take decades."

"So why the rush now? Why suddenly abandon everything?"

The captain glared at Joe. "I don't fucking know," he snapped. "I just..."

"'*Do what I'm told.*' You already said that."

Calming down the captain spoke evenly. "I was told that we were to move out immediately, but that got interrupted by having to get you."

"You could have left us alone."

"Yeah, well you know the answer to that."

"And you think the local townsfolk will riot or do something drastic if they think they're being abandoned to their fate? Whatever that is..."

"How the hell would I know? Not everyone can go at the same time."

The wall monitor continued to flash jagged lines of colour. The captain gave it a thump on the side, and for a moment an image of a large room, empty except for a huge table in the centre appeared, before once again collapsing into flashing patterns. "Useless piece of shit," he mumbled.

Doesn't matter when you are, if the technology fails, everything falls apart.

"Must be an electrical storm somewhere," the captain said to Joe. "They've been getting worse lately. Never had them this far south though…"

"That's how we got here. An electrical storm, a massive anomaly. Something more dangerous than a mere electrical storm. Damn near killed us, but it shifted us from our time into the future. To your time now."

"So that's why the top brass want to talk to you." A spark of interest flashed briefly in his eyes.

"I guess so. But they'll learn nothing from us. We got caught in that… anomaly thing and found ourselves here. That's all. We don't know any more about it than you do."

"Can I ask when?"

"Right after a huge tsunami wiped out every coastal city in the world…"

"Fuck! The Big Wipeout! An absolute disaster. Luckily a few groups had already started rebuilding inland before that." He stared at Joe while trying to process what Joe said. He was having trouble imagining how something like that could be possible. "Shit, that was a thousand years ago," was all he could think of.

"It takes a bit of getting used to." Joe said cheerfully. "Apparently not all arrivals came in a boat."

"That's right. Most of them are confused with no idea of who they are, where they are, or when they are. Not like you."

Joe said nothing, waiting for him to go on.

"I've never had anything to do with the arrivals, until now. The few that seemed 'undamaged' I was told disappeared into the general population before they could explain how they got here."

"You mean before they could be interrogated?"

"Mm, you could put it that way."

"I would. So, what are you planning to do about us?"

"Nothing. I've no orders regarding that."

Joe calmly watched confusion and uncertainty wash across the captain's face. In a way, he felt sorry for the man. He obviously had no idea what to do next, always following orders and when none were there, he was struck with confusion, at a loss even to think for himself as an individual.

"Why don't you get your men, take your patrol boat and join the ships leaving?"

"That's what I was supposed to do, but orders came in to get you instead."

"And now that you've got us?"

"I did what I was told" and after a pause to think about it he said, "after that I don't care." He pointed to the monitor on the wall, now filled with grey static. "If those on top can't interview you, or don't send someone to do it, That's their problem." He seemed relieved to have come to that conclusion.

Suddenly, he turned and rushed out of the room.

Shaking his head, Joe followed.

Outside, the sky was still clear, but a little darker as the sun was low in the sky. The hairs on Joe's arms stood up. The air was dry and dusty. It was unexpected, unusual, being so close to the sea, and it seemed to Joe that it was full of static electricity. *Must be the dust particles rubbing against each other as the wind blows them across the desert and onto us here.* At any moment he expected to see dry lightning bolts. It was the same feeling in the air, he remembered, just before they were caught in the anomaly that sent them here.

Back on the jetty, the captain ordered his two waiting men to board the patrol boat. He turned to Joe and said, "We'll pick up the two teams sent into town and then we'll escort the ships out of the harbour. You can hang around and wait for someone to come from the capitol to interview you" He looked at Joe intensely and smiled for the first time. "As far as I'm concerned, you can do what you want."

"Are you coming back?"

"No, we're supposed to escort them to Antarctica and stay there. That was the original plan."

"I wish you all the best."

"Thanks," the captain said. "Maybe we'll meet again."

"You never know," Joe said with a smile. "The world's not such a big place anymore."

16...

"What do you mean they went into town?"

"They took the dinghy and rowed across to see what was going on," Mary explained.

"Fuck..."

Mary seemed tired, weary, as if the weight of the world rested on her shoulders. He sat opposite her in the galley. "I'm sorry," he said contritely. "I didn't mean to swear like that."

"It's all right Joe, I've heard worse before."

"Why can't teenagers ever do what they're told?"

Mary shrugged her shoulders.

"We're free to go anytime we like. We should leave as soon as possible."

"We'll have to wait until Helen and Billy come back."

"Yes, but there's a bad storm coming. There's a lot of dust and static electricity in the air." He sucked in a deep breath and let it out slowly before adding, "it feels like an anomaly developing. We shouldn't be here when that happens."

"Oh, that's not good." Mary immediately looked worried. She would never forget how terrifying it was in that weird storm. She leaned across and took Joe's hands in her own. "I don't think I'd survive going through that again."

"We can't go anywhere until Helen and Billy come back."

"They've been gone awhile," Mary said. "What if they don't come back?"

"Let's wait for an hour. If they don't come back, I'll go and look for them."

17...

While they waited for the sun to set, wind gusts ruffled the water off the beach. Further out it was increasingly choppy.

"If we don't go now," Billy said, "it'll be hard to row back." But he didn't move. He stood there under cover of the trees along the back of the beach staring out to sea while the sky became noticeably darker.

"Smell the dust in the air," Helen said. "It must be blowing over from the desert country to the west."

A brilliant flash of dry lightning zapped across the sky with a loud crack. The hairs on their arms stood up. More streaks of lightning zapped across the sky above the bay. The tree they were standing under along with the other trees on either side of them shook and rattled as waves of thunder rolled over. A patrol boat passed by several hundred metres offshore, crashing through ever increasing waves, heading towards the pier where the two larger ships were located.

"Isn't that the boat that towed us in?" Helen asked.

"Yeah, looks like it."

"What do you think happened to Uncle Joe, and Mary? We have to go back..."

Billy remained silent, his attention on the patrol boat approaching the two ships moored by the long pier. It didn't tie up but sat alongside them. "There go the enforcers," he said.

The two teams of three enforcers they'd seen earlier in the square scrambled aboard the waiting patrol boat, dropping down from a rope ladder on the side of the first ship. Within minutes the patrol boat moved back out into the harbour and waited.

"They must have finished loading," Billy said, as one of the ships started to move away from the pier. When it was well clear, the second ship did the same. The air between their vantage spot and the piers with the ships and boats became darker as more dust filled the space between them, swirling in waves of small whirlwinds. It was getting denser by the minute. The two ships and the patrol boat made their way out to deeper water and slowly vanished as the swirling dust filled air obscured any vision of them.

Suddenly, all hell broke loose. A lightning bolt smashed a tree several hundred metres away, splitting it half, sparking a fire. The noise of the exploding tree almost burst their eardrums. Both held their hands over their ears while staring fearfully at each other.

"It's too late," Helen mouthed the words knowing Billy couldn't hear her. She couldn't hear herself either. "We have to stay here and sit it out."

An incredibly bright flash of lightning filled the sky directly in front of them, momentarily blinding them. The crack of thunder almost knocked them over. They held onto each other for stability as a sudden roar of wind swirled around them lifting leaves and small sticks, dragging sand up off the beach, and moments later sucking up water as the vicious whirlwind moved off the beach and out to sea. The tree next to them exploded as it too was hit by lightning. Billy felt a thump on his back as a small branch slammed into, knocking him to his knees before being carried off into the swirling sand and dust.

They huddled together on their knees, each with an arm wrapped around the other as well as the tree trunk they huddled against.

Lightning and thunder raged around them. The wind, like a malevolent entity, became momentarily a vicious whirlwind sucking at them, as if needing to devour them.

"Hang on tight," Billy yelled over the noise of the wind trying to drag them away.

They closed their eyes as tears welled up to wash away blinding dust particles and buried their faces into each other's shoulder to avoid breathing in the dust. The dinghy tied to the tree twisted and bounced ferociously against the ground, before something underneath it burst one of the inflated sides. The rubber flapped and tore away.

"I don't think I can hold on much longer," Helen said desperately into his ear.

"Don't let go!" Billy screamed, holding on as tight as he could. Dust and sand spun around them, stinging like wasp bites, feeling like knives scratching exposed skin as sharp windborne sand particles lashed them. The dinghy tore away from the rope tethering it to the tree and flew off looking like a mad manta ray frantically swimming to escape a dangerous monster.

"Shit," Billy couldn't help screaming out. "Shit, shit…"

Suddenly the local whirlwind raced across the beach and out to sea to join other twisters and swirling waterspouts. The force of the wind around them abated slightly, but the air was still full of dust and sand ripping past them.

Their last glimpse of the town square by the piers and jetties before the dust thickened so much it obscured it showed it was deserted. If the people they'd seen earlier weren't on the ships that left, they had retreated to the protection of their solid stone homes.

18...

Joe raced around on the deck and made sure all the vents, lockers and hatches were closed tight against the sand and dust blasting them. Below deck he made sure all portholes that could be opened were sealed shut. The last thing was the hatch, then he and Mary settled down in the galley to wait out the storm. There was no way he could venture out in search of Helen and Billy while the storm raged insanely around them. The yacht rocked and bumped against the pier as the waves fiercely agitated by the wind slapped against the hull, but the dust blowing down onto them tended to flatten the waves so the water in the harbour near the pier wasn't as rough it would be further out into the bay.

He looked at Mary. "I hope Billy and Helen found somewhere safe to wait out the storm," he said.

Mary said nothing. She just sat and listened to the sand and dust blown by the wind, blasting the hull and rigging. It was too loud to talk over, and she felt too weary to make the effort. She nodded to let Joe know she'd heard him.

The wind screamed in the rigging, and stroboscopic lightning flashed momentarily blinding them before waves of thunder rolled across them. After what seemed an infernally long time, but was not more than half an hour, the wind abated as suddenly as it had begun. The yacht stopped bouncing against the side of the jetty, while a modicum of light penetrated the interior as the dust in the air outside diminished.

Joe stood up. "I think it's safe enough now to go and look for them."

"Be careful," Mary said.

The wind still gusted and red dust and sand covering the deck and other exposed parts of the yacht lifted and shifted continuously, intermittently blown off the yacht into the water. The amount of sand and dust in the air had dissipated to a degree that resembled a light haze rather than a heavy fog. The wild whirlwinds that buffeted them earlier had disappeared.

"I'll try not to be too long," he called out to Mary before he stepped off the yacht and onto the pier.

The only way into the town was to follow the road from the other side of the compound. Leaving the pier and the yacht, he crossed the quadrangle passing the building where he'd been with the captain. Beyond it was a gate open to a short path going to the edge of a two lane road. On the road he headed in the direction of the town by the main harbour next to the inlet where they were moored. Visibility was still not good, but a lot of dust had already blown away or settled down. Small clouds of fine dust stirred up with every footstep he took, floating momentarily before being scattered by intermittent wind gusts. Everything he could see was covered with red dust giving the impression it was rusting away. Most of it, once the worst of it passed overhead, would be blown away by the wind, or if it rained, quickly washed away. He thought it unlikely they would get any rain anytime soon, so the damned dust would linger.

He was concerned that Helen and Billy may not have found shelter from the storm. He wasn't angry that they had taken off to have a look at the town, he probably would have done the same. But he hoped they'd found somewhere safe to sit out the storm, refusing to consider what might have happened to them if they hadn't.

As he walked along the road the air became noticeably clearer. The worst of the dust had blown away towards the east, and what remained in suspension had started to dissipate. Though it was close to sunset and getting darker, visibility was much clearer than it had been only fifteen minutes earlier.

The road ahead took a bend around a clump of trees that had been smashed and ripped apart. *The town should be just beyond there.* He picked up the pace. Out of the murkiness ahead, two figures emerged walking towards him.

Thank God!

"Hey," he called out. "I've been looking for you two."

"We're okay," Helen called back.

When they got closer, Billy said apologetically, "We lost the dinghy."

"The wind tore it apart," Helen said. She threw her arms around Joe and gave him a desperate hug.

"Take it easy," Joe said. "You're all covered in dust."

Stepping back, she shook her head and dust floated up out of her hair to be blown away by what was left of the wind.

Billy said, "We had it tied to a tree trunk, but the wind was ferocious. It ripped it apart."

"And it blew away," Helen added.

"Doesn't matter," Joe responded. "The main thing is you're safe. Let's get back and get you cleaned up. Mary was worried…"

The four of them slept fitfully as the wind picked up again overnight, buffeting the yacht moored to the pier by the quadrangle. It kept bouncing and rocking as waves pushed it up and down and against the shock absorbers lining the sides of the pier. There was no real damage done to the yacht, but it was an uncomfortable night. Lightning flashed and thunder rolled ominously for the first couple of hours but eventually stopped leaving only diminishing wind gusts to rock them. That too finally stopped early in the morning and the sun rose over the harbour which surprisingly didn't look much different to what it had been like when they arrived. A few badly moored boats had been washed ashore and wrecked, but the majority seemed fine. Several fishing boats were heading out to sea. People wandered into the town square to compare their experiences of the sandstorm, to sweep away accumulated sand as fine as talcum powder, to hose down the streets, but mainly to stare at a vacant lot where two buildings had stood before the storm.

Stepping onto the deck Joe took in a deep breath. The air had a mild freshness to it. It had changed overnight in the aftermath of the storm. Before, and they'd gotten used to it, were hot summer days, much hotter than summer in their time before the shift forward. They had become accustomed to it, and almost ceased to notice it, accepting it as normal. Now suddenly it felt like autumn, a pleasant surprise. They still have seasons.

A movement in the quadrangle caught his eye and he immediately focused on it. There was an aircar sitting off to one side in the shade of a building. He hadn't noticed it until a figure started to emerge.

Shit was his immediate thought.

He was expecting to see three enforcers, but only one person stepped out and started walking towards him. He wasn't dressed in a dark uniform, so the tenseness that had instantly permeated his body, vanished. He recognized the young 'observer' he'd spoken to the other day.

As the young man stepped onto the pier and walked towards him Joe called out "You again," and as the man came closer, he asked, "Did the controllers send you? You do know the patrol boat's gone, escorting the other ships to Antarctica?"

"I'm aware of that. And no, the controllers have no idea where I am."

Joe stepped off the yacht and onto the pier. He wasn't going to invite this young man on board. He also heard movement behind him as no doubt the others below had woken up and were coming up on deck to see what was going on.

"So why are you here? Are you still 'observing' us?"

"I took cover here from the storm."

"You weren't here yesterday." Joe interrupted him.

"I took cover in town. I saw the storm coming so I decided to stay rather than try to outrun it. They have a communal centre where aircars can be parked during stormy weather. I stayed there. I shifted here half an hour ago, but decided to wait until I saw you were awake. I didn't want to disturb you earlier. But I didn't want to wait too long. I was about to come and wake you when I saw you come up on deck…"

"Good morning, Aaron," Helen called from where she was standing half in, half out of the hatch to the main cabin. "Are you joining us for breakfast?"

"No. I would like to but I'm here to warn you."

"Warn us about what?" Joe asked.

"Two teams of enforcers are on their way in aircars, they say, to interview you. But I wonder why they need six men to do that."

"Now that's interesting," Joe said.

"It should be an hour before they get here. I thought you should know."

"I do appreciate it Aaron, thank you. Billy says aircars have problems flying over the sea, is that correct?"

"That's right. Circuits get scrambled by reflections off the sea's surface of the power broadcast. That's why I wanted to warn you. If you leave now, you could be well out to sea when they get here. They won't be able to follow you."

"Then we'll be gone by the time they get here." Joe affirmed.

"I'll leave now as well, so they won't know I've warned you."

"How come they don't know where you are?"

"I disabled the transponder. When I get back, I'll say it was damaged in the storm, and that the last time I saw you was when you were being towed in by the patrol boat."

"Thanks Aaron. You're a good person."

"You know, not everyone agrees with the controllers and how they run everyone's lives. I've seen towns like Billy's, where people manage quite well without the controllers directing their every move, in the guise of protecting them. Especially now that they have accelerated their shift to Antarctica. They want to set up a new society there but not everyone agrees with that. It would be regressing back to how it was after the disaster. I think they don't like the fact they have lost control over the years and want it back, that's what's behind the move to Antarctica. It has nothing to do with what they insist is a continuing rise in global temperatures along with worse storms than we've had before. People are looking for a way out, and Eyresea shows us how it can be achieved."

"There is no way out," Joe stated. "You adapt and learn to live with the world the way it is. If it's still warming up, that can't be changed."

"I suppose," Aaron said.

Joe suddenly realized the reason why dome shaped buildings were so prevalent. Domes were strongest form for warding off serious windstorms as the air would flow around and over them rather than buffet them as it would the more conventional buildings.

"You'd better get going." Aaron said. "Standing here talking is wasting time you could be sailing. And I want to be well gone before those enforcers get here. As far as anyone knows, I left an hour ago."

"Okay," Joe said. "Then I wish you the best of luck. And thanks once again for the warning."

Aaron nodded and smiled. "I'll see you around," he said, and with that he left Joe standing beside the yacht and walked back along the pier towards his aircar in the quadrangle.

Joe watched until the aircar spread its wings before lifting from the quadrangle. It made a circle in the air above it before heading towards the east, quickly becoming a small speck that soon vanished from sight in the immensity of a deep blue sky.

Before jumping back on board, Joe untied the stern rope from the stanchion on the pier, then did the same with the rope tying the bow to the pier. With both ropes safely coiled on deck he pushed against the pier after he jumped back on board and the yacht immediately drifted away. He said to Helen who was still half in half out of the hatch, "No point sitting here while enforcers are on their way. Wake up Billy and send him up to help with the sails. There's a good breeze which is fine for sailing. I'd rather not use the motor in case they can track it. Let them think we're still here."

He immediately unfurled the mainsail, hauling it up the mast. Billy appeared as the sail was beginning to flutter and fill with air. Without saying anything, Billy went to the foresail and did the same. While he was doing that, Joe began steering the yacht to take advantage of the wind rapidly filling the sails, sailing away from the small cove where they'd been moored.

Withing a few minutes they were out into the harbour already busy with fishing boats heading to favourite spots for the day's work. Glancing briefly back towards the domed town buildings as they sailed past, he thought for a moment the skyline appeared different, as if there was a gap between some buildings that hadn't been there before. But he couldn't be sure; he hadn't given the town much more than a cursory glance while they were being towed in behind the patrol boat. With fishing boats out and about, he assumed everything must be normal. He brought his focus back to sailing away as quickly as possible.

Half an hour later, they'd left the seaside town way behind and were heading towards the open ocean, that great Southern Ocean which encircled the world, and the newly regenerating continent of Antarctica far to the south.

The sun glistened on the waves rolling by them. The wind blew sea spray over the bow which with an occasionally heavier gust of wind, splashed him, making his eyes momentarily sting. A dolphin sprang out of the water in front of their bow and cavorted joyously for a minute before swimming off after a school of fish.

A beautiful day, he thought, feeling as free as the wind that filled their sails.

19...

The deep blue waters of the Great Southern Ocean filled him with joy, with massive swells rolling ponderously around the globe pushed by a steady driving wind giving them a decent forward speed. The yacht was at home, sailing in the place where it was created to sail. Harold had followed the designs of the boat builders of Chiloe, an island off the bottom end of Chile famous for its boat builders who built craft capable of withstanding the enormous storms prevalent in the Great Southern Ocean that forced its way through the bottom of Cape Horn and the northernmost tip of the Antarctic peninsula. Although Harold had used steel instead of wood for its construction, the design closely followed that of those famous boat builders. It was Mary who told him that. He would not have known otherwise. But the ease with which the yacht sailed these waters told him all he needed to know.

He wished he'd met Harold. The man was a genius, but unfortunately, he passed away after the initial inundation of the rising sea. He remembered his only glimpse of the man had been the night the first of the smaller tsunamis that initially raised sea levels hit the city during a fierce summer storm. He had seen Harold in the cockpit steering this yacht through the city's flooded streets while he was rescuing an old man trapped on a rooftop before the building collapsed. The yacht, the next time he saw it, was moored by the temporary floating docks at the edge of the flooded city. Mary had been on board, but her husband Harold was in hospital in a coma where he later died. *He never got see how beautifully his creation performed.* A touch of sadness washed over Joe momentarily, but was soon dispelled by the beauty of the day.

The wind that propelled them was cool, and Joe relished its coolness after the heat he'd experienced in the inland sea. It was a pleasure to feel cool again. *No wonder people want to move south to*

Antarctica. It would be centuries before that place gets too hot, or maybe it never will. Maybe a tipping point could be reached that starts to bring the climate back towards something cooler... Another ice age in a hundred thousand years? He smiled at the thought of that length of time. *I won't be around to see that...unless of course we encounter a seriously bad anomaly... And I never want to see one of those again.*

He set the steering to keep them on a southeasterly course, heading towards Bass Strait between Tasmania and the mainland. In the back of his mind, he was thinking they should sail to South America, to Argentina where the future of humanity was in the efforts to colonize the Moon and Mars rather than trying to live in Antarctica. They would have to stop before crossing the Pacific for essential supplies. They didn't have enough for such a long crossing. But it was nothing more than a vague idea. At that moment, he was happy sailing far enough offshore to avoid any patrolling aircars that might be looking for them.

Joe couldn't help smiling as he watched the two teenagers who had their backs to him as they sat in front of the cabin on the foredeck, joking and laughing while they chatted about — *who knows what?* It was good to see them so comfortable with each other, and it made him realize what a great decision it was to allow Billy to come with them.

Helen needed someone her own age to be with, rather than an old woman who wasn't really her grandmother, and a middle aged man who wasn't really her uncle but an old friend of her father whom she always treated as if he were a part of her family. That circumstances had forced them to be together was not something she thought about anymore. Too much had happened over the last few months with the death of her father, her kidnapping, and subsequent rescue by Uncle Joe, being introduced to Mary, and a safe living place on the yacht, the degeneration of civilized behavior and their fleeing the slowly collapsing city only to be engulfed by a tsunami followed by a mysterious but vicious electrical storm which brought them here. It was overwhelming, yet she had the resilience to push through it, almost forgetting it as she lived each moment relishing every new day as an exciting adventure. She had never felt so alive before…

To Joe she seemed happy about their relationship and that's all that mattered as far as he was concerned. He also like Billy. He thought he was good kid, and that he and Helen liked each other was a bonus. He had come to think of them as his family, and as the person responsible for taking care of them, he promised himself he would always protect them.

Every so often, spray from a wave the bow cut through cascaded over the fore deck, producing gouts of laughter from the two teenagers. The wind sighed in the rigging, the sails created gentle noises as they flexed, and the yacht moved in harmony with the rolling waves while leaning slightly to one side as Joe tacked closer towards the mainland. Over the horizon to the southeast he could see banks of cumulus clouds building up and he guessed that Tasmania was somewhere beneath or beyond them. But their destination wasn't Tasmania.

He had talked about it with Mary. They were curious about what had happened to their city after they left and wanted to see what had become of it. In fact, Mary had insisted on going there, so he agreed. It worried him though; Mary was not her usual cheerful self. She was sad and withdrawn, no doubt remembering her husband Harold had died there after surviving the first of the tsunamis that raised sea levels before the city was abandoned. They had cast his ashes into the sea from his runabout before it had been blown up by a para-military group attempting to kill him. He had moved onto Mary's yacht after the riots that overtook what was left of the city, during which he'd rescued Helen from her kidnappers, and had almost lost his own life. They left the city not long after, which was fortuitous because they were well out at sea when the giant tsunami hit, destroying the coastline from one end of the country to the other, changing the world forever.

He understood wanting to visit what was left of the city was Mary's way of paying respect to her late husband; it was no different from someone visiting the grave site of a departed loved-one.

"You know," Joe said to Mary as they came closer to what had once been the southern coast of Victoria but was now considerably altered after the incursion of the sea, "this yacht doesn't have a name. Why is that? Every boat has... should have a name."

They were in the galley sharing a cup of tea, while Billy and Helen were above, making sure the yacht sailed safely in coastal waters notorious for centuries for causing many shipwrecks. The waters were deeper now, but it remained prudent to keep watch for possible dangers. Hidden reefs, partially submerged bommies that might once have been sandstone islands offshore, just beneath the surface were scattered along this coast. Hitting one would be a disaster.

"We had no time to consider it," Mary said hesitantly. "We weren't ready. Everything fell apart... with wild storms, the sudden rise in sea level flooding the city... Harold having his heart attack soon after we'd we sailed through the streets out into The Bay... being rescued by the navy... Harold taken to hospital for treatment... the confusion... It was chaotic."

She took a deep breath and slowly exhaled as she gathered her thoughts. "Then you came along with Helen needing somewhere to stay... the riots... Harold passing away, his burial at sea, for which I am ever grateful for your help, and out departure... just so much..."

"Yeah, it was," Joe agreed.

"I haven't thought of it since. But you're right. Do you have any suggestions?"

The yacht leaned as it changed course, and instantly Joe was on his feet, popping his head up through the hatch to see what was happening. Billy saw him, reassured him everything was under control.

"Saw some rough water up ahead. Looks like a big reef just under the surface."

Joe joined him in the cockpit where he could get a better view.

Helen, strapped to the rail around the cabin, was in front on the fore-deck. "It's very rough," she called out confirming Billy's statement.

Ahead was a wide area of choppy water with waves crashing and breaking on something solid barely beneath the surface. *If the tide was out,* Joe thought as he studied it, *you could probably stand on it quite safely.* But the tide was in, pounding it with smashing waves. Spumes of spray belched into the air.

"Give it a wide berth," Joe said redundantly since Billy was already doing that.

The three of them watched silently as Billy took the yacht well inside the channel between the submerged island and the mainland. The island was almost a kilometre long, with the water on the lee side relatively calm. On the seaward side waves smashed into it, rolling across it to cascade off the calmer side in shallow waterfalls. Wind whipped spray from the waves up into the air, some of which blew across them as they sailed by with room to spare.

"If I remember right, there should be a couple more islands like this one," Joe said.

"Don't worry," Billy assured him, "We'll keep clear of them."

They had barely passed by the submerged island when Helen called out, "There's another one ahead."

"Yeah, Joe said. "I can see it."

A white patch of foaming water like the one they'd just passed.

"I see it too," Billy stated.

"Those islands used to mark the ancient coastline before the softer stone and land behind them was worn away by the sea over thousands of years. In my time the remnants of that ancient coastline were a row of flat islands. Now with the new sea level they're a bunch of dangerous reefs just beneath the surface."

Billy smiled at the 'history' lesson.

He's a natural, Joe thought as he turned to step back down the hatch into the main cabin. He's grown up living by the sea, fishing, sailing… He's in his element out here. Confident they were in safe hands, he felt relieved to have some moments to relax, to not worry about the yacht which they depended on.

"Is everything all right?" Mary asked as he sat back down at the table in the galley.

"It's fine. "We're sailing past a trio of sunken islands. Billy's good at the helm so we don't have to worry. What that means though is we are perhaps a day away from where the entrance to Port Phillip Bay used to be. It all looks so different now."

"I trust you won't miss it."

"I hope it's recognizable. Everything's changed so much."

"After a thousand years," Mary said. "I'm not surprised. But I have every confidence in you."

"That's good, and speaking of good, you did say some time back that this yacht was your home, a good home…"

"And?"

"I thought that would be a proper name for the yacht."

"A good home?" She looked skeptical.

"Yeah, but not in English. In Spanish. You told me Harold built this yacht to the design of similar boats constructed by the fishermen sailors of Chiloe, off the coast of Chile, that it was built to withstand the wild weather of the Great Southern Ocean."

"Harold spent a lot of time studying those boat designs."

"I thought we should name her *Buen hogar*, which in Spanish means Good home."

"I like it," Mary said after barely a moment's thought. "It does seem appropriate. I think Harold would be pleased…"

"Then *Buenhogar* it is."

According to Joe, the land they were passing should appear familiar. They should be near the opening to Port Phillip Bay, but there was neither of the two peninsulas pointing at each other to delineate the shape of The Heads they had sailed through when they left the city before. Nor were there any coastal towns that could have helped him determine their position. There was a wide open bay that appeared large enough to have drowned what was once Port Phillip Bay and Westernport Bay, and everything along their shorelines. Nothing was recognizable. There was no GPS to indicate their position and he was not able to use a sextant to determine it. If there had been one on board along with printed tables for calculating position, he would not have known how to use them —besides which, the tables would be so out of date as to be useless.

He had been relying on his memories of this coastline, also useless. Everything he saw was pristine with no indication of any inhabitants to give him any idea of location. His only option was to follow the coastline as it became an enormous open bay and hope that they would find the remnants of the city they had left —to them still only a few months ago— a thousand years in the past. *Would anything be there? Anything recognizable?*

The bay was so wide he couldn't see the other side or how far it extended. He could no longer think of it as a Bay; it was simply a massive indent in the coastline. Billy was steering while he stood on the fore-deck in front of the cabin searching for anything familiar. Far away to the east, almost on the horizon where sea and sky blended into a soft haze, he saw two dark shapes heading south. Ships, obviously, so, somewhere ahead of them must be the location from which these two ships had sailed.

He moved around the cabin, back to the cockpit and said to Billy, "There's two ships ahead heading south. So there will be a town or a city further in, from where those ships departed. At least we know we're heading in the right direction."

"Do you think they're going to Antarctica, like the other two?"

"Probably. We won't know until we find where they came from."

"If we follow this coast, we'll find it. Will it be the city you came from?"

"That's what I'm hoping. Those ships had to come from somewhere with a port large enough to service them, which means a reasonably sized city."

"Do you think my father could be there?" Billy asked hesitantly.

Joe looked at Billy's anxious face, the glint of hope in his eyes. He didn't want to disappoint him, but finding his father was extremely unlikely. He didn't know how to respond.

"Sorry," Billy said. "It was a stupid question. I can't help hoping though…"

20...

The next morning, they sailed leisurely along the indented coast towards a general greyish haze in the air indicating an industrial city. *Nothing's changed,* Joe thought as he eyed the grey haze ahead. *Wherever humans congregate in large numbers they fill their immediate environment with shit.* Since being in this time he'd accustomed himself to clear skies and clean air. The thought of being immersed in a partially polluted atmosphere again did not sit well with him.

All four were on deck. Mary was tranquil, almost smiling as she looked for anything familiar. Helen and Billy were bursting with excited energy and looked as if they couldn't wait to go ashore once they got there; Helen, because she felt this was home even though it appeared totally different from anything she could remember, and Billy, because this was the biggest city he'd ever seen. The only city, because the other place he'd thought of as a city compared to Eyresea, was nothing more than a seaside town.

The low rise city extended from the shoreline back up into a series of undulating hills. A wide channel between the piers and jetties along the shoreline fronting the city, separated it from many lines of almost vertically shaped densely overgrown islands that looked like volcanic lava cores left standing after the softer volcanic ash surrounding them had weathered away. Most of them were only a few metres above sea level, but there were several much taller ones in each row. One or two were possibly forty metres tall and they stood out against the others. Covered totally with shrubs and trees, with tropical vines and creepers wrapping around tree trunks obscuring what lay beneath, the islands were beautiful, extending over an area roughly ten square kilometres with straight line gaps between the rows of islands.

"Does that not look familiar to you?" Joe asked Mary.

She held his arm to steady herself. Her emotions were running high as she remembered how with Harold, they had escaped the first wave of massive flooding, sailing through city streets out into a wild ferociously stormy bay, only for Harold to suffer heart problems, and once they were rescued and towed back to safety by a navy patrol boat, he had been taken immediately to hospital for treatment, to later die there, his heart unable to stand the strain of the years spent building the yacht and struggling to control it during the worst storm they had ever experienced. Somewhere between those island remnants of the city and the shoreline of the new city is where they'd scattered Harold's ashes into the sea, only there was no new city there then. Her heat gave a few flutters as she wondered if they would be able to find the spot.

Billy was steering the yacht, and Helen was staring at the rows of vertical islands with intense curiosity.

"I'm not sure," Mary finally replied to Joe's question. With her free hand she wiped away tears running down her cheeks.

"The regularity of the islands, the spacing between them… Doesn't it look to you like they could be remnants of city buildings and the streets between them? I think over a thousand years the smaller buildings washed away but the bigger ones, the taller ones stayed, collapsing down on themselves as the foundations eroded. Now they're tall narrow islands."

Mary and Helen stared at the nearest islands, trying to discern the shape of the city they once knew. They couldn't be certain.

What else could it be? Joe thought.

Birds flew over and around the tops of the vertical islands. Joe knew those islands would be inhabited with all kinds of wildlife. *Life always fills whatever niches it can find.* They saw a few small boats or dinghies with people fishing in some of the wider channels between the islands.

Joe felt tempted to sail along one of the wider spaces between two rows of islands but thought better of it. There could be all kinds of rubble below the surface that could cause problems. It was better to maintain a wide berth around these islands as they approached the new city on the shores beyond.

Passing by the last of the island conglomeration, they entered the wide channel between the islands and the shoreline where many jetties and piers indicated a busy marine way of life. Hundreds of small boats, yachts, fishing and work boats were either moored at many of the piers or at anchorages close to them. Out on the water beyond the sea moorings, boats were heading out for the day's activities. Far over the new city the occasional sparkle of reflected light indicated aircars flying in and out of the city well away from the sea.

"Wow," Billy exclaimed. "It's huge."

"Do you think anyone will notice us?" Helen asked.

"Probably not," Mary said. "We're just another boat returning."

Joe had reefed in the mainsail, leaving only the smaller foresail still filled with air to give them a gentle forward momentum. With this done, he stood beside Mary, holding her arm to make sure she maintained balance. He pointed towards a distant range of hills rising behind the city along the foreshore. "I remember those hills," he said. "They haven't changed, although everything is different. It was somewhere in this area that we scattered Harold's ashes; I think."

Tears welled up in Mary's eyes as she remembered that moment, now so long ago in the past, but so very recent in her memories.

"I can't be certain," Joe clarified, "so much has changed…"

Mary gripped Joe's arm and squeezed it slightly to acknowledge what he'd said. They remained silent until Mary's tears stopped. She wiped her eyes with her free hand. "Promise me," she said softly so only Joe could hear, "when I die, you'll bury me or scatter my ashes here, so I can be together again with Harold."

Startled, Joe looked closely at Mary who gave him a wan smile. "Don't say things like that," he whispered back.

"I'm dying Joe. I know it. I can feel it in my bones, in my heart…"

"Mary…"

"You know it's true. My journey comes to an end here, so promise me…"

He could see it in her eyes, the truth he didn't want to admit to himself. She had grown progressively weaker and more infirm since the moment they'd arrived at Eyresea… since the moment they'd come though the time storm into this place. She'd tried to hide it from them, even initially from herself, but it was obvious to Joe, especially now that she'd pointed it out to him. He wondered if Helen and Billy had noticed yet. Probably not…too wrapped up in each other… But it would soon become obvious to them as well.

"I promise…"

This time Mary gave I him a smile that lit up her face. "Thank you."

The wind had dropped as they came closer to the city and the yacht slowed. Joe didn't want to use the electric motor. *Best not to let any observers know they had that capability. Never know when we might need it.* Leisurely sailing in gave them time to unobtrusively assess the situation.

He wasn't expecting any trouble, but he did expect someone would be waiting for them. They went to a lot of trouble earlier to talk to them, so he had no doubt they were aware of them arriving and would send someone for them.

What kind of reception they would receive was anybody's guess.

Powered vessels gave them plenty of room as they sailed towards the harbour. The yacht gently rocked and undulated over the wakes of passing boats. People waved to them from these boats, and they waved back. Joe tacked around a cluster of moored yachts into a clear space leading towards a jetty that had only a few boats moored beside it. There was a lower section near the end of the jetty where yachts could temporarily tie up, so they maneuvered their way towards that. Billy was by the bow, ready to jump onto the lower section of the jetty so he could tie them securely to one of several bollards. Helen released the foresail. It flapped gently, devoid of air and the forward momentum of the yacht slowed to a gentle drift.

As soon as they were secure, Joe reefed in the foresail, then went aft and used another rope to tie them to the jetty. They ignored the people who had wandered along the jetty to watch them arrive.

There were always people on piers and jetties watching boats and marine activities. If they weren't sitting and fishing, they watched with endless fascination those who did things in boats on the water, some dreaming that they would like to be out there, others simply curious.

By and large, those on the boats doing stuff tended to ignore those who were watching from ashore, subconsciously thinking of them as part of the background scenery. Joe, however, was surreptitiously observing those watching and those who walked along the jetty towards them. He didn't see anyone wearing the black uniforms of enforcers, which was a relief. He went about making sure they were properly moored to the landing jetty, that *Buenhogar*, was secure, before any of them stepped ashore.

"Don't go far," he told Helen and Billy who could hardly contain their excitement. "We may need to leave in a hurry."

"Really?" Billy said, looking towards the buildings lining the foreshore "it looks pretty good to me."

"Keep us in sight. I'll run a flag up on the mast to let you know if we must leave. You come back immediately you see it. Okay?"

"What kind of flag?" Billy wanted to know.

"Doesn't matter. Whatever we've got. You see a flag you come back."

"You worry too much," Helen said, "but okay, we'll come back right away if we see a flag."

"I hate to point this out," Mary said quietly, "but we don't have any flags on board."

"No? Then I'll tie on a bloody T shirt and run that up. All right?"

"Yeah, we get the picture," Billy said.

Then they were off, talking to people on the jetty briefly before heading towards the buildings lining the waterfront where they could see shops and eateries doing a roaring trade with crowds of people moving in and out of them.

Joe sat back down in the cockpit with a sigh. Mary sat beside him. "What next?" She asked.

"Let the kids have their fun while we wait. I suspect our arrival has been observed and we should soon receive an official visit. So, let's relax and enjoy the sunshine and fresh air."

"There," Joe said after they'd been sitting awhile. "Two aircars are coming in for a landing near the jetty…"

He stood up to watch the aircars drift over across the edge of the city, slowly losing altitude until they were above the road and the parking spaces where the jetty extended from the land. Mary didn't stand. She watched nervously. The two cars dropped quietly down to the ground.

Three sets of legs extruded on each side for them and the instant they touched the ground their dark wings folded back against the upper sides of each vehicle. Having landed in unison close to each other, nothing else happened. *Giant fucking cockroaches with bulging eyes and wings folded back against their sides*, was the image popped into his head the moment they finished landing. He wondered if they were deliberately built that way to frighten people.

"What are they waiting for?" Mary asked.

"Maybe they want to intimidate us. But I can wait as long as they can, so they'll gain nothing that way." Joe shifted in his chair, ready to stand up. "Perhaps I should take a walk along the jetty, take the initiative and approach them instead of waiting."

"Joe. Let's just wait and see what they do."

"That's probably best…" He sat back down making sure he had a clear view along the jetty to where the aircars waited, silent, black and glistening with the sun shining on them.

No one walking along the street by the waterfront came near them. It was almost like the *cockroach* cars had invisible screens around them that repulsed people. The aircar Aaron had used wasn't like those, nor were the ones used by the enforcers at their first encounter. These were different. *Military? Certainly not civilian types.*

It took fifteen minutes, which seemed twice as long, before the wing on one side of both aircars raised up to expose an entrance. Black ramps slid down to touch the ground. From one, a single black clad man emerged. He started to walk along the jetty towards them. Behind him, two other black clad figures emerged from the other aircar to follow him. Those two had vicious looking weapons held in a position enabling them to be fired quickly if needed. Their faces were obscured by black helmets with darkened visors.

Mary looked at Joe and he knew exactly what she was thinking —*they probably would have shot you if you'd approached them first.*

"Yea," he mumbled, "not very friendly by the look of them."

The man in front of the two armed enforcers stopped beside the yacht and looked at Mary and Joe sitting in the cockpit, waiting. He raised his visor so they could see his face. It was hard, as if sculpted from granite, too hard to crack a smile. The two behind also stopped and positioned themselves on either side of him so they both had clear shots if there was any trouble. He couldn't see their faces behind their helmets, but their intention was clear.

Before the man could say anything, Joe said," Is this how you always welcome visitors?"

"I ask the questions," the man stated.

"Then ask away."

Mary gave Joe a surreptitious nudge. Don't antagonize them.

"Is anyone else on board?"

"No."

The man nodded to one his assistants and that man stepped forward to come on board.

Joe stood up, and both armed men instantly aimed their weapons directly at him, intentions clear.

"You ask permission to come on board," Joe said quietly. "That's the usual custom. Or is it different here than anywhere else?"

"Would you rather we shoot you first, and then come on board to look around?"

Joe raised both hands palms forward. "Okay, you made your point. Your man can come on board."

They stood silently while the heavily armed enforcer stepped onto the deck, went to the hatch and dropped down into the main cabin. They waited silently, each staring at the other until he emerged a moment later, to step back onto the jetty where he took up his previous position with his weapon aimed at Joe.

"So, where are the other two?"

What is it with these arseholes?

"They're teenagers. They went to have a look around town."

He considered that, his unwavering gaze upon Joe. "All right. My men will wait here for them. Both of you will come with me."

"Hang on there. Mary's rather elderly and not very able. She should stay…"

"Not important," the enforcer said interrupting Joe. "She comes too."

"It's alright Joe," Mary said as she stood up slowly. She held onto his arm to steady herself.

The man, and one of the enforcers turned and started back along the jetty. The other stayed beside the yacht. Joe followed at a pace slow enough to allow Mary some dignity. She was struggling, and it wasn't easy, but she put on a brave face.

Joe noted impatience wash across the lead enforcer's face as he waited beside his aircar for them to arrive. The other man stood beside the second car with his weapon aimed in their general direction.

What does he think I'm going to do? Joe glared at him, abandoning any willingness to cooperate with them.

He didn't like being pushed around or ordered to do something without adequate explanation. They were arrogant, and overbearing. He was no longer interested in this society realizing it was nothing more than a police state.

But with weapons aimed at them, it was better to comply.

He paused to allow Mary to get her breath. The man with the weapon by the second car immediately pointed it threateningly at Joe, but his superior waved his hand, and the weapon was lowered. When they finally got to the side of the aircar, the leader indicated the open door. "Get in and strap in," he ordered.

His impatience got the better of him as he watched Mary struggling to get into the aircar. He stepped onto the ramp and gave her a shove to push her in. Mary stumbled forward and almost fell. Joe spun around and was about to shove the man off the ramp when he saw the other enforcer raise his weapon to shoot. He glared at the impatient man on the ramp who held his gaze without blinking until he turned back to help Mary get into a seat.

He made sure she was properly strapped in before sitting next to her, also fastening his seat belt. The lead enforcer settled himself into the front seat.

The ramp retracted and the door hissed shut.

Joe was seated in a position where he could see what the enforcer did to start the aircar and how he used the controls to rise off the ground to fly away. *That seems simple enough,* he thought, filing it away for future reference. If they could escape from where they were being taken, they would need an aircar to fly back.

The second aircar stayed where it was. The two enforces left were waiting for Billy and Helen, and Joe hoped they would see them there and stay out of sight, at least until he and Mary could get back.

Of course they would, he reassured himself. *They're both smart enough to keep away while that aircar is parked there, even if the enforcers aren't visible. They'll wait to see 'the flag' up the mast to tell them it's safe.*

But the important question was, *Will we be able to get back?*

21...

As the aircar swung away from the waterfront and headed over the city he lost sight of the waiting enforcers by the jetty where they had moored *Buenhogar*.

They flew inland over a wide expanse of low rise buildings that eventually gave way to what could only be private houses extending back up into the hills. Eventually they flew over scattered houses interspersed with farmland, before the greenery petered out, becoming dry and desolate over the other side a low range of hills.

"Where are you taking us?" Joe asked.

The man ignored the question. He focused on entering a set of numbers via a small keyboard on the dashboard in front of him. Coordinates for their destination Joe suspected. With that complete, he turned and glared at Joe. "Sit back and enjoy the ride," he said brusquely before turning his attention back to the dashboard.

Pissed off with the enforcer's arrogance towards them and his expectation of their compliance, Joe fumed. Mary was staring through the window but not seeing the land slip by below them. She looked as if she was in a trance, and that worried Joe.

Fuck this, I've had enough.

They had been in the air for almost fifteen minutes and the enforcer hadn't uttered another word. He didn't appear to be flying the vehicle. He was sitting there staring into the distance ahead while the vehicle flew itself. He naturally expected the passengers to do as he told them. People always obeyed enforcers, but this time his arrogance and belief in his power over others would be his undoing.

Joe thought that they were heading for the capitol where a committee wanted to question them. Their earlier attempt at communication had been cut off before it had begun during the dusty electrical storm. They'd obviously been tracking them as they'd sailed along the southern coast, and as soon as they had arrived at this major city, they'd sent someone to get them. The pilot hadn't radioed to tell them he was returning with 'prisoners' and Joe wondered if anyone was aware of where they were and when they were supposed to arrive, or even if the 'prisoners' had been taken into custody. It was time to do something before they got too far away.

He quietly unbuckled his seat belt; certain his action had not been seen. He leaned forward and suddenly wrapped his arms around the pilot's neck in a choke hold. The man must have been day dreaming. His body jerked with a spasm of shock. He brought his hands up to try and release the hold, but Joe applied sufficient pressure to make the man start to black out.

"Turn this fucking thing around and take us back."

The man was stunned. People he took in for questioning always did what they were told because they knew the consequences if they didn't.

Joe applied a little more pressure. The man would soon be unconscious. He struggled, and writhed, but soon stopped. Joe released a little pressure to allow some blood to circulate. He didn't want the man to be unconscious just yet.

"Turn it around," Joe repeated menacingly.

"You won't get away with this…" the pilot started to say, but Joe cut him off.

"If you don't want to be dead, do what I say. I'll give you a few seconds…"

"Okay," the man gasped. He had no illusions that Joe wouldn't do it. No one had ever attacked him before. But this renegade was threatening to kill him. Fear washed through his body, something he'd never experienced until now. "Okay, I'm turning around."

He reached forward and did something to one of the controls, tapped the small keyboard and the aircar immediately banked to the right and commenced a wide circle before straightening and heading back to coastal city, Joe presumed, along the path taken when they left.

"We're heading back."

"Thank you," Joe responded. He increased the pressure on the carotid artery and within a second the pilot slumped in his seat, unconscious. Joe released him and reached down to extract the man's weapon so he couldn't use it if he woke sooner than expected.

"Is he dead?" Mary asked tentatively.

"Unconscious. He should stay that way for the time it takes to get back. I'll wake him when we get there so he can land the car."

"The others will see us."

"I'll make sure we land before we're near them, so they won't see us. I'll sneak up and take them out. Then I'll run that T shirt up on the mast so Billy and Helen will know it's safe to come back, and we can get out of here."

Mary slumped back in her seat, her face pale. She seemed to be gasping.

"Are you okay?"

"No. It feels like my heart is going to burst."

"Take a few deep breaths and let them out slowly. It'll help bring your heartbeat down."

He felt her pulse and it was racing. But as she followed his instructions her pulse slowed, and colour came back into her face. She smiled, which was encouraging.

"It won't be long before we get back. I can see the green fields behind the city so we're almost there."

Joe leaned forward and woke up the pilot, who seemed dazed and uncomprehending for a moment before he suddenly remembered what had happened. His hand went down to discover an empty holster, before he twisted in his seat to look at Joe.

"Who are you?" He demanded; his voice raspy.

"Nobody important. Just land this aircar in that park I can see back from the water's edge."

They were about half a kilometre from the jetty where Buenhogar was moored, and he was hoping that the other two enforcers would not notice this aircar returning and landing.

"And if I don't?"

"You won't live to regret it." Joe whispered harshly.

From behind, Joe took hold of the man's head on both sides,

cupping his ears firmly. The man was strapped into his seat and couldn't turn to attempt a counterattack.

"I'll snap your neck if you don't land us, and we'll take our chances of getting out when this car flies over the sea and falls out of the sky." Ahead, beyond the edges of the city, the sea sparkled in the sunlight. "It's up to you. I don't give a fuck."

"Alright. Let me reach for the controls."

Joe relaxed his grip enough to encourage the man who leaned forward and did something on the control panel. The car immediately slowed and drifted down towards the small park Joe had indicated. It landed on the grass as soft as a butterfly landing on a flower in search of nectar.

"Very good," Joe said. "Now open the door."

"No,"

"You sure about that?"

"You're stuck in here. I won't open the door. Fuck you."

"That's too bad," Joe said. He instantly wrapped his forearms around the man's neck again and re-applied the choke hold, rendering the pilot unconscious within seconds.

"Now how are we going to get out?" Mary asked.

"I'll shoot the control panel. It might activate an emergency exit. If that doesn't work, I'll shoot the door lock, and force it open."

Mary shrugged as if to say, why not?

Joe aimed the gun he'd taken from the pilot's holster at the control panel and pulled the trigger.

Nothing happened. *Useless piece of shit!* He was about to try smashing the windscreen to see if it would break when he remembered; the weapons were genetically coded to only work with the persons they were issued to. *How did I forget that?*

He reached forward and placed the weapon in the unconscious man's hand, lifted it up and as tiny lights flickered intermittently along one edge of the weapon, he aimed it at the control panel. He forced the pilot's finger to pull the trigger. There was an instant flash and the control panel burst apart, electricity sizzling and sparking as circuits inside shorted out.

The car vibrated as the side door opened and the ramp slid down.

"That's better than I expected," Joe said.

Searching the pilot's side pockets he found two plastic restraints, one of which he snapped on the pilot's wrists locking them tightly together. Leaning over and reaching down he strapped the man's feet together with the other restraint making sure it also wrapped around the metal leg of the seat.

He sat back up and released the clasp of Mary's seatbelt.

"What did you do?" Mary asked.

"Strapped him to his chair. If he wakes up sooner rather than later, he won't be getting out and chasing us," he explained. "It's time we got a move on."

"At least you didn't kill him," she said as he released her seat belt and helped her to stand. Together they edged cautiously down the ramp into a field of freshly mowed grass.

"Some of the people in the park might come and release him."

"I don't think that's likely. From what I've seen, people keep well away from enforcers. I doubt anyone's going to release him. He'll be there until other enforcers come looking for him."

There had been people in the open grassed area as the aircar was descending but looking around as they stood at the base of the aircar's ramp, there was no one to be seen. He felt eyes watching him, but those watchers remained hidden. They'd vanished the moment they saw the aircar descending.

"Come on," he said as he held Mary's arm to support her.

He led her slowly towards a narrow street going towards the harbour. He'd noted it as the aircar descended. It was the only one going towards where they were moored. Other exits from the grassed park went into roads going in different directions into the harbor-side city. He had been looking forward to learning about this city that had grown around this new coastline, but exploring the city was no longer an option.

We need to get away before this bastard is discovered, he thought as he glanced back at the black brooding aircar with its door wide open standing starkly by itself in the middle of the grassy park.

No one will go near that, he told himself.

Joe led Mary cautiously along the narrow street which had bushes and low fences on either side creating a shady path leading back to the waterfront with its piers and jetties where he hoped there was enough activity to hide them from the enforcers waiting near the other aircar.

We do have one advantage, he thought as they made their way along the shady narrow street, *they won't be expecting us.* And that gave him something to smile about.

22...

Billy and Helen, partially hidden by a tall tree with several clumped bushes at its base, studied the jetty and their yacht moored beside it, and the black aircar of the enforcers sitting on the pavement at the end of the jetty where it joined the walkway along the foreshore.

"There's no flag up, so it's not safe," Helen said.

"I can't see any enforcers…"

"They're probably inside that aircar waiting for whoever returns to the yacht."

"Do you think they've got Mary and Joe?" Billy asked.

"It looks awfully quiet," Helen noted. "They've probably taken them somewhere."

"This is not good," Billy stated. He was beginning to feel scared, mostly because he had no idea of what to do. But also, like everyone else he knew, he didn't trust enforcers. They were often violent, but what instilled fear more than anything else was you couldn't see their faces or know who they were with the black helmets they wore. You could never gauge what their intentions were, what they were likely to do so you avoided contact with them unless they spoke directly to you. When they did, you would do without question what they asked because they were more likely than not to shoot you with a paralyzing jolt if you didn't, then ask questions later. They didn't care whether they hurt you, or even killed you once they got what they wanted to know. You meant nothing to them. And knowing that, he was frightened about what they might do to Mary and Joe if they'd taken them.

"I don't know what to do," Billy whispered to Helen.

"Let's wait back here and keep an eye on them," she said, referring to whoever might be in the ominous looking aircar.

Back, along the way they'd come, there was constant activity around the jetties and piers with boats and yachts leaving or arriving to be moored, fishermen coming and going, or simply people sightseeing, as they themselves had done recently. The cheerful noises emanating from that activity floated almost inaudibly around them, reassuring them life was normal, pleasant. But around the jetty where their boat was moored, it was bereft of activity, as if an invisible wall had been extended for a hundred metres all around the silent aircar with no one going anywhere near it.

"If we wait until it gets dark, we might be able to sneak past them and get back on the yacht, "Helen suggested.

"They're probably waiting for us to do exactly that. They can see in the dark with special night vision amplification built into their helmet visors."

"There you go, pessimistic again."

"Realistic. I know what they're like, you don't."

"So, what's the plan then?"

"Observe, evaluate, then we can act. Rushing in blindly only leads to disaster."

"Observe and evaluate… Alright, we can do that. We've got all the time in the world."

"What are you two whispering about?"

The unexpected voice behind them made them jump.

Billy and Helen spun around to see Joe standing less than a metre away with Mary beside him, holding his arm for support. Mary was smiling even though she looked a bit wobbly on her legs.

"Where did you come from?" Helen asked, trying to keep her excited voice down. "Are you alright?"

"We're fine," Joe said. "One of the enforcers took us in his aircar, but we got him to turn around and bring us back."

"We…?" Mary said. "It was Joe who convinced him to return."

Billy stared at Joe with an unspoken question.

"There was only one of them." He said nonchalantly. "I left him tied up in his aircar in a park over there," he gestured vaguely somewhere behind. "He won't bother us. But there are two still here, presumably in that aircar over there."

"We thought there might be one on the yacht waiting for us," Billy said.

"Possibly. There were three altogether. Their leader took us in his car, but I'd had enough of being threatened and dragged off to be interrogated. Besides, I didn't like the way he treated Mary… He won't bother us. But we need to get rid of the two waiting for you to return. That's what they said they were doing. They don't know we've come back."

"I won't ask what you did to make him bring you back…"

"Right, now we need to get rid of the two enforcers still here, before they find out what happened to their group leader, and call for reinforcements."

"I'm ready," Billy said with trepidation.

"We'll need a distraction. They are expecting two young people to return to the yacht, that's you…"

"What do you want us to do?" Helen asked.

"I'll work my way around until I'm behind the aircar. Once I'm there you stroll casually along, heading back to the yacht. Pretend to be so absorbed in each other you don't see the aircar."

"That shouldn't be too hard to do," Helen said cheerfully.

Billy grinned.

"Exactly. When the enforcers see you, they'll get out of the aircar. They won't expect me because they saw us being taken away. With a bit of luck, I'll get them both before they realize what's happening. At least I'll take them by surprise and that should slow down any reaction they might have to being unexpectedly attacked."

"Sounds risky," Billy said.

"Everything's risky. You need to weigh up the consequences to see if it's worth the risk. Odds would be better if I had a weapon."

"But you don't."

"Not yet. I'll look for something as I make my way around."

"Be careful Joe," Mary implored.

"Don't worry," Helen said, "I've a good idea of what he can do."

"Okay, we're all agreed. Mary, you stay here out of sight. Helen and Billy, wait until I signal you to move, okay? —they both nodded in agreement— Then I'm off. Give me about five minutes. As soon as I'm behind the aircar you'll see me, then you do your part." He slipped back and went into the bushes that formed a ragged hedge beside the fence line of several houses bordering the walkway along the foreshore.

The aircar remained unmoving, the sunlight bouncing off the glossy black surfaces of the wings and the darkened glass windows. It sat near the beginning of the pier, like a hideous statue of a giant cockroach, several metres away from the hedges along the other side of the walkway. There was no sign of Joe. None of the bushes along the fence line were disturbed which would indicate someone moving through them.

The wait dragged on and on, and the longer it took the more nervous Billy and Helen became. *How long is it going to take?* Billy asked himself.

"If I get any more nervous," Helen whispered, "I'll wet myself." Which made Billy smile. Suddenly he wasn't as tense anymore.

Then they saw Joe step out from behind the bushes. He had a length of fence paling in one hand. It was a bit over a metre long. *He must have torn it off an old fence*, thought Billy. They watched and waited until Joe had reached the back of the aircar. He looked towards them and nodded.

They stepped forward pretending to chat casually to each other as they walked along the footpath by the foreshore towards the pier, ignoring the waiting aircar sitting ominously to one side. They passed the front of the aircar and started walking along the pier towards the yacht moored at the end of it.

There was a hiss behind them and a soft rumbling noise as the aircar door opened, rising while the ramp slid down.

Helen was about to turn and look, but Billy gripped her arm. "Don't look back."

"Hey," a voice called to them. "You two. Stop right there."

They stopped. They waited a couple of seconds before turning to see one of the enforcers standing by the foot of the ramp. Billy looked beyond the enforcer to see where Joe was, but he couldn't see him. He was hidden behind the aircar. A second enforcer started down the ramp.

The first enforcer took a step towards them. "Are you heading for that yacht?"

"Yeah, we thought we might take a look at it," Billy said, trying to inject a touch of enthusiasm and curiosity into his voice.

The second enforcer stepped off the ramp.

It was then Billy saw Joe move silently out from behind the aircar. He stepped forward and shoved the fence paling, flat like it was a shovel, into the back of the second enforcer's right knee. The man went down with a scream. The first enforcer spun around to see what was happening while attempting to draw his weapon. He was slammed in the chest with the fence paling and shoved back. Joe leaped forward, grabbed the man's arm that was drawing his weapon and pointed it towards the second enforcer who was struggling to get up. He forced the first man to shoot the second man who collapsed in a heap, jerking spasmodically as the electric charge ran riot with his nerves. He then jerked the man's gun arm up and snapped the elbow. The gun flew out of his hand. Joe let go of the broken arm and grabbing the man's helmeted head on both sides, gave it a vicious twist. The man collapsed without uttering a sound, inert the moment he hit the ground.

Billy was again stunned at the speed with which Joe took the two men down.

"Get on board and get the motor started.' He told them. "Untie the ropes holding us there. We don't have any time to waste."

Mary was already walking towards them. The two teenagers ran along the pier to the yacht.

"You never cease to surprise me," Mary said once she was by Joe's side.

"Take my arm milady, and I'll escort you to your yacht."

"Thank you, I would like that."

Together they strolled along the pier as fast as Mary's ability to walk allowed. The instant they stepped on board, Billy engaged the motor and the *Buenhogar* moved rapidly out into open water.

23...

Buenhogar surged through the gentle waves close inshore, leaving a frothy wake behind. The only sound made was the splash of water and the rush of it passing by their hull. The motor George and his friends had installed to replace their original diesel one was more powerful, and he was grateful for that. Because it was broad daylight, he thought it best not to attempt to leave the area. The likelihood of the enforcers sending a powerful patrol boat to search for them meant they wouldn't get very far even with a good head start. They probably had an hour before the incapacitated enforcers were discovered and a less friendly lot came after them.

"There's no way we'll get far enough out to sea before they come after us," he told Billy who was beside him in the cockpit. Helen had taken Mary down into the main cabin where she could rest.

"So, what do we do then?"

"We make our way around the edge of the islands that were the original city as if we're heading out to sea. I'm hoping they'll assume were heading out as fast as possible and will be looking for us in the wrong area, but the moment we get far enough around to be obscured from shore, we turn and get in amongst the islands. We'll find somewhere to hide where we won't be visible to satellites. There's got to be hundreds of places where we can stay out of sight. We can slip out later when it's dark enough to avoid being seen."

It didn't take long before the new city was hidden behind the rows of ragged islands.

"Slow down and turn into one of the wider canals."

Their forward momentum suddenly dropped as Billy drew back the throttle and turned towards the rows of islands.

"That's it. Slow and steady. We don't want to hit something beneath the surface."

They motored quietly past a tall vertical island festooned with creepers and vines. Colorful birds flew out in a raucous flock screeching furiously at being disturbed. They quickly resettled once the yacht had passed, going further along what was once a road between rows of tall buildings. Fish darted beneath the hull as the yacht drifted through the water. Ripples created by the slow passing yacht slapped softly against the sides of the vertical islands.

"It's like being in a tunnel," Billy said as they passed under a series of overhanging vines.

Light splashed intermittently as they went between rows of vegetation covered mounds set between taller islands. Large lizards scuttled up tree trunks, birds flew out, circling around before re-settling back into the trees and bushes, and sometimes an animal screech made them wonder what else inhabited these overgrown mounds and vertical islands.

Cruising slowly, Joe spotted two tall islands the tops of which were so overgrown they had merged creating a shadowed place, almost like a cave between their bases. It was once a junction be-tween a main and a lesser street which meant the building rem-nants were close together. There was enough height for the yacht even with the mast, to be able to get under and be hidden from any satellite above There was such a huge area of waterways be-tween the hundreds of islands and mounds; it was unlikely they would be found anytime soon.

"Stop under there," he told Billy. "That's perfect. No one will see us from above, and I doubt if they'll come in here looking for us. I suspect, when they think we might be in here; it'll be too late to do anything, and they'll wait until morning. We'll slip out once it gets dark and should be long gone by then."

Billy maneuvered the yacht under the overhang and cut the motor.

Joe walked to the bow and using a rope he tied the yacht's bow to a large, twisted vine, so they would remain under cover and not drift into the open when the tide changed. He didn't want to drop the anchor in case it got tangled in something underwater and hindered them if they needed to make a fast exit.

When the yacht became still, they were surrounded with the buzz of insects, the slight lap of water as ripples brushed against the hull, the distant squawk of sea birds, and the occasional screech of parrots mucking about in the upper branches of the trees and vines covering the remains of the ancient city buildings. At times a splash as something larger breached the surface or leaped out of the water before falling back in stood out.

Looking over the side Joe caught glimmers of fish flashing by beneath them, and wondered if they might be able to catch some for a meal later. That would be nice. The only unpleasant thing about being here in amongst the mangroves he realized after a moment was the humidity. There was not much movement in the air, and now that they were also not moving, the humidity began to weigh on them. It made it seem a lot hotter than it was.

It might be safe but it's not a good place to stay for too long.

Mary, helped by Helen, came up on deck and sat in the cockpit.

"It's too hot to stay below," Mary said. There was a slick of moisture making her forehead glisten. "I'm having trouble breathing."

"Sorry," Joe said. "Do you think you can hang on for a while? It's not safe for us to leave yet. We need to wait until it gets dark."

Mary shrugged. It looked as if she didn't care one way or the other. She was pale, her eyes glazed, a slick of perspiration glistened on her skin. She was breathing with short shallow breaths.

Joe took Helen aside. "You know that small fan Mary uses... Do we have an extension cord long enough to bring it up here?"

"I'll have a look."

A few moments later Helen re-emerged with the fan connected to an extension cord. She placed it in the cockpit and aimed it at Mary, switched it on to blow a gentle breeze towards her.

"Ah..." Mary sighed. "Thank you. That feels good."

She still looked pale, but the sheen of perspiration disappeared, and her breathing improved.

They settled down to wait until sun set.

They heard passing boats, but none ventured into the spaces

between the rows of islands where they were hidden in the shade of overhanging growth, where it was slightly cooler out of the sun, although no less humid. The air barely moved between these rows of islands and the small fan set up to keep Mary cool was a godsend. Mary seemed comfortable sitting in the cockpit. Joe put a pillow behind her head and back, so she wasn't resting against the hardness of the deck. She had fallen asleep and was breathing easily, which was better than when they'd arrived several hours earlier.

Billy and Helen were fishing from the bow. They'd caught several decent fish which they immediately cleaned and put into the boat's refrigerator. The entrails they threw over the side attracted more fish which only enhanced their catch. Their voices were soft, nothing more than a murmur creating sense of calmness while they waited under cover of the overhanging vegetation.

Taking advantage of their safe position, Joe decided to catch up on sleep after too many long periods of being awake while sailing. *Who knows when the chance for a good sleep might come again?*

He slept sitting in the cockpit beside Mary, alert for any odd sound or disturbance. He was like a cat sleeping; any unexpected noise would bring him instantly awake. He would quickly look around, listen, and if nothing seemed out of order, would drop back into sleep again.

When Joe woke up the sun was about to set. Long shadows spread across the channels between the rows of islands. He looked around and saw Mary sitting beside him smiling.

"Are you okay? Why didn't you wake me?"

"I'm fine, and you were sleeping beautifully. I didn't have the heart to wake you."

The delicious aroma of the fish cooking wafted up through the hatch reminding Joe he'd not eaten anything all day.

Joe stood up and stretched. His back was stiff where he'd been leaning against the hard surface in the cockpit.

"Can you help me up?" Mary asked .

"Of course." He reached down and taking her arm he gently helped lift her to a standing position.

"Thank you."

She took a deep breath, letting it out with a sigh and then with Joe supporting her, she took tentative steps towards the hatch. It was much cooler and less humid than earlier which was a relief. In the gaps between the rows of islands stars began to punch bright spots in the sky above.

"I need to freshen up a bit." Mary said.

They had some awkwardness getting down the few short steps into the main cabin, but Helen rushed forward to help while Joe steadied Mary from above. Together the two women went forward so Mary could freshen up. Billy served the fish they'd cooked on plates set around the table in the galley.

"Sorry we don't have anything else to go with it," Billy said as he placed large portions on each plate. "But at least there's plenty of it. We caught heaps."

"It looks great Billy."

Mary and Helen returned, and the meal was eaten so quickly it vanished within moments.

They sat quietly in the gathering darkness, not wanting to put lights on in case they could be seen. A few times they'd heard boats moving along the various channels between the rows of islands, but none came near enough to discover them hidden beneath the overhang. They had no idea if the boats they heard were with people looking for them, or whether they were just fishermen working their way through the rich shallows, but as it got darker, the boats stopped coming and they were alone with the natural sounds of the life that inhabited the islands and the waterways between them.

Coming up on deck to an impenetrable blackness Joe could just see the channel they'd used reflecting faint light from the rising moon.

"Time to go," he said to the others below.

Billy untied the rope keeping them under cover. Joe used a boat hook to push them out into the open channel and once clear of any obstructions, he started the motor. Slowly they moved back along the channel and out into the open water. Without lights on— they didn't want anyone to see them —*Buenhogar* was invisible in the darkness; ephemeral bio-luminous sparkles in their wake the only indication something was travelling through the water, but this vanished once they left the dark islands behind. The moon was much higher and brighter lighting the surface of the sea.

Unfortunately, a passing satellite spotted the infra-red given off by the motor and the residual heat radiating off the metal hull. Their position and direction of travel was noted relayed to the capitol and that in turn was relayed to a patrol centre not far from the new city they were leaving behind.

A patrol boat was dispatched to rendezvous with them. A second patrol boat, which had waited for a superior controller to arrive, followed soon after.

They would both stop the renegade yacht.

24...

Around them, it was profoundly dark. The stars above were brilliant sparkles, bright enough at times to reflect off the surface of the sea, accentuating the absolute blackness of the deeps beneath. Joe still couldn't get over how sharp and brilliant the stars were compared to the night sky back in their time.

After forty five minutes of sailing in darkness, with only a dim glow far behind indicating the new city they'd not had a chance to explore, Joe thought it time to check on Mary. "I'd better see how the girls are doing," he said to Billy.

"I'll take the wheel," Billy said, jumping up to take a position by the wheel.

While Joe had been steering a direct course out of the huge harbour towards the open sea beyond, Billy had been sitting in the cockpit, relaxing, looking up at the stars, something he always enjoyed doing. He knew there were people on the Moon and on Mars, giving humanity a chance to survive elsewhere if things continued to get worse on Earth, and sometimes he even wished he could have gone on one of the expeditions to the planetary colonies. For a moment he wondered if his father might have gone to the Moon, then rejected that as a silly idea. He knew nothing about those colonies and how they were doing other than they were established by South Americans who thought conditions on Earth would continue to worsen until rising temperatures made the planet uninhabitable and decided humanity must become an interplanetary species to survive long term. But he and his people in Eyresea were of the opinion the world was reaching stability, and they were happy to stay where they were. They were exceptions because the controlling government also believed things were continuing to worsen and had already begun migrating to Antarctica. That cold barren continent was to be their future home. It was not something Billy could imagine.

I'm not going there, he decided.

But then he began to wonder where they were going. They always seemed to be on the run. He wasn't fond of enforcers, nobody was, so he accepted that getting away from them was the best thing to do, but after that... *What? Where would we go?* Yet strangely, he'd never felt happier. He was doing something different from what he'd done all his life and that was good. He was part of a family, odd though it was, and that was better than anything he'd recently felt. And then there was Helen, someone he really liked. *More than liked...* He sat back and smiled as *Buenhogar* sliced smoothly through the shallow waves towards an invisible horizon in the darkness ahead.

"How are you both doing?" Joe asked as he slid down the three steps into the main cabin.

It wasn't entirely dark inside. A faint glow came from a glow lamp in the corner of the cabin, enough to enable those inside to see where they were and not bump into anything if they needed to move around, but not bright enough to penetrate the portholes to be seen from outside.

"I'm okay," Mary said, but from the sound of her voice Joe thought she was having trouble breathing.

"You're not, really," Helen said with concern, confirming Joe's suspicions.

"Helen, why don't you join Billy up on deck? It's a beautiful night..."

"Yeah," she said as she reluctantly, but went up through the hatch. She didn't really want to leave Mary.

"Is it a beautiful night?" Mary asked.

"Yes, it is."

"I'm not so sure." She looked up at Joe who was still standing near the base of the steps leading to the hatch. "It's been a good run though. And I'm glad that it was with you and Helen, as well as Billy. I like him."

"What are you on about?" He moved over and sat down with

her at the small table in the galley.

"I can feel it, Joe."

"Feel what?"

"I was hoping you'd be able to bury me at sea near where we left Harold," she paused a second to take in a long breath, "all those years ago."

"Don't say things like that."

She ignored him. "But it seems circumstances will not allow that..." A sudden bout of coughing consumed her. Joe leaned forward to assist her, but she waved him back. "It's alright," she said as the coughing subsided. "Promise me you'll bury me somewhere at sea. Anywhere... That would be near enough to being with Harold after all this time..."

"Bury you at sea! What on earth are you asking me?"

"I'm dying Joe. Can't you see it? I can feel it."

He didn't know what to say.

"People know when they are going to die. That... anomaly... it did something to my heart"

"Mary..."

"It's been a good run Joe, and I must say, a wonderful experience."

"Don't..."

"A blessing you might say," she continued, cutting him off, "that you and Helen came into my life... and Billy too. He's a charmer. Promise me you'll make him look after Helen."

Joe looked at her in the dim light and could barely see her. It was as if she was becoming invisible, fading away.

"They make a lovely couple..."

"Let me turn on the cabin lights," Joe said, and stood up.

At that instant, a brilliant light bathed the cabin, so bright it momentarily blinded him.

The sound of klaxons blaring shattered the silence of the night.

"Shit!"

He flew up the steps to the cockpit to find the sea around them bathed with brilliant light, so bright it prevented him from seeing the dark shapes of two patrol boats lurking behind it.

"I can't see anything," Billy yelled above the ear shattering noise. "What's going on?" Helen yelled.

As suddenly as they'd started, the Klaxons stopped, leaving their ears ringing.

A massively amplified voice ordered: **"Heave to and prepare to be boarded."**

Joe reached over to the control panel and switched off the engine. *Buenhogar* immediately slowed and drifted to a stop. The brightness of the searchlights upon them dimmed slightly, enough for them to see two large patrol boats ahead, one on the port side with the other on their starboard side. Canons on the fore-decks were pointed at them, an obvious warning for them not to attempt to run.

The moment *Buenhogar* stopped moving forward and was drifting up and down with the waves, a fast runabout came from the starboard patrol boat towards them. There were two people standing up while a third one seated controlled the boat. They pulled up near the stern where Joe, Billy and Helen were standing in the cockpit.

They expected that they would be helped to board, but Joe, Helen and Billy didn't move. They stood watching as one of the men in the runabout tied a rope to the side rail to hold them against *Buenhogar's* stern.

"Are you going to give me a hand?" The officer in charge asked.

"No," Joe said. "You want to come on board? Understand you're not welcome, so don't ask for help."

"Who the fuck do you think you are," the boarding man asked belligerently.

"I could ask you the same question," Joe replied.

They watched the intruder climb awkwardly over the stern rail to finally stand straight, dignity intact.

"So, who the fuck are you anyway?" Joe demanded as the man straightened his uniform.

The intruder studied Joe and the others in the cockpit who glared back at him. He ignored the two teenagers to focus on Joe. He understood he wasn't from this time and so he allowed him a certain amount of leeway. He was also waiting for the other man in the runabout to come on board, the one with the weapon in case these strangers got out of control.

A second runabout headed towards them.

Seeing the other runabout on its way Joe said, "Excuse me." He stepped past the intruder who flinched at the unexpected move. Two steps and Joe was beside the rail where the second man was beginning to climb on board.

"No one said you could board."

"Doesn't matter," the man said. He had both hands on top of the rail and was about to pull himself up onto the deck.

"It does matter," Joe said harshly. "I don't give you permission."

"I don't give a fuck," the intruder snarled at him.

"Me either," Joe said.

The boarding enforcer had pulled himself halfway up and was about to step over the rail when Joe shoved him hard in the chest. Unbalanced he toppled backwards. He still had one hand gripping the rail, but he was so astonished to be attacked he involuntarily let go. He fell hard, hitting the side of the runabout, then bouncing off into the water. He vanished beneath the surface to come up a moment later spluttering and yelling obscenities, but his uniform soaked with water, and weighted down with weapons, started to drag him under. His furious splashing became desperate when he realized he was unable to swim without sinking let alone against the current to get back to the runabout. The patrol boats, the yacht and the runabout were drifting away as tidal currents dragged him further out. The second runabout quickly diverted course to collect the drowning man.

"What the fuck..." the intruder on board exclaimed. "We could shoot you out of the water."

"And they would do that with you on board?" Joe asked.

Silence.

"I didn't think so."

The second runabout quickly reached the struggling man in the water before he could sink properly. He was dragged on board, spluttering and coughing up water after which the runabout made directly for *Buenhogar*, pulling up and tying onto the runabout already there.

"You've caused problems for us, seriously injured our people, damaged equipment…"

"I've not killed anyone yet." Joe snapped back. "I've only responded in kind to the way you've treated us. You don't like the shoe on the other foot?"

"Do you know who I am?" The intruder facing Joe asked.

"No. And I don't care either," Joe replied.

"I could have you locked up right now and this yacht confiscated."

"And what good would that do?"

The man lifted his head up and straightened his shoulders attempting a formal stance which didn't impress Joe in the least.

Two more men climbed up onto the deck. Joe stared at them. He was outnumbered. One of them aimed a stun gun towards him while the other boarded. Joe didn't move. The half drowned enforcer stayed in the runabout. Helen and Billy also remained still, all they could do while stun guns were aimed at them.

"Why are you so desperate to talk to us?" Joe asked the man facing him. Then half-jokingly, "Do you think this yacht is some kind of time machine? That we can just vanish and pop out somewhere else in a different time?"

The intruder stared at Joe. "Isn't that what you did?"

"You are serious…" which surprised him. "You're deluded. But yes, we did just pop out of nowhere; out of a thousand years ago into this unpleasant present."

"My expert— and he indicated the last arrival who stepped forward to stand beside him while the other man kept the stun gun aimed at Joe — will take a look around."

The expert had several pieces of compact electronic equipment attached to his arms and was reading a small screen as he stood waiting to be told he could go ahead.

"I do mind, but objecting would be futile. Look around all you want. But if you upset the lady resting below, you will regret it."

"Don't threaten us," the intruder snapped at him. "We need to know," he said as his expert dropped through the hatch to the deck below, "to understand how you suddenly appeared here, and if we can replicate it on a larger scale to shift our people into another time, a better time. Colonizing Antarctica is a temporary solution. If the world keeps heating up…"

"You people are insane."

The intruder's expression hardened.

"What makes you think the future will be any better than what you have now? It could be a lot worse."

"We're willing to take the chance if it's possible."

"Then look for an anomaly and go into it; then you'll find out what you want to know." Joe said calmly to defuse their confrontation.

They wouldn't be able to get away from two patrol boats, one maybe, but not two. Even then outrunning a patrol boat was problematic, they were bigger and had more powerful engines than *Buenhogar*, not to mention guns that could sink them.

"It happened." Joe said calmly. "We had no control over it. Weird electrical storms were everywhere, on land, at sea. At one point they surrounded us, enveloped us… Damn near killed us… Then we found ourselves here. You arseholes have been chasing us ever since."

The intruder remained stony-faced.

"It's happened before I've been told, and it'll happen again," Joe said. "I've no doubt, but how and why I have no more idea than you do."

"If you wanted, could you do it again?" The man asked. "Just vanish and appear again at some time in the future?"

"Did you not hear what I said? We had no control over it. We were caught in a maelstrom of electrical discharges, or something weirder, which knocked us out, and when we woke up we were here sailing in a different sea, in a different time."

"Strange things follow you," the intruder stated. "There was one of those 'weird' storms in the town you were brought to by our patrol boat and several dwellings vanished with the people inside; nothing left but vacant land where the houses stood. It was as if they'd been scooped up and taken away. We've never had a storm like that here before."

"How could I know that? As soon as the storm passed, the patrol boat left, and so did we. None of us went into the town…"

"Then you had no idea?"

"No. It must have been a coincidence. Surely, you've had severe storms before."

"There are always storms, but like I said, nothing like that one. No houses or people ever disappeared before."

"And you think I know something about that?"

"You don't think it's strange that where you go, people vanish. Ever since you arrived, we've had an increase in violent storms."

"And you blame that on us?"

"This yacht has some connection that draws in massive amounts of energy."

"That's bullshit."

"We've been following you with satellites and they show abnormal energy readings surrounding you, something we can't quite measure. Can you explain that?"

"Maybe we're still connected to the anomaly that brought us here… some kind of quantum entanglement? Gravity waves, time streams? You tell me, because I've got no idea at all. I don't know. We found ourselves here and that's all there is to it. I thought you might have answers…"

"Then why keep trying to evade us?"

"I don't like being bullied with people trying to force me to do something or threatening my 'family'," Joe stated bluntly. "So now you leave us alone. Get off our yacht and don't bother us again. You have your own problems. Focus on those."

The man who had gone below came back up on deck to report that he found nothing, could not detect any excess energy, or anything else out of the ordinary.

"All right," the intruder acknowledged, obviously disappointed. "But we'll be monitoring you," he said to save face.

The two men abruptly turned and climbed over the stern into one of the waiting runabouts while one of the men kept his weapon pointed at Joe until both boats set off.

Joe, Helen and Billy waited until both runabouts and their occupants were hoisted up onto their respective patrol boat. Moments later the two patrol boats switched off their searchlights, plunging the area into darkness.

When their eyes compensated, there was enough moonlight for them to see the patrol boats had gone. They had silently backed away as the current from the outgoing tide carried *Buenhogar* past them giving Joe and his companions the impression they'd simply vanished.

Arseholes. But what if they were right, and somehow, we are still connected to the anomaly that transported us here... Could we be shifted again?

That was not something he looked forward to.

25...

"Turn back," Joe half in, half out of the hatch said to Billy manning the helm. Billy seemed perplexed. "We're heading back to the city."

With the two patrol boats having disappeared into the surrounding darkness, they had a clear passage out into the Southern Ocean. Billy thought it was an odd request, but rather than question Joe, he started to turn in a wide semi-circle to bring them around onto a heading back the way they'd come; no sails to shift, or tacking involved since they were running on the motor.

Down in the cabin Helen asked, "Why are we going back?"

Mary said nothing. She trusted Joe; he always did the right thing.

"Because we don't know where we're going. What are we looking for? A better place to live? We already found that, Eyresea. But as independent as they like to think they are, they are still monitored and remotely controlled by the central government that oversees everyone else. Running from them is pointless and gets us nowhere. We need to think about this. Before we even start to go anywhere, we need to stock up on supplies. I doubt we'd find much along the east coast and probably nothing at all if we headed south to Tasmania. Who knows what's left of that place. But back in the city there will be chandlers that supply ships and boats and while we have credit available, thanks to George, we should use it to get what we need if we must spend a long time at sea."

"Makes sense," Mary said softly to herself. She was past caring anymore and would go along with whatever Joe and the two youngsters decided. Let them worry about what to do... the future is theirs.

"What about looking for Billy's father?" Helen asked.

"You know we'll never find him. He could be a thousand years in the future, or somewhere in the past, if he's still alive."

"Billy keeps hoping…"

"I'm not so sure. I think he knows it's impossible but won't admit it yet. Apart from that, they don't expect us to turn back. They'll assume we are heading out to sea and around the coast in search of an anomaly we can use to transport us somewhere and will use satellites to keep track of us. There are none I could see up there now but when one makes the next pass overhead, they will start looking along our projected direction of travel. By the time they realize we are not anywhere they predicted, we should be back in the city and anchored amongst many other boats and will be harder to spot. Even if we give off a peculiar energy field, as we were told, it may be hard to see it in amongst the heat signatures from the other boats in the harbour."

"You don't think they've given up on us?" Helen asked.

"No. They couldn't find anything to connect us to the anomalies that exist in the weirder storms, but that doesn't mean they won't be watching or monitoring us."

"I don't like this place so much anymore," Helen said. "Maybe we should do what you said."

"Do what?"

"Find another anomaly and go through it."

"That would finish me for sure," Mary said.

"We could end up in a much worse place, or even dead," Joe said.

"It was just a thought…" Helen said. "I don't know. The only good thing about this place was finding Billy."

Joe smiled.

In the predawn light *Buenhogar* slipped quietly in amongst hundreds of boats from small dinghies to medium sized yachts, work boats, fishing boats, and a myriad other craft moored off as well as beside the many jetties jutting out into the harbour. They tied up at the end of a small jetty where three other yachts were also moored. Behind them the sun lit the tops of the rows of island remnants of the sunken city they used to call home a thousand years ago.

Even this early, there was activity. No one took much notice of them mooring but there were people on many boats preparing to up-anchor and head out for a day's fishing. Some of the jetties where work boats were moored had people coming back and forth, loading supplies. Voices from places along the foreshore echoed across the water letting everyone know they were preparing to open soon for business. Pelicans and seagulls crowded around a cluster of fishing boats that had been out overnight and were now unloading their catches to be taken to market. Beyond the plethora of moored boats, a patrol boat cruised past, an ominous reminder that enforcers were always somewhere nearby.

"See what canned or dried food you can buy with the credit chit your uncle George gave us," he told Billy as she gave him the card to use. Helen had several shopping bags draped over one shoulder. They were on the end of the small jetty where Buenhogar was moored. "We'll need more than you can carry with those shopping bags. And don't forget stuff like flour and dried beans, vegetables and meat that can be reconstituted. It doesn't take up much space but goes a long way."

"We can make as many trips as we need to get enough supplies."

"That's the idea. I'd come with you, but I don't want to leave Mary alone. She's sleeping, so I'll stay here." Then he added for Billy's sake, "Don't get distracted by the excitement of being in a large city. We're not tourists here."

Billy smiled and nodded.

"I'll keep him focused," Helen said jovially.

"Once we're done with food supplies, I'll look for a ship chandler and get other stuff like extra rope, another anchor and chain, an inflatable dinghy to replace the one you lost in the storm, life jackets —there aren't any on board…"

He watched the two happily heading off towards the increasingly busy shops facing the road that ran around the harbour. He watched until they disappeared amongst people thronging the street where the shops were now open for business.

Billy couldn't get over how many people there were hustling along the sidewalks, filling the shops, sitting at tables in front of food shops, eating and drinking beverages, conversing and laughing as if they had no troubles at all. The cacophony— the noise people made constantly talking and calling to each other as they went about their activities, combined with the traffic in nearby streets was overwhelming. He felt it battering his ears. He was used to the relative silence in Eyresea, which was a town barely big enough to occupy the space of one of these city-blocks which seemed to go on forever as far as he could see. He tried to look as if he belonged here but failed miserably.

Helen on the other hand relished the hum of human activity. She had for too long been isolated on the yacht often far out at sea as they escaped the riots and lawlessness that became endemic after the initial small tsunami and rising sea levels flooded coastal cities as the 'termination event' proceeded. She felt right at home in this crowded waterfront. She couldn't stop smiling, looking around, sniffing the smell of food cooking in restaurants as it wafted into the street. It was all delicious. She had to keep grabbing Billy and dragging along because he kept stopping to look at things he'd never seen before. Finally, she stopped in front a general store where she could see canned goods and fresh produce on display inside.

"A supermarket," she said. "This will do."

Billy gave her a soft nudge with his elbow. "I have no idea what to do," he said as they walked into the general store.

"Leave it to me," she said happily. "I know all about shopping, it was one of my favourite pastimes." She pointed to a row of trollies jammed together along a side wall. "Grab one of those and follow me."

When Mary woke up a short time later Joe prepared her a cup of tea and they went up on deck and sat in the cockpit where they could enjoy the benign weather while watching the endless activity around the harbour. Several times patrol boats cruised by, heading across the bay towards a distant section where three ships were moored beside a long wharf. One of those ships slowly departed, heading south, Joe thought, *for Antarctica?*

He wondered, how long it would take to shift a large proportion of the population there. Even if the population only consisted of a few million, it would still take a long time to get any serious numbers into Antarctica. *Were those going willing to disrupt their lives to start a new one in a not very hospitable place? Or did they not have a choice? Who decides who goes?*

He also wondered if it could be done before the imminent heat catastrophe overwhelmed them. Or if it was scaremongering to keep control of people and resources, so those on top could maintain their luxurious lifestyle, whatever that might be?

Nothing's changed. It was the same back in our time. Scaremongering to fire up the youth into believing in climate catastrophes that never eventuated but ruined so many young lives. And when a catastrophe finally did arrive, it was a natural result of the planet continuing to come out of the last ice age into a warmer period. Nothing humans ever did caused it, and nothing humans do would prevent it. We never lived in a time that wasn't fluctuating between warm and cold periods with gradual general warming the natural trend. It wasn't the end of the world; it was a new phase we needed to adapt to. The world is still here, and people are surviving, and still those bastards in control are trying to frighten everyone into believing their world's going to end... The same old bullshit as always...

His musings were interrupted by the return of Helen and Billy with full bags of supplies.

"We're back with the first lot," Helen announced as she dumped the contents of her bags on the deck beside the cockpit.

"Were you two daydreaming?" Billy asked as he also emptied his bags. "We'll leave you to store the goods below while we go for another lot. Okay?"

Without waiting for an answer, they grabbed the now empty bags and headed back along the jetty towards the shore and the shops along the waterfront.

"They seem to have done well," Mary said.

"I'll take it down into the galley," Joe said.

"I'll help…" Mary started to say.

"No, stay there. Don't worry. I'll leave it all in the galley and we can sort out where things go after they come back with a few more loads."

Several trips later the galley was filled with the goods bought. Joe left Helen to help Mary sort out where things were to be stored while he took Billy with him to search for the other stuff they needed from a ship's chandler. They hired a small trolley to bring back the new anchor and lengths of chain to replace the main anchor they lost while escaping the wild men attempting to storm them before they shifted to this time, coils of rope, thread for repairing torn sailcloth if needed, four life jackets, and a small inflatable rubber dinghy. Feeling satisfied that they had all they needed for an extended time at sea, they sat down for dinner and a discussion of where they could possibly go and for what reasons.

"There aren't many options," Joe said. "The eastern part of the country is controlled by what passes for a government. And from what we've experienced so far, it's not benevolent. There are obviously some freedoms… Have a look at this city. It seems open and free with people going about their lives with a degree of certainty, but generally everything is controlled by the government. They decide what you will do whether you like it or not. The people have no say in the matter, but if they don't cause too many disturbances, they are left alone to get on with their lives. As for us, because we are strangers, in their minds we represent a threat, an anomaly that needs to be explained, or worse, expunged. They imagine we have a way out, a means of travelling through time to a better place. It's a fantasy, but they believe it's a possibility. That's the only reason we are still 'free'. They'll continue to monitor us until they want something, then they'll come and get us."

"We could go west into the wild country. They'd never dare to follow us there." Billy suggested.

"Where those pirates came from?" Helen asked.

"All the way around to the other far side," Billy said. "There can't be pirates everywhere. The must be others who live in harmony with the land, with country, with nature…"

"I've no doubt." Joe said. "But going west is difficult. It would be against the prevailing wind directions and currents. Going east is much easier."

"East? To where?"

"South America? They have a space program and are sending people to colonize the Moon and Mars. Life there could be better than here."

"That's a long crossing," Mary said.

"How long?" Billy asked.

"Probably a month or two at sea, crossing the stormiest ocean on the planet," Joe said.

Billy's expression filled with trepidation.

"There are always islands we can stop at on the way," Helen said to allay his fear of such a long ocean crossing.

"Assuming," Joe reminded her, "that they aren't underwater because the sea level is hundreds of metres higher than it was in our time. All low lying islands and coral atolls would have disappeared. Only the biggest mountainous islands would still be there. "

He paused, thinking of what had happened to the inhabitants of Easter Island, or Rapa Nui, the most isolated island in the South Pacific, and the struggles they had there when they ran out of resources to support an ever increasing population. That could happen on any island isolated after the tsunami and the subsequent rise in sea levels. Who knows what they would encounter? He had a mental picture of wild savages pouring onto *Buenhogar*, killing them, stripping it of everything they could fined of value, especially the canned and dried food stocks.

The memory of them being attacked when they had anchored in a secure inlet only a few days after the tsunami had passed reinforced this possibility. *How much worse would things be now after all these years?*

"Unless it was an emergency, we should bypass them. They've been isolated for too long and if any of them have people still living on them, they most likely won't welcome strangers," he said, and then more emphatically, "I'd definitely avoid stopping at any island we see if we decide to make the crossing."

"Do you think a boat like this one could make such a crossing?" Billy asked still filled with trepidation at the thought of it.

"Without a doubt," Mary said emphatically. "My dear husband Harold designed and built this boat for sailing in the waters of the Great Southern Ocean," she added with a feeling of pride. She couldn't help a wistful smile as she remembered how Harold had toiled day and night for years to construct *Buenhogar* in their front yard, ignoring constant derision from neighbours in the street who looked upon it as a great folly.

They didn't think that when the sudden sea level rise inundated the city, drowning it forever, forcing them to evacuate while we sailed off through city streets out to safety in the Bay.

She had no doubts they could safely reach South America, no doubts at all.

Silence, while each of them considered the idea.

Helen was the first to break the silence. "I think we should do it," she said.

Mary nodded.

Billy hesitated but could think of no other alternative.

"I'll go wherever you decide to go," he said softly.

Joe looked at each of them in turn to see whether they were all in accordance. *Then that's settled...*

"Okay," he said, "If you're willing to take the chance... We should all get a good night's sleep so we can leave first thing in the morning."

26...

The clump of boots on the deck, the sudden rocking of the yacht as several people jumped on board, woke everyone up instantly. Joe grabbed a pair of jeans and a T shirt, slipped them on in a flash, opened the hatch, took two steps up until he partially emerged to see two black clad figures in the cockpit, facing him. One of them had a stun weapon pointed at him.

"What the fuck…" was all he managed to get out before being hit with a charge that sent agonizing pain through his body, freezing his muscles as if each one had simultaneously cramped. It hit him in the chest causing his heart to skip a beat before his body froze. Intense pain surged through him. His whole body shuddered as he collapsed.

The two intruders grabbed him and dragged him up out of the hatch into the cockpit where they left him. One stayed while the other dropped through the hatch into the galley. He heard Helen scream. Billy called out something incomprehensible that was cut off by the sizzling sound of a stun gun.

If they've hurt Mary, or the others… His mental threat remained unfinished.

The last thing he saw was two more men, neither of whom wore uniforms, each studying electronic equipment taking readings… as everything around him turned a brilliant white, like an exploding sun, before fading into… a deep blackness.

He awoke to find himself strapped to a chair in a glowing white room. A brilliant light above made the walls and floor glow with such brilliance his eyes watered. He couldn't wipe his tears away. There were also electronic sensors stuck to his temples, his neck and chest. There was something that looked like a blood-pressure measuring strap wrapped about his left arm, and there were two sensors stuck onto the ends of two fingers on his right hand. His legs and arms were immobilized but he could flex his muscles enough to let him know the straps couldn't be broken. A strap also held his head in place so he could only look forward. Flicking his eyes up and down and from side to side he discerned only absolute whiteness.

He couldn't see where the walls ended and the ceiling began, nor could he see where the walls blended into the floor. It was like being inside an incandescently glowing sphere.

A dark smudge appeared in the whiteness in front of him and two shadowy shapes emerged floating towards him. *Finally, something to focus on...* The two shadows became two people, and he was momentarily stunned to see one of them was Aaron. The other one looked like an older version of him, heavy set, cheeks beginning to sag, hair grey with steaks of white through it, but the resemblance was unmistakable. *Father and son?*

He was about to say something when Aaron put a finger to his lips in the age old signal to be quiet, to not say anything. He blinked several times since he couldn't move his head. Aaron nodded.

The older version stood silently in front of him, studying him with piercing eyes. Joe waited silently; his gaze fixed on the hard face of the older man who showed not a hint of empathy.

He couldn't escape, but he was not going to rant and yell, or to demand release. That would be useless, so he waited, continuing to stare defiantly at the older man. *Let him start first.*

"I've run out of patience," the older man said, finally relenting.

Joe flashed him the briefest of smiles which seemed to infuriate him.

"You've caused no end of trouble," he snapped harshly at him. "You've injured several good people..."

"Whom I must say were not very nice," Joe interrupted.

"They were doing their jobs." The man almost growled those few words.

"Yeah, they all say that" Joe said sarcastically. "Who might you be? You haven't introduced yourself."

"I'm asking the questions here."

"That's exactly the problem. You're not asking questions. You're demanding answers, solutions to problems I have no answers to."

The man spluttered. "I'm the Chief Minister," he said. "My son here has been observing you since your problematical arrival. We want to know how you got here, something thought to be impossible. But here you are. What device do you have on your boat that enabled you to travel through time? How can we replicate it? It could be a life saver for us, for our community."

"More than likely you and your cohorts want to use it for yourselves and fuck the general community."

Glaring at him, the Chief Minister pulled a small device from his pocket and pushed a button. A searing pain blasted through Joe's head. Worse than the worst migraine, he thought his head would explode. His body shook enough to rattle the heavy chair which was, he'd assumed, bolted to the floor. But it wasn't. He felt it move slightly as the pain coursed through him, then suddenly it stopped, leaving him limp, wasted, gasping, barely conscious. He was vaguely aware that his bladder had released, he'd wet himself. *Fuck...* Suddenly embarrassed. *At least I didn't shit myself.*

"My men are studying your yacht, searching it from top to bottom, stem to stern. We'll find whatever you have that generates the energy field we measured surrounding it."

"There's nothing to find." Joe mumbled. He felt his strength returning but was still unable to move much because of the straps tying him to the chair.

"Denying it won't do any good."

"You don't fucking listen, do you?" Joe snapped back, jerking uselessly against the straps.

"Oh, I listen. You're hiding something. I can feel it."

"You're paranoid. You and your fucking enforcers... Running around scared shitless..."

Pain slammed into him again. His body shook violently before slumping momentarily into unconsciousness. When he regained a semblance of coherence, he saw the Chief Minister smiling at him. Aaron, off to one side slightly behind his father, stared in horror.

"Calling us names isn't helping," the Chief Minister said softly.

Sucking in a shuddering breath, then releasing it slowly Joe glared defiantly at his torturer. He felt pins and needles coursing through his arms and legs in the aftermath of the electric shock.

"I've been telling your people all along how we got here," he said slowly while the tingling in his limbs receded to a dull throbbing. "It just happened that's all. You can torture me all you want, but you won't get answers to something I know nothing about. What did you learn from the others?"

"What others?" The Chief Minister pretended to look vague.

"Come on, we're not the first to appear here."

"The few we'd encountered," the Chief Minister reluctantly admitted, "were crazy. They couldn't tell us anything, not even about where they came from. We assumed they were part of a time travel experiment gone wrong. Most of them died soon after we found them. You are the only one who's able to tell us anything, and you refuse... I don't understand."

You probably fried their brains searching for answers. Even if I had the answers you want, I wouldn't tell you.

"Don't you understand you can't force people to give you answers they don't have?"

He wanted to ask what they'd done with his companions and if Mary was all right, but a sudden surge of pain rattled him again, surging through him for a brief moment before vanishing leaving him sweating and weak.

"Bastard," he mumbled.

"Think about it. I'll come back tomorrow, and we'll talk again once I know what's on your boat." He turned to his son. "Come on Aaron, we're done here for the time being. You'll see, he'll be persuaded."

As they left, Aaron, his face sorrowful, apologetic, turned back to Joe. He silently mouthed the word 'later'.

Later was an indeterminate period because there was no lessening of the glaring brightness in the room. Joe's only awareness that time had passed was because he was no longer wet where he had urinated involuntarily. He might have dozed but he had no way of knowing. Since the interrogators had left, he had not been aware of anything other than the blank whiteness in front of his eyes. If he closed his eyes, there remained a white afterimage that barely faded because of the intensity of the light in the room. He couldn't turn his head to see other parts of the room. He couldn't shake his head, a strap over his forehead kept it locked against the chair's headrest.

The room was silent, yet he could hear a slight hissing all around him. He was not used to hearing nothing. Perhaps his brain compensated by adding white noise only he could hear. He tried swallowing, but his mouth was devoid of saliva. Moving his jaw made his ears pop, but the white noise remained.

He wanted to scream but knew that would be useless. The room was probably soundproofed so no one outside of it would hear anything.

There must be a control centre with people monitoring, watching me, waiting to see me break down, to call out to be released, to yell out that I would tell them the secret of time travel… Fuck them.

He wouldn't give them the satisfaction of seeing him suffer. Determined to remain immobile though it became more uncomfortable by the minute, it took enormous willpower not to squirm, to not twitch even the slightest bit. *Let them think I'm relaxed, meditating…*

He tried to smile but couldn't. His face remained blank while he waited for something to happen. He let his mind go blank, to fill itself with the same whiteness that surround him… drifting into a state of almost non-being. His breathing slowed to the faintest of inhalations and exhalations. His heartbeat slowed…

He had no idea how long he remained in a state of almost non-existence, when a sudden movement of air indicated a door had opened. He blinked to clear his eyes of the whiteness and saw a blurred dark figure come towards and hover over him.

"Don't make any noise," the figure said softly. "I'm going to release you."

Joe felt the straps holding his arms and legs spring open with soft clicks. Then the strap holding his head immobile was released. He tried to move but seemed to have no control of his body.

"Let me help you," the dark figure said.

"Aaron?" Joe recognized the voice before his vision finally was able to focus on the man's face. "Won't you get into trouble for… this?"

"Shh, don't say anything. And yes, probably. But what are they going to do? I'm the Chief Minister's son. The monitors are on a meal break. I've inserted a loop into their computer showing you as you were before. When they come back, they might not realize you are gone because the screens will show exactly what they were showing before they left. Come on. Let me help you. We don't have much time."

Joe moved his arms and shoulders, feeling tingling sensations as muscles began to work. With Aaron's help, he slowly stood up. His first steps were almost a disaster, but Aaron held onto him keeping him from collapsing, holding securely as he took a few tentative steps. With each step towards the door in the wall his strength and control improved. By the time they'd exited the white room and were in the empty monitoring centre, and the door had closed behind them he was able to walk again although a bit shaky. He kept a hand on Aaron's shoulder in case he started to fall. Aaron pointed to the monitor screens and he saw himself still strapped into the chair apparently unconscious. Then they moved quickly out through another door quietly into a long grey corridor.

"What about the others?"

"They're in another room just down here."

After a few more steps the tingling in his nerves diminished completely.

"Another white room?"

"No, a normal room. They're being kept isolated while you were under interrogation. They're okay."

Ten metres along the corridor they stopped in front of another door.

"How come there's no one around?"

"It's the middle of the night. The only people here are a few workers that keep monitoring whatever needs to be monitored, because basically everything's on standby until the day shift comes back." Aaron explained. "You've been immobile for about twelve hours."

"Shit. No wonder I had trouble moving."

"Most people would have gone nuts by this time," he said as he keyed in a code and the door slid open with a soft hiss.

Inside the room, a lounge room with a large wall mounted TV that was not switched on Helen and Billy jumped up from the chair they'd been sitting on and rushed towards the door. Mary, Joe saw, remained seated, but she smiled broadly when she saw him about to enter the room. Helen threw her arms around Joe and gave him a huge hug.

"Take it easy," Joe said softly, "or you'll knock me over."

"Let's get going," Aaron said to them. "And be quiet. Try not to make any noise."

Joe went over to Mary and helped her to stand. He guided her towards the door without saying anything. She was happy to see him.

Once they were all out in the corridor, the door to their room slid silently shut. Aaron led them to a staircase, the emergency exit from the building, and as quiet as possible they pushed open the door and started down the three flights of steps to the ground level.

"We can't use the lifts; video cameras would record us. There are no cameras here in the stairwell," Aaron explained.

They shuffled down the stairs with hardly any noise apart from their ragged breathing. Out through the exit and into a wide open space where several aircars were parked. Aaron took them to a larger vehicle and once they were on board and strapped into their seats, the dashboard lit up with small lights casting a glow inside the car. Aaron fiddled with the controls and the car rose silently up into the air. It rapidly sped away from what Joe glimpsed as a massive prison like complex comprising of six buildings, most of which appeared barracks-like. The most forbidding one was the one they'd escaped from. Beyond this isolated complex, was broad expanse of rocky barren land.

They flew for half an hour to reach the city they'd been hijacked from. Aaron landed the aircar beside a near deserted industrial complex and led them out.

"No one takes any notice of aircars landing here, day or night," he said as he led them into a narrow service street. They followed close on his heels and within minutes emerged from the narrow street onto the wide street that ran alongside the harbour. Shops and businesses were closed and there was no one visible anywhere. Most of the boats moored by the piers and jetties as well as those in nearby waters were also dark. Streetlights were not the brightest, but still, they kept to the shadows as much as possible.

When they reached the pier where their yacht *Buenhogar* was moored. Aaron stopped. "This is as far as I go," he said. "Try to get away as far as you can before daylight, and you'll have a good chance."

"Why are you helping us?" Mary asked breathlessly. She'd managed to keep up with Joe's help, but her heart was racing, and her breath was ragged.

"To be honest... I don't really know. But I can not stand the way my father and his cohorts treat people. It's not right. He never used to be like that, but in recent years the power he has over people has gone to his head. He thinks he can do anything he wants and get away with it. I'm not the only one who doesn't agree with how they go about things, but at least I am able to help. When they realize you've gone, they'll find me asleep in bed, and though they'll suspect I had something to do with your escape, they won't be able to prove it, and they won't do anything because I'm the Chief Minister's son. At least I hope that's the case..."

"I don't know how to thank you..." Joe said.

"Just go, as quickly as you can."

With that, Aaron turned and went back into the shadows leading to the side street they used to get here, leaving them momentarily at a loss.

"The world's not such a bad place after all," whispered Mary, while they watched Aaron scuttle away. "There are good people everywhere."

"All right," Joe said, "We'd better get moving. It might only be minutes before they discover us gone and raise the alarm."

While Helen and Billy raced along the pier towards *Buenhogar* Joe, still feeling the effects of such a long time immobilized helped Mary, who was no less awkward. They walked slowly, each supporting the other, along the pier to their yacht.

Billy had already untied the ropes holding them in place and activated the engine. Helen helped Mary to come on board, and together they went down into the main cabin. After one last look back at the city, Joe stepped on board. He pushed against the landing pad they had been tied to and *Buenhogar* silently moved away from the pier, drifting into open water.

Billy engaged the electric motor and with hardly a ripple, the yacht moved away from the piers along the waterfront, and out into more open water. They moved slowly, barely leaving any ripples to disturb the many other boats moored against piers, and jetties, as well in the nearby waters.

Once they'd gone beyond the yachts and other boats moored in open water, Billy gave more power to the motor and *Buenhogar* surged ahead full throttle into the darkness.

They soon went beyond the regular clumps of islands that a thousand years ago were part of a great city. Heading into the darkness of the wide bay, they ran without lights using only moonshine and bright stars to show them the way.

Beyond was the open ocean where they knew they would be safe.

27...

The sun was barely up when the Chief Minister stalked into the control room, barely glancing at the monitor screens showing Joe strapped to the interrogation chair. He nodded to the two men sitting at their consoles but didn't bother speaking to them. He stopped in front of the door, to the white room, stepping through when it slid open with a hiss. He stopped after one step, stunned.

"Fuck," he screamed.

He stared at an empty chair.

He spun around and stepped back into the monitoring centre. The screens still showed Joe strapped into the chair.

"What the fuck happened here," he screeched at the two men who cringed down into their chairs.

When they stared at him, perplexed, he said, "Get up and have a look in there."

The two men did as they were asked and stood blank faced staring at an empty room.

Back in the control room the monitors still showed the chair was occupied.

They were about to speak when the Chief Minister said. "Did either of you leave this room during the night?"

They both nodded.

"I thought it was clear you were to be watching at all times, so why the fuck did you leave?"

"We took a meal break a few hours ago," one of them said.

"Together? A few hours ago? And you didn't notice anything wrong when you came back?"

They remained blank faced, contrite, aware of their horrendous mistake, fearful of what punishment they would soon endure.

"I'm surrounded by fucking idiots," the Chief Minister snarled at them. "Did either of you see my son Aaron here after we'd left yesterday? This looks like the sort of shit he'd get up to."

They both mumbled 'No'. Sweat beaded their foreheads.

"You'd better fix those computers," he said before storming out.

After ascertaining no one was in the other room either, in another part of the complex he interrupted the change of shift ordering the technicians to link to the satellite used to monitor the wayward yacht.

"Find out where the fuck they are," he demanded, then stood peering over their shoulders at the images on the various screens. "Well…"

"They're heading south. Looks like they're aiming to go along the west coast of Tasmania."

"Already?" *How long ago did they escape?* "Where the hell are they going?"

"There's nothing down there, apart from Antarctica."

"I know what's fucking down there," he snapped at them. "Find them."

Two other technicians walked into the control room, the morning shift coming in to take over. Voices in the corridor announced more arrivals for morning shifts in other parts of the building. The Chief Minister turned to the two new arrivals. "Do we have any patrol boats in the area?" He demanded.

When they looked puzzled, not knowing what he was talking about, he almost yelled at them. "Check the satellite feeds and see if we can get a patrol boat after them. I want those bastards back here."

They looked at the monitors, confused.

"What the fuck is wrong with you people?"

One of the original two night shift men said, "there is a patrol boat accompanying a group heading for Antarctica. It could catch them if we divert it now."

"Do it. Tell the captain the order comes directly from me. I want those bastards caught."

"Yes sir."

"Keep me updated," he ordered before storming out of the control centre.

28...

At dawn *Buenhogar* was far away from the mainland, travelling south. They had yet to pass by the western side of Tasmania. They were still running with the electric motor to save having to tack because they were heading slightly against the prevailing wind. The waves hit them at an angle, producing an uncomfortable sideways movement, but it would only be for a few hours. It wasn't as bad as he'd expected with the way Buenhogar handled the sea, the waves and the wind. He'd been expecting a patrol boat to give chase, but none had appeared. But since none had appeared he didn't think a patrol boat could catch them now. We've got too much of a head start.

Remaining in the cockpit while the others took a well needed rest below, he watched the sun peek over the horizon casting a warm light on high clouds far above and was filled with optimism. The air was cooler this far south, a welcome relief to the constant heat they'd lived with since their arrival.

He wondered how pissed off the Chief Minister would be when he found the interrogation room empty instead of him, comatose and strapped into the chair. He couldn't help smiling as he imagined how apoplectic he would be. He also felt momentarily sorry for Aaron who would bear the brunt of his anger.

People make their choices and must live with the consequences...

Far off their port side a dark shadow stretching south indicated the western coast of Tasmania. Cumulus clouds highlighted by the rising sun stood out in stark contrast to the dark shadow of the land hidden beneath them. He had no intention of getting closer but wanted to keep the distant land or at least the clouds above it in sight as a guide to the direction they were travelling.

Feeling exhausted after his ordeal in the white interrogation room and their subsequent escape, he wanted nothing more than to get into his bunk and sleep for hours, but they weren't safe yet. They wouldn't be safe until they had rounded Tasmania to begin the crossing to South America.

The sun got higher; the sea changed to a lighter colour with the tops of the waves almost translucent. The wind remained constant, but he continued to use the motor to avoid having to tack with the yacht in case it became too uncomfortable for Mary. He would switch to using the sails once they'd rounded Tasmania and were on their way eastwards. Slowly, the tension that had been consuming him drained away.

He contemplated setting the self-steering so he could take a rest, but decided they were too close to the Tasmanian coast.

Focusing on looking in the direction they were heading he didn't see the tiny dark speck near the western horizon gradually becoming larger as it approached from the west.

Billy came up on deck to join him in the cockpit. He'd had a short sleep and was feeling refreshed. "You should take a break," he suggested.

Looking around, he spotted the dark spot which was by then taking the shape of a patrol boat. It was a long way off southwest, but it wasn't coming directly towards them.

"Is that a patrol boat?" Billy asked.

"Shit," Joe exclaimed when he saw it. "How did I miss that?"

"Do you think it's seen us?"

"It doesn't look like it's heading towards us, so maybe it hasn't seen us yet. But if we maintain this course..." He swung the wheel as he spoke, changing course towards the coastline. "Close to the coast in shallow water, we might be able to lose them amongst the reefs."

"That's dangerous..."

"What choice to we have? Out here they can shoot us out of the water, but inshore, they might not be able to get close enough to do that."

"They have seen us," Billy said. "They've just changed course."

"We're closer to the coast. We'll get there long before them and with a bit of luck we might lose them."

The movement of the yacht became smoother as they were no longer running across waves but with them towards the coast. Joe pushed the motor to its extreme power setting and Buenhogar surged through the waves.

The distant patrol boat didn't get any larger; it still had a long way to go to catch them.

The coast rapidly loomed ahead of them. The waves became bigger, building to a good height before smashing into rocky reefs extending out from cliff faces where huge heaps of granite boulders formed escarpments above the waterline, before becoming dangerous reefs below the surface.

They turned and ran a bit slower parallel to the coastline, but this meant the waves smashed into them sideways causing the yacht to lean dangerously with much more sideways rolling. They were too close, and the incoming waves pushed them towards the hidden shoreline reefs. Joe turned back out towards the open sea to gain distance to get around a jagged island that appeared ahead of them. The gap between the island and the shore was wide enough for them to sail between, but the surface of the water in that narrow strait was an avalanche of froth and spray as waves coming around the island from both sides met in the middle and smashed together.

Coming closer to the island, it hid them from the approaching patrol boat, but then Joe realized it wasn't an island but was an extension to the coast further beyond with the shallow connecting part beneath the surface causing the turmoil in the water. Closer to the shoreline, as they slowly approached, he saw an inlet to what he hoped was hidden bay or the mouth of a river.

If we can get in there…

"They won't get is in there," Billy said. He'd seen the inlet as well.

"Let's do it," Joe said. He immediately steered towards the less churned up water flowing out of the inlet. It was only visible because they were close to it. Further out beyond the breaking waves, it could not be seen. *The Patrol boat is too big to come close enough to see it. A perfect place to hide.*

With enough forward momentum to maintain control, Buenhogar edged into the undulating water flowing from the narrow inlet. It was shallow, and a couple of times the keel brushed against gritty sand. For moments Billy and Joe feared they might run aground, but before that fear materialized, they were through the gap, over the sand bar and into a narrow river with deeper water. They motored slowly up the river until they were out of sight of the coastal inlet and were sure they couldn't be seen by the patrol boat when it arrived. They dropped anchor and cut the motor. The sound of the waves breaking nearby was muffled by the overhanging trees.

Joe immediately relaxed.

Assuming they had any idea of where they were, they would have to send people in to find them. He was dead on his feet but couldn't take a rest yet.

"We need to wait and see if they discover where we are," he said to Billy "They would have lost sight of us and will come close to this spot maybe expecting to see a shipwreck where we smashed into a reef. If they discover we've come in here to hide, they will send someone in to get us. I can deal with that," he stated unequivocally. Then seeing the worried expression on Billy's face he said, "But we need to keep a lookout to see when they arrive and what they might do."

"I can do that." Billy smiled confidently. "I'll make my way back through the trees along the edge of the river to the inlet."

"Make sure you can't be seen."

"Not a problem." He grinned confidently, happy to have something to do.

The bow of *Buenhogar* faced upriver, held in place by the anchor, but the stern was close enough to one side for Billy to jump across without wading through the water and getting wet. He immediately jumped ashore and vanished into the bushes beside the riverbank.

With his attention focused on the spot where Billy had vanished into the bushes he jumped involuntarily when Helen suddenly appeared beside him and touched him on the arm. "Mary's having trouble breathing. You'd better come."

Without a word, Joe dropped through the hatch with Helen right behind him.

Mary was propped up with an extra pillow to make it easier for her to breathe. Her face was pale, her eyes watery. A small dribble of saliva had wet the left side of her face, and the pillow. She looked at Joe with a weak but knowing smile.

"Mary…"

Helen carefully wiped away the dribble with a soft cloth.

Mary smiled her thanks then suddenly gasped raggedly for breath. There were gurgling sounds deep inside her chest indicating fluid in the lungs. Her frail body shook as she struggled to get enough air, then just as suddenly as it had started, it stopped. Her breathing eased again.

"It's time," she said weakly.

"No," Joe said softly.

"I'm sorry," she whispered slowly in between shallow breaths, "but I won't see the end of this voyage…" she gasped again, struggling to breathe.

"Can't you do anything?" Helen pleaded with Joe.

He felt completely useless. There was no one they could call for help; no way he could drain the fluid in her lungs caused by, he suspected, a heart attack. He desperately wanted to alleviate her breathing. All he could, all any of them could do, was to be with her, to comfort her and hope that she wasn't in too much pain.

"Don't look so worried Joe," Mary said quietly. "I'm okay with it."

"What is she talking about?" Helen said breathlessly, her eyes wide.

A renewed bout of wheezing, of struggling for breath prompted Joe to add another pillow behind Mary's shoulders so she could sit up straighter, which eased her breathing slightly. Helen wiped away more slight dribbling.

"These few months we've spent together," Mary spoke so softly they had to lean close to hear her, "have been the best in my whole life. You're my family… never forget that…"

Helen's eyes watered. Tears left faint streaks down her cheeks.

Joe felt hollow; a part of him had been torn out. He brushed the back of his hand across his eyes to wipe away the tears that formed.

"We should… thank you for… taking us in…" he mumbled almost incoherently.

"Don't look sad," Mary whispered. "I'm looking forward to joining Harold… after all this time…"

Her last words were so soft Joe thought he'd imagined them.

Her head eased back onto the pillow as she closed her eyes. A faint smile played momentarily across her lips. Her breathing slowed, becoming so faint they couldn't hear it above the ambient sounds of the bush obscuring the river Buenhogar was hiding in.

A moment later there was a slight shudder, after which Mary remained still.

Neither Joe nor Helen moved a muscle for a long time. Eventually Helen turned towards Joe, an unspoken question in her eyes.

"She's gone," he said sadly.

Helen wrapped her arms around Joe. Her whole body shuddered as she let loose the tears welling up inside her. Once again, her world was falling apart.

It was a long time before she stopped crying.

"What are we going to do?" Helen's voice was like that of a little lost girl.

They were standing in the galley.

"I'll take care of her. You go up on deck and wait for Billy to return, okay?"

"Where is he? Where did he go?"

"He went to the mouth of the river to keep an eye out for the patrol boat."

"He should be here, with us…"

"He'll be back… Now go on. Go up and wait for him."

She nodded, wiping more tears away with a swipe of her hand.

As soon as Helen went up through the hatch, Joe returned to Mary and carefully wrapped her bedsheets around her, so she was completely covered. He wondered what he could use to tie the sheets so they wouldn't unravel, and after rummaging in the Mary's closet he found her dressing gown and removed the cord. He wrapped it around her legs, tying it to hold the sheets together. He used several safety pins to pin the sheets together where they covered her face and head. That's the best I can do, he thought apologetically.

As light as Mary was, he would need Billy's help to get her out of the cabin and to bury her at sea, and he would need a weight to help her to sink, but he would worry about that once they'd left this hiding place. He hoped it wouldn't be too long because a body would soon begin to decompose, and that was not something he wanted to have happen with Mary.

Back up on deck he sat beside Helen in the cockpit. Neither said much, waiting for Billy to return. They heard him scrambling through the bush long before they saw him emerge beside the stern. He clambered aboard and his grin faded when he saw Joe and Helen distraught.

"What's the matter?"

Suddenly Helen started crying again. Billy sat beside her and put his arm around her shoulders, drawing her in close against him to comfort her. It was Joe who spoke.

"Mary passed away."

"No…"

"Not long after you left."

"I don't know what to say…" He looked at Joe then Helen who had stopped crying. "Are you okay?" He asked her.

"It won't be the same without her," was all she managed to say.

He looked up at Joe who was now standing. "How did it happen?"

"Her heart gave out. She woke up having trouble breathing. It got worse… there was nothing we could do."

"I tried to make her comfortable," Helen added.

"She did want us to say how happy she'd been to have spent these last weeks with all of us," Joe said solemnly.

"It's not fair," Billy said solemnly.

"No, it's not Billy. It never is." To change the subject Joe asked him what he saw during his reconnaissance.

"Yeah, sorry… I should have told you right away. The patrol boat cruised by the cliff, passed the bay but kept well away from the reefs. It didn't come in close enough to see the entrance to the river here. I watched them sail along the coast for a while, then they turned and headed back towards the west."

"They must have been diverted from accompanying the colony ship to Antarctica that we saw leaving earlier. Are you sure they kept going west?"

"I watched until they disappeared below the horizon."

"That's good. We'll wait for the tide to come in to make sure we get over the sand bar at the mouth of the river."

"What about Mary?"

"She asked to be committed to the sea, as was her late husband Harold… a long time ago."

"How are we going …?"

"To do that? I've wrapped her in a shroud." He paused a moment before continuing. "We need to find something to weigh her down, so she'll sink and not float away. We could use the anchor, but it's the only one we have, and we need it. The only thing I can think of is to weigh her down with rocks. If you could collect several reasonably sized rocks, we'll find something to put them in that we can attach so she'll sink when we commit her to the ocean."

Glad to take their minds off Mary's passing, Helen and Billy almost said simultaneously, "we'll go ashore and find some right now."

"That's the spirit," Joe said. He would get Mary and sit her in the cockpit while they looked for the rocks.

29...

"What do you mean they fucking disappeared?" The Chief Minister stared furiously at the screen linking him to the captain of the patrol boat dispatched to intercept the wayward yacht off the Tasmanian coast.

"We had them on the radar. We set a course to intercept them along the coast. Then they vanished. One second, they were there, the next…they were gone."

"You saw them vanish?"

"Yes. We were some distance away, but the yacht was clearly visible. They were close to the coast… then they… vanished."

"That can't be possible."

"I was watching them through binoculars. I saw it with my own eyes. What else can I say?"

"Was there any electrical disturbance around them?"

"Nothing. The weather was fine. They were cruising parallel to the coast, then suddenly they turned and headed directly towards the roughest section of coast… They must have seen us coming and changed course… that's when they vanished. We searched the coastline for several kilometres either side of the spot where they vanished. There was no sign of them."

The Chief Minister was lost for words, his thoughts tumbling like storm clouds.

"Should we still keep searching?" The tone of the question indicated the captain thought it was pointless to keep trying.

"Could they have hit a reef and sank? Did you find any wreckage?"

"Absolutely nothing. If they'd sunk, we would have found something. There wasn't a sign of anything…"

"Fuck!" The Chief Minister screamed uselessly at the monitor screen. He felt like throwing something at it, smashing it. He spun around in search of something he could throw but saw nothing he could use to vent his frustration.

"Those bastards lied to us," he yelled, his back to the screen. "They did have some way of controlling time." He sucked in a deep breath and held it for several seconds before letting it out with a loud sigh.

Much calmer, he said to himself, "I fucking knew it."

The Patrol ship's captain waited patiently, careful not to say anything that could further upset the Chief Minister.

"Where the fuck did they go?"

Realizing he was still being observed by the patrol ship's captain, and there could never be an answer to his rhetorical question, he turned back to the monitor and the waiting captain. "You'd better get back to your duties," he said calmly and switched off the monitor.

The four day shift workers in the control room remained silent, hardly daring to breathe while keeping their eyes on the screens in front of them. None attempted to look at the Chief Minister. After an intolerably long moment they heard him stalk across to the entrance and leave. They all breathed a sigh of relief when the door slid shut behind him with a soft hiss.

30...

It was early afternoon when the tide was at its highest and Buenhogar quietly cruised back down the river and into the small bay behind the headland and its previously exposed reefs. They had no trouble crossing the sandbar while the water was still with only shallow swells rolling in to shore. It was so clear Joe could almost see individual grains of sand on the bottom between clumps of green sea lettuce and brown kelp patches where small schools of silvery fish darted about only a few metres beneath their hull.

It's too shallow here, he thought as he glanced again at the shrouded figure seated in the cockpit with a stitched bag of rocks sitting on her lap. Another bag was tied around her feet. We need to be in much deeper water… Won't be long now.

He patted Mary's knee as a way of reassuring himself that he was doing the right thing.

Helen and Billy were standing on the deck in front of the main cabin, searching ahead for any sign of the patrol boat. There was nothing between them and the horizon.

Even the sea beyond the shoreline was quiet, expectant. The swells of the day before had flattened out, becoming smooth and glassy, making their motorized path into deeper water a soft undulating movement that relaxed all on board *Buenhogar*.

It's like the sea's allowing us time and space, Joe thought. *Time to mourn. Its never this calm normally…*

"It's all clear ahead," Billy called out.

"Thanks Billy," Joe responded. "We'll stop when we get another kilometre or so offshore."

The water was still as clear as it had been close to shore, but it was too deep to see the bottom. All they could see was a deepening blue with shifting shafts of light refracted by the movement of the flat waves fading into the depths below. The occasional flash of silver as light reflected off a fast moving pelagic fish gave them an indication of the depth.

It's deep enough already, Joe thought, but then he didn't want to take the chance that Mary might be washed ashore during the normally rougher weather that prevailed along this coast. A bit further out where it drops into more abyssal depths is what he wanted.

She would rest peacefully there...

An hour later with the rugged coast nothing but a shadow behind them, and ahead of them the vast emptiness of the ocean, Joe switched off the motor and *Buenhogar* drifted slowly to a stop, finally rocking gently up and down as the flat smooth swells undulated caressingly beneath them.

"I think now is a good time Mary," he said softly so Helen and Billy couldn't hear him. "This is a good spot."

The sun was lower on the horizon and the light cast gave the sea's surface a welcoming golden tone. Joe wondered how he was going to lift Mary and position her in a manner that was dignified. With the two bags of rocks tied around her waist and her legs at the ankles, it would be hard for him to lift her by himself. He could simply drag her across the deck and push her over... *NO, not like that.*

"You'll need a hand," Billy said.

Joe almost jumped. He hadn't expected Billy to be there beside him.

"Thank you. If we can both lift her and get her seated on the edge of the deck at the stern..."

While Billy took hold of Mary's feet and the bag of rocks attached, Joe took hold of her around the waist on one side with Helen assisting on the other, and together the three of them lifted her out of the cockpit. They inched their way to the stern where they sat her on the deck. Joe opened a section of railing used as a gate to give them clear access to enter and exit the water if they ever needed to dive below the stern to clear debris around the propeller. They sat Mary in the opened space on the stern with her legs over the edge. Helen stood behind with Mary leaning back against her, holding her in a sitting position.

"Are you going to say something?" Helen asked Joe. He was standing on her right side.

Billy, on the other side, said, "You should say something."

"I don't know what to say..."

He was greeted with silence as Helen and Billy waited expectantly. Hanging over the stern, Mary's feet rose and fell with the soft rocking movement of the yacht allowing them to briefly touch the glassy surface every few seconds creating a series of expanding ripples.

"Mary was kind, and loving," Joe started hesitantly.

Billy and Helen nodded encouragement.

"She took in a desperate young girl who'd lost her father, giving her a home, and much needed love...in a world gone mad." He paused, struggling internally to gather his thoughts into a coherent form.

"I'm also extremely grateful that she accepted me as well as part of her family, and I'll always love her for that." He looked down, speaking directly to her. "I'm sorry Mary, that we can't commit you to the sea where we left Harold, but as you reminded me, the sea is all encompassing and anywhere in these beautiful waters is the same..."

He looked out over a calm sea, took a deep breath before slowly exhaling. "Mary, we commit you to the sea from whence all life on Earth began... and we hope that somewhere in the vast depths of this ocean you will be with Harold again..."

He stopped, unable to think of anything else.

"It won't be the same without you," Helen said. "I miss you already..." There were tears in her eyes.

Billy struggled to keep from crying.

Without saying another word Billy and Joe lifted Mary up so her legs could slide over the stern. They held her for a moment in an upright position before letting go.

She slid feet first into the ocean beneath, rapidly disappearing into the deep blue depths.

The three of them hugged each other without saying anything

as tears ran down their faces. They stayed that way until the sun vanished below the horizon, its golden rays turning red before fading to purple and the first stars appeared above them.

When they finally let go of each other, a freshening wind ruffled the waters, heralding their calm respite was over. The sea had given them time to commit their friend and to mourn her, now it was time for them to move on.

The waves began to increase in height. Gusts of stronger wind created erratic whitecaps further to the south.

Together, Joe and Billy ran up the sails and set a course to the southeast.

When they'd passed the lowest extremity of Tasmania a full moon had risen casting silver streaks across ocean swells. Joe turned more to the east but still maintained a southerly angle enabling them to pass by the lower extremity of New Zealand. They needed to skirt the bottom of New Zealand before they could head across the enormous distance to Chile and Argentina.

Taking advantage of the constant winds in the Great Southern Ocean, the movement of *Buenhogar* steadied as, like a living being, she accommodated herself to the movement of rolling swells and constant wind driving them forwards.

There was nothing for them back in their own country.

What the future held was unknown, but being optimistic, Joe knew it could only be better. Their goal was South America and the opportunity for Helen and Billy to make a good life there, or in the fledgling colonies on Mars or the Moon if that opportunity arose.

Joe was no longer concerned for himself. He'd had an interesting life, of that there was no doubt, but... *The future is for them. I've had my time.* And it was being created in South America with their expansion into space, to the Moon, to Mars, and beyond.

That's where they needed to go...

Where they were going...

www.ingramcontent.com/pod-product-compliance
Lightning Source LLC
Chambersburg PA
CBHW011403010726
47495CB00009B/2752